RUTHLESS Heart

EVE L. MITCHELL

Editorial services provided by Helayna Trask with Polished Perfection.

Cover design provided by JJ's Design & Creations; jjsdesigncreations.wixsite.com/mysite/services-pricing

Cover Photo provided by Wander Aguiar Photography: www.wanderbookclub.com

Cover model: Joey Lagrua

RUTHLESS *Heart*

To coffee, for getting me through the late nights to hit this deadline.

Note from the Author

This is a book of fiction, general landmarks, places, cities etc are referenced, but my knowledge of them is from maps, wikipedia and my imagination.

Please note that the deviations that there may be from the cities or places mentioned in this book or surrounding area are to fit in with the story.

I am a British author and although I have tried to make this story as universal as I could, there will be some British spelling, phraseology, and terminology that I can't (and won't) eradicate from my writing. I'm okay with that, I hope you are too.

Ruthless Heart

She is his enemy. He is her nightmare.

Three football stars who have it all: looks, money, talent and the world at their feet. No one messes with the Devils. You're either with them or against them...and you'd have to be stupid to be against them.

Ava isn't stupid, but one night of being in the wrong place at the right time is coming back to haunt her. One of the Santo boys —Jett—is out for blood. Specifically, *her* blood. Thankfully, he doesn't know who she is, and Ava plans to keep it that way.

Sophomore year threatens to stop Jett's progression to the championships and, more importantly, his plan to play in the NFL. All because of some mystery blonde. But he has a plan: find the threat and *eliminate* the threat. Jett is ruthless in his pursuit to find the girl who threatens his career.

They say there's a thin line between love and hate, and neither is prepared for the consequences when they cross that line.

Three guys, three girls, one game. Are you ready to meet the Devils?

Content warning: please note that there are elements of this story that may be disturbing to some readers. The story involves an incident of drink spiking but there is no non-con involved.

When the truth is a weapon
And you know you can't hide from it
Do you run?
Or do you play the game?

EVE L. MITCHELL

The Morning After

Bright light pressed against my eyelids painfully, the morning sun demanding I open my eyes and wake up. Moving my head away from the brilliant light, I turned onto my side. I wasn't ready to admit that I was awake, not even to myself. Moving hurt my head. Pounding started from what felt like an inch behind my eyeballs all the way to the back of my skull where the throbbing sensation resonated off of my cranium and bounced back to my eyeballs, which seemed to be pulsing in rhythm.

I had a hangover?

I'd never had a hangover before. I'd only been drunk a few times before, and it didn't feel like this. I'd definitely never had this thumping in my temples before. Sleep. I needed more sleep. My friends told me that sleeping was the answer and then coffee. I peeled an eyelid open…coffee? That was a reason to bear the blinding pain that rushed into my head as my open eyelid allowed light in, and I hastily closed my eye again. No. Not even coffee was worth this pain. *There's a sentence I never thought I'd say,* I thought ruefully.

Sleep, *that* I could manage.

Settling in under the sheet, pulling it high up over my face to block out the light, I promised myself five more minutes.

Running water had my eyes peeking open again, and slowly, I moved my head from under the sheet to look around. I could hear the shower? As my eyes adjusted to the horrific brightness, I slowly realised three things.

This was not my room.

These were not my sheets.

This was not my bed.

Cautiously, tentatively, my hand slipped under the blanket and explored as worrying realisation crept into my foggy head. *I'm naked? Why am I naked? Where are my clothes?* Alarm and panic were quickly replacing the pain in my head from too much alcohol the night before.

The bathroom door opened, and I hastily dropped my head under the sheet, closing my eyes as the rest of my body froze.

"I can't believe you're still here," a male voice muttered.

So, he knew I was here, and from the sounds of it, he wasn't happy about it. But the more important question to me was, who was *he*?

"Yo, chick."

Chick?

"Yo, girl."

Slightly better.

"*Woman!*" he said loudly, his irritation bleeding into his tone. "Wake the fuck up and get the fuck out. I don't have time for this."

I will never drink again, Lord, if you send me a sign that I did not have sex with this guy.

I heard a door being flung open, as it bounced off what I assumed was the wall, announcing that there was another person in the room. "There's a girl in your bed?" the new person said, and I wasn't sure in my hungover, dying-of-humiliation state if he was stating a fact or asking a question.

"Yeah, she's not waking up either."

"Fuck." I heard the hesitation. "She dead?"

"Are you fucking stupid?" I heard the scorn in bathroom guy's voice, and between the pain in my head from the hangover and the burning embarrassment, something niggled that I recognised his voice. "You think I fucked her to death?" I could hear his amusement as his movements sounded louder in the room, and I guessed he was getting dressed.

Cue snort laugh from the other guy. "Maybe she's just passed out in bliss?"

"My dick feels red raw, so I definitely fucked her more than once…so…not impossible."

He did? Cold horror crept slowly up my body. *I had sex? With him?* He sounded like a complete dickhead. It was taking all my willpower to lie there and breathe evenly when, in reality, I wanted to bolt out of the room and then crawl into the nearest hole that I could find.

"Well, that was TMI," the other one said with a small laugh. "You better have wrapped it up."

"*Obviously*. Can't remember much, but I picked up enough wrappers when I went to the shower this morning," I heard him tell the other one, and then I heard him stamp his feet. Was he putting shoes on? "She isn't waking up." The irritation was back in his voice.

"Back up a minute. You? *You're* fuzzy on the details?" the other guy asked curiously. "I thought you weren't drinking last night?"

"Yesterday was fucked, you know that." I heard bathroom guy sigh. I needed out of this room. "I must have had more to drink than I thought," he added quietly. "You know what those parties are like, the cups have more alcohol than soda."

"Yeah, but still, you shouldn't be drinking the night before."

Even under the sheet, I could feel the unspoken tension between the two of them, and I was now rigid waiting for the fall-out. The other chuckled softly in what I think was his attempt to lighten the mood before he changed the subject. "So who's blondie?" he asked casually. "You do know who it is?"

Which confirmed that they couldn't see me, which was great, I thought as relief washed over me. However, it was clear the asshole I slept with didn't know who I was any more than I knew him. The bright side of this was that I may still get out of this unscathed. Well, apart from the damage to my dignity, but if it meant I could avoid a face-to-face confrontation this morning, I was okay to deal with my dignity later.

"Fuck knows, some girl," my sleeping partner answered casually. "Not sure I could pick her out of a lineup."

I could almost *hear* his shrug. *Asshole.* He obviously did this a lot, and that realisation made me feel worse.

"You really were wasted, was that wise? Damn it, how are you standing right now?" Again, the amusement leaked through the reprimand, and I also would've liked to know how he had no hangover. Reprimand Guy spoke again. "What do we do with her? We're going to be late, and we can't be late today." He was now sounding less amused and more frustrated.

Welcome to my morning.

"Fuck." I heard the footsteps approach and forced myself not to cower. "Girl?" the guy snapped at me. I lay immobile, forcing my breathing to be calm and steady, which would be funny if the rest of my body hadn't been drenched in nervous sweat.

Could this be any worse? I will never ever drink again, please don't make him pull the sheet back. My stomach churned, and my eyes opened in horror. *No.* My mouth flooded with saliva. *Please no.* My stomach roiled again, and I had no choice but to bolt upright and shove past *whoever* as I launched myself at his bathroom and hurled up the contents of my stomach.

"Fuck, that's nasty," I heard his friend mutter. "Fine ass though."

Even over my retching, I could hear the guy's answering grunt. "*Fuck*. I don't have time for this shit," he protested.

"We really don't, you're going to have to leave her here."

"Shit." I heard him swear again just as another wave of nausea hit me.

"Just lock up the goods and make sure all the used condoms are gone. She could be a crazy clinger looking for a meal ticket."

I heard the bathroom door slam shut as I said another prayer to the porcelain throne my head was halfway down. Even as I threw up and clung to the toilet bowl, I heard them moving around in the bedroom. There also seemed to be more voices now. As my stomach tried to turn itself inside out, or what felt like it, I was very, *very* conscious that I was stark naked. Tears from my violent gagging ran down my face, as did snot from my nose, and I could almost *taste* the vomit in my nose.

Oh my God, I'm dying.

The door opened as another wave of sickness left my body.

"Ugh, *Jesus*." I heard him hesitate. "There's water by the bed, painkillers too, take them and leave. Do *not* use my shower." He hesitated. I could feel him behind me, and I was suddenly grateful that my head was hanging down his toilet so I didn't have to look at him.

My head was on my arm, which was currently across the toilet bowl, my blonde hair a curtain around me giving me some privacy as my body shuddered in aftershock of the violence of my vomiting. I tried to nod that I heard him, acknowledge his stern disgust that he wasn't bothering to hide from me.

I could feel his eyes on me and then heard another curse as he seemed to make the decision that he had to leave me. With effort, I managed to lift my head and look up as I heard another heavy sigh. A mirror above me allowed me to catch a look at his side profile as he turned and stormed out of his bathroom, slamming the door shut behind him.

Even with him gone, his presence lingered in the bathroom, and as I crouched there, the image of him burned into my brain. Thick black hair with a clean sharp jawline, a nice straight nose. Even side-on, he was gorgeous. Nausea washed over me again but not from my overindulgence in alcohol this time.

No.

It was because of *who* was leaving me to throw up in his bathroom. I knew *exactly* who he was, even if he didn't know me.

The infamous quarterback for the Cardinal Saints, my college.

Possibly the most arrogant, *dangerous* guy I had ever met.

Jett Santo. *Shit.*

I knew who he was, the whole of Tennessee knew who he was. What I didn't know was how I ended up in the same orbit as him, never mind his bed, and as I leaned over the toilet again, my focus shifted to getting out of here.

And him? Well, he didn't know who I was, and since I had no intention of ever letting him find out, I could deal with this whole *experience* later. For now, I needed to stop vomiting, pick myself up off his bathroom floor, clean up, and leave without letting anyone see me.

Totally doable.

CHAPTER 1

Ava

"AVA? ARE YOU EVEN LISTENING TO ME?" MIA SNAPPED AT ME AS I looked up from my phone.

"Yes," I lied. "I completely heard you."

My friend narrowed her hazel eyes at me as a frown marred her face. Thick auburn hair hung in waves over one shoulder, and I envied her hair colour as the sun picked up the highlights of chestnut and toffee, which shone through the natural red hues of her hair.

"Well, what did I say?"

"Um..." I winced at her glare. "I don't know, I was reading the stats from this weekend's game," I explained hurriedly.

"Why? Was there a yard that you missed on Saturday?" Mia mocked as she rolled her eyes.

"Rushing or passing?" I teased her as she took a drink of her soda.

"Ugh, who cares?" Mia threw her hands up as she laughed at me. "As long as they move it down the field, does *anyone* care *how*?"

"Yes!" I answered with a long-suffering sigh. I loved football. Even after my less than spectacular experience on Saturday morning, I was not letting that deter my passion for the game, and still watched in the afternoon. Mia, who had been my best friend since we were four years old, knew I adored the sport. "How can you still not know this after fifteen years?"

"Because, Ava, darling, I stopped listening to you talk about football when we were about, hmmm"—she pretended to think about it—"four?"

"You're full of shit, Mia Davis," I laughed as I swung my bag of chips at her.

"Am not," Mia giggled as she snatched my chips off me and stole a handful.

"I thought you were off carbs?" I smiled knowingly as I lay back on the grass, enjoying the afternoon sun.

"I am," Mia moaned as she lay beside me. "I'm just so *cracking* hungry."

I snort laughed at her terminology. Mia refused to swear, and her alternatives always made me laugh. I closed my eyes against the bright August sunshine. "What did you read this time to tell you carbs were bad?"

"It was in the college newspaper."

One eye popped open as I turned my head to look at her. "Serious?"

"Yes, Hayley's health piece this week was about how carbs destroy your weight loss goals."

I rolled onto my side as I looked at Mia. Even lying on the grass in a short jean skirt and a pale pink T-shirt, she was stunning. "Mia, what are you losing weight for *this* time?" I saw her frown of annoyance at the inflection of my voice and belatedly realised she was hangry. *Shit.*

"*This* time, as you put it"—she shot me an annoyed glare—"I need to lose eight pounds."

I cast my eye over Mia's frame. She was taller than me by about two inches, and her five eight height allowed her to have some of the best legs I'd ever seen on a female. "Where do you have to lose it from?" I teased. "You have nothing *spare* to lose, Mee."

"I think I'm carrying excess water."

"I think you're an idiot," I replied with a smile as I rolled onto my back again and closed my eyes.

"Whatever," Mia muttered beside me. "Anyway, as much as I *am* wonderful to talk about, I was asking how *you* were?"

"I'm good."

"You're full of poop."

I grunted in amusement. "Honestly, I'm good."

"You never talk to me," Mia complained. I didn't answer; I *did* talk, I just didn't have much to say. Mia stood suddenly. "Okay, I need to go get a salad or something before I start chowing down on the grass."

"Try eating something more substantial than a carrot," I advised as my hand dipped into my bag of chips.

"We're not all you, Ava," Mia snapped.

"Ugh, pleeeease go eat a baked potato or something." I groaned as I sat up and looked at her, shielding my eyes from the sun. "You're horribly bitchy when you're hungry."

"Are you coming?" Mia demanded. I swear her foot almost stomped the grass.

"No. I have Leitch next, and you know I need to find my zen before he starts telling me I'm a terrible failure in his class."

"Oh." Mia frowned as she looked down at me. "I might eat candy if you're not with me."

"Then eat candy!" I laughed at her answering eye roll. "Grab some peanut M&M's—peanuts are protein, they're positively healthy."

"You suck," Mia declared as she picked up her tote bag. "I'm buying a *salad*."

"Good for you," I encouraged her as I ate more chips.

"You sure you're okay?" Mia hesitated.

"I'm good," I assured her.

"I really shouldn't have let you walk home alone." I looked up at her as she chewed her bottom lip. The sun shone strongly behind her, blocking out my ability to see her face clearly, but I knew Mia, I recognised the tone of her voice. "Is that why you're mad? Because I ditched you?" she asked me quietly.

"Mia, I'm *not* mad. I've told you a hundred times. You met tall, dark and, unfortunately for you, dreary. I wasn't that drunk, and I walked home to the apartment. No big deal." I forced a smile. "If anything, *I* ditched *you*, and you should be mad at me, but you're not. And I'm not mad at you. All is good."

"Okay. But next time, you have to stick to the buddy system; you're not supposed to walk home alone." Mia crouched back down beside me, enabling me to see her properly. "*Anything* could have happened to you. You're not invincible, Ava."

She was right, and I maybe would have been reckless if I had walked back on my own. But I hadn't been alone. "I solemnly swear I will break up your lovefest with whichever victim you've chosen, and I will not walk home alone when drunk, again," I said, my hand raised to my temple in a three-fingered salute as I simultaneously crossed my fingers at my side for the lie.

Mia squinted as she considered my salute. "What is that even supposed to be? Boy Scout or soldier?"

I examined my hand and shrugged. "Which one do you want it to be?" I asked her with a grin, easing the slight tension. Reaching over, she swatted my hand playfully, her smile chasing away her frown. I licked my bottom lip as I half sat up and looked around quickly. The grounds were busy, but there was no one really nearby. "You definitely didn't see me leave?" I asked her.

"No." Mia's smile was replaced by a look of sadness and worry. "One minute you were talking to some dude with amazing blond hair, I mean, like it was totally shampoo commercial worthy, and the next you were gone." Her fingers pushed her hair off her face as she looked at me. "Hair guy was where I had seen you last, and I did go over and check, but he said you wanted fresh air and then you were heading home. I called and texted, but you didn't answer." Mia huffed in derision. "But *that's* not unusual, and of course, it turns out you didn't even have your phone!" Mia wailed.

So I hated being available twenty-four seven, sue me.

"Hey," I said gently as I reached out and caught her hand, giving it a gentle squeeze. "I was fine. I came home, fell into bed and died a thousand deaths when I woke up."

Mia hastily covered her mouth to stop her giggle, but her laughter was not to be contained. "You looked *so* bad when I came home."

"I felt *so* bad when you came home," I agreed as I rubbed my forehead in memory of the misery that was Saturday. "Why do people repeat that process every weekend?" I shuddered in memory of my hangover.

"You don't need to drink as much as you did," Mia admonished gently. With a quick smile, she pushed herself to her feet again. "I'm glad you're not peeved. I mean, I know you would have told me, you just, you know…I need to ask." She saw my amused look and rolled her eyes. "*Again*."

"I *know*, Little Miss Needy," I teased her. "Now go feast on lettuce."

With a shake of her head, Mia turned and started to walk away. "See you later, Ava!" she called over her shoulder.

"Not if I see you first, Mia!" I yelled after her. Her one-fingered salute over her shoulder was my goodbye, causing me to laugh loudly.

Grinning, I ate more chips and checked the time on my phone. I had another twenty minutes before Leitch ruined my day with his harsh criticism of every word I wrote. Mia's continuous need to ensure she hadn't upset the balance of any relationship was one of her biggest downfalls. I knew this as her best friend, and maybe, in this case, it was justified. And maybe if I *had* actually walked home, I would feel a little miffed, but I hadn't. Somewhere between leaving the party and arriving home before Mia on Saturday morning, I had fallen into Jett's bed. I couldn't tell her, I knew exactly where her thought process would go, and even though I had no recollection of hooking up with Jett when I woke, my brain *knew* that what had happened between us was consensual.

Loud, wild laughter caught my attention, and my easy smile

faded as I watched the group of guys cross the quad.

He caught my attention immediately as he walked with his brother, Gray, and their cousin, Ash. They were on either side of him, with Jett in the middle, and they looked...*godlike.* A handful of other players from the team crowded them as they passed a ball easily between them.

Jett's dark wash jeans were in the distressed style but still clung to his thighs, and I noticed when he turned to look over his shoulder, that they sculpted around his ass. A black T-shirt half tucked into his jeans hung loose on him but still managed to pull across his broad shoulders. Dark sunglasses hid his eyes, but his trademark smirk was, as always plastered on his too handsome face.

Slipping my own sunglasses on so that I could observe them discreetly, I watched a group of girls flock to the three Santo boys like bees to honey. I had no fear that they would look over at me, I could blend into the background like a pro.

Jett laughed at something Gray said to him. The two brothers were similar in looks and height, as you would expect for brothers but not necessarily for twins. Although as I watched Jett duck his brother's playful punch, I did think the universe had been kind to every one of us for not giving us *identical* twins. Gray was slightly smaller than his brother, his hair cut close to his head, his face more rounded, making his cheekbones not as prominent as Jett's were. Basically, neither was too shabby to look at. I groaned out loud. Who was I kidding? Both were what my mom would say, "look twice, 'cause twice is nice," meaning you would see them and look again to make sure you saw their hotness.

At six four, Ash stood taller than them both. He played tight end on the team, and due to my love of the game, I knew their stats. Ash's hair was always messily styled, and in the warm summer afternoon, his guns were out in honour of the sun shining above us. Actually, all three of them were showing the goods today. Even from my spot under the tree, I could see the definition of their muscles, my eyes running over Jett's heavily tattooed arm. I was not complaining at the view the guys were happily providing.

Still, as I watched them, I wondered how the hell I had ended up being in the same bed as *those* muscles? I had absolutely no recollection of even *speaking* to Jett on Friday night, never mind getting up close and personal. God, I'd been more than up close and personal. My cheeks reddened as my whole body burned at the thought. Despite myself, I shrunk down against the tree, trying to disappear. Which was ridiculous considering, from what I knew and had heard from his bed on Saturday morning, Jett was no clearer on who I was or how he had ended up with me either. My ears had been pinned back all of this morning for any gossip involving Jett hooking up with a girl at a party on Friday night. It wasn't uncommon, the guy was never with the same girl twice, and he didn't appear to care that he had a reputation as a manwhore.

I had been drunk, *so* drunk. I knew I was. Even though I'd only been drunk a few times, that wasn't my first time where I got wasted and had no recollection of what had transpired. However, I had the uncanny drunken ability to appear completely sober. I'd been told before that I didn't seem drunk; my words, my actions, my behaviour, all were exactly the same as when I was sober. The only thing that was different was that my inhibitions were lower and I had absolutely no immediate memory of the evening once the alcohol took over.

Which is one of the main reasons me and alcohol didn't mix. Rarely would I drink if I went to a party. I was happy as the designated driver or sober buddy.

However, on Friday, Mia had been sad because her most current love interest had been promoted to *numero uno* on the douchebag list. Mia had a shit track record with guys. She always picked the too handsome, the too perfect looking, the blinding white teeth toothpaste model wannabe, whose looks hid that he was less than perfect underneath.

But, in true Mia style, she was never moping about a guy for long. If they pissed her off, she went out and found a new one, and she was so darn friendly and enthusiastic she ended up with no hard feelings towards her most recent breakup.

I knew all this. We'd been best friends since forever when our moms shared a babysitter to keep costs down.

When Mia said to me on Friday that she wanted to forget recent number one, she caught me at the right time. I had received another rejection from a publishing company about my short story. No reason given, just the generic *thanks but no thanks.* I'd been ready to drown my sorrow at a college party. The fact that I'd annihilated my sorrow was perhaps a question for later, I mused.

Jett caught my eye again. I'm not sure he had *uncaught* it, to be honest. I looked him over curiously, as the idea of me being in bed with him was just so ludicrous. I was close to believing aliens had abducted us both and put us in a sticky situation.

And sticky I had been.

I gulped audibly.

Jett may have used multiple condoms in our *tryst,* but I had remnants of a night of passion on my body that left me with no doubt that we had been *active* with each other. My lower body had ached in a way that I hadn't expected. I knew the stories of how good in bed Jett Santo was. His bed-hopping expertise was as legendary as his quarterback skills, and I'd heard the girls in his group gossip about his "blessed" size. After I had finally stopped throwing up on his bathroom floor, I'd ignored his warning and crawled into his shower to clean my skin of sweat, of everything, but mostly of *him.* I'd found my clothes scattered about his room, and slowly I had gotten dressed. It was game day for the Saints, he wouldn't be returning anytime soon.

His room was clean, neat, almost obsessively so. It was bigger than my bedroom, but then it would be. The Santo brothers were legacies. This college was named after them after all, Cardinal

Saints College. Their "dorm" house was an old plantation style white building with numerous rooms, which stood proudly amongst the trees at the edge of the sprawling college grounds.

As I had looked around Jett's room, I'd realised that the only thing messy was the bed, which I'd tried to avoid looking at, but eventually I'd approached the wide double bed and saw the evidence of our night. The faint bloodstain on the sheets marked the end of an innocence, in body if definitely not in spirit.

Over the weekend, flashes of us together had begun to seep through, beginning to fill in the blanks. Slowly, I was remembering his touch, his kiss, his lips, which had been…everywhere. I felt my cheeks heat as I watched him now making his way to the cafeteria, completely oblivious to who I was and what we had shared.

I lost my virginity in a night of drunken sex with a guy I disliked, and I only had a fuzzy recollection of what had happened.

Some girls said they wished they could forget their first time. The irony was, I really wish I could remember mine.

CHAPTER 2

Jett

"SANTO. MY OFFICE, NOW!"

All three of us turned to the coach, and I saw him huff out a frustrated sigh as his eyes met mine. "You. Now."

"What the fuck's up his ass?" Gray asked as he watched our coach disappear into his office.

"Who knows," I answered as I bent to pick up my book bag. "I knew Monday mornings with him would be a bad idea," I grumbled as I started to make my way to the office. Glancing over my shoulder, I looked back at the two of them with a grin. "Wait for me, I'm starving."

Ash nodded as he sat back down and pulled out his phone, content to wait. Gray scowled, but I saw him sit beside our cousin as I turned back to walk into the office.

"Coach," I greeted as I closed the office door behind me. He sat behind his huge desk, which seemed to take up the whole space of the room. Accolades, certificates and pictures of past stars littered his walls. I found the room almost suffocating each time that I was in here. It felt crowded, and every time I left the office, I would take a deep breath as if I could finally breathe again. Coach Bowers was a small thin man, clean shaven, with thick dark hair peppered with silver, small beady eyes and a heavily lined forehead because he was constantly frowning. He had been the football team's coach for six years and was perpetually pissed off because we had yet to achieve a championship victory.

However, he was confident that he had the winning combination this time with me, my brother and Ash. I'd heard him tell my father that the reason he stuck with the college was because he had been promised the Santo boys. I was a quarterback, Gray a running back, and Ash a tight end; we basically *were* the Cardinal

Saints' offence, and according to Coach, we were all he needed to make the championships. Our defence was also shaping up to be shit hot, and already our freshman year had progressed us further in the league than the football team had done for years. Coach was sure we would be lifting that trophy before our senior year, and I was in full agreement with him. In this, we shared an understanding as we had the same goal.

The three of us trained relentlessly. We would play in the NFL, hopefully drafted to the same team, but the odds of that were slim. However, all three of us were aiming for the draft, and each of us working together was how we were going to get there.

Coach Bowers looked at me, and I felt a moment of confusion as to why he looked so pissed off this time.

"You're not stupid, Jett," he began, and I knew that was more rhetorical than an actual question. "You have a perfect four point oh average, so I know you have the smarts. You're ambitious, you train as hard as anyone on this team. You're a leader, I see that when you're training. You motivate this team, which is why you are captain."

"Coach?" I could feel the unspoken *but*.

"Your brother, a loose cannon, but you keep him in line. That boy can run and catch a ball with the best of them. He's a goddamn powerhouse for a running back, which means he has the wow factor. I like the wow factor."

"Gray's good," I agreed. Where the hell was this going?

"Your cousin, best goddamn tight end this team has had in years. Ash is a coach's dream, with his ability to defend when needed, and add on to that he can *run* like he can, one of the best damn catchers on this team. Him and Gray, gifts from the football gods."

I nodded in agreement. It was true, we were all talented. We worked hard, we deserved the praise.

"And you, the quarterback for the Cardinal Saints."

"Is there a problem, Coach?" I asked as I straightened my spine, standing at my full six three height.

Coach's lip curled, and I felt uneasy as he watched me, his face giving nothing away. "Do you think that I don't know your nicknames? The Devils?" He looked me over derisively.

"We don't hide it," I answered equally as coolly. "Given that our last name means saint." I met his cold stare with my own. "We're anything but saints."

"Oh, I know." Coach stood, his hands flat on the desk as he leaned on it and glared at me. "You're not saints. The three of you are a goddamn handful, but I didn't think you were entitled little shits who think they are invincible because of whose name's on the college walls."

I bristled. "That's bullshit, we worked hard to get in here. All three of us deserve to be here." It was true, we had worked hard, and we each had good grades. We hadn't coasted into this college because we were *legacies*. We had asked for no favours and received none. "What's the problem?"

"The problem? *This* is my problem," he barked at me as he tossed a clipboard down onto the desk, with a chart on it, and as I looked at it, I couldn't believe my eyes.

Snatching the clipboard up, I read the result again. "What the fuck is this?" I asked him as I looked up.

"Watch your language," Coach warned me. "That is a drug test result."

"I know that," I answered him as I clenched my jaw. "Why does it have my name on it?"

"You're smart, figure it out." Coach grunted as he sat back down.

"This is bullshit." Tossing the clipboard back on the desk, I looked at him. "This isn't mine."

"We don't make these kinds of mistakes."

"Newsflash, you just did." I met his hard angry stare with my own. "I'm telling you, there's no way in hell that's mine."

"It was taken from you on Saturday morning. Only eight players were tested. *This* is yours."

Saturday morning, I remembered, I had pissed in the cup as easily as I would in the bathroom. They'd handed me the cup as soon as I walked into the locker room, and the assistant coach had been on hand to supervise my *deposit*. I vaguely remembered him labelling it as I left to get ready for the game. *Fuck*, I'd been a little fuzzy from the booze the night before and had been too busy hiding my hangover from the coach.

I realised that if this result were right, it wasn't a hangover I should have been hiding.

"Coach," I began as my mind raced. "I don't take drugs. All we do, all *I* do is train for the game, you *know* this."

"I thought I did." Coach Bowers shook his head as he looked at the wall with his prized accomplishments on it. "I thought wrong."

"You didn't," I corrected him quickly as I pulled a chair out and sat down, without his permission, but I wasn't thinking straight. This could mess up my entire year, hell my entire *career*. "I was at a party on Friday night. I don't remember much about it," I admitted as he glared at me in anger. "I thought I'd had one beer, but on Saturday morning, I woke up beside a girl." I ignored his look of disgust. "Ash came to get me for practice. I'm *never* late, but I almost was on Saturday. He asked me about her, and I told him I didn't remember." My hand ran through my hair. "I swear to God, Coach, I thought I'd drunk too much, but I wouldn't." My anger was mounting rapidly. "I *didn't*."

"You shouldn't have been out before a game," Coach reprimanded me automatically as he sat on his chair and considered me. "You're saying that your drink was spiked?"

Was I? I nodded slowly. "I wouldn't pull this shit, this is all I want. The game, the NFL, I wouldn't risk *anything* for my chance, Coach."

His small dark eyes watched me longer than I was comfortable with. "You need to prove it," he said eventually.

My eyes closed briefly. How the hell would I do that? I had no idea who she was, and even if I did, how would I know if she was the one who spiked my drink? "I will."

"You have two weeks."

"You're not reporting it?" I asked him with incredulous hope.

Coach levelled me with a flat glare. "You *do* train hard, you *do* appear to be committed, but I've been fooled before. This once, I will give you a pass. This will go on record in two weeks *if* you can't prove in that time that you, *Jett Santo*, got your drink spiked. *If* you can, then you will be absolved of the offence you have committed."

"I didn't commit an offence," I retorted angrily.

"I don't fucking care!" Coach suddenly screamed as he leapt to his feet. "If you were stupid enough to get tricked, you're as fucking reckless as I feared. This team is not for reckless, stupid, arrogant *devils*. Now get the hell out of my office, tell no one, and I want you back here in two weeks or before, with *proof* that *you've* been played."

"Two weeks?"

"Yes, you've got an injured ankle."

"I have an injured ankle…" I stood slowly as his meaning sank in. "I'm suspended?" I demanded, outraged at the outcome.

"Yes. What? You think I would let you *play*?" Coach snorted in contempt as he sat back down heavily. "You may be privileged, boy, but you get no *privileges* in my team. Now get out, get proof, and keep your mouth shut."

I had no choice but to leave him, and as I slammed the door behind me, I heard the crash from his office. I didn't give a fuck what he had thrown, as I was pretty close to destroying something myself.

Gray was already on his feet as I stormed towards them. Ash was looking past me to the closed door.

"What is it?" Gray asked as I walked past them.

"I'll tell you outside."

We exited the locker room, and I jogged down the steps as my mind raced with the last ten minutes. Gray and Ash were silent as they kept pace beside me. When we were far enough from the sports building, the stadium rising behind it, I turned to them both.

"What did I drink on Friday?" I demanded of Gray.

"What? I dunno." Gray looked at Ash, who shrugged. My brother tapped his hand off his thigh as he thought about it. "I wasn't there long enough," he said. "Why?"

"My drink was fucking spiked," I spat out as I looked around to make sure there was no one else nearby. "I failed the drug test."

"For real?" Ash asked in astonishment.

"I'm suspended for two weeks," I added as I glared back at the modern sports building, as if the sandstone walls were the cause of my problems.

"Are you joking?" Gray demanded as he stepped closer to me. We were twins, but I was taller slightly, where my brother was broader. Our features were similar, but we weren't identical; however, there was no denying that we were brothers. Our twin bond was just as strong, although some days that worked against us rather than for us.

"Do I look like I'm fucking joking?" I snapped at him, and his eyes narrowed at my tone. "Sorry," I muttered as I shook my head.

"How did this happen?" Ash asked as he shoved his hands in his pockets. "The girl?"

"I think so," I told him as Gray looked between us both.

"What girl?" he asked as we began to walk slowly onto the

campus. Gray hadn't come home Friday night, choosing to stay with whoever's bed he had fallen into.

"Some blonde in my bed on Saturday morning," I explained as we walked under the heavy tree canopy.

"I didn't see a girl when I came back to get ready for practice," Gray said as he looked between us. "Why am I just hearing about it?" Ash nor I said anything as we walked on, each deep in our own thoughts. "And you don't know who she was?" Gray probed.

"No clue."

"So, she hooked up with you after you were spiked?" Gray surmised. "Otherwise, you would remember who she was if it happened before you took it."

Ash looked thoughtful as he stopped walking. "Yeah, that's a good point. We need to trace back to everyone you spoke to from the minute you turned up at the party to the last thing before you can't remember."

Nodding in agreement, I saw four of the guys from the team, heading out of the library. They saw us and hollered. Forcing a smile on my face, I reached into my back pocket and put on my shades.

"We say nothing to anyone," I told them both as I gestured towards our teammates heading towards us. "Act like nothing has happened. All they need to know is that my ankle got tweaked in practice and we're being careful."

"This is bullshit," Ash muttered under his breath as he raised a hand in greeting.

"Play the game, Ash. We'll figure this out later," Gray said as he shot me a worried look.

Falling into step with our teammates, we made our way to the cafeteria for lunch. I had three classes this afternoon, and I needed to eat before then. A football was passed easily between us as we walked, and as we got deeper into the campus, I started eyeing every blonde who walked past me.

"Even behind the shades, you look like a perv," Ash murmured as he caught the ball and threw it back. I smirked despite myself at getting caught. "Play it cool, we'll figure this out," Ash repeated Gray's words from a few minutes ago.

The cafeteria was packed as it would be at lunchtime, and as I looked around the crowded room, I tried to keep my expression neutral. Our usual table was at the very back, positioned with three chairs along one side, with only the wall behind them. It enabled me, my brother and my cousin to sit and see everything. We hadn't intended to claim the table on our first day here last year, it had just happened.

The football team knew who we were before we even got here, and just seemed to have migrated to the back of the cafeteria to be with us. It was a thing, it happened throughout school. People wanted to be beside the Santo boys, fuck knows why. I was definitely not a people person, Gray was hostile to the point of violence, and Ash, well, Ash was popular because he was actually the only one who was *likeable.* Maybe if we ditched our cousin, Gray and I could enjoy the silence. Even with my temper high, the thought of trying to remove Ash from our lives caused me to smirk. It had been the three of us since we were seven years old. Through elementary, junior high and then high school, we were inseparable. And now college.

Cardinal Saints College was a D1 college, and as I looked over the cafeteria, I could practically map out the varsity teams at the tables, as each sport grouped together. Like liked like after all.

Gray practically vibrating with rage beside me brought my focus back to my current problem. Pressing my knee into my brother's to warn him to keep calm, I remained outwardly unaffected. Ash was leaning back in his chair as he surveyed the room coolly. He was equally as angry but hiding it better than my brother, probably better than me if I was honest.

"How the fuck do we hide this from dad?" Gray asked me with his voice low.

"You don't," Ash answered quietly as he flashed a smile at a girl crossing the floor. Short skirt, tight top, wide smile. My eyes narrowed as I watched her; her blonde hair wasn't the right shade of blonde. She wasn't the girl from Friday.

"Coach has to tell the dean," Gray answered him with more bite than he probably meant. "And that prick will fucking burst with happiness when he finds out. Dad's going to be the first one he calls."

"Coach won't say shit," I said to my brother as I saw Ash agree out of the corner of my eye.

"You don't know that," Gray reasoned as he jerked his leg away from mine, causing me to turn and give him my full attention.

"I *do* know that, because Coach knows he needs me on his team, and I can't *be* on his team if I fail a drug test." The three of us sat in silence as we continued to watch and assess every person in the room.

"And you don't remember what you drank?" Gray asked me with concern as he picked up his chicken wrap.

"I remember a beer," I replied as I took a drink of my bottled water. "I remember saying I was only having one and then I would move onto water. I fucking *knew* that hangover was shit, I would never drink that much before a game."

"We all had shit to deal with after Friday afternoon," Ash said quietly. Gray grunted as he picked up his lunch, his scowl aimed at anyone who was stupid enough to look our way.

"You're sure that you only had one beer?" Ash asked me as his head turned to look at me curiously.

"I don't know. It's fuzzy after that."

"What a complete shitshow," Gray growled as he tore a chunk off his wrap. "I don't even know how this could happen." He tossed his wrap down on the plate as he glared at everyone and no one. "She better have been a good lay at least."

I saw Ash glance at me and then quickly to the line of footballers heading our way. "You said you slept with her, but what if you didn't?" Ash whispered fiercely.

"I did," I told them as I fought to push down the rising anger again.

"You sure it's not just your ego talking?" Gray asked bitterly.

"No, dipshit," I retorted as I smacked the back of his head. "I picked up the *evidence*, and even if I didn't, she took the bedsheet."

"What?" Ash looked at me, perplexed. I had no reasonable explanation. When I returned to my room after the game on Saturday, my bed was made. Finding that suspicious in itself, I had pulled the covers back and found only the mattress staring up at me. What the hell was on the sheet that would incriminate me?

Looking around the room, I took in all the students, watching the ones who sat with friends, laughing, or the ones who sat alone, studying. I noticed what I always did. Almost every set of eyes was at one time or another on the three of us.

Always fucking watching.

"I don't know what's happening or why," I told my brother, my voice heavy with anger. "But I know that someone on this campus spiked my fucking drink, slept with me and took my bedsheet. What the fuck do they want it for? Evidence?" I looked at them both. "I will find them, and when I do, I will take great joy in ripping their fucking body apart."

CHAPTER 3

Ava

LEITCH OFFICIALLY HATED ME. I KNEW IT, THE CLASS KNEW IT, AND he made no effort to hide it. I wanted to die as he stood on his small podium and read my work to the entire class, derision heavy in his tone as he read word for word…slowly.

"The wind cracked against the window as the rain fell heavily from the sky..." He paused, and in true complete asshole style, he looked at me over his glasses that were perched on the end of his nose. "Ms Bryant, remind me again what you propose to do with your undergraduate degree in English."

"Editor, for a publishing house," I told him as I felt my body slide lower in my seat. I could feel every pair of eyes on me as the professor zeroed in on me.

"*Book* editor?" he asked with such scepticism. I heard a few answering titters in the class. At my feeble nod, he seemed to positively radiate with glee. "Tell me, Ms Bryant, as a potential editor, does the opening line of this...*story* that you have produced make you quiver with excitement?"

"My role as editor is not to be excited by a book but to know whether it would be a good fit for my publishing house, if it would sell." Fuck you, asshole, you don't scare me.

"Wrong," Leitch spat as he spun on his heel and marched to his whiteboard. In the day and age of laptops and online classes, Leitch was old school and liked whiteboards, paper submissions and red markers. He *especially* loved red pen. "As an editor, *you* are the reader. If that book does not grip you, why would it grip others? How can you market and promote a book that you do not believe in?" He held up my submission with his fingertips. "If *this* does not excite you"—he shook the paper lightly, causing more snickering in the class—"tell me, why would you think it would therefore excite *me*?"

My mouth opened to snap at him when the doors to the lecture room were swung open, the looser one on the right flying back wildly and bouncing off the wall. The guy stood there, looking at the wall and the door and then at Leitch.

Ash Santo. The third god of the football triad.

He smiled widely at Leitch, completely oblivious that the look he was receiving from the professor made us mortals run and cower in fear.

"Am I late?" Ash asked casually as he closed the door behind him. "Like a little bit late or so late I shouldn't have bothered?" It was quite clear he didn't care what the answer was as he made his way into the lecture hall. He was so tall and broad I doubted even Leitch would challenge him.

"You shouldn't have bothered," Leitch drawled. "Who are you, and why are you"—he glanced at his watch—"fifteen minutes late for this class?"

"Ash Santo. Practice ran late, therefore lunch ran late, hence… I'm late."

I looked between the two of them. Ash was solid looking. He had to be, he was the team's tight end. Leitch was average height, potbellied, with old man stubble and grey hair. Ash, with his light brown hair, clean shaven jaw, stunning good looks, and his arms bare showing his biceps, stood out for all the wrong reasons for Professor Leitch. Quite simply, Ash did not look like he belonged in this class.

"I told administration to stop sending me jocks," Leitch muttered loudly as he motioned for Ash to come further into the class.

"Pretty tough to do in a varsity college with sixteen sports represented," Ash retorted with a snort as his eyes ran over the class, making me suddenly very conscious of the empty seat beside me. "Anyway, I opted for this class, I'm not looking for easy credit." Ash walked past Leitch, whose face was turning purple. "I was told you were good, was I misinformed?"

Ash ignored the swell of laughter as he made his way to my end of the row. His bag dumped on the floor at my feet as he somehow crammed his massive frame into the seat beside me.

I watched the professor open his mouth and then close it again. I almost felt sorry for him. Here he was being upstaged by a football player who didn't appear to know Leitch's fearsome reputation. What could he say, his class wasn't easy credit? By doing so, he would be acknowledging Ash's intelligence for opting for this class. If he said it was easy credit, easy for jocks, then he was saying the *class* was easy. This class was anything but easy, and I knew this as I had already had a year of Leitch in the introductory class in freshman year.

"Don't be late again" was all the professor had as a comeback.

Ash shrugged, and again I felt myself staring at him out of the corner of my eye in awe as he sat there unfazed. That he was being so nonchalant to the meanest man I had ever met made me almost admire him.

I think Ash Santo just became my hero.

"Yo, blondie," Ash whispered when Leitch turned and decided to demoralise another victim and their writing. "Got a pen?"

Glancing at him, I met his wide, dark blue eyes, and my throat closed up. With horror, I recognised the whispered voice. Ash was the other person in Jett's bedroom on Saturday morning.

He had seen me naked.

Throwing up.

Naked.

My butt facing them as I threw up.

Naked.

"Wow, I'm not used to being propositioned so early," Ash told me with a wink. "A pen will do for now, if you can?"

What? Oh my God, I had totally blurted out the word *naked* to him. I was going to die. This was the worst afternoon of my life. Wordlessly, I handed him my pen. He looked at it and then at me and my now empty hand.

"What will you use?" he asked curiously.

Shaking my head so my hair surrounded my face, I shrugged slightly.

"Okay, thanks." I heard him give a low whistle as he sat back in his chair, the creaking noise telling me the chair was also regretting him sitting beside me. "Weird girl," he muttered.

I *was* weird but not because of him. Not really.

The rest of the lecture, I had no idea what Leitch said. The only good thing was that he ignored me, and I think I had Ash to thank for that. The professor had only looked at me once when I had rustled in my bag for a substitute pen. With an apologetic look, I pretended I dropped it, and with a resigned long-suffering sigh, the professor had resumed his lesson.

As I hurriedly packed my book bag, Ash held my pen out to me, inviting me to take it back, but all I could focus on was the chewed pen lid. I shook my head in refusal. He could keep his saliva, thank you very much.

"You look familiar."

My stomach dropped like a stone. "You can keep the pen."

"Have we met?" he asked me as he unfolded from the chair. It was a sight to see, and I wasn't a hypocrite—it was enjoyable seeing those muscles flex up close.

"Hmm, no?" Scooping up my bag, I smiled briefly and then hastened across the lecture room floor.

"Ms Bryant, a word."

No! Turning slowly, I trudged back to Leitch's desk. "Sir?"

He made me stand there until every student was out of the class, and considering I had been almost sprinting across the floor to avoid Ash, I waited a while. The Saints tight end grinned at me as he passed, casually strolling out the door as casually as he had strolled in. I envied him so much right now.

"Ms Bryant," Leitch began.

"Do you know it's Ms because, in the 1950s, if you were unsure of a woman's marital status and age, you called them Ms because *Miss* was deemed to be for a girl or young woman? It was almost the equivalent of mister."

The professor raised his eyebrows at me as I snapped my mouth shut. Me and my useless knowledge.

"Fascinating," he said drolly. "You will not be surprised to know that I have never once considered your marital status."

"No," I mumbled as I looked at my feet in embarrassment. "Sorry."

"I want to talk to you about that paper you submitted. The assignment deadline is not for another week, yet you submitted early. Did you think it wise?"

"Well, I did at the time," I said weakly as I looked over his shoulder at the whiteboard, trying to avoid his heavy scrutiny.

"Hmm."

"You want it rewritten?" I guessed. I had tried to get ahead on assignments so I could spend some free time designing posters and flyers for my friend Wade's band.

"I want it burnt and forgotten."

Feeling my eyes widen, I stared at him in astonishment. "You didn't even read it," I protested.

"I don't need to read it to know it's fanciful garbage."

"This class is *creative writing,*" I said to him as I tried to keep my temper. "Your job is to teach fiction, non-fiction and poetry. I *gave* you fiction."

"You gave me washed-up, run-of-the-mill dross," Leitch said as he crossed his arms, resting his back against his desk as he considered me. "Do the work in the time assigned, do not rush it, and actually try to keep to the assignment, and next time? Well…you *may* be better. You will thank me for this once you realise that I am doing you a favour." His hand made a shooing motion. "Go, you are dismissed."

Biting my tongue, I turned and marched out of his lecture hall. It took every inch of my willpower not to slam the door shut on my way out.

Angrily, I made my way to my next class, History of Writing. In freshman year, I had found it to be stale, but the promise of dissecting Shakespeare's plays had me eagerly enrolling in this course for this semester and next.

Because Leitch was an overbearing prick, I was now late and had most probably lost my seat in the middle row. As I slipped into the auditorium, I saw Professor Matson had already launched into *Romeo and Juliet*. The lights were dimmed as she used the overhead projector, and thankful for the cover of darkness, I quietly made my way to the back seats. Stealthily, I spotted an empty seat second to last row, and with more grace than I knew I had, I lowered myself into the chair, dropping my bag at my feet.

My cry of surprise as I sat on a person echoed off the walls, stopping Professor Matson in her stride. A hundred pairs of eyes swivelled to look at me as the professor strode across the room and flicked on the lights.

Jett Santo grinned back at me as he straightened, fixing his jeans before he casually flung his arm against the back of my intended chair. Wordlessly, I noticed the girl, who had been half draped over the chair beside him, slipping off the seat and scuttling along the aisle, trying to keep out of sight as her friends giggled at her and covered her as she reached them.

"What is going on?" Professor Matson demanded.

Jett raised one perfectly shaped eyebrow as he looked at me in question. What the hell was I going to say?

"Speak!" the professor demanded.

"I..." I swallowed past my building fury and turned to the

professor, my hands raised in supplication. "I thought I saw a rat." Technically speaking, I wasn't lying.

Several answering squeals and the sounds of shuffles as many students raised their feet from the floor ensued, and it took several minutes for the professor to regain control of the class. The whole time, I sat rigidly in the seat that the girl's *body* had been in, while Jett sat smugly beside me, his smirk in place as his shoulders shook in silent laughter.

How had this turned into my afternoon? Ash, Leitch, and now Jett. Where was Gray? They might as well have just thrown them all at me and gotten it over with.

"Have you all calmed down?" Professor Matson asked sternly while she glared at me. When she heard enough mumbles of assent, she motioned to the TA to dim the lights. "As I was saying," she said as she turned back to the screen.

"You owe me a finish." Jett's smooth voice caused my jaw to clench and my hand to curl into a fist.

"Don't be a pig," I whispered back furiously. "You're disgusting."

"Didn't stop you looking," he said smugly as he leaned back in his seat.

I opened my mouth to reply and snapped it shut again. Angling away from him, I tried my best to focus on the lecture, but the presence of *him* sitting next to me was distracting.

The mounting horror that he may recognise me was making me nervous. How would the conversation even go? *Hey, I'm the girl you slept with, you took my virginity, and I then hurled in your bathroom for an hour. Wanna grab a coffee and tell me how we hooked up in the first place?*

No, thank you.

And look at him, in History of Writing class and he had a girl giving him a blow job. What a complete asshole. I couldn't believe I fell for his shit. If there was shit to fall for, which I still wasn't clear on...either way, he was an asshole.

I was never drinking again.

Ever.

I always knew he was a dick. He proved it on Saturday morning, and he hammered the fact home just now. They were the Devils, they were the complete antithesis of not only their own last names, but the school they played for. They didn't give a fuck about anyone but themselves and football. They broke rules, they partied where they shouldn't, and they took what they wanted. They had an almost cult-like following, and they pissed me off.

In high school, our football team was also made up of the popular kids, but here, the Santo boys took it to the next level. They were considered gods on the field, and they were considered gods off of it. All three of them were free with who they slept with, and I'd heard the rumours, they were apparently not lacking in skill in the bedroom either. The fact that they all had the smarts to be here rubbed salt in the wound even more.

I detested them and had done long before I got my scholarship here. Their high school team played mine once in junior year. Gray had caught every pass Jett had thrown, and then Ash had scored the winning touchdown. Then, when our team was commiserating our loss, the three of them and their teammates had torched a devil sign into the front lawn of my school.

No one could prove it. The fact it had been a devil's trident meant nothing. It could be someone trying to make trouble for them, the authorities said.

Bullshit.

I'd been told that, when our team had asked if anyone had actually asked either the Santos or the rest of their team, no one had been able to answer them.

This afternoon only confirmed what I already knew, Jett Santo would never know what I gave him on Friday night, and if I never spoke to him again, it would be too soon. As my resolve strengthened, I started paying attention to class. As my focus became more about Romeo Montague and less about Jett Santo, I felt my inner calm settle.

One night didn't mean anything. I made a mistake. I was a nineteen-year-old girl at college. It wouldn't be my last mistake, but I knew as I got lost in the greatest tragedy ever told, that *he* was a mistake that wasn't worth getting worked up over.

As the lecture finished and the lights turned back up, I stood and gathered my bag. A large hand encircled my wrist, preventing me from leaving. The tingles running up my arm caused me to hesitate fractionally before I jerked out of his grip.

"What?" I snapped at him.

"Wait," he told me as his eyes ran over my jeans and T-shirt.

"Why?" I scoffed as I put my book bag over my shoulder. "Not interested in the second take of your live porn show."

"I haven't seen you in this class before," Jett said as he stood, and I had to take a step back to look up at him.

"Given what you were doing during class, I can understand why."

"Judgmental," he murmured as he stepped into my space, and I instinctively stepped backwards. His head tilted as he studied me. "Uptight little thing, aren't you?"

"No, asshole. I just know a sleazeball when I see one." He was far too close to me. My stupid body was reacting to him, like it *recognised* him. Good God, he was intimidating, but sweet baby Jesus, he really was *hot*.

"I don't think I like you," Jett declared as he looked me over again.

Asshole.

"I don't think I care." With a tight smile, I turned away from him and made my way down the stairs. *What a complete douche.* At the doors, I couldn't help myself, and I looked back up at him. The girl from the floor was talking to him, her hand on his arm, her thumb rubbing his bicep as she plastered herself to his side.

Jett wasn't paying any attention to her, his eyes were locked on mine. His trademark smirk appeared as he stared at me. Swallowing past the sudden lump in my throat, I flicked him the finger before I turned my head away and walked out of the class.

Tossing my blonde hair over my shoulder, I headed outside. Putting my sunglasses on to cut out the glare of the Tennessee sun, I decided today's encounter was actually a good thing. We didn't circulate in the same groups, and chances were this was the last time we would ever be face-to-face with each other again, and I was fine with that.

Jett Santo was nothing but a hiccup, and I was ready to move past it. Notch him down to experience, I told myself. A bad one? Possibly. But an experience, nevertheless. And in my favour, he had no idea who he had *notched* into his bedpost, and he would *never* know.

I knew that this was a win for me. As I walked out into the sunshine, I recognised that, as crummy as it felt *right now*, I would take the win.

CHAPTER 4

Jett

THE GOOD THING ABOUT BEING LEGACIES WAS THAT WE GOT THE RUN of the house. The other guys who shared with us deferred to us, and we got the best rooms. The worst thing about being legacies is that there was no peace or quiet; people were everywhere, constantly.

Which I usually complained about, but after the conversation with Coach today, I was on a mission. Whoever the blonde was from Friday, someone in this house must have seen her.

Gray was already in the kitchen, talking to a few of the guys. In total, twelve of us lived in the house. Gray, Ash and I had the top floor. The game room was in the basement, along with two bedrooms where the freshmen were usually dumped. On the ground floor, there were three bedrooms as well as two reception rooms and a dining kitchen. On the next level up were four bedrooms along with the main master bathroom, which none of us used, so we usually allocated that bathroom for parties. When we had them. Which was rare.

The house used to be known as a party house, but neither myself, my brother nor my cousin were here to party our way through college. We were serious about getting our degrees and more serious about our spots on the team.

My spot was in danger, and there was absolutely no way I was losing it because of some loose pussy and a spiked drink.

Anger coursed through my veins as I thought about it. I didn't know what I'd even taken, for fuck's sake, and had my senses not been so fucking numb from Coach telling me that I had failed a drug test, then I would have paid more attention to the drug results other than the small, neatly printed "failed."

Gray took one look at me and angled his body so that he was

blocking my sight of the other guys. That was my brother's subtle hint that I was wearing my emotions, something both of us had been taught from an early age by our older brother to never do. It was a trait we taught Ash when we were younger, which is why so many people thought we were heartless assholes.

Well, we *were* heartless assholes, but even if we weren't, we wore the masks of indifference well.

"Guys," I said as I walked around the kitchen island to see who exactly my brother was talking to.

"Hey," Gray greeted when he turned to look at me over his shoulder. "How's the ankle?" His quick look at my ankle reminded me I was supposed to be injured. This was so much shit.

"Annoying," I snapped angrily, catching my twin's quick grin at my tone.

"Heard you took a knock from Ash," Jamie said as he looked me over. He was one of our defensive ends and was a complete dick. He tried to wipe me out every practice despite the fact we were on the same fucking team.

"Yeah, my cousin forgets his own strength."

Jamie snorted but said nothing. Again, I caught my brother's look and, swallowing my temper, headed to the fridge.

"So, is Quinn going to come over to *massage* you better?" Derrick asked with a grin to his friends.

"Shut your mouth, dickhead," Gray snarled before he turned to me. "I'll take a water," he said as he joined me at the fridge. "Ash is going to be here a little bit later," he told me quietly as he took the bottle off me.

"Why?" I asked him as I scanned the fridge for something light and easy.

"Because he is." Gray reached past me and took out some cold cuts of chicken. "Get the tomatoes and the lettuce," he instructed as he headed to the island, where a chopping board was already set up. Within moments, he was making sandwiches for us both, while I sat on a bar stool and watched him.

"Hey, so when I heard you got dragged into Coach's office, I thought it was because you had been to the party on Friday night," Derrick said as he propped up against the counter I was leaning on.

"You drinking the night before the game?" Jamie asked me as his eyes narrowed.

"Just one." The lie wasn't really a lie. I only remembered one beer. "He was there too." I pointed at Derrick.

Derrick looked at me before he glanced at Gray and then back at me. "Yeah, I spoke to you for like fifteen minutes and then left. Wasn't really *there,* you know."

He did? I thought hard about it, and I had a dim recollection of him talking to me about the game the next morning. "Huh, that's right, you were talking about routes again." I shook my head slightly in mock despair as I rolled my eyes at the others and Gray, who laughed on cue.

Derrick flushed but joined in the laughter. He played corner and was always yammering about plays and routes, which I didn't mind, he just got on my fucking nerves at the best of times.

"Where'd you go after?" Gray asked him casually as he sliced the sandwiches.

"Met up with some guys from class, played some pool. I was wired, there was no way I was sleeping." He crossed to the cupboard and took out some plates. "You know I'm too worked up the night before a game, but don't worry," he said with a pointed look at Jamie, "I didn't drink, and Jett was nursing his beer, he said he was going to leave and go home."

"Well, he wasn't alone," Jamie muttered dryly as he watched Gray make the food.

"Thought you weren't at the party?" I asked him shrewdly.

"Wasn't," Jamie huffed as he eyed the steady pile of sandwiches

Gray was preparing. "The whole fucking house could hear you getting laid."

Gray's hands paused slightly before he continued to slice the sandwiches. "You got laid?" he asked me with fake humour.

"Course he got laid," Jamie snorted as he looked over at me. I could see his distaste for me clearly, and I had to remind myself that Coach would not appreciate me giving the lead defensive end a minor concussion. "Heard the bitch screaming for more even with my headphones on."

"What can I say," I replied coolly as I stood and accepted the plate from Gray. "I aim to please."

"Yeah, well can you *aim to please* when it's not the night before a game? You set the rules when you came into the house. No drinking before a game, no parties before a game, no fucking in the house before a game." Jamie pulled himself up to his full height, and with the height and weight of him, other guys would be intimidated.

I wasn't other guys.

"Yeah." I took a hearty bite of my sandwich. My brother made the best chicken sandwiches. "You got something to say to me?" I asked Jamie around my mouthful.

"How come you get to break *all* the rules?" Jamie asked as he leaned forward, resting his meaty forearms on the counter.

"Because he's a Devil." Gray stacked the sandwiches onto two other plates, leaving some on the chopping board. "Now eat your fucking sandwich before he shoves it so far down your throat you'll finally know what fucking deepthroating feels like."

Grinning at my brother, I took my water and my sandwich out of the kitchen, Gray on my heels.

When we were in my bedroom, the two of us ate in silence before Gray sat back on my couch, his head against the wall.

"No one saw you with your screamer."

"Not one person?" I asked in disbelief as I sat forward, my head falling into my hands.

"Nope." Gray popped the *p* as his hand ran over his face. "If I didn't know better, I would say you imagined her. But she was still here in the morning, Ash saw her ass, and Jamie just confirmed that you were *heard* at least, if not seen."

"Why can't I remember any of it?" I turned my head to look back at Gray, and in the quiet of my room, he looked worried.

"You know what it sounds like, don't you?" he asked me quietly.

"Yeah, I know *exactly* what it sounds like." Shaking my head, I stared at the bed.

"Yo," Ash said as he walked into the room, closing the door behind him. "Tell me that's for me." He pointed at the two sandwiches sitting on the plate.

"Like I would leave you out," Gray scoffed as Ash flopped backwards onto my bed. "Thought you'd be longer. Find anything?"

"Nothing," Ash groaned as he sat back up. "She's a fucking ghost."

"How?" I demanded as I shot to my feet. "Do you know how *often* people are *watching* us?" I looked between the two of them. "Every fucking moment. How the fuck did no one see me with her?"

"Because you're a *Devil*," Gray answered me as he held the plate out to Ash. "No salt, no mayo, no butter, just chicken, lettuce, tomatoes."

"My man," Ash said gratefully as he accepted the plate. "Thanks."

"Welcome," Gray murmured as he watched me. "Jett, we know how to move without anyone seeing us. If you didn't want to be seen, no one would have."

"Except the girl," Ash mumbled around his food.

"Which confirms that you didn't meet her *at* the party, but on the way home." Gray was looking on his phone. "Between the other end of campus and here, there is a whole lot of ground, but more importantly, the woods to the east. Would you have taken a shortcut?" He looked up at me, his light blue eyes calculating. "It would make no sense, but if you weren't thinking straight…"

"What a fuck up." I started to pace as I racked my brain about Friday night. We had no classes on Friday afternoons as we all had practice. Practice had been fucking merciless, and Coach had been worse than normal. His wife had recently passed away, and he was channelling his grief through avenues of torture on his players. When the centre started throwing up from the intensity of the workout, Coach had eased off. But it had been brutal.

After practice, I went to the gym to use the pool and then the spa. My body had been stretched too tight. When I got home, I spoke to Quinn for an hour on the phone. Ash had gone home straight after practice to see his little sister, who had been sick with a bug. She was better and no longer contagious and wanted to see her brother to wish him luck for the game the next day, since her mom deemed her still too poorly to attend. There was not one Santo man alive who could deny Tilly anything. After I spoke to Quinn, I'd gotten a text. "Where's my phone?" I demanded as I looked around the room.

"Why?" Gray asked as he looked up. "It's not like you would take her number."

"I got a text to go to the party. I don't remember who though." I looked at my brother. "Do you?" Gray shook his head in answer.

"Here," Ash said as he picked it up from the side cabinet and tossed it to me.

Scrolling through my messages, I searched for Friday night. "I must have deleted it," I said as I read. "There's nothing here except…"

"Except?" Gray demanded as he stood.

"Who the hell is Wade?" I asked as I looked up at them.

"Fuck knows. Why?" Ash asked as he looked over my shoulder.

"Because I have a message from him after one saying it was nice meeting me." I looked between Ash and Gray with a raised eyebrow. "It's never *nice* to meet me."

Ash laughed despite the situation, and even Gray cracked a smile as he looked at his watch. "As true as that is, brother, we need to move if we're doing this tonight."

"Yeah." I nodded as I stared at the phone. "How long we got?"

"Fifteen." Gray picked up the plates and headed to the door where he hesitated and looked once at Ash before he spoke to me. "You're going to need to call Quinn, she may help."

"Shit, really?" Ash groaned as he stretched, his hands touching the ceiling easily. "Why do we need to bring her into this?" he protested sullenly.

"Because she knows everyone, even if she is a giant bitch." Gray gave him a tight smile. "She also hears shit we would never be told." Gray shook his head in admiration as he thought about our childhood friend. "To be honest, I'd be surprised if she didn't already know," he added with a fond smile.

I agreed with my brother, but I hesitated as I looked over at Ash, who rolled his eyes. "Whatever, just don't expect me to be there." With a shake of his head, he left the room.

"It's been almost two years," Gray said softly after Ash was gone.

"Quinn has a lasting effect on people," I quipped.

"He'll go apeshit when he learns how much you both still talk."

"Will it be more or less apeshit when he finds out it was you who told her to break up with him?" I asked with mock curiosity. Gray gave me his full attention, and after a long moment, he raised an eyebrow. "What?" I challenged him with a smirk as I crossed to the bathroom. "You think you can get anything past me, *little* brother?"

"Up until Friday, I would say no. But that was before you got your drink spiked and got more or less date raped." Gray's voice was cold. "Now I think you're probably the pussy I always thought you were."

I turned to look at him. He was slightly shorter than me, a fact I knew pissed him off. His hair was dark brown rather than black, his face rounder, fuller, and in my opinion—not that I ever told him—better than mine. I was all sharp angles, whereas my brother was softer. Not in temper though, in temper we were both explosive.

"Did you *really* just go there?" I asked him as I took a step towards him.

"Yes, I did." Gray stood tall. "Because *my* brother would never be sitting fucking *worrying* about who some slut was. Instead, he would be wrecking fucking mayhem, finding the bitch who drugged him and then"—Gray leaned forward as if in challenge—"be mopping up her blood with her blonde…*fucking*…hair."

We stared each other down for a few more minutes before I looked him up and down. "Man, you're a bitch." I felt my top lip curl in a snarl. "Bitch-slapped by Gray Santo," I added with a shake of my head.

"Anytime, big brother," Gray said as he turned back to the door. "Any fucking time."

When the door closed behind him, I gave another shake of my head as I thought about it. He was right. I was too caught up in the aftereffects. I needed to focus not only on the *who* but the *why*.

Why would anyone need to drug me to get me to sleep with them? I wasn't overly fussy about my bed partners, and from what I had seen of my puking *partner* on Saturday morning, she had curves in the right places. From what my dick had told me as I showered, it had definitely had no problem carrying out its job. I'd picked up four wrappers and, much to my annoyance, three used condoms from the floor on my way to the shower after Ash, almost breaking down my door, had woken me up. I was always careful with the disposal of my shit, so the fact I had merely tossed them aside as I kept on going should have been a warning on Saturday morning that something wasn't right.

That and the fact I hadn't heard my alarm. I never overslept. Now I wasn't sure if that was an effect of whatever had been in my system.

Why hadn't I looked at her? She hadn't moved an inch when Ash hammered the door. She hadn't grumbled when I prodded her, hadn't stirred when I nudged her. Hadn't woken when I spoke to her before I went to shower. I recalled Ash asking if she was dead. Fuck, the amount of care I had taken in regard to her well-being on Saturday, she could have been.

I'd been so fucking lucky. Coach hadn't noticed my hangover, which I now knew wasn't a hangover. Our game on Saturday had been against one of the lower league teams. They couldn't score a touchdown even if we hadn't shown up.

No one had anything to gain from that team for spiking my drink.

Suspended for two weeks, maybe more. I peeled my T-shirt off as I fumed internally. If it was more than two weeks, I would miss the trip to Texas, and I always enjoyed beating the smug fuckers on their defence. Also meant I would actually have to attend Friday classes.

As I threw my jeans in the laundry basket, I stopped. After our game in Houston, we were at home to Alabama.

Cursing savagely, I pulled my clothes on for tonight before I went to speak to my brother. I knew exactly who had fucking drugged me.

Now, I just needed to find the blonde to prove it.

CHAPTER 5

Ava

"AND THEN LEITCH WAS LIKE, YOU'LL THANK ME FOR THIS." MY hands waved as I talked, and I glared at Mia as she stifled her giggles. "And *then,* I was late for History of Writing class, and I sneak in, sit down second row from the back, and *sit on a girl*!" I screeched. "Go on, ask me *why*."

Mia coughed back her laugh as she waited for more. "Why did you sit on her?"

"Because she was giving head to a stupid man child," I grouched as I fell onto the couch in despair, my anger at Jett surfacing once more.

Mia laughed out loud before she followed me to the couch, her iced coffee dripping onto the wooden floor. "In the classroom?" she asked me in disbelief as she sat down.

"Yes! It was horrifying, and of course I yelped like a goddamn puppy, and the whole class stops and looks at me, and the professor turns the lights up, and everyone's staring, and she's crawling along the back row and…ugh." I stopped as I rubbed my hand over my eyes. "It was *humiliating*."

Mia laughed loudly, her head thrown back as she clutched her sides. "Why were *you* humiliated? You weren't getting down and dirty in the class." As she prodded me with her toe, I thought about Jett's smug smirk again. *Asshole.* "Who was it?"

Mia knew I held a harbouring resentment towards Jett Santo as it was. Before Friday, we had never actually met in person—and now I *had* a reason for my irrational dislike of Jett—but I was a football fan.

And he was a football star.

And I *didn't* support the Cardinal Saints football team. Or their cocky smirking quarterback.

I got into this college through sheer luck and, of course, academic credit, but this was a private university, and I was on the lower half of the food chain when it came to money. Actually, I was so low down I was lucky I could *see* the chain at all. However, I had been given one of only three English scholarships due to my submission entry, which was a thesis of twenty thousand words detailing why I was worthy of the scholarship. My 3.9 GPA helped too.

My mom went to college in Alabama, and I was all set for their state college, but my chance to stay "local" arose when my guidance counsellor recommended I apply for the scholarship to Cardinal Saints College. I'd laughed at first and then thought, *why not?* never in a million years thinking I would actually be successful. The scholarship was a rarity in itself, but it was a *full* ticket, it even included a meal plan. It was a godsend and meant neither mom nor I would need to worry about college debt.

However, despite our gratefulness for the scholarship, my mom's football blood ran white and blue; therefore, *my* football blood ran white and blue. Not the silver and black of the Saints.

Dante Spence was the quarterback I followed. Dante was the college football star who I dreamed of. Dante was the footballer who I had imagined myself in several positions in the bedroom with. *Not* Jett Santo. With his stupid messy black hair and his stupid tattoos and his stupid low husky voice that made me want to listen to him all day.

"Ugh, no one really." I shrugged it off, and out of the corner of my eye, I saw her smile fade.

"You don't know, or you don't want to tell me?" She placed her cup down on the table without a coaster, and I hurriedly snatched it off the wood.

"Mia!" I protested. "There's a coaster *right* there."

"Gosh, you're as bad as my mom," Mia muttered as she pushed herself to her feet. "You're such a worrywart, Ava." She held her hand out to me, and I placed the cup back in it, watching her as she drank her coffee as she settled back onto the couch. "Now, tell me who it was."

"Jett Santo."

Mia was on her feet again, her coffee forgotten as it dangled in her hand. Her mouth was open, and I knew I was about to be asked a hundred questions. "Are you for real?"

"Unfortunately, yes."

"Oh my gosh, did you see it?" Her eyes were wide with excitement, and I was already shaking my head. "You had to have *seen* it. They say he's not shy in that area, is it true?"

"He's definitely *not* shy," I grumbled. "I didn't see anything," I added as I headed to the kitchen to distance myself from her questions. I didn't add that I could still *feel* him in my nether regions either.

"How?" Mia followed me, sliding onto the bar stool at the breakfast counter. "How didn't you see anything?"

"I guess he must have put it away when I screamed."

Mia snorted as she started laughing again. "Oh my!" She gasped between laughs. "You're *such* a prude, I wish I'd seen your face!" As she wiped her eyes, I remained silent. Mia had no hang-ups about hooking up with guys, and truthfully, I envied her. I just didn't feel the need to sleep with the people I went on dates with. Mia always went on about the chemistry. I think my pH level was neutral, as I had never encountered a chemical reaction yet.

You did today when you spoke to Jett.

Yeah, that was an aftereffect of Friday. *Not* him. Not after he had...*parts*...of him in someone's mouth in a classroom. Pig.

"He probably needed consoling, poor thing." As she poured her remaining drink down the sink, I stared in horror at the waste of coffee before her words penetrated.

"Why?"

Looking at me over her shoulder, my best friend shrugged. "I didn't want any more."

"No, doofus." Swiping at her hair playfully, I giggled as she ducked out of the way. "*Why* would Mr-I'm-The-Best-Quarter-back-Ever need consoling?"

"Oh he's injured. Didn't you hear?"

"Injured?" I was already on my phone, looking at the team news. "He didn't even take a tackle on Saturday."

"You're so weird." Mia rinsed her cup before putting it in the trash. "He got injured in training."

"When?"

"Dude, I am not his PA." Mia crossed her arms as she watched me. "You seem *very* interested in him. You sure you saw nothing?"

Not that I can remember.

"I saw nothing," I stressed. "I just had to put up with his shit-talking afterwards."

"He *spoke* to you?" Mia was excited again.

"Mia, I stopped him getting his finish," I said, using the appropriate air quotes. "I told him he was disgusting."

Mia was once again speechless. "Are you *kidding me*?" she squealed. "You told one of the hottest guys on this campus that he was disgusting?"

"Mia, he was getting a *blow job* in class!"

"Ava, Jett Santo could be in a threesome in the middle of a class, and people wouldn't say a word."

"Well, that's a disturbing thought." I picked up my book bag and headed to my room. "He's a male chauvinist pig!" I yelled over my shoulder.

"You're a prude, Ava Bryant. You need to get rid of that V-card and come join the rest of us in the dirt!" Mia's words carried down the hall, and even though she was laughing and I knew she was only joking, her words still stung.

"I was in the dirt," I said to my empty room. "I don't want to go back down there."

Mia and I had secured a two-bedroom suite with a shared kitchenette. A small living room off of the kitchenette and a shared shower room made up the rest of our tiny dorm suite. The college housing actually marketed it as an off-campus apartment, which even with a very artistic licence, I thought, was pushing it. Firstly, there was no *off-campus*. The whole entire built-up area in the middle of lush forestry was campus. There were stores and restaurants, but the whole entire economy of the town of Cardinal was the college, administration and student body.

If you drove about two hours from Knoxville and an hour north of Nashville, you'd found us. Being a private college, the student population was smaller than most, but the fan base for the varsity teams was huge. The football stadium sat over forty thousand spectators, and at every home game, there wasn't a seat to spare.

The actual town was a few miles west of the college campus, and that's where some of the students came from. Like the Santo boys. Rumour was they had owned their high school as much as they now owned the student population in college.

In my opinion they were arrogant boys, who thought they were above everyone. I watched them play, and they *were* talented, but they ruined it, because they knew it.

Privileged, entitled assholes.

And I slept with one of them.

Like so many before me, with many more to follow. I wasn't delusional. I knew having sex with Jett on Friday would make me no more than another girl in his long list of conquests, I just struggled to understand how *I* was on the list. Why didn't I remember meeting him? Talking to him? Why was I only getting X-rated flashbacks of him having sex with me?

I'd read a book once where the girl hooks up with the guy in the bathroom in the very first chapter. Some random guy walks into the bathroom, and they have some sort of insane chemistry and end up going at it without a word spoken. I loved reading that sort of attraction in books.

But those books were fiction. Fantasy.

Hooking up with random people without *saying* anything, did that happen in real life? With no consequences? No guilt? No *care* for their health?

I needed another shower. I still felt dirty. Used. It wasn't rational; I *knew* I had been drunk, I *knew* he wouldn't have known how incredibly out of character it was for me, I *knew* Jett wasn't to blame for my recklessness on Friday.

Yet still…I hated him.

I hated him for what he unknowingly took, and I hated myself for not being able to remember.

Talking to him today merely emphasised how much of a dick he was. The best news I had heard since Friday was that he was injured. Reading the update on the college football's newsfeed, I grinned when I saw he was out for two games.

What a result! Mom's hometown college team played here in a few weeks, and the Saints' backup quarterback was nothing compared to Jett. Looks like the Blues would be winning.

With a smile on my face, I settled down to do my assignments and promised not to give one more minute of my attention to Jett freaking Santo.

I WOKE UP SWEATING AND PANTING, COMPLETELY DISORIENTED. My tank top was stuck to my body, and my sleep shorts were twisted around my hips and thighs.

"Ava?" Mia's voice sounded from outside my door. "Are you okay?"

"Huh?" Wetting my lips, I tried again. "Yeah, um, sure," I said as I rose up onto my elbows and looked around the dimly lit room. There was no sound and little light. Sliding my legs out of bed, I crossed the floor and opened the door.

Mia was on the other side looking as dishevelled as I felt, her skin tacky with sweat.

"Generator out?" I guessed.

"Yeah, I think so."

"Fuck, it's like an oven in here." Gathering my hair up into a pile, I tilted my head back.

Our humble little apartment lost electricity more than it probably should. We'd spoken to the college housing department, and they assured us it was a fluke that would be fixed. That was twelve months ago. Every month, sometimes twice, the generator would fail, and for an evening, we would either freeze or overheat. This month it was overheating.

Tennessee nights at this time of year were hot, muggy and sticky. I wanted a shower.

"How long's it been out?" I asked Mia as I headed to the fridge.

"Not sure, your moaning woke me up."

"Wh-what?" I stammered as I turned to look at her.

"I thought you were having a nightmare at first," Mia told me as she leaned against the counter. "And then I thought you had a guy in there with you."

"A guy?" I knew my eyes were wide as saucers as I stared at my best friend, who was watching me curiously.

"Yeah, you were *moaning*."

"A bad dream, I'm sure." Turning my head away from her, I ran the water and filled two glasses. I avoided eye contact as I handed her a glass. "Whose turn is it to complain to housing?" I asked her as I took a sip.

"Yours."

"Dammit." With a resigned sigh, I headed back to bed. Pushing the window open, I hoped for a small breeze to cool the room. When I felt nothing except more heat, I tidied up the covers and climbed onto my bed.

I should have bought a fan. But then they only worked with electricity, and we currently didn't have any.

"Night, Ava," Mia called through the closed door, and I mumbled a goodnight back to her.

I sounded like I was moaning? As I lay on my bed, staring at the ceiling, I tried to think about what I was dreaming of. Closing my eyes, I decided it wasn't worth worrying about. I needed sleep because I had a full day of classes tomorrow, and I had to fit in a trip to housing.

Strong hands slid down my sides as my body arched to meet his. His mouth captured mine in a hot searing kiss, his tongue stroking mine as his hips drove relentlessly into me...

My eyes flew open as I sat up straight. *Oh shit.*

I was having a wet flipping dream about Jett? As I shifted restlessly on my bed, my lust rose once again, and the throbbing in certain *parts* of me intensified.

Biting my lip, I turned onto my side. It had felt real. Like he had been here. My subconscious was remembering him more than *I* actually remembered him.

"He got a blow job in class, Ava," I reminded myself crossly. "You're lying here thinking about someone who doesn't deserve it, and he's already moved onto someone else."

Flopping over onto my back, I took in a deep breath. The ache between my legs was still there. The need to be satisfied hadn't lessened, even with my sharp reminder of who my body was craving. I was a healthy nineteen-year-old girl, I had urges, and my hand had always been enough. These walls were a little thicker than paper but not much. In the apartment I lived in with mom before I came here, the walls were thin. I didn't make loud noises at any time, but as I lay in the dark, staring into the shadows, fragments of images and sounds danced out of my reach. I remembered a cry, a gasp, an elusive feeling with the promise only he could deliver.

One night.

I was with him for one night, and now he was haunting my dreams. Nightmares more like. The fact that my subconscious was throwing up visions of us tangled together was not welcome, or something I wanted to experience again. Thumping my head back onto the pillow, I groaned and then hastily covered my mouth. I did *not* need Mia coming back to the door.

With a disgruntled sigh, I spread my legs more and slipped my hand under my shorts. I would take care of this. I would not think of him. This was perfectly natural. I had nothing to be ashamed of. This would get him out of my system. That's all this was: residual want.

I didn't *actually* want him. My body just needed release.

My fingers started to work on my problem, and as I closed my eyes, willing the finish line to be quick, I steadfastly refused to think of the cause of my discomfort.

Seriously, how long would it be until I was free of this guy?

CHAPTER 6

Jett

THE THREE OF US SAT IN THE CAR, WATCHING THE HOUSE, WAITING for the last light to go out. The light above the porch finally vanished, signalling that the occupants were in bed. Finally.

Gray's knee had been jittering for the last half hour, and even if he was my twin, I was close to amputating the fucking thing before I lost my mind. Ash sat in the back, relaxed and easy, as always.

"Time?" Gray asked for what felt like the millionth time.

"Ten minutes since you last asked," Ash drawled from the back. His head was resting against the seat, and his eyes were half closed.

Gray twisted in his seat to glare at him, which gave me time to hide my grin at my cousin's snark.

"Thirty more minutes," I told them both quietly. "You remember your positions?"

"We're not stupid," Gray mumbled as his leg took up its rhythmic tapping again. After another twenty minutes, my hand shot out and I placed it firmly on his knee, pressing his leg down to the floor of the car.

"I will cut it off," I warned with a hard glare to my brother. His answering scowl made me grin, but I didn't remove my hand until he nodded.

"Are you sure they'll sleep through this?" Ash asked me as he leaned forward, alert for the first time since we had parked halfway down the road.

"Yeah, I'm sure."

"Okay, I'll check the back now then." He opened the car door and, pulling his hoodie low, he took off over the grass. Blending into the night, he was hard to spot, and I smiled with grim satisfaction at how well he had adjusted to our night-time "escapades."

"He's gotten good at this." Gray echoed my thoughts as he too watched Ash disappear into the night.

"Like a duck to water," I murmured as I checked my watch. "You okay?"

"Yeah, I'm ready." Gray pulled his own hoodie down low over his face before he adjusted his black bandana over his mouth. "You have the codes?"

"I do." I checked my watch again. "Three more minutes."

Gray nodded and opened the car door. Following, I locked the car and then, ensuring there were no casual observers in the street, I placed the car key on top of the tyre out of sight. My phone lit up with a message from Ash telling us the back was clear, so we both jogged across the street and slipped undetected into the yard surrounding the house. Stealthily, we made our way around to the back and joined Ash, who was already at the back door, a small black folded-over case in his hand.

"You have five minutes," I whispered to him.

Gray stood sentry at the bottom of the steps, pressed against the wall to keep out of sight but still able to watch.

As Ash started to pick the lock of the back door, I watched for any movement from inside the house. We had been watching the house for over a week. The routine was the same, the inhabitants very much keepers to the same schedule.

"I'm in," Ash said as he stood and tested the handle. A low whistle to Gray, and my brother was coming up the steps.

"The study is the only thing we want," I reminded them as Ash slowly pushed the door open.

When no answering alarm sounded, I felt a smug thrill of victory. I knew the people who lived here had an alarm system, and I had been fairly confident that they didn't set it at night-time.

Swiftly, the three of us crossed the kitchen, into the hall, and taking the second door on the left, we entered the study.

Pulling out my phone, I opened the note I had with the safe

code. It was one of three, and my research told me, for the make of the safe these people had, you had three attempts before you were locked out.

Ash uncovered the safe, which was hidden behind a painting, and Gray snorted. "One time, I'd just like to come in and the fucking thing be on display."

Three-five-one-seven-two, I punched the code in and waited. The safe beeped loudly in denial, and all three of us froze, waiting for the sound of movement to tell us that the occupant had been woken.

Seven-four-eight-nine-zero. The safe beeped, and I pushed the handle down. "Bullseye," I told the others. The safe had the normal stack of cash, some boxes that would contain jewellery no doubt, and a few folders with paperwork. "Gray," I instructed as Ash stayed by the door, watching.

Gray snapped a picture of the layout of the safe, and then quickly we took the contents out.

"Hurry," I urged him as we divided the folders between us. We started searching. When I was almost through my search, I looked at my brother. His face was twisted in a scowl, and I knew he hadn't found anything either.

"Anything?" Ash asked from the doorway.

"No," Gray said as he stepped back and let out a long sigh. "Another fucking dead end."

"Let's put it back," I told him as I held back on my own sigh. Quickly I checked the boxes and, with no interest in the contents, moved the diamonds, emeralds and other precious stones aside as I checked for hidden compartments. Gray was doing the same to the inside of the safe, and I could almost feel his irritation before he stilled.

"What is it?" I asked, closing the boxes and stepping up beside him.

He said nothing, but his look of determination made me wait

patiently. A creak sounded above us, and all three of us stilled. Ash had his finger to his lips as he slowly opened the door a fraction more.

The creak sounded again, and Gray looked at me. "Bathroom?"

I nodded, but we made no move as we heard a door close, and then a few moments later, a steady stream as someone relieved their bladder.

"They sleep with the bedroom door open," Ash whispered. "We need to be extra quiet."

Gray started pressing again, and then I heard the soft click. With a triumphant smirk, he pulled out two items. A USB stick and an envelope.

"Harry? Are you okay?"

The three of us stood still at the sound of the voice.

As quickly as we could, Gray and I put the contents of the safe back together, even as we heard the answering murmur from the bathroom.

"I can get you some painkillers?" Harry's wife called, and we all looked up as we heard her feet hit the floor.

"Hurry," Ash urged, and I snatched Gray's phone off of him to check the layout before we hastily closed the safe. The two of us replaced the painting, and then the three of us were at the study door, waiting.

The bathroom door opened as the toilet flushed.

"Dude didn't even wash his hands," Gray muttered in disgust.

"That's the least of our problems if they come downstairs," Ash warned.

"They won't," I whispered as I tucked the USB into my jeans and the envelope into my back pocket. "Let's move. One at a time, like always."

Ash was the first out of the study, and for a guy of six four, he was almost dainty as he crossed the hall and disappeared into the kitchen.

"Are you sure, dear? It won't take a minute."

"No, honey, let's just go back to sleep."

I grinned at Gray, who rolled his eyes at me for being right, before he left the study and crossed the hall and entered the kitchen. Casting a quick look around to make sure the room was as we found it, I followed them out. When I got to the kitchen, they were already outside, and I followed, Ash closing the door behind me.

We waited on the back porch for a few minutes before, one by one, we ran from the house back to the car.

Within ten minutes of being in the house, we were driving away with a USB stick and an envelope hopefully telling us what we needed to know. No one spoke during the trip back, not even as I parked the car outside the house, and as quietly as we had left it this evening, we made our way to the top floor.

In my room, Gray and Ash disrobed of their black clothing and pulled on their pyjama shorts. While they got ready to look like they had been in bed in case anyone came looking for us, I fired up the spare laptop I kept in the back of my closet.

"Was easier than I thought," Gray said as he pulled a chair up beside me. It was the first any of us had spoken since we left the targeted house.

"Too easy?" Ash asked as he sat on the bed, his eyes on the screen. "What's in the envelope?"

"A code," I told him as I tossed it over to him. "I would guess it's the passcode."

"Yeah," he nodded and then looked at the screen. "Swap seats. If it's encrypted, I'll get in quicker than you."

Not a lie. Ash studied computer science, I did economics. Both of us were shit hot on computers, he was just better at coding and, in this case, *decoding*.

As we waited for the USB to come to life, I peeled my own clothes off. Unlike my brother and cousin, I slept naked, so I had no sleepwear to change into. However, they were used to seeing me in my underwear, and it was too humid tonight to be keeping my jeans on. Ash was grumbling about idiots and easy codes as I tossed my stuff in the hamper.

"It's so hot," I grumbled as I took Ash's vacant spot on the bed.

"I'm in," Ash said. "Looks like a video, we watching?"

"Fuck yes, we are," Gray said as he leaned closer.

Twenty minutes later, not one of us had spoken a word.

"Fuck," I finally murmured.

Ash huffed in agreement, his eyes on the now black screen.

"I..." Gray trailed off before his hand ran over his hair. "I will never unsee that."

"What a sick bastard." Ash shook his head as he stood up. "What a sick, twisted fuck."

"We need to identify her," I spoke softly as I looked at the two of them. "She probably has family who have no idea where she is or what happened to her."

"We need to identify the four bastards in the video also." Gray's voice was hoarse.

"Well, *Harry* wasn't one of them," Ash spat. "But I bet he knows who they are."

"We'll figure it out," I told them. "Jesus, I don't think I can sleep after that."

"We have to." Gray stood too. "Who's keeping it?"

All three of us stared at the USB stick like it was a deadly snake. "I will." I picked up the innocent looking USB.

"Will the laptop show that we watched it?" Gray asked Ash.

"No, I'll clear any traces of it."

"Tomorrow," I told them. "It's almost two in the morning. Go to bed."

They left, and I stood alone in my room, my fingers curled tightly around the offending item. With great care, I put it and the envelope in my own safe, which I kept hidden under the floorboards in my closet.

Over an hour later, I still couldn't sleep. The scenes from the film we had inadvertently uncovered were still fresh in my head. Grumbling under my breath and getting out of bed, I flung on some training shorts and a T-shirt from earlier.

I needed to clear my head.

Seeing the low light from under Ash's door told me he was also still up. I could hear my brother pacing in his room, and it made me feel slightly better knowing the film had caused them the same amount of unrest as it caused me. I knew they both would have heard me, but neither of them stopped me from leaving the house, and I knew none of us would sleep much tonight.

Walking the campus at almost three in the morning had a surreal feeling about it. The buildings were in darkness, while the halls and dorms only had a few lights on, depicting either late night studiers or those who had more interesting things to do in bed than sleep. The humid night air made me thankful I had pulled these workout shorts on, as already I could feel sweat trickle down my back.

The more I walked, the more my head was filled with the images of the girl on the film. We had watched it on low sound, but even with the barely heard audio, her screams would linger.

Reaching the other end of the campus, I debated about walking back in a straight line and went on a detour instead, weaving in amongst the buildings, heading in the direction of the stadium. I always found inner peace on the turf.

I saw her before I recognised her. Sitting on the steps of a simple apartment block, I hesitated before I decided to approach her.

The girl from class today didn't notice me at all. Her long slim legs were stretched out in front of her on the lower steps as her elbows rested on the step behind her, her head tilted backwards as she stared up at the night sky. Her hair was a tangled looking mess as it hung loose around her shoulders and rested on the step at her back. For as engrossed as she was watching the stars, the position didn't look comfortable.

With a sigh, she sat up, and I watched her back curve as her hands gathered her long blonde hair into her hands before she twisted it on her head, her breasts catching my attention in her thin top as they stood out proudly.

With her hair off her face, I could appreciate her beauty. I hadn't noticed in class, but she was more than pretty. A small, delicate button nose sat over thick plump lips. I almost wished it wasn't as dark—I had paid no real attention to her looks this afternoon. I hadn't paid attention to *her* really. Her loose jeans and loose T-shirt had been hiding a body that curved in all the right places if her shorts and tank were anything to go by.

"Don't scream," I said to her as I approached her, knowing she was completely unaware of me walking towards her, and her startled yelp reminded me of her reaction earlier in class.

"You creepy fucker!"

I grinned at her as she stood hastily and looked around uncertainly. "Not creepy, just out walking."

"It's after three in the morning," she hissed at me as she looked around again.

"I know, why are you out here? Can't sleep?" I leaned against the wall of her building. At least, I assumed it was her building.

She watched me for a moment before she looked around again. "No, it's too hot."

I looked at the AC units on the side of the building and looked back at her in question.

"They broke, they break regularly."

"Housing will fix it if you ask them."

She rolled her eyes at me as if I had just told her water was wet. "Yeah, I know. Only they don't seem to fix them for long."

"Why do you hate me?" My question surprised me as much as it did her. I had no idea why she disliked me so much, and for the life of me, I didn't understand why. But she was not shy in hiding her aversion to me, even though I was fairly confident I'd never met her before.

My question obviously flustered her as she was putting her hair up again. Gray did the same thing, fidgeted when he was agitated or nervous. I was guessing she was nervous. Because of me? It didn't make sense.

"How's your ankle?" she asked me instead of answering. "Should you be walking so far on it?" When I raised an eyebrow, she lifted her shoulder in a half shrug. "Students talk."

"You're concerned for me?" I heard her huff of derision, and for some reason, this made me grin wider.

"No, not at all." She glanced over her shoulder to the door. "I better go inside."

"I make you nervous." She had turned to leave, but she hesitated at my question. "Why?"

"You don't make me nervous," she answered as she looked over at me. "It's late, I'm tired."

"You tell yourself that." I smirked at her as I resumed my walk.

"You don't affect me at all," came her angry hiss, and I smiled wider. I knew I was getting to her, but I didn't know why. I just knew it pleased me in some way.

"As I said, keep telling yourself that," I called softly over my shoulder. I laughed when I heard her door slam in response. With a smile and a lighter step, I headed back home.

I had a lot of shit to sort, but now I was ready for sleep.

CHAPTER 7

Ava

IN THE MORNING, I WAS CRANKY, AND I KNEW EXACTLY WHO I WAS pissed off at. Jett Santo. Every single time I tried to get rid of him from my brain, he turned up, like some form of narcissistic junkie who sensed I was *moving on* from Friday, so he popped back into the forefront of my awareness in case I *could* forget him.

He was like a freaking whack-a-mole just waiting to be swatted.

I would quite happily swat the fucker with a baseball bat if I could.

Sleep had not come to visit me last night. I had gotten up and done some course work, hoping it would help me sleep. Then I had merely lain in bed and watched my alarm clock move ever closer to getting up time. An hour before I was due to wake up, I was using a washcloth to give myself a sink bath since the generator was still out, which meant no shower, and at the stroke of eight thirty, I was arriving at the housing administration building with a vengeance.

Much to my annoyance, there was already a line forming, and I was eyeing the guy-in-front-of-me's coffee with rabid want. Was it assault if I tackled him to the ground for his coffee? On top of theft? My crazy inner ramblings made me giggle and caused the carrier of the object of my desire to turn and look at me quizzically.

Lame hand wave later, and he had not only turned back, facing front, but also moved a step further away from me. It did not lessen the soft sultry smell of caffeine though, and I was almost salivating by the time he was called forward.

My horror as he casually tossed the three-quarter full cup into the trash was only surmounted when Jett came out of the side office, looking impeccable and well-rested, wearing a white T-shirt and dark blue jeans with ripped out knees.

Hiding behind my hair so he wouldn't see me, I studied my scuffed white Chucks. Even had I not known he was in the same room as me, I would have felt his presence as he came and stood casually beside me.

"Morning," he greeted cheerfully.

I hate you.

Looking up and pretending I hadn't seen him before he was beside me, I forced a carefree smile. When his head tilted slightly to the side and his beautiful blue eyes narrowed infinitesimally, I can only imagine what my face must have looked like.

"What?" I asked him rather forcibly, and my good Southern manners internally balked at me. "Sorry, morning."

"Are you always this uptight?" Jett asked me with a casual sweep over me, and I remembered that I was practically unwashed, my hair probably looked like I'd been on the back of a hay cart, and I was pretty confident this was yesterday's T-shirt.

"I'm not uptight, I'm just not a morning person," I explained patiently.

"You were like this yesterday, and it was the afternoon. You were like this last night, or should I say earlier this morning." He looked me over again critically. "I think you're just uptight."

"Well, thank goodness I don't really care what you think." Again the tight smile, but this time I wasn't forcing myself to be nice to him.

"I knew I'd regret doing this, but yeah, you can come out of the line. You're holding everyone up."

"Huh?"

Jett looked at me with that damn smirk on his face. "Your generator will be fixed this morning."

"Huh?"

"How quickly you go from hostile to speechless." His lip curled up in a smile at the corner, and I was torn between wanting to lick it or smack it off his face. "I think I like it."

"You don't even know my name." I looked around as I stepped out of the line. "I was next, so you better not have been fucking with me."

Again the cool appraisal, and again I felt like an uncouth bug. "I'm not *fucking* with you. I don't know your name, but I know the building."

"Oh." I glanced around again, and when Coffee Abuser left the counter at that very moment, I darted into the open space before the guy behind me could take my place. "Hi," I greeted the lady behind the counter. "I live at the suites off of Blossom Parade, and our generator is down."

The admin woman clicked on her computer. All the while, he stood beside me, casually leaning his back on the counter, his elbows propping him up, with his head turned towards me. I could feel his smugness, and I desperately didn't want what he had said to me to be true, because I genuinely couldn't cope with the thought that I would be indebted to him.

"Yes, this is already listed as a repair. We'll have someone out there this morning, probably after ten," she said as she looked at me, and I felt the weight of weary resignation hanging around my neck. Like a noose.

"Oh, um, thanks," I mumbled as I went to turn away. "Do I need to be there?" I added as I half-turned back.

"No, it's an old fault outside," she told me with a firm but polite "move along" smile, and with heavy feet, I walked away from the counter.

I didn't look at him until we were outside the admin building, and he seemed content to wait for it. Biting my tongue from any harsh words escaping, I wrapped my arms across my chest, gripping my elbows as I stared over the quad. "Thanks."

"Physically hurts you, doesn't it," Jett said, humour thick in his voice.

"No." It really did. "Why?" I dared a glance at him, and when I saw that self-satisfied smirk, I knew I would punch him.

"Figured I owed you after yesterday," he told me with a casual shrug. "Even though it's a closed campus, girls shouldn't be sitting out in their PJ's at three in the morning to cool down because their housing facilities are screwed."

I huffed out a laugh despite myself. "It's not the heat, it's the humidity," I uttered the well-known saying, and he gave a low rumble of laughter.

"Exactly." Jett still sounded amused. "Call us even?"

"I wasn't aware I owed *you* anything." Why did my mouth have to speak without my brain intervening?

"I told you that you owed me a finish." His slow smile was almost my undoing. No one, I mean *no one,* should be able to look like that before nine in the morning.

"Right, you did. I ignored you then too." Too bad my tummy was fluttering like it was full of butterflies. My body was not on my side when it came to Jett Santo. Jett laughed out loud, causing a few people to turn and look at us, which made me tilt my head down so my hair covered my face, hiding me from curious eyes.

He noticed. "You ashamed to be seen with me?" he asked me curiously.

"No, I don't know you to be ashamed of you." *Lie, I know you better than I should.*

"You're a smartass."

"You're a dick."

"You enjoyed looking at my dick." He leaned against the wall, completely at ease.

"When?" I gasped in horror as I finally made proper eye contact with him. *Had he remembered who I was?*

"Yesterday, in class?" Jett had lost his smile and was looking me over with more interest. "Or…do we already know each other?"

I did not like the way his eyes suddenly narrowed as if he was trying to place me. "Absolutely not," I told him hurriedly. "We've never spoken."

"You really are very uptight."

"Yeah, you said." Looking around at the grounds filling with students, all of whom knew exactly who he was, I knew I needed away from here. "Look, it was kind of you to use your connections, I guess, in helping me. The suite is a shit place to be in the heat, so thanks. But if you wanted anything else..."

"Are you fucking kidding me?" Jett snapped to attention, and I took a hesitant step backwards. The irritation was clear on his face, and this time when he looked me over, it was less complimentary.

"Wh-what?"

"I was messing with you earlier, I didn't help you so I could fuck you."

"Whoa, that is not cool to say out loud, dude!" My look around us now was more frantic, and I hoped to God the guy walking past within three feet of me hadn't heard.

"Not cool to say out loud, but okay to *think*?"

"I didn't know what you meant; if I thought wrong, well, can you blame me?"

"What the fuck does that mean?" Jett demanded.

"Well, you're, you know...you."

"No. I *don't* know. Why don't you tell me?"

Could you die on the spot from mortification? I didn't know if there were actual cases of it, but I was possibly close to being the first one recorded on campus.

"I didn't mean to cause offence." Tucking my hair behind my ears, I refused to look at him. "I said thanks, we're even as you said. Can I go now?"

"I wasn't aware I was keeping you." Jett's tone was no longer friendly. His look was hard, and I was more than ready to leave.

"Okay, um, have a nice day." I turned and quickly left him standing there. *Have a nice day?* Seriously, after telling him he was basically a manwhore? Well done, Ava. I didn't look back, but I could feel his heavy stare on me, and I had to stop myself from running, anything to put distance between us. He didn't remember me. He didn't remember Friday. Or I was just one of so many, he couldn't remember me even if he wanted to. If that wasn't a slap in the face, I didn't know what was. I was grateful that he got the generator fixed, but I didn't think we would ever be even.

Not by a long shot.

I made it to my first class by the skin of my teeth, and I heard nothing that the professor said in the fifty-minute lecture. Not one word. I was the same in the next class, my attention focused inwards rather than outwards. What I did hear was my conversation with Jett on a constant loop. I told him I didn't know him, and then I told him he was a slut. Wonderful.

My fingers continuously threaded through my hair as I wondered for the hundredth time how the hell I had met him on Friday. I was at the party. He was not. I had too many drinks. I knew that my stomach had been tender right into Sunday night. Even drunk off my ass, I would know if Jett was at the party. I would know if any of the football guys were there, but it was the night before a game. They shouldn't have been out. *He* shouldn't have been out. I would remember if they were there.

Wouldn't I?

"Ms Bryant, are you listening?"

My head shot up, and my mouth dropped open. "Huh?"

"I'll take the lack of articulation as a *no,* shall I?" Professor Windsor asked me with an easy grin.

"Sorry." I knew I was turning red, but the professor was now openly laughing at me. "Didn't sleep last night." I immediately regretted my words, because the catcalls and whistles were expected even if they were juvenile.

"What kept our Ava Bryant awake?" Professor Windsor asked me. His name was Joe, and he encouraged us to use it, but it felt odd, and I hadn't managed it yet. Not even in my head.

"Generator broke, no AC."

"Ouch, and we're not even in the first week of September," he said with a shake of his head. "Southern heat is a killer."

"I did spend about three hours during the night going over the assignment," I told him as I hoped that this would distract him from the fact that I hadn't been paying attention.

"In the Southern heat, whilst overheating, you thought of Blanche?" The professor gave a cheerful laugh as he turned to the whiteboard. "Okay, Ava. Tell me how *A Streetcar Named Desire* reflects your inner turmoil in a hot room in the middle of the night, with no air."

"Well," I began, and I was off. It was one of my most favourite plays, and I had been thinking about her last night as I lay and thought about *him*. A desperate woman confusing illusion with reality. Was I confusing my fragmented memories of Friday with something they weren't? I was having flashbacks of a hot and heavy sex-a-thon, but what if it wasn't? What if I had simply passed out and all the sexcapades were in my head? *He didn't even know who I was, for God's sake.* Maybe some small—very small, possibly minute part of me—*wanted* it to have been a sex session, but in truth, my virgin inexperienced self had actually been so bad in bed, and drunk, he had simply rolled over and gone to sleep?

Giving the class my attention, as it should have done, and talking about the play lessened my inner ramblings, and I became more focused.

Packing up my things afterwards, I was pleased that I had started a good discussion in the class, but like so many other times, my mind wandered back to him. Realistically, I knew I had to take the hit. My ego was bruised. I should have meant more than I did to him. But then, truthfully, he should have probably meant more to me than he did.

So…was I any better than Jett? Really?

I didn't remember the night much, and he didn't seem to remember me…so…maybe he was just as drunk as me? And honestly, did I actually *want* him to remember? God no. I could quite happily live my life without him having that knowledge.

He had done a nice thing for me today.

In return, I'd been a bitch.

We would never be friends, but I should do the honourable thing and thank him properly. Civilly. I hadn't been polite with him so far, but maybe me being purposefully nice to him would shock him so much that I could deliver my apology and get out of there before he could reply?

If unicorns were real, they'd fart rainbows.

I texted Mia after my third class when I received the email that the AC was fixed. She sent me a trophy emoji for killing it in the admin building. I would tell her later who we should actually be thanking. Or to avoid the conversation, I could keep it to myself. Mia wouldn't care who really got it done, as long as it was done.

Heading to the cafeteria, I thought about lunch. I needed carbs and energy. Possibly an energy drink. And coffee. Maybe a burger. With fries. No, was that too heavy? But if I had a food coma happening in the afternoon, I could snooze through Leitch. No, that would never happen.

As I debated my food choices, I really should have paid more attention. A sudden whack to my head knocked me flying. My cry of alarm and my arms flailing like a windmill would have been comical if I hadn't just landed on my ass.

"Ow! Sonofabitch!" Rubbing my head, I sat up as I realised my book bag was spilled all over the grass too.

"You okay?"

I looked up into familiar light blue eyes and a handsome face, only this time it wasn't the Devil that I was used to. Gray Santo? Seriously? Was someone just fucking bored up above and *trying* to make me miserable?

"You hit me?" Shaking my head to clear it from the thumping, I refused his outstretched hand as I stood.

"Nah, not me, him," Gray said as he jerked his thumb over his shoulder.

I half expected Jett, but it was the backup QB, and he was currently heading my way. "His aim's shit," I snapped as I rubbed my head again, not too sore. The ache would fade quickly.

"Yeah, we were trying a new play."

"Try your new plays and routes in the stadium," I growled as I bent down to pick up my belongings and put them back in my bag.

"Hey, you okay?" The backup quarterback had arrived. I knew him. I knew the whole team on paper, but I wasn't in the mood to be nice.

"No, jackass. Be more careful." With a glare, I stomped angrily away from them. Twice in one day I had been the source of attention from a Santo brother.

"Yo, chick?"

I stopped dead and turned back to Gray, who was holding something out to me. "Chick?" I asked him incredulously. "Do I look like poultry?"

"Whatever, you dropped this." He tossed it to me with casual indifference and had turned away before I had clumsily caught it, realising it was my wallet.

"Thanks," I called out after him, his back broad and straight as he walked away. He flicked his middle finger up at me, and despite myself, I grinned. That was how I expected a Santo to behave. Complete indifference to the lesser minions.

Maybe the knock on my head was my world shifting back onto its rightful axis.

"So, is it just any man that you're rude to, or do you reserve your aggression just for us Santos?"

Fuck my life. I turned and met his cool sardonic stare with trepidation. "Hi."

Jett didn't smile.

"You saw?"

"Hard to miss."

"Apparently not for your backup," I muttered as I rubbed my head again in remembrance. He said nothing. *Okay then*. "So, earlier," I started and then faltered. His eyes were glacial, and I felt nervous. "I was rude."

"You were."

"Okay, well, thanks for that, anyway…" My sarcasm was hard to rein in, but I had to try. "*Anyway*, I should have said thank you. Properly."

"Properly? So now you want to give me a blow job?"

"What?" My eyes were wide as I met his cool look. "What is *wrong* with you?"

"What's wrong with you?"

"*You!*" We stared at each other for a long moment. Me in incredulity, him with apathy. This was getting me nowhere. "I just want to say thanks, it's fixed. I appreciate your help." I waited, and when he gave no response, I was content to tell myself I'd tried my best. "Now we're even."

"Fine."

"Fine." I waited again. "Oh fuck off, you know I'm trying to be nice. You didn't have to help me, you did, I've said thanks, again, now please, we don't ever need to speak again, okay?"

I hastily walked past him, and when I heard him say, "No problem," I didn't even falter. *Now* the last few days could finally be over.

CHAPTER 8

Jett

"You know her?" Gray asked me as I approached him and Ben, our backup quarterback.

"Met her twice, happy to never meet her again." I took the ball off Ben. "Your aim was on point."

"Didn't mean to knock her down," he admitted as he looked at us with a grin. "She dropped like a stone."

"Yeah, when I said aim for her, I didn't mean knock her out," I told him with a grin. "Thank fuck she's too prickly to realise she could probably sue us."

"You want to tap that?" Gray asked me as he turned to watch Uptight and Angry march into the cafeteria.

"No, even horizontal, that girl would still have a giant stick up her ass, and it wouldn't be mine, know what I mean?"

Gray snorted as he tossed the ball in his hands. "She does have a point, we probably shouldn't be doing this in the quad."

"She irritates me," I told my brother. "I wanted to see her knocked on her ass. Mission accomplished." With a grin to Ben, we started to head to the stadium. "Thanks to our fine quarterback, I got my wish."

"It sucks you're out for two games," Ben said casually as the three of us walked along the campus. "I really didn't think Ash landed on you that hard."

"He's two hundred and forty pounds. Trust me, him landing on you, hurts," I told him easily.

Gray walked beside me quietly, his eyes on his phone, and then his head was up and he was looking behind him. "She's going for lunch," he told me. Turning back the way we had just come, I saw the familiar long-legged, black-haired girl head into the cafeteria.

"Where's Ash?"

"Stadium."

"Let's go." Turning back to Ben, I tossed him the ball. "See you in a bit."

Gray and I headed to the cafeteria. I needed to enlist help for what happened on Friday.

Quinn was already at a table when we got there, two plastic containers in front of her. Her long hair gathered over one shoulder as she settled down to eat her homemade lunch. We'd known Quinn since we were ten. She was the girl next door. Awkward. Shy. Braces. Hideous hair. She was also wild. Her parents lamented that we led her astray. If they only knew what their beautiful daughter was capable of, they would owe Gray and me a thousand apologies.

"Queeny," I greeted her as I took the seat opposite her, and Gray pulled a chair from the neighbouring table, ignoring the cry of protest from its intended occupant.

"I hate that," Quinn said without raising her head from her food. "What do you want?"

"What's up your ass?" Gray asked her as he leaned over, plucking one of her carrot sticks out of her container and popping it in his mouth.

"Your brother," Quinn snapped as she glared at him. "Maybe it was your dad? I can't remember, all the Santo dicks merge into one giant pain in my ass."

"Jesus fuck, what's your 'tude for?" Gray glared at her, and I knew I had to intervene before they ended up killing each other.

"Quinn." I leaned forward to get her attention. "Can I have a chance to speak?"

"What's happened this time?" Dark brown eyes met mine, and for the first time since we sat down, a small smile graced her face.

"It's like you expect there to be a problem," I joked with her lightly.

"I have the Santo twins interrupting my lunch when their

cousin is nowhere near them, which means you've been looking for me. Or waiting for me. Which usually means…you need me for something." Quinn took a small bite of her chicken salad. "Who is she? How much do I need to know? How bad do you need it resolved?"

I started to tell her, keeping my voice low. "I was at a party on Friday—"

"Before a game?" Quinn frowned at me, and I hurried on to avoid the lecture.

"Yeah, I planned on having one beer. I was there checking something out."

"What?"

"It's not important," Gray interrupted me as he looked around. "He had one beer, then Derrick saw him leave and go home."

"The cute corner?" she asked before she rolled her eyes at Gray's scowl. "So?" Quinn was looking between the two of us, her food forgotten.

"I have no memory of getting home."

"You were drugged?" Quinn asked me with concern. "I knew that ankle injury was bullshit. Who?"

"I don't know."

"That's not all," Gray said as he took another carrot, ignoring her glare. "He woke up with a girl."

Quinn sighed, shaking her head in disappointment as she laid her fork on the table. "You're a complete asshole. How did you even manage?"

"I *don't* remember. *Anything*," I stressed as I held her gaze. "I need you to find out who she is."

"What's the last thing you do remember?"

"The beer."

"You took an open drink?" Quinn was ready to launch into another lecture.

"No. I opened it."

"You laid it down? Unattended?" She looked even more ready to start yelling.

"No."

Sitting back, she tossed her hair over her shoulder. "Pinpricks?"

"What?" I exchanged a glance with Gray.

"If you didn't drink it or swallow it, then it was injected into you." Quinn stood abruptly. "Let's go."

Ignoring her food, she picked her book bag up and headed out of the cafeteria, not giving Gray nor me any choice but to follow.

Quinn walked into the men's bathrooms with no qualms. "Everyone out." Stunned, a few students looked at her before they started to react, either in horror or humour, and then they saw us. "Move it, boys, no need to be shy. I'll make sure I tell whoever asks it was a weapon." She winked lasciviously at them before she jerked her head towards the door. "Today, guys," Quinn urged them.

Gray checked the stalls as I held the door open for the students to leave. Quinn stood in the middle of the bathroom already looking me over.

"Last memory of the night?" she asked when we were alone.

"The beer and talking to Derrick about routes for the game the next day."

"Whose party?" she asked as she approached me, handing her book bag to Gray before her hands started running up my left arm as she studied me.

"I don't remember, some guy."

"Jett, I honestly—"

"C'mon, Quinn, you know it could have been anyone's. He got a text, he went, enough said. Ask around, people saw him, you'll learn whose it was." Gray was also now studying my skin intensely.

I felt like a lab rat. Quinn exhaled in exasperation but nodded. "I'll find out." Her hands were now lightly prodding over my right arm, which was heavily tattooed. "I'm never going to find it in this mess."

"Hey," I protested, turning my head to look at her. She jerked my head forward as she moved up to my neck and then was pulling my earlobe forward to check the skin behind there.

"You're sure you didn't drink it?" she asked as she moved around to my back.

"I'm sure. This is weirdly relaxing," I teased her as she pulled my T-shirt up and ran her hand over my back. "Like a pregame warm-up massage."

I heard her huff out a laugh as her hands kept moving. "You're funny," Quinn told me lightly. "Okay, I have nothing." She stood back and then moved to the side of me so I could see her. "Who were you looking for at the party?" she asked casually as she took her bag off of Gray.

"What do you mean?"

"I mean, *Jett*, that I've known you for ten years give or take, ever since daddy dearest left the navy and settled down in the house right beside yours." Her eyes flicked between me and my brother. "I know when you're speaking bullshit. Now, if you want me to help, you tell me what I want to know. Now." Quinn gestured to the door. "Or I walk."

Gray caught her arm to stop her in case she went through with it. "Quinn, we told you—"

"You told me shit," Quinn interrupted him. "Jett doesn't go to parties when he doesn't know who's having them, who they are, or what they have going on. And he sure as fuck doesn't go alone!" Wrenching her arm from Gray's grip, Quinn turned her angry stare my way. "Who were you *both* looking for?"

"Quinn..."

"I told you!" Angrily she stepped towards me. Quinn was tall, but still she needed to look up at me. "I told you *all* to leave it alone."

"We're never going to do that," I bit back angrily. "That fucker messed with what's ours."

Throwing her arms up into the air, she pushed past me. "I'm done. When you can listen, and *respect* my wishes, then I'll talk to you."

The door slammed behind her. Gray and I stood awkwardly for a moment longer before I turned to the urinal. *May as well take care of business since I'm here,* I thought.

"We stopping?" Gray asked me as he stepped up to the one beside me.

"No."

"She'll be pissed."

I grinned as I unbuttoned my jeans. "She's always pissed," I replied grimly as I started to piss. "I don't give a fuck if she's pissed, nothing stops us."

As we headed to the stadium, I thought about what Quinn had said. I knew she wasn't happy about what we were doing, and even though it had caused more of a rift in the friendship we had, she had to know we would never stop.

Quinn Lawrence was like a sister to me, no one in this world would *ever* hurt me or my family.

No one.

Ash was running routes when we got to the stadium. Coach was glaring at both me and Gray, and without a word, Gray ducked into the locker room to get changed while I dropped my pissed-off self onto the bench.

Ben came over to talk to me, and I spoke to him briefly about nothing. Me not mentioning his arm, and he not mentioning the fact that I was sitting on the sidelines like a spare prick in a brothel.

"Why are you here?" Bowers said to me after he pointed at Ben and then the twenty-five-yard line. Ben took the less than subtle hint and jogged over to meet up with the rest of the offence.

"I'm recovering from a *slight* injury. While I do so, am I not supposed to make it to practice?" I couldn't look at him. If I did, I might punch him, and then "Two Weeks' Suspension" headlines become "No Longer Plays for Cardinal Saints College" breaking news.

Bowers rested his foot on the bench and rested his arms on his raised knee so that he was eye level with me. "Don't pull shit with me, son. You and I both know that this team does not need to have you glowering at them from the sidelines. Pick your butt off that seat, go away."

"Go away?" I asked him disbelievingly as I met his heavy stare.

"You have something more important to be doing, no?" He straightened before he took a step back. "Go find what you need to be finding."

I sat for a few seconds, my temper flaring, but instead, I rolled my head on my shoulders and stood swiftly, causing Coach to stand back abruptly. My smile was not friendly, perhaps had too many teeth, and I knew my eyes told him exactly what I was feeling. "I'll see you soon."

I didn't bother saying anything to Gray as I passed him coming out of the locker room. He knew when to leave me alone. Outside of the stadium, I looked around. As much as it pissed me off, I reluctantly agreed with Coach.

Find the threat to my career. *Eliminate* it.

Quinn would be networking, it's what she did best. And even if she said she wasn't helping me, she would be. It's what we did. Plus, it would be easy for her; she looked like a goddamn supermodel. Everyone spoke to her, even if she was as hostile to people as I was.

Well, I wasn't hostile to everyone.

I did well with women. I needed to find the girl from Friday. What better place to start than my female *friends*? Most girls wanted back in my bed, which meant most girls, even though they disliked me or themselves, either or, they still spoke to me. I needed to use that to my advantage.

Checking my phone, I headed to the campus coffee shop. Hot afternoons and free periods meant one thing: iced drinks. Whether they be coffee or tea, they were the welcome distraction and sustenance most people wanted. I was looking for one particular girl, and I was pretty confident I would find her at the tables outside the coffee shop.

As I walked, I thought more about last night and the video we found. Were they connected? The girl from Friday? My steps slowed, no. No one knew what the three of us were doing, we'd be in jail. No amount of money or *legacy* would prevent that from happening.

As I walked, I realised I had taken the longer route, passing by Uptight's dorm. I could hear the steady hum of the AC, and I felt slightly smug as I walked by. Maybe she would be nice to the next guy who offered to help her out of the goodness of his heart.

I hesitated. Fuck. Whoever that guy was, it sure as hell wasn't me. Looking over my shoulder, I eyed the AC unit. I had half a mind to go over and pull the wires. But then, did the next guy actually deserve the sharpness of her tongue?

No. I wasn't too sure they did.

I still wasn't sure that *I* did. With a smile as I thought about her getting knocked over earlier, I was whistling when I approached the coffee shop, and the girl I was looking for, *right now*, was holding court in the centre of the tables as I knew she would be.

Elise sat at the table, her two best friends beside her. They all looked the same. They looked similar in middle school, and in high school, they had morphed into clones. Which is why Ash had managed to sleep with all three of them and think they were the same girl. Which was fucking hysterical when he found out, not that he had laughed. Gray and he just called them Elise One, Two and Three, and I had started doing the same.

I knew them apart. I just didn't like them enough to call them by their names...until I wanted something, and then I knew One would drop and suck at the mere hint of boasting about being in my bed, Two would lay back and spread them to get one over on anything One may do better, and Three wasn't at all fussy which hole you aimed at.

"Elise," I greeted as I sat down opposite them.

"Hey, baby," she said with a sly smile.

I fucking hated being called *baby*. "Heard there was a party on Friday that you weren't at?"

"No, I was at *the* party. There was another lame party over at Cedar, and you know us classy girls don't mix down there."

Say nothing.

Cedar Avenue was literally three rows of student housing over from where she lived on campus. However, with one sentence, she told me more than I knew before sitting down. That's why no one I knew outside of my football circle was talking about the party I was at. They were all somewhere else.

"We were at Chip's. Hardly any of the fun people were there," Two pouted. I think she thought it was cute, but to me, she looked like a blowfish.

"Game day's Saturday," I said as I looked around, pretending to check out for eavesdroppers. "Elise, I need a favour, but I would prefer to keep it quiet."

The three of them leaned forward as one. Honestly, they were more in sync than Gray and I were. It was creepy.

"Anything," Elise whispered with wide eyes.

"I was on Cedar on Friday, briefly," I added when I saw three identical expressions of horror. "Had one, then left. But..." I looked around again. "Some bitch took something from me." Not a lie.

"You slept with someone else?" Three looked distraught.

"I went home," I said to her, making sure my smile held promise.

The things I fucking did for my football career.

"Oh." Two looked happier.

Elise glared at them both before her hand reached across the table and stroked over my arm. Nails perfectly manicured and as long as talons stroked over my fingers. "Poor baby, what do you need?"

"I don't know who she was. All I know is she was blonde and at Cedar on Friday. Can you find out who she was? I want to keep it discreet." There was absolutely no chance of that happening, which is why I told her. If I couldn't find the blonde myself, I would flush the bitch out.

Elise's smile was eager. "Consider it done."

Standing, I gave her a quick once over. "Let me know when you have something." I left them tittering behind me and knew without looking that either she, Two, or Three...hell, maybe all of them, had just sent the text message offering sex. Pulling out my phone, I shook my head as I saw I was right.

As I read the message with the offer to console me, I had another message, this time from Quinn.

Queeny: **I think I know what it was, call me.**

Me: **Where are you?**

Queeny: **Class**

Me: **Meet you outside when you're done**

Queeny: **Ash? Gray?**

Me: **Practice. See you in ten**

CHAPTER 9

Jett

LEANING AGAINST THE TREE, I WELCOMED THE SHADE FROM THE HOT sun as I waited for Quinn to come out of class. When I saw the doors open and students coming out, Quinn was easy to spot, tall and graceful. I noticed she had changed her clothes from earlier into three-quarter-length yoga pants and a pink T-shirt knotted at the back. She came down the stairs of the phys ed building, ignoring most of her classmates. With her hair now in a high ponytail, she cut an impressive figure as she crossed the lawn to meet me.

I watched her as she put her sunglasses on before offering me a wide smile. We were all hoping to head to the NFL, and Quinn had never been happy about being left behind, so she'd decided when she was fourteen, if she couldn't *play* beside us, she would *treat* us, and she held onto that determination. She was now studying sports therapy, and she was damn good too.

"Hey, twice in one day," she murmured when she was close enough to be heard without drawing attention to us. Which would be impossible. She looked hot, and I was the school's quarterback. We were probably already on someone's Instagram or TikTok.

"It's how rumours start," I told her, causing her to look around uncertainly at my comment, but she laughed despite the underlying truth of it. "They're both at practice," I told her quietly as I pointed at my ankle. "I'm not, I'm injured."

"Bullshit story." Quinn lowered herself gracefully to the grass, and I followed. "You okay?"

"Yeah." I hesitated, but this was Quinn. "I'm fucking furious."

"You have a right to be." As she pulled at the grass, she looked a little uncertain.

"What is it?"

Handing me her phone, she gestured towards the screen. "It's open."

As I read the article she had open on a website, I felt my insides twist. "Is this shit legal?"

"Yes, it's used sometimes as an anaesthetic. They call it twilight sedation." Quinn leaned forward to scroll on her phone. "See here," she said as she pointed. "It's used for *conscious sedation*. Many people are awake and talking when they are given it, and after the procedure, they have no idea what happened."

"Is it possible," I asked her as I kept on reading, "that this is what I took?"

"Yes. It's called *Versed*, and it gets given in liquid format as well as IV. In a drink, it can be slightly bitter, it says…so I *assume* you would notice…but in beer? I don't know if you would. I think it can also be diluted down, from what I understand reading it all."

"I didn't put the beer down though," I said as I looked up at her in concern. "I don't remember much, but I *know* this."

"You had to have. Or you drank something else?" Her brow was scrunched in thought as she read on her phone. "Are you sure you only had one beer?"

"Positive. The only other thing I drank was water."

Quinn's head snapped up as she tore off her sunglasses to glare at me. "You said one beer, nothing else."

"No other alcohol. I picked up a bottle of water when I left." Rubbing my jaw, I thought about it. "I don't even know if I opened it."

"You dumbass," Quinn grumbled as she stood. "It was *in* the water."

"How?" I said as I rose to my feet with her. "How would anyone know which bottle of water I was going to pick up?"

Quinn hesitated, looking thoughtful before she looked at me in horror. "Unless *you* weren't the target and everyone at the party was."

Taking a step back, I looked at her. "How long does it last? You said it can be diluted down, but how long does it stay effective?"

Quinn read down her phone, and then her fingers were flying over the screen as she looked it up. As she relied on her medical references, I tried my hardest to remember Friday. I had the beer, I spoke to Derrick about routes as I searched the room, but the prick I was looking for wasn't there, so I left. Did I pick up the water? Or was it given to me?

I couldn't remember.

Shit.

"Depending on what else it's mixed with, it can stay as potent in water for up to twenty-four hours." Quinn looked at me, her brown eyes wide with concern. "Well, that's just horrifying."

"How long does it stay in your system?" I asked numbly.

"Four to six hours."

That wasn't long enough. "I don't think it was that. I left around one." I wanted to punch something. "I was tested at nine, that's too long." Saturday morning came rushing back to me. I had been fuzzy, which I thought was due to alcohol, but my memory was clearing, and now...now I was going to kill someone. "I drank from a bottle of water in my room when I took a painkiller before I left for fucking practice," I groaned in realisation. "Come on, we need to tell Gray and Ash. Don't fight me, Quinn, I need you there to answer their questions."

With a curse and a lacklustre punch to my arm in protest, she started to follow me, grumbling the whole way about asshole Santo men.

When we got to the stadium, practice was over, and I texted Gray to tell him to meet us in a box. We needed quiet, and we needed somewhere without the team seeing us, so I opted for one of the boxes, and even though we had access to most of them, I'd gravitated towards our family one.

It was adequate in size. Eight plush comfy chairs covered in black leather. Silver and black was very much the theme in Cardinal Saints College. Light grey walls with black uplighters gave a more muted effect. Overhead spotlights were an option if you wanted a brighter atmosphere. The carpet was a dark grey, but the main area of the floor was black wood, easier for cleaning up spills, which happened often during a game. Fans would never learn to put the drinks down before jumping to their feet to cheer, no matter how well-bred the family. A faux black marble countertop with five bar stools in front of it separated the *guests* from the booze and the three fridges behind. Quinn had already grabbed a soda as I waited by the windows for my brother and cousin.

When Gray and Ash joined us and had also taken drinks from the fridges, I quickly ran down what Quinn had learned. It was gratifying that Ash and Gray were as speechless as I had been when I read the articles.

Quinn stood slightly behind me, answering their questions with what she had gleaned from the internet and also from her professor when she had asked careful questions. His answers had made her start looking into the drug.

"How long does the memory loss last?" Gray asked.

"It can be a few days."

"So it will come back? He'll remember who this was?" Ash spoke as he studied her phone. Neither of them ever made eye contact when they were in the same room now. That ship hadn't only sailed, it had sunk.

"Possibly," I said.

"How did it even get in the water though?" Gray asked as he looked between us. "You said it was unopened, was it sealed?"

"Gray...I don't know."

"We would have heard if the whole fucking party lost their goddamn memory over the weekend," Ash spoke suddenly. "Those parties can be wild, but not everyone's smoking or snorting."

"Or drinking alcohol," Quinn said softly in agreement. "Who else would have seen the water?" she asked me.

"I don't know."

"Can't you even think about it?" Gray asked me in exasperation.

"Brother," I warned him as my jaw clenched.

"His memory from right before it could also be affected," Quinn said as she took her phone off Ash. "I hate to say it, but I think you need to just wait."

"I'm not waiting," I snapped as I turned away from them and looked down over the field. The gridiron looked welcoming, and I wanted to be down there, throwing balls, not up here, trying to recapture a lost memory.

"You think you drank the water before you left right on Saturday morning, right?" Gray started to pace. I could hear him crossing the carpeted floor. "Why do you remember practice before the game?"

"That's a good point," Ash said as I turned to look at them. "You were kinda hazy, lethargic even, but you were aware."

"I was?" My head was spinning trying to make sense of it all. "Quinn?"

"I dunno." She shrugged as she leaned against a seat, her foot tapping as she thought. "Unless...the familiar is so routine that you didn't notice?"

"He didn't notice he lost his memory?" Ash asked with more bite than he needed.

"You fell asleep," Gray exclaimed suddenly. "At break, you ducked Coach, and you sat in the bleachers, remember?" he asked me as he crossed to stand in front of me. "I woke you up. It wouldn't have been more than ten minutes." When I started to nod in recollection, Gray looked over at Quinn. "That's not normal, not on game day." He turned back to me. "You said it was the hangover, and I said you were lucky we were at home to a shit team."

"I..." Jesus, this was hell. "I think I remember that."

"And all you did after that was throw and catch, Coach didn't want you too tired for the game." Gray was practically vibrating with excitement. "It pisses me off that we didn't notice."

"Why would you though?" Quinn said thoughtfully. "You were hungover, you were active, talking, walking, playing. You were normal."

"He's never *normal*," Ash quipped before he scowled when he realised that he had made a joke to Quinn.

An uneasy silence followed, but I knew better than to push it.

"I have the three Elises on it," I said, breaking the tension. "By the end of the day, I'll be well *versed*." I sneered at the name of the drug even with my play on words. "Again."

Gray snorted in contempt, and Ash was suddenly looking anywhere but at Quinn, who was looking at me with her lip curled in distaste. "You went to Elise?"

"Queeny, you said you weren't helping."

"I know but...*Elise*?"

"The more the merrier, isn't that right, Ash?"

Yes, I went there. Yes, I was a bastard. Yes, it made Quinn's lips twitch into a smile.

"Still, we didn't have to go to *desperate* so soon," Quinn said regally as she collected her bag from the counter. "Okay, I'll find out more about this, and if you find out more about who, let me know."

"What are you going to do when we know who it is?" Ash asked as he stood, his arms extending high over his head as he stretched. "Glare at her?"

"Enough." I stopped Quinn's or my cousin's reply. "I got this now, thanks for finding out what it was."

"I'm not done with this," Quinn warned me as she secured her bag on her shoulder. "Not by a long shot."

"What do you mean?"

"Jett, are you serious?" Quinn looked more pissed off than normal. "I'll deal with this bitch."

"No."

"*Yes.*" She gave an angry toss of her hair and I was ready for a lecture, but when she met my gaze, her look was one of concern. "She drugged you, she *slept* with you, because she's twisted or to make sure you had it in your system for practice?" I realised Quinn was as furious as I was and wanted to cause harm. It pleased me how much I was on board with that. "This bitch is mine, I'll kill her."

"She's *mine*," I growled as I met Quinn's fierce look.

"You're going to hurt a girl?" Quinn mocked me slightly, a perfect eyebrow rising in question. "You would never hurt a woman."

"Hurt her? No." I looked around the room at my family. "Annihilate her? Absolutely."

CHAPTER 10

Ava

I WAS SITTING IN CLASS WHEN I GOT THE FIRST HINT THAT something was happening. The usually dull, stale atmosphere of finance was almost throbbing in intensity. I hated finance, but being an English major, mom had convinced me that even editors needed to live in the real world, and a few backup courses in practicality weren't such a bad idea. She was wrong, they were a *terrible* idea.

Jett was in this class, I knew, but it was so huge I never usually saw him. *Because he was probably getting sucked off in the back row,* I thought maliciously. The only time I actively looked for him was after a game, checking to see if he took any knocks or dents that would've rendered him injured.

He was never injured.

As I doodled on my page, I did need to remind myself I didn't *actually* wish bodily harm on him. Well, not before Friday. Before the weekend, if he got a torn ACL, I would have felt genuinely sorry for him. Now I wanted to tear every ligament in his body and watch him squirm in pain.

Okay, Ava, that may be too savage, even for you.

The flower I was doodling had now become a little flower garden, and I was shading them happily as I waited for the class to commence when the seat beside me scraped back.

"We illustrating for children's books now?"

Quickly I sketched some headstones and looked up at my friend Wade, who was watching with interest.

"You're a sick fucker, Ava," he said as he plucked the pen from my fingers and, in a few strokes, had added both our names to the gravestones. "Sweet and innocent on the outside with something sinister lurking beneath," he teased.

"You know it," I agreed as I turned the page in my notebook to a fresh one. "What time do you need me tonight?"

"Gig starts at eight, need your pretty little butt at the van at a quarter to."

"Cool." I kicked my feet out in front of me. "I have to go to the print shop to pick up the flyers for next week, but they came out...amazing."

"Course they did, my favourite artist drew them."

I smiled at the compliment. I met Wade through an online ad last year. He was in a country rock band and played bass guitar, and Wade needed someone to design and distribute his band's flyers and posters.

He was also the only original member in his band. There seemed to have been a revolving door of band members, but only Sticks remained from the tail end of last year. Sticks was the drummer, obviously. I had no idea what his proper name was, he was just Sticks. Neither of them looked like country rock would be their jam. Wade had a faux mohawk, neck tattoos and several piercings. His black gauges were usually the conversation starter. I had looked him up on Facebook before I met him for the first time and had drawn a few samples of heavy metal themed posters. He had laughed his ass off at my assumption, and we were pretty much friends from then on. Sticks had long hair and also several piercings and always wore a dog collar on his neck. Dog collar and shorts were the only thing he wore on stage; he didn't even wear shoes. Sticks was odd.

The band paid for the printing of the posters and flyers I designed for them, and paid me fifty dollars for every new design. They played regularly twice a week in the campus bars and maybe an additional set in Cardinal itself. Because Wade hated the familiar and was always looking for variety, he had really pushed my drawing, always wanting something new. He hated the mundane and comfortable. It was hard work sometimes, but it was fun, and we had formed a tight friendship.

Despite Wade's need for change, one of the things that was steady was his girlfriend, Bea. She was the complete opposite of Wade: long blonde hair that she always wore up, pretty dresses, not a piercing or tattoo in sight. Day and night had nothing on those two, but they were absolutely perfect for each other.

Which gave me hope that opposites did attract and in some cases, stuck.

"The natives are restless," I said to Wade as he looked around the class from our usual corner in the large classroom.

"Hey, did you hear? Your favourite quarterback got mugged or something…I dunno…something."

"Dante?" I gasped as my hand flew to my throat in horror.

"No, *this* school's QB. Something was stolen?" Wade thought about it. "Who really cares?"

"Jett?" I felt my frown as I looked around in confusion. "Who would be stupid enough to steal from a Devil?"

"Dunno, and when did you start calling him by his name?" Wade looked at me with interest.

"I can't call him *cocky asshole* all the time," I mumbled as I resumed drawing. "That girl almost decapitated me last week when she heard me," I reminded him dryly. The girl was obviously unhinged. No one, I mean no one, should react that violently to an offhand comment that the lead quarterback of the Saints was a cocky asshole who couldn't throw for shit. I may have *slightly* overexaggerated his throwing skills, but I was having a private conversation with my friend, not plastering it on social media.

"Don't tell me...you've got a crush on the footballer. Please, Ava, don't do this to me." Wade laughed easily. "I refuse to allow you to become just another groupie. Groupies are for my band only." Wade nudged me playfully. "If it *has* to be a Santo, make it the brother or whatever the other big guy is."

"Cousin. And Ash is the tight end for the team. I don't know why I have to keep explaining football to you. You're from Texas, for goodness sake, shouldn't you *bleed* football?"

"I *bleed* rock 'n' roll, as you well know." Wade plucked my pen from my fingers as he took my pad and flipped the page back to my previous doodle. He added some music notes to the sky, and then beside one of the headstones, he sketched a quick ball. He grinned at his work and proudly handed me the pad back. An *RIP* was under the football, and I slapped his arm in protest.

"You'll be *under* that headstone if anyone sees this," I hissed at him.

"Guys and their balls," Wade snorted. "Bunch of bullshit. Plus, football terms are so sexually driven," Wade said as he stretched, almost knocking me in the face with his elbow. "Tight end, sack, muff, spearing...whoever invented this game was fucking horny at the time and needed to get laid."

"So, you do listen, but only to the dirty sounding words?" I laughed at my friend. "You're such a boy."

"Sweet Ava, you say 'spearing the tight end' to me in any sentence, and I don't give a fuck what you're talking about, I'm listening." Wade winked at me before we were both giggling, trying to settle down as the professor came through the doors. She looked frazzled, and as I watched her cross the floor, I wondered why she looked so...dishevelled. A few minutes later, Ash Santo strolled into the class, and I was pretty sure I wasn't the only one putting two and two together and getting sexcapade as the answer.

"Only a Santo would fuck the teacher before an assignment allocation," Wade muttered to me.

"Devil," I corrected him as I watched Ash take his time to climb the low-rise stairs to the back of the class. His last name was Santo, which meant he and the twins were untouchable. In my opinion, it meant they were dicks.

A dick that I had slept with, and if that didn't make me the biggest fucking hypocrite, I didn't know what did.

"Hey, why so sad?" Wade asked me. "I thought I warned you it was assignment day?"

Looking up at him, I forced myself to look happier. "You did, I'm ready to ace it, you?"

"Yeah, sure." Wade rolled his eyes as he strummed his knuckles off the desk to a beat only he heard.

"I'd offer to help you, my friend, but we both know I need *you* for this class."

"In that case, we're both fucked."

With the mood between us lighter, we turned our attention to the professor, who had finally started the lecture. As she started running through what the assignment would consist of, I did wonder idly who would mug or steal from Jett? He had been fine earlier. Wade nudged my leg with his to get me to pay attention, and it worked. It really had nothing to do with me if Jett had something taken from him.

Nothing at all.

ARRIVING HOME LATER THAT AFTERNOON, I HEARD HER VOICE BEFORE I'd even come up the steps to our apartment. Mia was practicing. I hated to disturb her when she was practicing, so I always tried to make as little noise as possible. Dumping my bag, I started getting stuff from the fridge so I could make dinner.

Mia never ate properly unless I cooked. She went through fad diets constantly, and before freshman year ended, she had given up solids and was on a liquid diet. Not the fun kind either.

I had done a store run recently though, so hot chicken was on the menu tonight. Knowing she would complain about the carbs from the bread, I was making it with white rice instead. Still carbs, but Mia had a love-hate relationship with bread, and currently she was in hate mode. How anyone could choose to hate bread…I didn't understand, but there were some crazies out there.

Listening to her sing as I cooked relaxed me. Mia had the most beautiful voice and had been so happy when she got accepted into the music programme to do a Bachelor of Arts in music with a side helping of computer science. I never questioned her minor. She was good at design and was eager to learn code…or something equally mind-numbing, mind-numbing to *me* anyway.

Music was where she excelled. Her voice was her instrument, and she had a huge range. Mia was tall, but I swear her lungs were triple in capacity. Wade had begged her many times to be his singer in the band, but Mia always refused. Country rock was not for her. Even when he swore he would change the whole band's genre and dynamic, Mia said no. He didn't know that even though she could sing like an angel, Mia hated the limelight.

Which was kinda odd because she was insanely popular. In our high school choir, she had blended in and downplayed her voice until junior year when she knew she needed the credit for her application here, so one day, she stepped forward and floored her fellow choristers with her voice.

As I poured canned tomatoes into a saucepan, I listened to her as she was currently singing gospel choir songs. Making the tomato sauce for dinner, I found myself humming along with her as I cooked, the tension from the last few days easing away.

When dinner was ready, I knocked on her door gently. "Mee-Moo," I called. "Supper's ready."

The door flung back, and she launched herself at me, arms wrapping around me as she squealed with happiness. "Did you hear me hit that C sharp?"

"Sure."

"You work for a band, you live with a major in music; how can you not even know what C sharp sounds like?"

"Was it the screechy part?" I teased, pulling her behind me as I went back to the kitchen. When she peered over my shoulder, I turned my head slightly to see her frown at her dinner. "Shut up and eat. I don't care what you're dieting for, you need to eat."

"I do eat," she protested as she picked up her bowl and fork and headed to the couch. "Thank you for steaming the rice," she added as she sat down.

"Of course." It was best to let the subject drop. We didn't need to fight over this. Not again.

"Hey, did you hear about your favourite football player?" Mia asked as she took a forkful of food, her eyes rolling back as she groaned. "Oh my gosh, this is divine."

"Jett?" I asked. "Wade said he got mugged?"

"Jett?" Mia stopped chewing. "Santo?" Her eyes widened. "When did *he* become your favourite?"

I squirmed in my seat, uncomfortable that my head went straight to Jett. "Who were you talking about?"

"*Dante.* Dante Spence, you know your huge crush?" Mia ate more chicken, her eyes dancing with laughter. "But I'm ready to hear about how he was usurped by a Devil."

I snorted at the terminology as I shovelled food into my mouth. "Devil's right."

Throwing her head back on the couch, she yelled, "Tell me!"

"It's not important." Waving my fork at her, I urged her to talk. "Tell me all about Dante."

"He is apparently newly single."

My fork dropped. My jaw dropped. My face reddened. "No..." I breathed. "Mia, don't tease me."

"Yes, I saw it on his Instagram. You know it's over with if it's on social media." Mia laughed lightly. "How long do you think it will take him to get from Alabama to here to knock the door down?"

"Bitch." I grinned as I picked up my fork. "It *could* happen," I said playfully. "I'm sure he has thought about me as much as I've thought about him."

"Ava, the guy's an idiot."

"He's delicious," I corrected her.

"Ava, you've spoken to this nincompoop three times. Each time, he's been so unbearably dull. I swear I was asleep last time."

"You couldn't possibly have been asleep, you were sucking the face off the wide receiver."

Mia grinned at me and winked as she ate her supper. "Oh yeah, I knew something more fun than listening to *him* was happening." Tossing her hair over her shoulder, she looked at me critically. "Three times, and he hasn't even asked your name. All you spoke about was football."

"I like football," I reminded her.

"You're impossible."

"When did they break up?" I asked her eagerly.

"I don't know, his status changed to newly single." Mia eyed me as she scraped the bowl. "That was delicious."

Finishing my own food, I shrugged at the compliment. "Needed more seasoning, I think."

Mia said nothing as she took my bowl off me and went to the sink. "So, tell me about Jett."

"Huh? Oh, nothing much, Wade said he got mugged."

Mia looked far more interested in that than the object of my desire's newly single status. "Who, when, where, and what did they take?"

"I don't know." Standing, I checked the time on my phone. "Any of it. I'm sure, by the time we come back tonight, you'll be able to tell me."

With a shove, my best friend followed me to my bedroom. "Hey, thanks for getting the AC fixed. It was actually pleasant to come home to."

Should I tell her who she should thank? With her level of

interest in Jett, I thought it best not to. "I didn't do much." Which was true, I hadn't done anything. As I got my clothes out for tonight, I listened as Mia told me about her day. It was the most normal two hours I had spent since Friday.

Hoping that I was back to my normal self, I laughed along with my best friend. Which is why when we left later to meet Wade and the band, I was feeling happier and looking forward to a couple of hours of handing out flyers and listening to some good music. With Mia by my side and the two of us talking about anything and nothing, all was right in the world again.

CHAPTER 11

Ava

A STRONG HAND RAN DOWN MY SPINE AS THE OTHER HAND GRIPPED MY wrists in front of me, holding them together. My head was turned to the side, my cheek lay flat against the bed, and my moan, as fingers traced lightly over my ass, was loud.

His arm slid around my waist as he pulled me onto my knees. When he bent over my back, his grip on my wrists was gone. I felt a knee spread my legs more, and with one surge of his hips, he was inside me. His arm stayed wrapped around my waist as his other hand skimmed up my back, his fingers threading into my hair as he pulled me upwards.

I was nothing but sensation. Fingers loosening from my hair, his hand glided lightly over my skin before wrapping around my throat, his thrusts becoming harder as I practically sat in his lap.

"What do you want?" he whispered into my ear.

"More," I answered as my body bounced on his.

"Good." He shoved me roughly back onto the bed, and my cry of surprise was muffled as I landed face-first onto the mattress. On hands and knees, I begged for more. I heard myself demand he fuck me harder, and I heard his answering laugh as he did as I instructed.

It was too much. The feeling in my toes was spreading up my legs. Every feeling, every touch, every awareness of him *was all being drowned out by the rapidly building pressure in my core, I was going to erupt. I could feel it.*

And so could he.

"Come for me," he ordered harshly in my ear.

I did.

I heard his answering roar, and then I was falling.

My eyes snapped open as I lay on my bed, sweat trickling down my body. Awareness rushed back to me as I realised I was not in some heavy sex session, but I was in fact alone, in my bed, having another hot dream about my least favourite quarterback.

Sitting up, I wiped my hand across the back of my neck. I could still feel his fingers there. His phantom touch was screwing with my head.

Getting out of bed, I turned to look at the mess of the tangled sheets. It looked like I had been in a fight with the sheets and lost.

With an unhappy sigh, I headed to the kitchen to get some water. Running the faucet to let the water cool, I waited for a few moments. Because our apartment was so small, we didn't have a big fridge, and mom had bought us a filter that attached straight to the faucet. As I filled my tumbler, I focused on forcing his body from my subconscious. It had to stop. Two nights in a row. I was exhausted, and I needed to sleep without him waiting for me in my dreams.

I was not a person who did well with no sleep. In fact, I was a monster with sleep deprivation. No amount of Red Bull would save me tomorrow, or any other energy drink. Nothing would be able to elevate my mood. I had Leitch first thing tomorrow morning too; I needed the z's, or I may be in danger of getting flung out of his class if he bitched at me. There would be no holding back my snark if I didn't go to bed and sleep.

Checking the time, I fought my frustration when I saw it was ten after four. Three hours, before I was due to get up. *Please let me have three hours,* I prayed as I headed back to my room.

"You okay?" Mia asked me as she came out of the bathroom.

"Yeah, thirsty," I mumbled as I walked past her.

"You want the AC turned up higher?" Mia asked as she hesitated at her own bedroom door. "You're sweating."

"I think I'm getting sick," I lied.

"Oh no, should I get the cough medicine?"

"Nah, sleep is all I need." With a tired smile, I closed the door as I heard her run the faucet in the kitchen. Setting my water down, I turned to the bed, straightening my sheets and fluffing my pillows. "Fuck you, Jett Santo, you do not get to come into my bed anymore," I told the pillow in my hand fiercely. "Enough is enough, let me *sleep*." Finishing my water, I got back into bed.

Curling onto my side, I stared at the bedroom wall and thought about earlier. The bar had been fun. The bouncers and the wait staff knew we were underage, but since we were only drinking Coke, they left us to it. I had visited every table, spoken to a handful of people, and passed out every flyer telling them where the band was playing next week.

Wade's band was good tonight. The new guitar player was great, and the guy singing was cute as well as a good singer. Plus, they all seemed to like each other, and the look on Wade's face at the end of the set suggested that he had high hopes for this group to gel better than their predecessors.

Mia had also had fun, and she and the new singer had gotten on well. Mia would make anyone relax; she was bubbly, bright, and easy to talk to.

The new guitarist, Shane, had been quiet, but his light stubble, dirty blond hair and easy smile had made him easy to watch. Wade had teased me about liking him too much, but when I shushed him, he didn't say anything further. But I saw his pleased smile when Shane asked for my number. Mia of course took my indecision out of my hands as she put my number directly into Shane's phone.

Wade dropped us off at the apartment, and after chatting about the night over a cup of tea, we had gone to bed...where my night had taken a sour turn. A few hours later, I was awake, staring at the wall and once again thinking about an arrogant, entitled, dickhead quarterback.

Who had gotten my AC fixed.

With a groan, I flipped onto my back and stared sightlessly at the ceiling.

I'd thanked him. We both had a strong distaste for each other. There was nothing left to think about. So I lost my virginity to him. Fine. I couldn't get it back, and I needed to stop mourning the loss of it.

Shane seemed nice. Shane might call. Shane might even ask me out when he called. Shane had nice brown eyes. Shane was a step in the right direction. So why, when I closed my eyes to try and sleep, did only steely blue eyes stare back at me? Light blue eyes framed with thick dark lashes. With a strangled scream, I threw my now empty tumbler across the room.

"You okay, Ava?" Mia called to me through the wall.

"Yeah, thought I felt a bug," I called back, flinching at the lie.

"Go to sleep, it's late."

Yes, I know. I'm trying. With a hand pressed firmly over my eyes to keep them shut, I took deep calming breaths.

I knew why I couldn't sleep, apart from the porn rerun in my head; it wasn't the only thing keeping me awake. Mia had found out what happened to Jett on Friday. The rumours were rife that someone had stolen something from him. No one was clear as to whether it was his wallet or something else, but the word on campus was that the Devils were hunting because Satan himself was angry.

Is that how we met? Had I been helping him search for what was lost? Should I approach him and ask? But then how did that explain that he didn't recognise me? If someone had been helping me after I lost something, I would remember who they were. *Regardless* of my last name.

However, helping someone, even a Devil, was something that I'd totally do. I considered it more as I thought it through. He lost something or something was taken, and I offered to help him find it...on my way home? Absolutely not one person had said to me that they saw me talking to Jett Santo on Friday. I had been with Mia, we had run into Wade, and *he* was the one who told me earlier tonight that I lost at beer pong and took the forfeit of double shots. Ignoring warnings, I was insistent I could win but kept losing…hence the complete wastedness.

By that time, Mia had met whatever-his-name-was and was in the land of exploratory hook-up bliss. Wade left early, but he said that he saw me and a guy getting *cosy*. The guy was Mia's hair shampoo commercial guy, but no one knew what his name actually was. What they both confirmed was that neither Jett, his brother, nor Ash…had been anywhere near our party.

I still had a gaping hole in my already blank memory of *when* and *how* I met Jett. But it did narrow it down to the fact I really must have met him on the way home.

Sitting up in bed, I drew my knees to my chest. The party was on Oakwood, I lived on Blossom, there was half a campus between my apartment and the party on Friday. Even with the distance, I still had no reason to pass where the football stars stayed.

Had I decided to walk the campus? Alone? It wasn't something I usually did, but then getting wasted wasn't something I did either. My head dropped onto my knees as I gave up. I would probably never know. I was getting flashbacks of X-rated memories but nothing that led to the before *or* the after. Not until I woke up and heard him and Ash in the room. The only signals my brain was receiving was the *during*, and sure, for my first time, I seemed to have done well if the moans I heard when I closed my eyes were anything to go by…but I needed more. I felt my body heat at the thought of *more* with Jett, but I think my body and my brain knew it was a one-time thing.

Lying back down again, I fleetingly thought of asking him. As briefly as the idea came, I shoved it away. After all, there was no need to deliberately poke the beast. Especially one that was already on the hunt.

IT SEEMED ALL MORNING THE ONLY THING PEOPLE COULD TALK about was that someone had stolen off of a Santo, and the Triad were out for blood. I tried not to listen, but as with all things like this, the more I tried not to, the more I heard.

First it was his wallet. Then no, it wasn't his wallet, it was his watch. By mid-morning, after said "victim" was seen with his watch on, it was his car key. This one made no sense to me as I would have guessed that his key was easy to replace since the car was sitting on the driveway of their house. Sure enough, by lunchtime, it wasn't his car key but his car. Again, that was preposterous—the car was *right* there. I was beginning to lose interest in the whole "who stole from the Devil" saga, but I grudgingly felt bad for him if he had lost something. However, if I were honest, I felt worse for whoever the poor sucker was who stole it from him.

Their life wouldn't be worth living.

As I sat under my tree on the quad at lunchtime, I waited patiently for Mia. The tree was giving me shade from the sun, and it was a hot one today, which is why I was grateful I was wearing a strappy tank top and the lightest pair of shorts I could find. Nice respectable length, not short shorts like I had seen some girls wearing, while wishing I had their confidence.

With my head leaning back against the tree, I watched the students amble past, the heat making us all lethargic and sticky. My eyes dropped shut, and I think I dozed off a little, jarring awake when a shadow appeared over me and my foot was nudged.

Wade and Mia grinned down at me as Mia waved a can of Coke in front of me. I could see the condensation running down the side of the can, and my mouth watered at the thought of the coolness.

"I think I fell asleep," I admitted as I took the drink and pushed my sunglasses on top of my hair.

"You slept badly last night?" Mia asked me as she uncovered her salad box.

Nodding, I took a deep drink of the cold soda. "And to what do

I owe the pleasure of your company this lunchtime, Mr Wade Gordon?"

"Bea's at some sewing thing, some event her department's involved in. Only time I'm that close to a needle is either on the record player or the tattoo gun, know what I'm saying?"

"I thought the secret to a happy relationship was doing what your partner wanted, even if you didn't want to?" I teased him lightly as I uncovered my own lunch that Mia had bought me.

"Tell that to my mom and dad," Wade snorted. "Mom did everything dad wanted right up to the day he *wanted* his secretary more than mom and left us."

Mia raised her eyebrows in surprise at Wade's outburst but said nothing.

Looking over at me, he grinned. "Your favourite Saint is the talk of the campus," he said before biting into his sandwich. "*And* I heard that the fact everyone is talking about it is only making him more pissed off."

Mia dropped her fork as she clapped her hands excitedly. "Oooh, and I heard that Friday is why he isn't playing." She looked between us both with a grin, knowing she was telling us new information. "So they're saying he wasn't injured, he was suspended."

"Suspended?" I asked her, aware that I was leaning forward eager to hear more. "For what? His game on Saturday was on point. I mean, he had a sixty-eight percent completion rate, what more do they want? Blood?" I shook my head in derision.

"It freaks me out when you rattle off the stats like that," Wade said as picked up his can of Coke. "You're weird."

"No, not the game," Mia said, bringing my attention back to her. "Apparently, he was out Friday night before the game, and he was drinking, and he kept the whole house awake with some skank he took home."

I had no words. I was dimly aware that Wade was chuckling and giving Jett a virtual high five.

Please let me still be asleep. "He's suspended for sleeping with a girl?" I asked her, hearing the crack in my voice, and hastily swallowed more of my drink.

"I think so, that and the partying before the game," Mia nodded. "I think the team complained or something."

"So nothing was stolen, that's a lie?" Wade asked. He looked a bit too disappointed in the mundane fact it was just Jett and another nameless girl.

"Oh no, apparently *she* also stole from him, which is why he's looking for her."

The can of Coke dropped from my hands, and as I failed to catch it, the one small mercy was that I didn't splash anyone. "Slippery," I murmured as I hastily moved slightly away from the spilled drink.

Mia snorted and looked at Wade with a twinkle in her eye. "Apparently, the girl from Friday is *also* slippery, as it seems the star QB doesn't know her name and is fuzzy on her details."

"Fuck off." Wade almost spat his sandwich out in disbelief. "He banged her, kept the whole house up, and he doesn't know *who* she is?"

Mia shook her head in amusement. "Nope. Charming, isn't he?"

"I saw him on Friday, met him for the first time, he seemed like an okay guy." Wade shrugged. "Didn't seem that drunk to me." Wade grinned. "But I was, so maybe I'm not the best judge."

"You did? *You* met him?" I asked Wade. "Where were you?"

"Heading to Cedar, you know they throw the best parties. Sticks was already there," Wade said with a wink.

Cedar? Jett had been at Cedar? None of this made sense to me. I'd been at Oakwood.

"Well, drunk or not, I don't fancy being the girl when he finds her," Mia commented as she finished her lunch. "In fact, she may be safer transferring. Can you imagine what's going to happen when he finds her?"

"Why?" I swallowed hard. "It's not that bad, is it?"

"Seriously?" Mia looked at me in question. "I know nothing about football, but she's the reason he's suspended from playing, which even *I* know is the only thing he seems to have any interest in. He's going to make her life miserable. And even if he doesn't, everyone in that house *heard* them having sex... Her life's going to be so miserable."

"For sure," Wade agreed.

Well, when you put it like that...*shit*.

CHAPTER 12
Jett

"HEY, BABY," ELISE GREETED.

I looked down at her as she stepped into my space. The urge to push her away from me was strong, but I needed something from her, and therefore I had to bite my tongue from cursing her out. "Elise," I said as I saw Ash look away, trying to hide his grin. Asshole.

Those talons of hers snaked up my chest, over my shirt, and one ran down the side of my neck. Jerking my head away from her, I sidestepped, ignoring her frown. "Not good enough for you?" she sneered at me.

No. "Do you really want me to answer?"

Smoothly ignoring me, she carried on. "I heard that the *whole* house heard you on Friday night fucking this girl that *I'm* helping you find." Elise glared at me as she crossed her arms across her ample chest, pushing the girls up in her low scooped T-shirt.

"Who told you that?" I asked as I looked up and over the students milling about in the hall of the economics building.

"Jamie."

That fucker.

"When did you and Jamie get cosy?" Ash asked her as he slung an arm casually over her shoulders. "Not like you to go defence."

"Jamie doesn't speak shit," Elise answered as she stared right at me.

"Really?" I mimicked her pose as I crossed my arms and leaned against the wall with a casual look over her. "He tell you that you're the tightest pussy he's been in? You're not."

Ash laughed as he pulled Elise closer. "Or did he tell you he's never ass fucked anyone? Because he's already been through the back door with Three," he whispered as his tongue licked Elise's neck before he bit her earlobe. He gave a light laugh when she winced as he gave her a slight push away from him. "He tell you that you were special?" Ash mocked.

Elise glared at both of us, and I saw her anger building, but I also watched as she contained it, and I felt disappointment at her desperate attempt to pretend we didn't matter. To girls like Elise, we were *all* that mattered. Which was sad, because she was hot enough, and more importantly, she wasn't stupid; she was just deluded that she thought banging her way through the football team meant she would eventually snag herself a football player.

"You're dicks, both of you." Elise tossed her hair over her shoulder before she turned and started to walk away from us both. "Find your own fuck buddy," she called over her shoulder.

With a smirk, I looked at Ash, who was grinning openly as he watched her stalk off. "Bless her heart," I mimicked and snort laughed when he clutched at his heart and batted his lashes.

"She's pissed you banged someone else, but she's hooking up with Jamie to make you jealous?" Ash was grinning as we started to go into class together. "At what point does that make sense?"

"She's *special* in some things," I said as we climbed the stairs to the back row. The lecture room was vast and held over two hundred students. Anyone who took economics as a minor or took this course as an elective all sat this class together. It was also an hour forty lecture, and Ash and I claimed the back row the very first week, where we could sleep through it before our four-hour training practice that followed.

"You coming to practice?" Ash asked me quietly as we settled into the almost comfy seats.

"Yeah, Coach can fuck off if he thinks he's keeping me away this time." Pulling out a notebook and a pen from my backpack, I slid down my seat a little to get comfier. "Plus, I want to know who told half these fucking rumours I'm hearing."

"I like the one where you got your car stolen while you were in the back seat getting fucked, and neither you nor the thief noticed."

I stared at my cousin, who was grinning as he set up his own notebook and laptop. Ash always brought a laptop. He had hideous handwriting, and by typing his notes, he was at least guaranteed to be able to read them later.

"That isn't even plausible."

"People are idiots." His glance at me with his half shrug was dismissive. "Even being robbed, you're still a legend," he grunted good humouredly.

"It's all lies and bullshit." I frowned at my lined notebook and started drawing out the gridiron. "This is the only thing that matters."

"Yup." The professor started the class, and the rustling as people settled down quietened. Ash shifted in his seat so he was closer to me. "Quinn have any luck?"

"Not yet, but I have more faith in Queeny than the Elises." Turning my head slightly, I took in his side profile. "She's more invested."

Ash huffed out an acknowledgement but said nothing further about her. "We need to remind Jamie who's his team captain," Ash murmured.

"Already on it." I showed him my phone and my text messages with Gray.

Me: **Jamie spilled to Elise**

Gray: **Which one?**

Me: **One**

Gray: **Prick! Put Ash on him in practice**

Gray: **I'll get the fucker in the locker room**

Me: **Nah – I got it**

Gray: **No. You can't afford to get caught, Coach will have your ass**

Gray: **Fucker needs taught some respect**

Ash was grinning as he read, and he pulled his own phone out and joined the chat.

Ash: **I'm ready to teach**

Gray: **Preach to that**

Me: **We still need him for the season**

Gray: **Do we? Pity...**

Ash and I shared a grin before we both put our phones away, and as Ash began to pay attention to the lecture, I closed my eyes and rested my head against the back wall.

A warm hot mouth was wrapped around my dick, and I was thrusting into her willing mouth at a steady pace.

"That's it, just like that," I encouraged as I tightened my fists in her hair. Her mouth was going to suck me dry if she kept this up, and I wanted to fuck her first before I came, but her mouth was too fucking good. My head tilted back as I kneeled on the bed before her, her body crouched in front of me as her tongue stroked me in rhythm. I was going to come, fuck, she better swallow. "Shit," I cursed as I filled her mouth. Her small choke was not enough to deter me from gripping her head tighter as I held her in place.

Sitting back, she released me with a pop, her blonde hair covering her face as she wiped her mouth with the back of her hand. I gave my dick a couple of hard stokes. How the fuck was I still hard? "Turn over," I commanded, and she willingly flipped onto her stomach. "Ass up, it's your turn."

A sharp dig into my side had me jerking upright. Ash was looking at me with wide eyes before his eyes flicked to my crotch, and I realised I was hard.

"Seriously?" Ash asked incredulously as he packed his laptop away. "I hear those fucking moans enough when I'm in the room next to yours, I don't need them beside me in fucking economics."

"Shit," I muttered before I grinned at him. "What cologne you wearing? It's really doing it for me." I shoved my notebook into my backpack before I pulled my shirt over my junk.

Ash knocked the back of my head as he stood. "Dick. Who was it?" he asked interestedly as I stood and we made our way out of class.

"My Friday blonde," I answered him grimly. "Man, she can suck dick," I added on with another groan.

"You remembered something?" Ash asked me excitedly as he grabbed my arm, pulling me to a stop. "Who is it?"

The images were faded and didn't feel real, wisps of memory that were too fragile for me to grab onto. "I don't know," I bit out in frustration. "I can't see her face."

"Figures," Ash said as he resumed walking. "It wasn't her face you were interested in."

I almost agreed when I was hit with the feeling of how I felt in her mouth. "Not too sure about that," I mumbled as we left the building. Bright sunshine blinded us as we both put our shades on. "Ugh, practice is going to be brutal."

Ash grunted his agreement as he looked over the campus. "Easier to take down number ninety-seven though." His grin was vicious. "You gonna tell Coach about Versed?"

I thought about it and decided I had nothing to lose. "Yeah, he's not going to move if I can't point him to a *who,* but I hope that a *what* is progress." Sunlight reflected off of the buildings as we walked, and I revelled in the bright afternoon.

Ash tracked a group of girls as they passed, long legs, short tops, flirtatious glances over their shoulders as they passed us.

"Your tongue's hanging out," I said dryly.

"Better than my dick in economics," he snarked back at me with a wink.

"You're an asshole," I told him good-naturedly.

"I am," he agreed. "Dickheads run in the family."

"Ain't that the truth."

"Aw, fuck," he complained, his good humour vanishing as Quinn came into view. "She's got *that* look."

"Which look?" I asked as I watched our friend cut through a throng of students.

"The determined look," Ash muttered as we slowed down to meet her.

"Assholes," Quinn greeted with absolutely no preamble at all. "Who leaked the juice?"

"Jamie," I told her.

"How the hell am I supposed to work around the thousands of rumours?" Quinn snapped at me. "I'm not a freaking miracle worker."

"You giving up?" Ash asked her as he pushed his shades up to make eye contact.

"No, asshole. Of course not."

"Then what you bitching for?"

"Stop, before you both throw down," I cut them off. "We didn't teach you to fight to fight *us*," I reminded Quinn.

"I could take your ass." Quinn's sharp tone as she looked Ash over derisively didn't help.

"Pegging? That your freak now?" Ash asked her, equally scathing.

"All you think about is sex, you're so fucking predictable."

"Is that—"

"I swear to God, I will knock you *both* out, and I really don't give a fuck that you're a girl," I barked at them both. "It's been *two* fucking years." I looked between the two of them, and as they stared in opposite directions, I briefly thought of knocking their heads together. "You still on the girl?" I asked Quinn, changing the subject.

"Yeah, I had practical this morning, and they let me loose on the volleyball team. Jada the captain is really nice. She's putting out feelers."

"Jada…" I racked my brain.

"End of freshman year, you hooked up with her at a party the basketball team had in their dorm house." Quinn looked bored as she reminded me.

"Oh yeah." I nodded. "She *is* nice."

"Well, I'm glad you approve." Quinn's tone was dry and bored.

"He's starting to remember having sex with his blonde," Ash said to Quinn without making eye contact. Still, it was better than a few moments before. "That good?"

Quinn nodded enthusiastically. "This is great news! *And* I have it on semi-good authority from three different people, that you were not with anyone at Cedar and you definitely left alone."

"Why semi?" Ash asked.

"Well, they were all drunk, but they remember more than he does." Quinn shrugged. "I also have a confirmed sighting of you on Oakwood where there was another party. Do you remember that?" When I shook my head, she chewed her inner cheek. "Well, something is better than nothing, even if it is sex… Okay, I need maybe…two more days?"

I leaned over and planted a kiss on the side of her head. "You're a queen."

With a grin, she pecked me on the cheek. "I know. Later, losers."

I watched her walk away before I turned to Ash. "You need to stop the shit. It's tiring as fuck."

"It's *my* shit."

"No, it's not. It involves us all, she isn't going anywhere." As we headed to the stadium, I could feel my cousin struggle with his anger. "Just spit it out."

"She fucking cheated."

"I know."

"And that's okay?" Ash demanded as he ran his hand through his hair in frustration. "We'd have cut anyone else loose."

"This is Quinn," I reminded him.

"So she's exempt because we've known her for longer?" he asked me scathingly.

Stopping, I grabbed his arm and forced him to stop walking. "No, asshole, not because we've known her since we were ten. She's exempt because we made a pact not to fucking hook up with her, and *you* broke it."

"We made that pact when we were twelve," Ash said as he threw his arms in the air in frustration. "We didn't have any idea what the fuck we were agreeing to."

My hand shot out, thumping into his chest. "That's *your* excuse. Quinn stays."

Ash's eyes widened in disbelief. "So I go? Is that what you mean?" he asked as he knocked my hand away. "Bullshit."

"Where the fuck would you go?" I asked him as I started walking again. "Don't be a pussy, she stays. *You?* You'll get over it."

"And Gray? What does he think?"

"Gray thinks like I do." My brother was completely neutral and *silent* in this fight; I knew it and so did Ash. "Now, concentrate on more important things like taking this fucker down in practice."

Ash suddenly laughed as he slung his arm over my shoulder. "I do suddenly feel the need to hit something, *hard*."

"See, and you say I give you nothing."

CHAPTER 13

Ava

As the week passed, I got more and more nervous. The rumours were becoming more ridiculous, but the fact remained that Jett was on the hunt, and the *girl with the blonde hair* was the topic of almost every conversation. I'd even heard that some girls had approached him and claimed to *be* the girl. Seriously, they needed their heads looked at. It was like a modern-day version of Cinderella, these girls offering themselves as the wearer of the infamous slipper. Only there was no slipper, and it was all just a bit more desperate and sadder.

He haunted me. At night, I could feel him, and I lived through what felt like a complete rerun every night in my dreams. During the day, I ducked whenever I saw him, and twice I just hid. My only consolation was he really didn't seem to know it was me, and having spoken to him numerous times at the beginning of the week, my brain felt that I should be able to relax, but my heart wasn't listening.

Ash and Gray were no better. Gray was almost growling at everyone, and I heard that in practice yesterday afternoon, Gray had punched out Jamie Woods the defensive lineman. One Devil gunning for you was bad...but the girl with the blonde hair had three.

Not the girl with the blonde hair. *Me*. My pen tapped off my desk in a rapid rhythm as I waited nervously for the lecture to start. This class I was Santo free, but one of their female friends was in it, Elise something or other. She was classic high school bitchy, and I'd been fortunate enough to never be on her radar. High school was over, but for the reigning bitches, they never outgrew those years of honing their skills of scorn and vapidness.

Jesus, I was turning into the bitch. For all I knew, Elise was really nice and volunteered at a cat sanctuary or something. As I watched her hold her group of friends captive with her storytelling, I decided she probably wore fur, and if she was at a cat sanctuary, it was more likely to skin them for a new coat.

As I despaired internally at my cynical self, I turned my attention to my notepad and started to sketch out a new design for one of Wade's new posters. The band had written a new song, and Wade wanted a poster with the song in the design. The song was called "Kiss Me in the Rain," and I was debating how to get the song and the band's name, Atticus Dawn, into the poster.

"Hi, can I sit?"

Looking up, I smiled in surprise at Shane. "Hi, I didn't know you took this class?" I said as he sat beside me and I turned to talk to him.

"Yeah, just for this semester." Dirty blond hair, too long, but it suited him. Warm brown eyes, and today he had thick framed glasses on. His polo shirt and long shorts were topped off with bright white sneakers. He was as far removed from country rock as I was from the Queen of Sheba.

"I don't think I'd have recognised you," I admitted as I looked him over. "You are completely different from the other night."

"I scrub up well, you mean?" he teased with an easy smile. "Which do you prefer? College me or Atticus Dawn me?"

My laugh was light as I shook my head at his teasing. "You're still you no matter what you wear."

"Oh, so it's what's *inside* that counts," he joked as he smiled down at the top of his desk.

"Bingo!" I gave a light clap of applause. "I was actually thinking of the new poster design," I told him as I showed him my notepad.

"You're so talented," he murmured as he studied it. "It makes no sense to me that you don't study art and design."

"I'm not that good," I protested slightly. "If I was, I would know how to make it rain…"

"Go out with me?"

I blinked as I looked up at him from my drawing. "Huh?"

"A date, with me, go on one?" Shane squeezed his eyes shut. "Okay, in non-Yoda, that's will you go on a date with me?"

I hadn't been expecting it. I mean, I knew—well, I thought I knew—that he liked me, but this was our second conversation? I wasn't used to being asked out. I wasn't sure of the etiquette. Did I just agree?

"Ava?"

"Um, yeah, sure."

Shane smiled widely at me, and I shyly smiled back. The door being closed brought my attention back to the front of the class, and I was unsure whether I was grateful there was no further conversation or disappointed. After fifty minutes of purple prose, my head was weary and heavy. Which I belatedly realised was the point of the lecture, but still, I think I needed an Advil.

Shane and I walked out of the class together, and at the walkway to my next lecture, he told me he was heading in the opposite direction.

"You still have my number?" he asked me as he reached for his sunglasses.

"Yeah, I do." As he checked his phone to make sure that Mia had indeed given him my number, I noticed Jett and Ash walking towards the stadium. Jett looked amazing, there was no other word for it. His thick black hair was pushed back off his face, his shades hiding his eyes. His head was held high, his broad shoulders were straight, his T-shirt tight across them detailing his sculpted muscles. His sleeve of tattoos caught my eye, and I noted how even in today's intense humidity, he still wore jeans. Ash was similarly attired, his usual drop armhole shirt displaying his muscles and ripped jeans. Both wore dark sneakers, and both looked *good*.

"You heard the rumours?" Shane asked me with a curious look.

Nodding, I turned my attention back to him. "Yeah, crazy, right?"

"The life of the infamous," he said, but I caught the bitter edge to his humour and wanted to probe more when his next words caught my question in my throat. "Hey, *you're* blonde."

No no no no no no. People can *hear*. "As are many." Was it suspicious if I suddenly turned up tomorrow with my hair coloured brown?

"True," Shane said as he grinned at me. "So…you're not the thief?"

"Err. No."

"But would you admit it if you were?" His smile was wide, and had he not been so horrifically close to unveiling me, I would have laughed also. "Didn't Wade say you're a football fan?"

"I am. But not a Saints fan."

"Oh." Shane looked momentarily confused. "I'm only joking."

"Yeah, no, it's funny." I pretended to look at my watch. "Well, I better scoot."

"Yeah, sorry."

As I turned from him, I walked straight into the brown-haired girl Elise. "Sorry," I mumbled as I almost ran past her. When I was far enough away, I turned back to see her talking to Shane, who looked *far* too relaxed and casual with a girl after just asking me on a date. I didn't miss her head turning and looking my way either before I rounded the corner out of sight.

I had a very bad feeling about this, and the feeling lasted all day.

Yet another night of restless sleep, and I woke up with a banging sore head and a temper to rival a bear who's just found out some bastard ate his porridge.

"How are you feeling?" Mia asked me as she sipped her coffee.

"You've asked me five times," I replied as I shoved my notebook into my book bag. "And for the fifth time, I'm fine."

"You don't sound fine."

"How do I sound?" I asked as I picked up my own coffee cup and swallowed the contents in a few gulps.

"Irritable."

With a snort, I kissed her cheek before I was out the door and heading to class.

I would have loved some fresh air to clear my head, but it was September, I had zero chance of feeling *fresh.* I needed more coffee. Maybe an IV right into the vein this morning would do the trick. Checking my watch, I had time if the coffee shop was quiet. Putting more speed into my steps, I walked with single-minded purpose to get more of my morning fix.

The line was stupidly long, but I'd stayed in it, and my caramel latte was in my hands and tasted like heaven in a cup.

With a deep gulp, I swirled the coffee goodness around my mouth before swallowing. Ugh, whoever said coffee was better than sex was obviously right. This was much more satisfying. I ignored my inner denial and the projected porn show in my head as I hurried to Leitch's class.

All the coffee in the world wouldn't have been enough to get me through the fifty minutes of hell he unleashed on me. I wish I knew what his problem with me was. By the time class was finished, I was emotionally and physically drained. As I walked outside in a daze, my brain in danger of quitting for the day completely, I knew the only thing to get me to the next class was more coffee. Or watching Leitch drown...

Coffee. I needed coffee.

"Hey, can I have a caramel latte please?" I ordered, and as I stood back to wait, I looked around the coffee shop.

How I missed seeing Jett when I came in was a feat in itself. His head was bent together with his brother and the girl who was sometimes with them. I didn't know her name, I just wished I had her legs. She was beautiful and always looked out of place when I saw her, like she shouldn't be carrying books with her in college but, instead, be on a runway somewhere or have her face on the cover of magazines.

Jett must have felt me looking as his head raised, and angry eyes met mine. Quickly, I looked away but not before I saw him hit Gray's arm to get his attention. Hastily, I picked my order up, and with a glance over at them, I saw all three of them glaring at me now.

What the actual hell? My feet were not slow in getting me out of there.

I didn't even know he was following me until I felt the hand on my arm before he jerked me to a stop.

"Dude, *not* cool!" I squirmed trying to get out of his grip. Jett ignored me as he began to walk us across the grass. "Hey." I tried to get his attention. "Hey!" My voice was louder, and I saw several people look our way.

"Shut up before I shut you up."

"Who the fuck do you think you are?" I wrenched my arm again, and still his hand held me in a punishing grip.

"I know exactly who *I* am, tell me"—he looked down at me as we walked—"who the fuck are you?"

"Wh-what?" Digging my heels in, I made it so he had to drag me, and I really think he would have if he hadn't heard the same sniggers I did from passing students.

Roughly he turned me to look at him, his hand still tight on my arm. "Where were you Friday night?"

No! My horror froze me for a moment. "Where were you?" I countered glibly.

Sky blue eyes now looked like a heavy storm was coming in. He was not happy. In fact, he looked kinda scary. This was *not* where I wanted to be. "Cut the bullshit."

"I agree, you should." I finally jerked out of his arm. "And I'll bruise, thanks for that."

"Where were you on Friday night?"

"Is it your business?" I snapped at him. Why did he want to know now? Had he figured it out?

"You're her?" he asked me as he looked me over one more time. I didn't like the fact he was looking at me with barely concealed contempt. Maybe it wasn't contempt, maybe it was astonishment? Either way, it was non-complimentary.

"I'm who?" I hoped that I sounded confused, curious even. I didn't *feel* curious, I felt like I was three short seconds from a complete panic attack, throwing my coffee at him, and running very, *very* fast away.

"Fuck, it really *is* you."

"If you're so sure, then why are you asking?" I tore my eyes away from his stupid perfect face and looked out over the quad, desperate for an intervention and praying that I appeared indifferent, searching faces of the other students in the hopes of seeing someone I recognised, someone who would save me from this embarrassment. *Please, God, make him leave me alone.*

"I can't believe it would be *you*." His hand dragging slowly over his face emphasised his growing horror at the realisation, and I forgot that I was supposed to be appearing cool and casual if not slightly irate. Instead, I felt nothing but mounting anger that he was being such a complete jerk.

Asshole.

"Wow." I looked him over as coldly as he had looked at me. "You really do know how to make a girl feel *special*."

"How the fuck did it even happen?" His eyes were narrowed in anger, and I knew that the longer I stood in front of him, the more questions he was going to ask.

Personally, any other time, I loved questions but only when it was the right time, right place and the right person.

Right here? Right now? This was not it.

I didn't have enough answers to make me look good coming out of this.

Biting back the rapidly building hysteria inside me, I sent a quick silent prayer to the angels above to forgive me for the sin I was about to commit against caffeine, and then I actually did it.

I threw my coffee at the star quarterback of my college's football team.

Catching him by surprise, I took the opening, and turning, I sprinted across the campus grounds like the devil was nipping at my heels. Because he was, and he was gaining on me...fast.

Ignoring the catcalls and the shouts of encouragement as he chased me across the campus green, I savagely cursed myself for being a couch potato and not a fitness freak as I felt my lungs scream in protest at the sudden unwelcome exercise. Strong hands grabbed me, and I was half carried, half dragged into a building and thrust into the first room he came across. Thankfully, it was empty, so no one would see my humiliation.

"What is your problem?" I demanded as I turned and realised it could be that he was wearing my caramel latte on his white T-shirt.

"You bitch." Jett stepped towards me, and on instinct, I backed away as he advanced. "No, you don't fucking *run*."

The door opened, and I turned in hopes that someone had come to save me from whatever the hell was going on, but instead, Gray came in. Closing the door behind him, he leaned against it, folding his arms, his unfriendly glare telling me there was no help coming from him.

"What's going on?" I asked them as I tried to keep my voice calm.

"Why did you do it?" Jett demanded.

Seeing no compassion from Gray, I turned back to look at Jett. "I don't know what you mean."

His fist came flying past my head and met loudly with the wall behind me. I flinched. He didn't. His body was mere inches from mine, and I daren't look up at him.

"Tell me *why* and who gave it to you." His voice was low and sinister.

I was either going to throw up or faint. I think he'd seen enough of me throwing up, and I wasn't sure he would take kindly to me passing out either. "I'm sorry, I don't know what you mean." My voice cracked as I stared at the tattoos on the arm that caged me in.

"Ava?" he asked. "That's your name?"

"Yes," I croaked. Great, he only learned my name today? I felt cheap.

"Tell me what I want to know, and I won't make this worse." His voice was cold in my ear.

"It gets worse?" I tried to joke. I heard Gray's sharp inhale, I felt Jett press closer, and for the gazillionth time in my life, I wondered what possessed me to speak before I thought.

"Why?" He drew back slightly so he could look down at me. "Who gave it to you? What did you have to gain?"

I knew I looked confused because I *felt* confused. "Why what? Gain what? Why did we...have sex?" My face flamed, but this was too intense, and I needed to leave. Now. "I dunno. Why do most people have sex? It felt like a good idea at the time?" I suggested wildly. "Why do *you* normally sleep with girls?"

A hand wrapped around my throat as he tilted my head backward to look at him. Furious eyes met mine, and I should probably have been grateful he was holding me up, even if it was by my neck.

"You're hurting me."

Jett leaned closer, and I forgot to breathe as I felt his hate envelop me. "Hurt you? I'm going to *destroy* you."

He shoved me away from him, causing my head to bang off the

wall as he stormed past me and left. Silently Gray met my stare. With a quick glance over me, he followed his brother out of the room. My knees gave out as soon as the door closed behind him, and sliding down the wall, I brought my knees up to my chest. Tears ran down my face as I dropped my head down onto them.

I don't know what he thought had happened, but I knew I was in deep shit, and I had no way of knowing how to get out of it. What did he even think I had taken? Wiping my eyes, I got shakily to my feet. There was only one thing I *could* do, and that was find out. Even if it meant I had to talk to him again. Not knowing if I would survive another encounter with him, I left the classroom behind me. One thing I was sure of, it wouldn't be today. I wasn't *that* reckless.

CHAPTER 14

Jett

I'D BEEN WALKING OUT OF MY MORNING CLASS WHEN MY PHONE beeped with a text, and I had almost not read it when I saw who it was from.

Elise: **Hey baby, I found your thief**

Me: **Who?**

Elise: **What will you give me for my knowledge?**

Me: **Tell me what I want to know**

Elise: **So demanding when I have the cards**

Me: **Cards? Don't piss me off, who is she?**

Elise: **Come over later tonight and I'll tell you**

Me: **You want sex?**

Elise: **So blunt**

Me: **Name? Now**

Elise: **Always so dominant...I love it when you're angry**

Elise: **She's no one btw**

Me: **Name**

Elise: **Ava Bryant. Trust me, she isn't anyone, what time will you come over?**

I'd shown Gray the texts and been surprised when he had started laughing.

"Why is this funny?"

Gray shook his head as he looked at the name and then at me, the humour gone. "Because you know her."

"I don't," I corrected him. "Apart from Friday, I don't know her. And even then, it doesn't count until I *actually* remember."

"Yeah?" Gray saw Quinn approaching and gave her his usual dip of his head. "Ben bounced a ball off her head earlier this week at your request."

I stared at him with my jaw slack. "No," was my automatic reply.

"When she spilled her purse, I picked up her wallet, checked the ID out of habit, it's her."

"She's been in my face since Monday, acting all pissed off and angry," I told him in bemusement. "Who the fuck is she?"

"Send the name and the address of her dorm to Ash. He's in class right now, he'll find out everything you need to know."

"Hey, what's up with you two? You look like you just got told you can't be assholes anymore," Quinn greeted us.

"We found who the girl is," Gray told her bluntly.

Quinn lost her teasing smile and met my glare. "Before me? Ugh, coffee and strategy," Quinn ordered.

We'd just sat down when I'd looked up and she was standing there, staring at me. Looking so fucking innocent…I wanted to rip her head from her shoulders. When she saw all three of us, her eyes had widened, and then she was practically running out of the coffee shop. I'd been chasing her before she could get far, with no idea what I was going to say when I caught her.

I couldn't believe that the girl who drugged me in order for me to fail a drug test, and fucked me on top of that, was *her*. Sure, she was annoying from what I had met of her, and self-righteous, but she *still* didn't seem to fit. I had recognised her derisive look on Monday when she caught the girl with my dick in her mouth. I thought she was merely uptight, I didn't think it was because my dick had been in *her* a few days before.

Some people needed to get laid to loosen up, and she seemed to tick all the boxes. I thought she was one of those people. She was an uptight, judgmental woman who needed to take the stick out of her ass.

How well she'd played me.

Gray was silent beside me as I walked away from the classroom I left her in. Wide green eyes flashed in my head, and I struggled between my need to go back and *make* her tell me what I needed to know or to keep walking *away* from her.

I saw Gray pull his phone out, but I couldn't hear what he said to whoever he called over the roaring in my ears. I'd been *nice* to her. Everywhere I turned since Friday, she was there. I had never seen her in my class before, and she just *happened* to need to sit beside me on Monday?

Suddenly, every encounter with the snake felt contrived. I had *helped* her. No fucking wonder she looked scared to see me on Monday night, she must have thought I was coming for her. Fucking bitch.

"You need to rein it in, brother," Gray murmured beside me as he placed his shades on. "Put your shades on."

"I can see fine," I snapped at him.

"Yeah, and everyone can *see* you. Hide the rage and remember you're injured, even though Coach let you practice yesterday."

"Fucking bullshit."

"I know, but let's play the game." His tight smile held warning, and I looked in the direction he flicked his eyes. The three Elises were heading my way.

"I don't have time for this," I said as I turned my head from them and slipped my Ray-Bans on.

"Let's hear what more they found," he said to me quietly. "Where the hell is Ash when you need him?" he grumbled as I watched him brace for the impending arrival of Elise and her clones as I thought about this morning.

"Hey, baby," Elise greeted me with a wide smile. "We've been digging." She gestured half-heartedly to Two and Three beside her. Elise looked over my white T-shirt. "What happened?"

Her fake smile was grating on my last nerve. "Nothing you need to be concerned about," I snapped. "You got anything for me?" When I saw her eyes widen with excitement and her lips pout, I barely held my temper in check. "On the *girl*," I stressed, cutting off whatever goddamn innuendo she was going to spout.

"She's no one," Elise said. It was pissing me off she kept repeating herself. "She does English or creative writing or something, has absolutely *no* social life, parties now and again. I think she dates some guy in a band."

Gray had been watching Quinn walk towards us, but his eyes flicked to Elise and then me when Elise said Ava partied *now and again*. Well, something told me that information was shit.

"What band?" I asked as Quinn met us and wordlessly handed me a black T-shirt. Ignoring three pairs of eyes basically eye fuck me in the middle of the campus, I tossed the ruined shirt in the trash before I put on the new one.

"It's some country thing. She promotes them or something," Wendy spoke up. She was Three, but she was actually the more tolerable one.

"You know any more about them?" Gray asked as I straightened the T-shirt.

"Main band guy is Wade…something. Think he's her boyfriend."

"Wade?" Gray asked as I let out a low chuckle. The Wade in my phone from Friday? There really were no coincidences.

"Anything else?" Quinn asked the three of them with no effort to hide her dislike. They had all slept with Ash on the same night after all.

"No," Elise answered with a saccharine sweet smile.

"Then fuck off," Quinn told her, mirroring her fake smile before she turned her back on them.

Elise's glare at Quinn's back was full of hate, and when she saw I had seen her, she paled. "So…baby…later?"

"No."

The three of us walked away from them as Quinn muttered inaudibly beside me.

"What did she say?" Quinn asked when we were far enough away.

"Nothing," Gray answered. "But…Ash pulled her records, he'll meet us at the house. Seems she's a scholarship student," he added with a sly look.

I looked at him in surprise. "Is that right? What kind?" I asked as we headed towards the house. "I just love how fragile those things are, don't you, Queeny?"

Gray smirked as Quinn laughed while we walked along the tree-canopied paths. Scholarships were few and far between for this college. They had strict rules, firm guidelines, and a stern no fuck-ups policy.

She'd talk. She'd tell me everything I needed to know, or she was gone. She was a conniving bitch, but when it came down to it, what was more important to her? Her loyalty to whoever gave her the drug or the scholarship that she worked hard for?

I would bet money it was the latter, and that…that I could use.

Ash came into my room with a spring in his step until he saw Quinn, his good mood vanishing as their eyes clashed. "We just letting anyone in now?" he muttered as he took a place on my bed, our previous conversation obviously forgotten.

Gray was sitting on the couch with Quinn. Their heads had been bent over her phone as they researched the infamous Wade. I looked between the three of them and suppressed my sigh. I had more important things to worry about than his hurt feelings and his ex.

"What'd you get?" I asked him instead.

"More than I ever need to know about her," Ash replied dryly. Pulling out his laptop, he flipped it open and turned it towards me.

Her high school records were in front of me as well as her information and academic record from freshman year too.

"Nice," I complimented him as I looked through it all. "Ava Bryant, nineteen, from Knoxville, single child, parents divorced, lives with mom..." I trailed off as I read more about her boring life. "Fuck, she's dull. Good grades," I mused.

"She's in Professor Leitch's class, and he does *not* like her," Ash told me as he kicked off his shoes. "I sat beside her on Monday, and he was ripping into her when I arrived and held her back when class was over."

"Which is why she was late for the class I have with her." I looked back at her record thoughtfully.

"Yeah, the speed she was trying to leave Leitch, she probably gets to the next class before you would from Macroeconomics." Ash gestured to the laptop. "She's been in all of our classes either this year or last, we just haven't noticed her. He was on her again this morning. Seriously, I actually felt sorry for her; the guy's brutal, more so to her."

Quinn snorted as she sat listening. When three pairs of eyes looked at her, she shrugged with casual indifference.

"I still don't know how she ended up being fucked in my bed."

"Charming," Quinn deadpanned as she leaned back on the couch. "Is she in any of my classes?"

Scanning the records quickly, I shook my head in answer. "No." I flicked through her admin record, roommate was Mia Davis, same town, same school, same dorm here. "Roommate's her best friend?"

Ash nodded as he reached forward. "Yeah, to be fair, that struck me as curious, but they don't seem to have pulled any strings. Friend is a music major, and she's in two of my computer science classes."

"She's a music major with a side helping of geek?" Gray asked curiously. "How does that work?"

"Means they both have brains if not money," Quinn spoke from the couch. "Is the friend on a scholarship too?"

Recognising Quinn's angle, I checked and shook my head. "No, she's paying her way."

"Can't use that then," Quinn thought out loud.

"Use it?" Ash questioned her before he looked at me. I returned his stare and saw his sudden understanding in his grin. "Nice."

"The little bitch will talk or...she'll walk, her choice," I grumbled as I went back to reading about her.

"Gimme my laptop," he told me, and I handed it over. With a few clicks, he was handing it back to me. "See what I see?"

Her Facebook page was in front of me, and on it was a photo. Grainy at best, it looked like it had been taken a few years ago. Ava was standing with a trophy. I didn't give a fuck what it was a trophy for, what I noticed was what she was wearing: an Alabama Lions jersey. I looked up at Ash, and he nodded grimly.

"There's your *why*," he said as his eyes narrowed in anger.

"Now I just need the *who else*," I said, passing the laptop to Quinn and Gray so they could see also.

"Son of a bitch," Gray cursed as he looked closer.

"I see it now," Quinn said quietly.

"What?" I asked as I stood, stretching.

"The attraction, she's pretty." She studied the photo more. "I didn't see it today 'cause all I saw was her fleeing, but I see why you would pick her."

"He didn't *pick* her," Gray said as he closed the laptop. "She picked *him*." Gray's knee was jittering again, and I knew he needed to let off steam.

"I need more," I told Ash. "I need to know what she does when she's not in class. She may be scholarship for the full ticket, but what else does she do?"

"Yeah, I have feelers out."

"I can work on this," Quinn said as she stood. "There won't be a thing I don't know about her by tomorrow," she promised as she picked up her bag. "I'll be in touch."

When she had left, the three of us looked at each other. "So she's definitely back in?" Ash asked, his eyes on the floor before he lay back on my bed.

"She was never really out," I answered with a quick look to Gray, who sat quietly. "We've known her forever. Quinn could bury each and every one of us in this room in a heartbeat, and you know it."

Ash huffed in derision as he stared at the ceiling. "So she's here in case she blackmails us?"

"Shut the fuck up, and don't be an idiot," Gray bit out as he stood. "Quinn's like family."

"And are you forgetting the other thing we're doing?" I asked Ash. "*For* Quinn?"

"That's different."

"How?" Gray and I asked at the same time.

"Because Quinn getting used and hurt is not the same thing as Quinn eating fucking dinner with us again." Ash rose off the bed. "She shouldn't get a free pass."

"She hasn't!" Gray said with more sting than I think he realised. "You've ignored her for almost two fucking years, we've kept her out *for* you. But fuck, you've fucked more women than she has men, you've proven you're over her, she gets it. We *all* get it. Stop being a whiny bitch." Gray shoved his hands deep into his front pockets of his jeans. "Move the fuck on."

Ash and he stared at each other for a long time, and I sat between them, waiting for either the punch to be thrown or the acceptance. I hadn't been in the middle of this shit at any time, and I sure as hell wasn't starting now.

"Whatever," Ash eventually shrugged. "We done?" he asked as he looked at me.

"Yeah."

With a curt nod, he headed to the door.

"Where you going?" I asked him as he pulled the door open.

"To get laid." The door closed firmly behind him, and I turned to my brother.

"Went well," I commented as I crossed the room to the bathroom.

"He's been a pussy for too long."

"She did cheat on him," I reminded Gray as I dropped my shirt in the hamper before I came back into the room.

"Yeah, well, he's over it." Gray chewed the inside of his cheek as he stared out my window.

"I don't think he is." I gave my brother a sceptical look as I pulled off my jeans.

"He is," Gray insisted as he sat back down on the couch. "He just doesn't like that she cheated first."

"First?" I queried as I pulled on my shorts.

Gray's eyes flicked to mine before he looked away again. "They were hardly perfect." His tone was slightly defensive, and I considered my next words carefully.

"Tell me again why you told her to break up with him?"

Gray stood and met my gaze. "One of them had to, it wasn't healthy for any of us."

"So…you did it for our friendship?"

"Yeah." Gray gave me a smile. "And because he's stubborn. He has the Santo bullheadedness."

Slowly, I nodded as I regarded my brother. "Okay."

"You going for a run?"

"Yeah, exercise for the ankle," I said mockingly as I put my running shoes on.

"Coach will skin you if he sees you. He already cast doubt on your injury when he let you practice yesterday."

"Coach can suck my dick." I left my bedroom to the sound of

my brother's laughter. I didn't give a fuck if Coach found out, he could hardly be pissed that I was damaging my ankle.

A good run and a clear head, that's what I needed before I planned my move against Ava. My lips curled in distaste as I left the house. Ava... *Snake* suited her better.

The best way to deal with a snake...cut its head off.

CHAPTER 15

Ava

"So I heard a wild rumour this afternoon," Mia said with no *hello* or anything as she burst into our apartment. I was making dinner and knew by the look on her face, she had heard about my sprint-a-thon across the quad.

"The Loch Ness monster is actually a large eel?"

"Huh?" She paused for a second before her hand tossed her hair over her shoulder. "No…amazingly enough." Her look was sharp. "But it's almost as mythically impossible as an imaginary sea monster. Did you..." Again she hesitated. "Did you...*throw* your coffee at Jett Santo?"

"I did."

Mia's mouth dropped open as she stared at me. I carried on stirring the sauce as she walked over to the couch, sinking down onto it slowly. "Why?"

"He's an asshole."

Mia's eyes widened slightly, but she still looked confused. "You threw your coffee at him because he's an asshole?"

"Yes."

"Ava?"

"Mia?" I countered as I put the pasta in the boiling water.

"You can't throw your coffee at people! Not *him*!"

"Why? He isn't God."

"He may as well be, *here*."

"Ugh, no. He's an ass and a dick and a cock."

Mia looked at me in wonder before she started to giggle.

"Why are you laughing?" I asked as I stopped stirring the pot to look at her.

"You seem fixated on his anatomy," she teased. "I can't believe you threw your coffee. I mean, you're you...*you* would never waste caffeine."

"He deserved it. I'm just sorry I ordered a latte and not a filter."

"He would have been scalded!" Mia admonished me as she stood and made her way into our kitchen. "Lemme taste," she murmured as she picked up a spoon.

"Good?" I asked her as she dipped the spoon back into the pot.

"Not sure, need another taste." Her laugh was loud when I snatched the spoon off her.

"Greedy! Supper will be ready in fifteen. You need a shower?" I asked her, returning to stirring my pots.

"Yeah, it's so cracking hot outside, thank goodness we got the AC fixed." She headed to her room. "And because I'm not even complaining you're feeding me carbs *again*," she called over her shoulder, "I want all the details over dinner!"

Her comment about carbs actually made me smile briefly because there were no details I wanted to share. Jett seemed incensed or insulted, I wasn't sure which, that he slept with me. Half of what he had said to me made no sense. The other half seemed like a complete overreaction. I knew people had regrets over one-night stands. When the beer goggles came off, the truth could be sobering. Pun completely intended.

That was fine, because I could handle rejection. I wasn't fragile. I just didn't like the guy, *any* guy, who pushed me against a wall with his hand around my throat. He did not get to touch me without my permission, and the next time he thought about putting a hand on me, I'd rip it off and shove it up his ass. Dick.

As I stirred my pasta, I thought back to the afternoon. I had left the classroom and skipped my next class as I hid in the library from prying eyes. Even in the library, I couldn't escape the whispers about the girl who'd thrown a drink over Jett Santo. There was so much speculation, but as I listened and hid, I realised everyone thought that girl was the one who mugged him. How was I to defend that?

When I heard one girl say he could chase her any day, my head lifted from the book I was pretending to study to look at her, partly to welcome her to be in the position I had been earlier and then see if she still wanted to be chased and partly because he wasn't *that* desirable…was he?

Then I realised I was being stupid. They thought I had stolen from him, if only they knew the truth. I'd been wrestling with his touch all afternoon. Hands that had brought me such pleasure on Friday had been restrained from causing me harm this afternoon. And I had no doubt that he wanted to wrap his hands around my throat and squeeze.

"Maybe I hurt his ankle," I blurted in realisation. Had I somehow caused him harm on Friday, which meant I was the reason he was injured to play? I had been tender on Saturday, maybe he had too. Is that what I had taken from him? The ability to play? More importantly, was I brave enough to ask? I didn't really have a choice.

"You're deep in thought," Mia said from behind me. "How did you hurt his ankle?"

"What?"

"You just said maybe you hurt his ankle?" Mia got drinks out of the fridge and then forks before placing them on the breakfast bar as she watched me. "Heard a few people say his ankle seemed fine as he was chasing you over the campus." Mia giggled again as she winked at me in humour. "I would have loved to have been there."

"It wasn't funny."

"Why? Tell me, did he hurt you?" She instantly sobered.

"It's nothing." Turning my back on her, I drained the pasta. "He was slightly aggressive, and I threw my coffee at him in a temper." As I emptied the pasta into the pot with the sauce, I concentrated on it rather than meet Mia's stare.

"Aggressive how?"

"Just...I dunno. Demanding." I served two portions into the bowls. "And rude."

"Well, if he was rude, he deserved to be latte'd."

"It was the perfect cup too." I mourned the loss of my caffeine. "I should have hit him with my book bag."

Mia snorted as she picked her bowl up and went to the couch. "Not sure you should have *hit* him at all," she chided as she sat down. "Violence breeds violence, remember." Scooping up a forkful of her supper, she looked at me as I ate my own. "You're going to have to apologise."

"No."

"Ava, he's the most popular guy on campus. They're already talking about you damaging him. These football people are crazy." Her shrewd look made me flush. "*You* know this better than anyone."

"I didn't damage him." Staring sullenly at my dinner, I set the bowl aside. "He needs to tell people he chased me."

"People *know* he chased you *because* you threw a hot drink at him." Mia was looking at me with concern. "Please tell me why."

"It's nothing, I spoke to him on Friday." I assumed I had...I don't know what I said, but I'm sure we must have said something at some point to get to where we ended up.

"*Friday!*" Mia screeched. "Why am I only hearing about this now?"

"Because I don't remember."

"Oh." Her incredulous excitement at me talking to the star quarterback faded when she realised I was *that* drunk. "Oh no, you won't know what you said...at all." Her hazel eyes were wide again, only this time in realisation. "You're screwed."

"Eat your dinner," I told her even as I nodded in agreement.

"I bet you criticised his game," Mia said knowingly. "You would have mouthed off about football, and he probably took offence."

Complete guesswork on her part, but it wasn't unlikely. I just knew he hadn't taken offence, or if he did, he had a strange way of showing it. "Who knows, I didn't get the chance to ask."

"Well, we can fix this," Mia told me confidently as she resumed eating. "We'll explain you're a forgetful drunk, and he will understand."

It was my turn to be incredulous. "You do know who we're talking about?"

"Yes."

"Mia. They aren't called the Devils for no reason," I reminded her. "They pull shit on people for less than this."

"This is different." Mia could be completely oblivious sometimes. "Don't worry, Ava, we'll fix this. I'll think of something."

I didn't have her confidence as I ate my supper. In fact, I felt the pasta sitting heavily in my stomach in trepidation at Mia's idea of fixing. I possibly would have more luck with him on my own.

Should I stick to the plan, corner him on his own, and hope he had a conversation with me? I wondered. He didn't seem to be averse to talking…before. Setting my food aside, I met Mia's worried stare.

"I can talk to him," I told her quietly.

"Okay." She nodded in enthusiasm. "We'll find him tomorrow at lunch and let him know what happened."

Standing, I picked my bowl up and took it to the sink. "I think I would be better talking to him myself," I said to the sink, keeping my back to my best friend.

"Really? I don't." Mia laughed, her tone light and cheerful. "You're terrible at socialising and will probably end up telling him that he needs to work on his arm or something."

"His arm's fine, he needs better footwork inside the pocket," I told her as I grabbed the dish cloth and wiped my hands.

Her knowing look as she finished her supper was enough to make me groan. "Which is why I will talk, and you just say sorry, okay?"

"What if it has nothing to do with his game?" I thought perhaps giving her the entire information of the evening may have been a bad idea. She knew I was drunk, now she knew exactly *how* drunk I was, and I couldn't have her knowing any more. I was thanking every angel in heaven she hadn't put me as his bed partner together in her head.

"Well, what else could it be?" Mia rose to her feet as she carried her bowl to me, and taking it off her, I once again turned to the sink.

"I dunno," I mumbled as I rinsed and washed her dishes.

"Just let me handle this, okay?" Mia said as she hugged me from behind. "I'm going to practice," she told me as she gave me another squeeze, and I nodded before she was humming to herself as she walked down the short hallway to her room.

Staring out the window to the surrounding dorm houses and apartments, I once again dried my hands before I folded the tea towel and put it on the side of the counter. My fingers traced over the grey and white imitation marble countertops before they landed on the slightly yellowing grey and white checked vinyl flooring.

We'd been so lucky to keep the apartment from freshman year. Yes, we both complained about the small size of it, but the only people sharing the bathroom was us, and we weren't sharing kitchen facilities. Nor did we have to stick to what the cafeteria served us three times a day. Even though my scholarship covered meals, there was only so many times you could eat cafeteria food.

I had been inside some of the other accommodations, and there was worse than our apartment, but then, there was better. I had a dim recollection of the size of Jett's bedroom and bathroom, although I was fuzzy on the details. I looked at our humble apartment, taking in the two-seater sofa and single armchair. The TV was tiny, but neither Mia nor I cared about TV, and plus, if we wanted to see anything, we used our laptops.

I often lay in bed with my iPad and headphones if I got caught in a binge-worthy series. *The Walking Dead* came to mind, which I had watched on my own. There was no way in hell Mia was going to watch it, as there was too much gore.

I was restless. The need to sort this shit out with Jett was making me struggle to focus. Checking the time, I made my way to my own bedroom. Slipping on sneakers and checking my hair was tidy, I quickly brushed it before putting it in a ponytail. A moment later, it was loose again—easier to hide behind. I contemplated lip balm for my dry lips, or would that look like I was desperate…or making an effort?

I didn't want either option to be a possibility, never mind considered. I wanted him to only listen to what I was saying to him.

Hesitating at Mia's door, I heard her singing her scales, and knowing not to interrupt her, I left the apartment after leaving a note on the breakfast counter.

The walk through the campus was sticky and not entirely pleasant. Halfway to Jett's house, I ended up scraping my hair off my neck and face, tying it up. My thin T-shirt with a cartoon dog on it and the slogan *Coffee...because murder is wrong* had seemed cute when I picked it to wear this morning. Now it seemed juvenile. My denim shorts were modest, not short shorts like Mia wore. Just normal denim shorts with a woven belt. My white Chucks still needed a good clean.

As I walked, I realised I probably should have made more effort in my appearance. Jett was not used to laid back and easy-going Ava. He thought I was uptight. Looking down at my scuffed sneakers, I grinned. Well, I would never be accused of being high maintenance.

My feet faltered as I stood off to the side of his house. It was huge. I mean, I knew it was big, I'd been past it before, never really paying attention to it, thinking of it as the "footballers' house," but now, knowing I had to go up and knock…my teeth worried my bottom lip. Maybe I needed Mia after all.

"Is there a reason you're here?"

Turning swiftly, I looked up at Ash. He was blocking the sunlight, making it hard to see his features. Looking him over, I took in the ripped black jeans and the drop armhole T-shirt with the slogan *I'm a Saint* splashed across it.

"Hi," I greeted.

Ash moved slightly, and I had to turn to avoid the sun, enabling me to see him better. Gone was the friendliness from Monday. Instead, his eyes narrowed in anger. "What do you want?"

Shoving my hands into my back pockets, I rocked back on my feet. "I came to see Jett."

"He's busy."

"It will only take a moment," I said to him as I looked toward the house.

"He's still busy."

"You can tell from being out here?" Yes, that's right, antagonise them all. This wasn't helping. "Look, I just need to speak to him for a few moments. There's been a misunderstanding."

"Like what?" Ash moved again, and I mirrored his movement until I realised the bastard was now between me and the house. What an effective blocker he was, no wonder they loved him as a tight end. "Tell me, I'll pass it on."

"Um…"

"You have no idea what you're going to say for what you've done?" Ash looked surprised.

"I really didn't think of it," I admitted as I lifted my shoulder in a half shrug. "I was hoping inspiration would hit me on the way here."

Ash grunted, but he didn't move from his spot.

Resignation settled around my shoulders. "You're not going to let me get to the door, are you?" I asked him.

"My cousin is not someone you want to piss off. At the moment, you're the number one reason he's not playing." Ash folded his considerable sized arms as he looked down at me. He had to have been a foot taller, or thereabouts, he was so…big. Everywhere. "You want to walk in there to meet his wrath for a few moments with no plan and fuck all to say?"

"I could come back another day," I offered as I realised he was actually doing me a favour.

"You do that," he said with amusement as he turned and walked away from me. "That'll be so much better."

"Thanks," I murmured, not knowing if he heard me. Still, I thought that he had just done me a solid. What was I thinking, coming here with no plan? Strategy. Football was a game of it, and I loved strategy. Jett would appreciate a good strategy. If I couldn't appeal to his human side, I would raise my game to *the* game he understood.

With a clearer head than I arrived with, I started walking back to the apartment with a plan.

It wasn't until I was halfway home that I realised Ash had been being sarcastic when he had walked away from me. *Well, damn.*

CHAPTER 16

Jett

I finished typing up my assignment as the door was knocked, and making sure I had saved the document, I called out for them to enter.

"Hey," Ash said as he poked his head around the door. "Safe to come in?"

With a grin, I spread my arms in welcome as I pushed the chair back from the desk. "What's up?"

"Just spoke to Ava." Ash sat down on my couch as I looked at him with surprise. "She was outside, literally hopping from foot to foot about approaching the door."

"She's here?" I was on my feet, anger pulsing through me.

"No." Ash watched me carefully as I crossed to the window, leaning out to see if I could see her. "I told her to go."

Spinning back to him, I tilted my head in question. "Why?"

"Because look at you," Ash spoke quietly. "You look ready to kill her."

"She spiked my drink and then fucked me." At his sharp inhale at my bluntness, I stalked towards my cousin. "Both literally and figuratively."

"I know." Ash nodded as he looked up at me.

My eyes narrowed as I looked down at my cousin. "Then why do I think you're helping her?"

"Because I've thought about it. I met her on Monday, she's...completely unassuming." Ash stretched his legs out as he seemed to think about it. "Look, you're right to be pissed. *I'm* pissed. But..." He trailed off as he looked past me to the other side of the room.

"But?"

As his eyes came back to mine, he grimaced slightly. "I think there's more to this story." He held my look and didn't shy away from it.

"You think she's innocent?" I asked him in disbelief. "Or tell me, is it because you saw her naked ass as much as I did on Saturday morning? You want a turn at her, that it?"

Ash wagged his head as he stood. "No, and don't be a fucking asshole." His shoulder bump as he passed me made me grit my teeth. "I sat beside her Monday. She does absolutely nothing to draw attention to herself, and earlier today, that fucktard Leitch ripped her to pieces, I mean it was fucking brutal. Someone should report the fucker. *She* should report him!" Ash sighed. "You don't sit through that...that...humiliation without a word spoken, not if you're the kind of person who drugs others."

"So? Maybe she's only tough when she's victimising someone."

Ash's laugh was loud in my room, echoing off my walls. "Dude! You? You're never a victim. The whole house heard you fuck her. They all heard her screams, and apparently you weren't quiet either. Do you know how many guys in this house jerked off to the sound of you fucking her?"

"I don't care," I snapped. "What's your point?"

"Exactly. *You* don't care," Ash bit back at me. "And my point? My point is that you may have been drugged, but have you read about Versed? It's used as an anaesthetic."

"So?"

"So, you stupid fuck, it makes you fucking sleep! You fucked her what, three, four times? Does that sound like someone who is almost fucking passed out?"

My next words died on my tongue. I hadn't thought of that. "So? Maybe I had a different reaction."

"Dude, all I'm saying is, if her intent had been to drug you and take advantage, you wouldn't be an active participant. Understand?" His furious look made me pause, but I was a Santo and we were stubborn.

"And?"

"And…I don't think *she* drugged you. I think something happened in between the two events." Ash sat back down again. "We're missing something."

"Yes, it's called my memories."

"Stop being a diva," Ash muttered as he leaned forward, his elbow on his knee, his head dropping into his palm as he stared at my wall. "We're missing something. Something vital."

"And the person who may be able to help, you just turned her away," I reminded him.

"I did." Ash sat back as he looked at me. "Look at you, you're ready to rip her head off. Gray already told me you were going to wring her neck earlier. She's not safe around you at the moment."

"Again, I would like to say that she drugged me."

"Again, I would like to say I don't think she did," Ash mimicked me.

I started to pace the room as I thought about it. No. She knew she did something wrong, why else would she run? You don't run if you're innocent. Do you? Christ knows she was mouthy; she would have had no qualms about telling me exactly where to shove it if she was innocent.

No, I'd been fooled by her before. She knew more than she was telling, and I wanted to know it all.

"You haven't listened to a word I've said, have you?" Ash asked me with a rueful look.

"I did, I listened."

"But you don't care?"

"No. I really don't. She's not as innocent as she looks."

"I know, I heard about her from Friday," Ash deadpanned.

The door swung open, and Gray pulled up short when he saw the two of us, reading the room in a heartbeat. "What's happened now?" he asked as he closed the door.

"You sound more like mom every day," I said to him, causing

both of them to give a light laugh. I saw the tension leave my cousin's shoulders as he relaxed when Gray dropped down beside him.

"Seriously, what is it?" Gray asked. I gestured for Ash to fill him in, and in truth, I wasn't happy when my brother started nodding alongside him. "It kind of fits," he mused. "I mean, when Ben knocked her over with the ball, she was more conscious of people staring at her than she was of who I was." Gray flicked his eyes over to me. "Even when she spoke to you after it, she was more...pissed than anything."

"Incensed," I mumbled as I crossed once more to the window.

"Yeah," Gray nodded thoughtfully.

"Have we learned anything else?" I asked as I turned to both of them.

"Yeah, the guy Wade, the band's his." Ash handed me his phone. "That's his long-term girlfriend—your fuck buddy isn't her. His band's been playing some of the campus bars here and in Cardinal. They sometimes go further out but not often."

Gray was scanning Ash's phone before he was showing him his. "Got this off Facebook: blondie draws and designs his band's posters." Gray grinned at me. "She gets paid for it."

"Does she indeed?" My twin always knew what to say to me to make me feel better. "Declared?"

"Nope." Gray sat back and closed his eyes. "I'd say she's in violation of her scholarship."

"Earning an income while receiving a full ticket, tsk tsk." I sat back down at my desk with a satisfied grin. "That's just unacceptable behaviour for a student of Cardinal Saints. What *will* the dean say?"

As I started to laugh, Gray grinned, and after a resigned groan, Ash joined in.

I'd hang the little bitch out to dry. I didn't give a fuck if she was the one responsible for giving me the water with the drug in it.

Ava Bryant was responsible by default, and therefore she was *not* innocent. Which made her guilty, and *that* meant she would pay.

Gray broke me out of my inner thoughts as he leaned forward intently. "We know more about the thing we found?"

Ash also sobered as he leaned back into the couch, his body stiffening. "I think I have an idea of who the girl is. The men in the video, no."

"We keep going?" Gray asked as he looked between us.

"We do," I told him as I looked toward my closet where the memory stick was before I turned to Ash. "You took it?"

"How else am I supposed to do anything with it?" he asked me with a roll of his eyes.

"Should I care that you know the code already?" I asked him dryly as I walked over to the closet.

"It was pathetically easy," Ash boasted as Gray high-fived him.

I snorted as I stared at the floorboards. "I'm changing it again."

"Why?" Gray asked me good-naturedly. "Should we have secrets?"

Good point. "No." I closed the doors and turned back to them. "You're right." Leaning against my desk, I considered them both. "Do you agree about her?" I asked Gray.

"Fuck buddy from Friday?" he guessed, knowing me better than anyone.

"Yeah."

Gray tilted his head to the side as he looked at me, and with a brief once over, he turned to look at Ash. "She fucked with a Devil. I don't give a fuck who or what drugged him, she fucked him when he didn't know better. She pays. We'll figure out who else it was, and *they* will pay after."

"We get her kicked out of school?" Ash asked, trying hard not to frown. "Even though he would probably have fucked her anyway?"

"She pays," Gray repeated firmly.

"But..." Ash once again leaned forward, his hands rubbing across his hair as he thought about it. "I dunno, from what we heard, I don't think you came off too shabbily." His head raised to look at me. "If anything, she put you more on the fucking map."

I saw Gray smirk, and he caught me looking. "Jamie did kick up a fuss about it. Even though the bastard's jealous, it still interfered with his sleep…before a game."

"Humiliate her." Gray and I both looked at Ash in surprise. "We don't know how involved she is. I think and truly do believe this, she was tricked as much as you were. Whether that be someone told her you were into her and she fell for it, I dunno. You've spoken to her, does she really seem like this is what she gets her kicks from?"

"No." Crossing my arms over my chest, I looked at them both, my thoughts recalling easily how tense she was. "*Fuck!* No…she doesn't. I would actually encourage her to get laid, she's so fucking uptight."

"See?" Ash looked at me with something akin to hope. "I think you should be willing to listen to what she has to say, and if you don't like it, then make her life hell."

Looking at my cousin, I gave a bitter laugh. "You were the one who chased her off," I reminded him.

"Yeah, because I needed a chance to talk to you."

All three of us turned to my door when we heard the light tap on it. "Yeah?" I called.

Derrick opened the door, and seeing the three of us, he hesitated. "Hey."

"What?" Gray growled from his seat. He wasn't a fan of our corner. Derrick paid too much attention to Quinn, and Gray was protective.

"Um, Jett?"

"Um, what?" I asked as I took my seat at my desk.

"So, I, uh..."

"Of for the love of fuck, spit it out," Ash snapped.

"Heard you had Ava here on Friday," Derrick rushed out. "I didn't realise that was who I was hearing." He gave us all a meaningful look, and a tight knot formed in my stomach.

"Who's Ava?" I asked. Her name didn't roll off my tongue, I liked *bitch* or *uptight* better, so the natural sounding hesitation worked.

Derrick looked genuinely confused for a moment before he gave me a sly smile. "Oh yeah, I get it, love 'em and leave 'em. Good one."

I saw Gray look at Ash, who looked equally annoyed. "Hurry this up," I snapped.

"The girl on Friday was Ava. Yes?" He looked unsure now, and I needed that set in stone.

"What makes you think that?" Gray asked. "You see her?"

"What? No, I heard her but didn't see anyone. Actually..." Derrick rubbed the back of his neck. "No one saw her. How'd you get her out?"

"Why are you here?" I asked him again. I was already tired of this.

"Well, you know how Ava is," he started. No, I really didn't. "She's like football mad."

"She is?" Ash asked quietly.

"Yeah!" Derrick came into the room more, his eagerness at telling us something we didn't know overriding his good sense. "You know, I heard that even the sports editor on the paper checks the stats with Ava after the game."

My attention was fully on Derrick, but I knew both my brother and my cousin were exchanging looks. "She seems great," I said to Derrick. "A true fan."

"Oh no, she is really shy. Or you know...so I thought." He was looking both excited and resentful at the same time, his feelings for Uptight not exactly hidden.

"You want a pass at the girl from Friday," Gray said from his corner of the couch. "That's why you're here?" His contempt was easy to pick up on, and even though Derrick didn't know him that well, it was plain Gray wasn't impressed.

"Yeah, she's like my dream girl."

"Your dream girl is the girl from Friday being fucked senseless and screaming to let the whole house know whose dick she was on the end of?" I asked him as I stood. Why was this even bothering me? I couldn't explain it, but I wanted to punch him for knowing what Ava sounded like when she came on my dick.

"Yeah," Derrick nodded eagerly.

"I don't know who Ava is."

"You chased her across the campus today," Derrick told me with a little more firmness in his voice than I liked, the hard glint in his eye pissing me off even more.

"Her?" I asked him. "The blonde?"

"*Yes*," he stressed.

"So? You think she's from Friday?" I looked back at Gray and Ash and smirked. "Why the fuck would I chase someone I already had in my bed?"

"What? But…everyone's saying that it was," Derrick's eyes were flicking between the three of us in confusion.

"What am *I* saying?" My flat stare wouldn't encourage any further questions.

"But—"

"If no one saw her, how do you know it was her?" Gray asked quietly. Too quietly for my brother.

Derrick looked completely confused now. "But everyone's saying that it was her," he repeated.

"Are you saying that Jett's lying?" Ash asked with seemingly casual curiosity.

"Yeah, Derrick, you calling me a liar?" I raised an eyebrow as I looked down on him.

"No!"

"Sounds like it to me," Gray said as he stood. "Weren't you talking with Jett at the party?" he asked him. "Was your Ava there?"

"No. Just one of the band guys she hangs out with." Derrick looked genuinely agitated about that, and I made a mental note to look into this further.

"So you didn't see her with me, you didn't see her here, and you didn't see her leave..." I trailed off as I took a step closer. "Tell me again how she's your screamer?"

"You chased her," Derrick mumbled almost inaudibly.

"So?"

"Man!" He scratched his ear as he looked at me. "I was so eager for it to be her, know what I mean?"

No. I didn't.

"I'd love to tap that," he said with an unhappy shrug. "She's smokin'."

She was? Yes, she was, but again I didn't like this little fuck noticing.

"So…" He looked at me expectantly. "Who was it then?"

"Get the fuck out of my room."

Derrick started to laugh before he registered the scorn on my face and the fact Ash and Gray were on their feet behind me. With a sound that reminded me very much of a squeak of a mouse, he turned and practically ran out of the door.

When I had closed it firmly behind him, I turned to the other two. "Bobby checks with her on football stats?" I looked at Ash. "Still think she's innocent?"

"Another piece of the puzzle," he answered thoughtfully.

"Douche told us something else though," Gray said, on his phone again. "Wade? He was definitely there. I'm thinking it's time we get some alone time with this guy."

"Agreed," Ash and I spoke together.

"They play Thursday at the Bar One," Gray told us as he stood and shoved his phone in his pocket. "Don't know why you're so adamant to deny it was her here, but if you aren't sharing *that,* then"—he grinned widely—"you need one of the Elises to cover for you for Friday."

"Fuck." He was right, I needed a cover story. Which meant I would have to pick one of them. Shit.

"Sucks to be you." Gray clasped my shoulder as he left my room, Ash chuckling behind him as he followed him out.

Fuckers.

CHAPTER 17

Jett

Ash pushed the handle of the door down, and silently the three of us entered the house. We knew the residents of the house were on vacation, but that didn't mean we should be careless.

"What's the point of alarms if no fucker sets them?" Gray hissed in a temper as we crossed the large living area, heading for the stairs.

"I already disabled it," Ash whispered back. "Did you not notice who *makes* their alarm system?" He gave us a cocky grin, and Gray let out a low chuckle.

Ash's dad had shares in an alarm security company despite knowing next to nothing about it. However, his childhood friend, Bill, our "uncle," did know about it, and it was from him that Ash caught the coding bug. The fact we were breaking into a house with our family's security company coverage was slightly ironic, and I saw Gray smirk at the paradox. *Santo Security Systems* didn't just provide alarm systems, but anything you may need for security, whether that be a house intruder alarm system, a panic room, a simple wall-mounted safe or the more elaborate editions that only the truly paranoid needed.

"Where's the office?" Ash asked us quietly as we climbed the stairs. Suddenly, Gray held his hand up in a tight fist, indicating we stop.

Frozen on the stairs, we listened. And then I heard it.

A soft drawn-out moan.

Gray looked back down the stairs at us as he pulled his hood low and covered the lower half of his face with the black bandana we all wore, his eyes narrowed in accusation on Ash, who had assured us that the house was empty.

The moan came again, louder, and you wouldn't need to be a

genius to know *exactly* what was going on in the room halfway down the hall.

"Fuck, baby, this ass is so fucking tight." The male voice was loud in the silence.

"Fuck my ass," came the answering moan, and Ash turned to look at me with surprise before he too was covering his face with his bandana.

Gray stealthily moved up the stairs, and I caught Ash from reaching forward and grabbing him. Shaking my head, I pointed ahead. Just because there were people here didn't mean we wouldn't go forward with the plan. I watched my cousin clench his jaw as he debated whether we were being reckless, and then he followed Gray.

"Baby! Baby, I'm going to come, I'm going to fucking come up your ass on this bitch's bed."

Tightening my jaw to stop the laugh from escaping, I realised at least we knew *which* half of the owners was on vacation, as her husband cheated on her with whoever the lucky recipient may be.

At the top of the stairs, Gray waited, and when the headboard banging off the wall reached fever pitch, he pushed the study door open, the slight squeak covered by the rhythmic thumping.

Gray stayed by the door, leaving it open a fraction. With them being in the house, we should really have had it more open, but none of us really wanted to listen to the sound of their fucking.

"It's under the desk." Ash was barely audible, but the two of us headed to the desk and very quietly rolled the office chair back. "We need to lift it," he told me, and we both hesitated.

Was it worth being caught?

"You got this?" I asked him as we considered the options.

With a terse nod, we looked at Gray. He held up his hand and flashed his fingers. Ash and I glanced at each other, and then with a nod, we moved the desk, but then we followed Gray's instructions and waited.

The headboard banging stopped, we heard the shout of pleasure, we heard the answering groan, and still we waited. Gray stayed at the door, and all three of us dropped when we heard footsteps on the hall.

"You want anything?" the guy called out.

"Only you," came the answering call from the other man.

Ash pretended to put his fingers down his throat at the cliché reply. We waited as we heard him move downstairs, and we waited more when he came back up the stairs, never once coming near the study. That didn't mean we weren't anxious at the thought of it though.

"I got strawberries, cream and a...banana."

Gray choked on his laughter, pressing his hands to his mouth to stop the giggle. Ash was bent over, his body shaking, and I could only hope that my own fit of hysteria would stay silent as my shoulders shook with laughter.

As we strained to hear the low murmuring of voices, I nudged Ash, and he uncovered the floor, pulling the rug back, which hid the safe underneath.

Quietly, we lifted the hatch, and with a look to my brother, I saw he was fully focused on the door.

"Does this beep?" I suddenly whispered to Ash.

"No, it's the latest model, only installed two weeks ago," came his low reply.

"Still default code?" I said with surprise.

"Fucker deserves to be robbed," Ash said quietly to me. "*Actually* robbed." He sat back on his haunches as we heard another moan. "Was hoping they'd sleep," he admitted.

With a grin for my cousin, I opened the safe. Ash pointed his phone into the safe, and we both stared as he took a quick photo. Money was stacked neatly in one corner. A folder of documents, which Ash pulled out and quickly started to go through. A long jewellery box, which I opened and nudged Ash when I saw the black memory stick nestled between a gaudy diamond ring and diamond stud earrings.

Gray jerked suddenly, knocking the seat by the door, and we all froze, waiting to see if the bedroom gymnasts had heard us. I saw the reason my brother reacted—a black and white cat moved slowly across the floor, looking as confused at our presence as we were by it.

"Meow." It looked straight at me as it stopped in the centre of the room.

Gray glared at it and then me. He wasn't fond of cats.

"You've got to be fucking kidding me," Ash murmured as he handed me a piece of paper.

Reading it, I looked up at him in alarm. He shook his head and carefully I folded the document, slipping it under my hoodie.

With another shake of his head, he let me know there was nothing else of interest. Quickly we reassembled the safe, and as I closed the hatch, the cat brushed against me. It stood at my feet and then began to weave in and out of my legs. I thought they only did that in cat food commercials. It was hungry? It could fuck off.

I stared at it. It stared back. Neither of us moved.

"Meeeow."

Ash gave out a sigh as he bent down and picked the furball up and placed it to the side. Swiftly the desk was put back, and then the stupid cat meowed again.

"It's the bitch's cat."

Gray was pressed against the door, ready to burst through it if he needed to.

"Should we see where it is?"

I think all three of us held our breaths for what seemed like eternity.

"No."

"Maybe it's hungry."

"I'm hungry."

I rolled my eyes at the dude as Ash and I crossed to Gray, and he slowly opened the door. The door creaked, again we froze, but when we heard a murmur about the *stupid pussy*, Gray looked over at me, and with a firm look, he slipped out into the hall.

At the top of the stairs, he disappeared, and then Ash was following him. Pressing against the wall, he waited until Gray was at the bottom, and then he was gone too. With a deep breath, I followed their lead.

"Meow."

I hesitated for a moment, and then I was moving across the hall and almost threw myself down the stairs just as the bedroom door opened.

"Kitty! Shut up!" came the harsh voice of the owner.

I was half crouched on the ground floor hall, completely exposed. If he looked over his bannister, he would see me.

Gray and Ash were at the kitchen door, eyes wide as we all waited.

"Meow."

I had never wished harm on an animal until that moment. All it needed to do was run down the stairs after me, and I was busted.

I saw the guy clearly then as he walked towards the cat, and as he passed and his back was to me, I flew across the floor to the safety of the kitchen.

"We have minutes if that," Gray whispered as we raced to the door, and with a slow calm precision neither of us felt, Gray softly opened the back door to the yard, allowing Ash out. I could hear Kitty's owner coming down the stairs, and as the lower lights went on, my brother and I exchanged a panicked look before we were both through the door, and then all three of us dropped to the grass outside.

We crawled across the grass on our bellies, our heads low to the ground. At the side of the house, we raised ourselves to a crouch, and again one by one, each of us left the yard.

I was the last one at the car, and when we were in, with Gray checking the area to make sure there were no observers, I started the engine and we pulled away.

When we had enough distance between us and the house, Gray started to laugh. "A banana?"

"A fucking cat?" Ash started to laugh too.

"Always knew pussy was likely to be the end of us," I joked before we all dissolved into laughter.

"What's on the paper?" Gray asked me when he sobered.

Ash looked out the window, his lips pursed, and with a sigh, I pulled it from my hoodie and handed it to Gray.

"Are you *fucking* kidding me?" Gray exploded in the back seat as he read it. "Take us back, take me back *right* now."

"You need to calm down," I told him as Ash turned in his seat to look at Gray.

"Calm down?" Gray was still staring at the paper as he practically vibrated with rage on his seat. "This will *destroy* her." His eyes snapped to mine, and I nodded.

"I know." I held his stare in the rearview mirror. "Gray, we're going to fix it."

"Fucking asshole," Gray growled. "We need to *end* him."

"Gray," I cautioned him as I drove, my eyes flicking once to Ash in warning.

"We'll get him," Ash assured my brother. "We can't tell her about this."

"Of course we don't tell her," Gray fumed in the back seat. "Why would *this* be in that guy's house?"

"We have a memory stick. Hopefully, it tells us more." Ash rubbed his hand over his face.

Thirty minutes later, we were making our way tiredly up the stairs to our rooms. I heard low moaning on the second floor coming from Jamie's room and smirked back at Ash as I carried on past.

"Not working it hard enough," Ash called out as he passed the door, thumping it loudly. "Work it hard, get your freak on. Girl, you even alive in there? Make him work for it, baby!"

With a grin at Ash, I hesitated on the stairs. "Jesus, Elise told me you were shit, but I never believed it. No wonder she only moans for the Devils."

Gray snorted as he climbed the stairs. The moans got louder, and my brother's laughter echoed down from the top floor as Ash and I jogged up the stairs after him.

In Ash's room, we kicked off our sneakers, and Gray held his hand out impatiently for the memory stick.

"Wasn't keeping it off you," I murmured as I placed it in his hands.

Ash swiped it out of Gray's grasp with a wink. "I'm quicker."

"Heard that about you," Gray quipped as he pulled his phone out of his pocket and started scrolling. "Remember to wipe the image from your phone," he said to Ash as he sank down onto the couch.

I'd taken the edge of the bed, but Ash had hit an encryption, and as he worked on it, I lay back, my eyes closing. When I heard his grunt of satisfaction, I sat up as the film began to play.

At the end, I turned to look at Gray whose face was white with fury. "At least this girl walked away."

"Yeah," I agreed as Ash remained quiet. "What is it?"

"The file says it has three more minutes."

We waited as the camera remained pointed at the bed. Ten seconds before the end, a face came into view and turned the camera off. It was a sloppy mistake but one we needed.

"Harry, what have you got yourself involved in?" I said quietly to the silence of the room.

"We go back to Harry's?" Gray asked as he stood.

"Yeah, and we beat the shit out of him," Ash growled as he

turned in his seat. "He wasn't in the first one, but is it because he's the cameraman?"

"We need more." I stared at the floor, knowing my brother was never going to agree to what I was going to say next. "We need to show her."

"No."

"Gray—"

"I said *no*, Jett."

"I agree."

I turned to look at Ash. I hadn't been expecting him to agree with Gray after seeing the film. "You do?"

"She sees this, she'll freak out." Ash met Gray's look. "She doesn't need this shit in her head." He leaned back in his chair. "It's bad enough it's in ours, she doesn't need it."

"It's already in *her* head," I reminded them both.

"We said no." Gray's look was pointed, his tone brooked no room for argument.

"Fine."

"Let's get some sleep," Ash, ever the peacekeeper, suggested. "We still have tomorrow to prepare for."

I walked to the bedroom door. "We hit the bar first. We need to know about this Wade guy."

"Class, practice, bar, fuck shit up," Ash said as he ticked the items off his fingers. "Got it."

Gray smiled suddenly. "Time to remind this place who we are."

"It is indeed," I agreed.

"You ready?" Gray asked me as he bounced on his feet in anticipation.

A slow smile spread across my face. "When am I not ready, little brother?" I gave a low laugh as I left them. Tomorrow night, this campus would remember what it meant to have the Devils at this school.

It was time to cause mayhem.

CHAPTER 18

Ava

"AVA!" MY EYES FLEW OPEN, AND I SAT UP AS MIA CALLED AGAIN.

"What?" I mumbled, swinging my legs off the side of the bed and opening my bedroom door. "Did I sleep too long?"

Mia popped her head out of the bathroom, her hair curled and down, her eyes smoky and her nude lipstick in her hand. "Yeah, you have twenty minutes."

"Who you trying to impress?" I asked her as I took in her skinny, dark grey jeans and a blood red off-the-shoulder top.

"No one," she scoffed as she went back into the bathroom.

"Lead singer of Atticus Dawn perchance?"

"Perchance?" Mia's light laugh from the bathroom had me grinning. "No one says perchance."

"Elizabeth Bennet does," I corrected her as I stared at the contents of the fridge. When I saw her thinking about it, I rolled my eyes. "*Pride and Prejudice,* Mia. Did we drink all the soda?"

"No, I made up mixers," Mia told me as she came into the kitchen.

"You look good," I complimented her as she took out a jug and poured us a healthy glass each. "How long have I got?"

"Fifteen?" She grinned at me as we clinked glasses. "You'll only need ten."

"So I get dressed quickly." I took a hearty gulp. "Ooh yummy. I'll be back in five."

My clothes for tonight were already laid out, and I tossed my sleep shorts and tank off, pulling on the black mid-thigh flippy skirt and simple black box top with a small shoulder-capped sleeve. Black and white Converse slipped on over my sneaker socks, and I went to the bathroom to brush my hair.

"Mia, come do a messy bun!" I called to her, and within

minutes, she had my hair in two high ponytails before she was pulling them through the hairbands and then looping them through each other. With a few bobby pins, she secured my messy bun, pulling a few strands of my blonde hair free to "soften" my face, as she called it.

"You need mascara and lippy," Mia told me as she pulled my makeup bag from the cupboard under the sink. "Use the extra volume one I got you," she said as she handed me the tube.

"You're so bossy," I muttered as I obligingly stroked the wand over my lashes.

"Red or rosy pink?" Mia held the lip gloss in her hands.

"Pink." I decided. With a final look in the mirror, I was ready. "Did I make it?"

Mia rolled her eyes. "With time to spare. Let's finish our drinks; I called a cab."

"You did?" I asked her in surprise, and I picked up my flyers for tonight's show.

"These pants are new, so I'm not sitting in Wade's van on those seats where he puts his drive-thru food."

I opened my mouth to ask how did she know what had been on the cab driver's seats, but one look from Mia made me simply drink from my glass instead. "This is all I'm having tonight, if we go to the party after the gig," I told her as I pointed at the glass. "I've had enough party time already this semester."

"I thought you would, that's why I only made enough for two glasses and used extra soda."

Briefly hugging her, I laughed when she squeezed me back. "This is why I love you." I headed back to my room to grab my purse.

"Cab's here!" Mia called as I entered the living room. "Got everything?"

"Yes, ma'am, let's rock and roll."

Wade's band was playing in Cardinal tonight, so it was a ten-minute drive in the cab, and Mia talked to the driver the whole time while I checked my flyers, admiring the new design.

When we got to the bar, I told the bouncer our names, and he tagged us as underage with pink wristbands. We were early, and Wade and the guys were still setting up. "Hey, I have them. Where do you want them?" I asked as I held up the flyers and assessed the tables.

"One on every table, then they said we can put them on the shelf over there," Wade said as he pointed to the shelf that ran the entire length of the bar. We'd been in this bar before. It was bigger than some of the ones at campus, and the floor was always sticky from years of people spilling their drinks when they were dancing. Sheryl, the lady who owned the place, was nice, and she always gave Mia and me free soda when we were here.

"Holy shit, you both look hot," Wade blurted as he finally looked at us. "You are staying here, aren't you?" he asked me worriedly.

"Yeah, but there's a party at the basketball team's house later," I told him as I looked over at Mia, who was talking to Alex, the new singer. "Mia wants to party."

"Cool, got that invite too. I'll tag along with you," Wade told me. "Posters are the shit, Ava. Love them."

"Aww, thank you." I batted my lashes at him, and he laughed. "Looking very JC tonight, Mr Gordon," I complimented him.

"Did you just tell Wade he looked like Jesus?" Shane asked me in confusion as he looked at the faux-mohawked, tattooed bass player.

"JC. Johnny Cash."

"Oh," Shane laughed self-consciously. "'Cause he's all in black?"

Wade grinned as he called Alex over. "First song tonight, as inspired by our poster girl, 'Man in Black,'" Wade told him, and Alex nodded.

"Sure, it'll take us right into the new song too."

"Agreed," Wade said as he squeezed my arm before they went back to the stage area.

"You look good," Shane said as he looked me over appreciatively. "For someone? Or do you have plans later?"

"Party at the Orchard later."

"Basketball guys?" He grinned at me slyly. "They told me football was your game of choice."

"So? I can't party?" I teased him, and he smiled at me in good humour.

"Okay if I join you later?" Shane asked as he looked over to the stage where Sticks was calling for him.

"Yeah, Wade's coming too."

His smile lost some of the shine, but he turned before I could clarify that I was aware of what he was asking me. I started putting the flyers on the tables and strategically placing them along the shelf on the wall.

"Why does the hot guitarist look like you threw up in his shoes?" Mia asked me curiously as she handed me a soda.

"He asked if he could come to the party later, and I said yes and that Wade was already going."

"Oh." Mia took a sip of her soda. "Maybe it could have gone smoother," she said with a small smile my way. "You can make it up to him later."

"How?" I pulled out one of the stools at the wall, sat and crossed my legs, and leaned on one of the flyers as I stared at her.

"Tell him he played well and he's a great addition to the band." Mia shrugged as she swayed her hips to the music coming from the jukebox, oblivious to the fact she had Alex's full attention from the stage.

"You okay here or do you want to move closer?" I asked her as I looked around the bar. "They won't mind if we get closer. They'd probably prefer us to be further from the bar," I added ruefully.

"We can move nearer the time."

Nodding at her plan, we spoke quietly as we watched Wade and the guys make the finishing touches to the setup, and then Wade was scribbling in a notebook, and I knew they were making up the set list. I shook my head at his casualness to the set, but he had explained to me before that he didn't like selecting the music too far in advance. He needed to feel his vibe on the night.

More people started arriving, and as they did, Mia and I left the comfort of our wall and started mingling and handing out flyers. Pretty soon, the band started, and that made my job harder as everyone seemed to unconsciously move forward as one. Wade had a good college following, and they were loyal supporters, mostly always showing up when they had an off-campus gig.

An hour into the music, I was glad I had worn sneakers and a skirt, it was so hot in here. The music was great, the crowd was enjoying it, and all my flyers were safely in people's purses or back pockets. Good result.

I was back at the side of the room, leaning against the shelf as I watched Mia dancing beside the stage. She was with a girl from one of her classes, and they were having fun. Wade started to play the intro to one of their best songs, and I pushed off the shelf to stand straight. I loved this one, it was called "Stars and Dusk," and he said he wrote it one night after watching a film about six demons and a witch. I loved this song.

As I sang along to the chorus, I felt a body press up against me, and I stepped forward. The presence behind me stepped forward with me, and as I turned to glare at whoever it was to back off, my words died on my tongue as Jett stared down at me.

He would never hear my protestations over the music, so I stepped forward again and startled when an arm slipped around my waist, pulling me back into his hard body. Again, I looked over my shoulder at him, and he raised an eyebrow at me in question before turning his attention to the stage.

So that was it? I was to just accept his manhandling of me?

Staying as rigid as I could, I jumped when his breath caressed my ear.

"Loosen up, Uptight, anyone would think you hated me touching you." I felt the nip at my ear, and I was glad he didn't hear my reaction. "We both know you have no problem with my hands on you." As he spoke, his hand slipped under my loose top, and his fingers stroked over my skin.

I felt him straighten, but his hand never moved, his thumb rubbing light circles over my skin, and along with it, my heart thumped in rhythm. Should I move? Would he let me? *Will he let me leave? Seriously?* I grumbled inwardly.

He doesn't *own* you.

He doesn't even like you!

Then why is he touching me? To throw you off-balance, Ava. And newsflash, it's working!

As the song ended, my hand covered Jett's, and I tugged. The guy had strong hands. I mean, he'd been flinging balls through the air since he was three, but seriously, were they glue?

Alex started to sing the cover version of a Michael Ray song, and as his gravelly voice wrapped over us, I felt Jett at my ear again.

"You trying to get free of me, Uptight?"

"Yes," I ground out. "You don't need to be holding onto me."

"I can't hear you."

Leaning back, I turned my head as far as I could so he could hear me. I saw the amusement in his eyes when my ass pressed into him, and when I tried to jerk free, he took a step back and turned us both before I was spun in his arms looking up at him. The move was so sudden I didn't know how I was facing him. Two shadows moved and stood in front of Jett, shielding us, and I realised Ash and Gray were here too. Why? This wasn't something they would normally be at.

I went to ask, but the hardness in Jett's stare made me bite my tongue. "Every time I try to find an answer about Friday, you're there."

"I don't understand."

He said nothing, but swiftly he stepped away from me. I realised the music had stopped and Alex was telling the crowd they were having a ten-minute break.

"Ava, there you are!" Mia looked at me and then Jett, her eyes widening when she realised all three Santo guys were there. "You okay?" she asked me as she looked over Gray and Ash, who had just turned to face us.

"I'm fine," I answered her as I maintained eye contact with Jett.

"Jett," Gray said quietly in the loud bar, and Jett flicked his eyes away from mine to look at his brother. Wade was heading to the bar, and Jett coolly stepped away from me without a backwards glance, Gray on his heels. Ash lingered, but his eyes were all for Mia.

"Don't you need to run after him too?" I snapped at him. Mia's eyes widened in surprise at my obvious animosity, but she said nothing as she looked at Ash.

Ash smiled, it was slow, and goddamn it was sexy. I was thankful that I wasn't on the receiving end of it, or else I was sure I would have felt my knees weaken. But Mia? She looked completely unimpressed.

"Ash," he told her.

"And?"

His smile was now a grin, and with a dip of his head to her, he walked past. I noticed his hand skimmed her arm as he passed her, and I don't know if he would have felt the goose bumps that ran over her arm at his touch, but there was no denying he had affected her.

"Holy shit, what was that?" I whisper-hissed at her when he was far enough away.

"I was hoping you would tell me," Mia said, giving me her whole attention. "What did Jett want?"

I stared at her, dumbfounded for a moment. "Huh?"

Mia blinked as she gave her head a quick shake as she looked at me, as if *my* reaction was confusing *her*. "Dude, you were just in a huddle with the Saints number eight."

She was either ignoring my obvious question, or she was so used to guys hitting on her she was now oblivious. I would probe later, I decided. I looked around and saw Jett and Gray talking to Wade and pointed them out to Mia. "He wanted to meet Wade."

Lame lame lame...*lame!*

"But you didn't introduce him," Mia said to me in confusion.

"Ladies, how did you like the set?" Alex asked as he came up to us.

"You were great," I told him truthfully and smiled when Shane joined us, handing a bottle of water to Alex.

As Mia talked to the guys, I couldn't help but track the Santos as they spoke to Wade. Wade looked like his usual self, and he was talking happily to them. There was no universe that existed where Wade and the Devils were in the same orbit. What on earth were they talking about?

"That okay with you, Ava?" Shane asked me, and I turned back to them.

What? "Of course," I agreed.

He smiled at me, and then both guys were heading back to the stage.

"You have no idea what you just agreed to, do you?" Mia said to me, her voice heavy with amusement.

"Tell me," I urged as I watched the Santos leave the bar. Jett didn't even look over his shoulder or in my direction at all. It was as if I didn't exist. He had held me to him and hadn't let me go when I tried, what did that mean? Did any of it mean anything?

"It's nothing to worry about, we're going to hang back at the end and then go to Orchard together."

I nodded and flinched back when her hand appeared in front of my face.

"Now, are you going to tell me what you were all up in Jett's space about?" Mia asked me curiously.

"I was?" I asked her incredulously. "Did you even see the way you and Ash reacted to one another?"

Mia looked around the room. "Ash?"

"You're ridiculous," I murmured as the band began to play and the music made it impossible to speak anyway.

Mia and I helped clean the tables when the music was over, and Sheryl was delighted with our help. When the band was all packed up and the bar had its normal Thursday night clientele, we waited outside for the guys to load the van.

"Who's ready to party?" Wade cried when we were all in the van, and I laughed as he waggled his eyebrows.

I felt my shoulders relax as we got ready to leave the bar. I was looking forward to the party.

CHAPTER 19

Ava

"It's a Thursday night, it's hardly going to be an all-nighter," I reminded Wade.

"Why? I got no classes until twelve tomorrow," Wade said smugly as he started the van. "We played really well tonight, and I'm up for getting *lit*."

"And Sticks doesn't go to class on a Friday," Shane said with an amused look over his shoulder at the drummer.

"You have no classes on a Friday?" Mia asked him in surprise. "Lucky."

"I have class," Sticks told her as he twirled a drumstick in his hand. "I just don't go, ain't got no time for that shit, it's Friday."

Mia looked at me, and I giggled at her expression. Sticks once told me he lived to the beat of his own drum and no one else's, and although I was sort of impressed at his own self-awareness at the tender age of twenty-one, I also knew he was stoned when he told me. In fact, Sticks was usually stoned.

"So, Wade, you got Devil groupies?" Mia teased as we drove, and my heart almost stopped in my chest at her complete lack of discretion as she just blurted it out.

"Yeah." Alex looked excited. "We need them to spread the word they were there," Alex said to Wade, leaning forward. "Word gets out we have Devils in our fanbase, man, we'll be made."

"They're just guys," I grumbled.

"Yeah, they are," Wade said with a grin. "But I don't think they're fans," Wade said cheerfully as he looked in the rearview mirror. "I met Jett last Friday. Guy was looking for his keys."

"His keys?" I asked Wade.

"Yeah, he lost them. Was pretty worked up about them too." Wade shrugged. "I asked him where he'd been, and he said he'd been at a party on Cedar. I was heading that way, and I told him I would give him a call if I saw them." Wade snorted out a laugh. "He full on tells me he doesn't answer unknown numbers, so I made him give me his number, and I texted him so he'd know who I was if I found them."

"He must have," I said more to myself than the van. "Found them, I mean."

"Yeah, or one of his brothers was home," Wade spoke to me.

"Brothers? Ash is his cousin," I corrected.

"You know a lot about the Santo guys," Shane said to me. His look was searching.

"Ava's a huge football fan, she knows the team's stats," Mia piped up, and for the next few minutes, I was tested on my football knowledge.

It broke any weirdness between Shane and myself and answered my curiosity about Jett. As we headed into the basketball players' dorm house, I tugged Wade's arm to get him to stop.

"He came all the way to the bar to say thanks for *not* finding his keys?"

Wade looked at me, his face thoughtful. "Why are you so curious?" he asked. "Thought Spence was your QB of choice."

"He is. It just seems so anti-Santo." I nudged him with my shoulder. "I'm just nosey, let's go."

"I'm fucking with you," Wade joked. "You give me or him, I'm not sure who, too much credit. I never told him I didn't find his keys, and he didn't come to say thanks. Either way, you're thinking about it too much. They were in town, heard the music, came in. He saw it was me and said hi. The brother, the fierce-looking one, he grilled me, but Jett told him to cool off. He's an alright guy."

Ha.

The party was in full swing when we went in, and we inevitably got separated before meeting again. The room wasn't as full as it would be if it were a Friday night. Sticks disappeared to the basement pretty quickly, and Wade saw a guy from his class he needed to talk to. Mia dragged Alex to dance, and then it was just Shane and me. We stood in companionable silence for a while, and then he said he was going to rescue Alex from the dance floor, and I suggested we take them outside. It was too hot in here, and I needed air. My top was sticking to me.

As I went ahead of them into the backyard, I was almost relieved to take a deep breath, even if the air was thick with humidity. I watched two guys get into an argument, and opting to stay out of the way, I crossed the yard to take shelter at the corner of the house. A flare of cherry red alerted me to the fact that there was someone further in the shadows, smoking a cigarette.

"Sorry," I told them. "Didn't mean to encroach on your solitude." I grinned to whoever stood in the darkness. They moved forward, and my jaw dropped. Jett looked at me, half hidden in the shadows. What was he doing out here, *smoking*? Wait, *why* was he smoking? "You shouldn't smoke!" I berated him, taking a step towards him in irritation. "You're an athlete. Your body needs to be at its best!"

He took a long drag of his smoke, his eyebrow lifting in challenge. "A full night in the bar and you're still uptight."

"I'm not uptight."

"Sure," he scoffed as he took another pull of his smoke before he stubbed it out on the side of the house. "My body *is* at its best, you know that." He gave me a sly look as he took a step towards the light. His attention was caught by the guys arguing, who were now swinging punches. A bottle went flying through the air, and Jett grabbed me, pulling me out of the way as the projectile flew through the air coming towards me.

I had no idea where the bottle landed, because I was pressed up against the side of the house with Jett pushed up against me, one arm resting against the wall as he leaned into me. I hated smoking, but weirdly, the smell of nicotine mixed with the scent of him, which was almost cedarwood-like with an undernote of vanilla, made me breathe him in.

"They missed," I said to him in a low voice when I realised that he knew I'd basically just sniffed him.

"Mm-hmm." Jett didn't move, and as we were away from the lights of the house, I could no longer see his face clearly.

"You can move," I reminded him.

His answer was to press his lower body into mine. "You're so...*nervous*. No. Not nervous, jittery."

"Jittery?" I gave a low chuckle as I looked up at him. "Well, a guy I hardly know has me pressed against a wall in a dark backyard," I hissed at him.

"Hardly know? Now, now, Uptight, you're forgetting we're old friends."

I felt his hand skim down over my hip and onto my thigh. He bent slightly, and feeling my skirt being gathered in his hand, I might have stopped breathing. "What are you doing?" I asked him as I felt air around the top of my thigh.

"Testing something," he murmured as his fingers trailed over the top of my leg.

"Testing what?" I was rooted to the spot, my head turned slightly to look towards the backyard, and somewhere I realised in my head that he had tugged up the side of the skirt so that no one could see if anyone came looking.

"Just…" He paused, and then his fingers skimmed over my pussy, and I gasped. I mean, I knew he was probably going to do something, but still it was a shock when he touched me. "Relax," he whispered against my cheek, and I knew he had to feel the racing of my heart as his fingers caressed over my panties again.

"I don't think—" I almost bit my tongue when he pushed my panties to the side and his fingers slid through my gathering wetness. My head fell back against the wall as I could feel Jett watching me as his fingers rubbed over the small bundle of nerves, which were the only thing my whole entire being was concentrating on.

"Keep your eyes open," he instructed as he slid one finger inside me, and my hands gripped his arms. "Jesus." I heard his low voice as he pushed another finger inside me, and then he moved them both, in and out, while his thumb rubbed gently over my nub.

My knees were close to buckling as my tummy clenched again and again with need, almost like hunger. I needed more.

"Fuck, your pussy wants this," Jett's voice was hoarse as he continued to finger fuck me.

I had no words. I could feel it building in my toes, I needed the release. My head tried to drop forward onto his chest, but Jett gripped my neck and held me so I was looking up at him.

"Eyes on me." His voice was harsh. "Are you close?" I didn't even get to answer before he was answering for me. "Yeah, I can feel you gripping me, hungry pussy." His head dipped, and I wildly thought he was going to kiss me. His mouth hovered over mine before he moved to my ear.

"Frustrating isn't it, to be on the edge of *something*, knowing it's just within reach and not quite being able to grasp it." Jett withdrew his fingers, fixed my panties and then stood back.

"What?" My voice was shaky, and my breathing was rapid. I was so close. What was he doing?

Jett popped two fingers in his mouth and sucked as he watched me, and then with a smirk, he walked away.

What the fuck was that? Hastily, I fixed my skirt, my panties dampening from his ministrations, and I leaned against the wall, trying to sort out what had just happened.

"I don't see her." I heard Mia's voice, and in my panic, I remembered I was supposed to be meeting my friends. My friends, who at any time could have seen me flat against the wall, with a Devil's fingers inside me.

What if they had seen Jett walk from this side of the building?

Shit.

Looking to the other side, I noticed the overgrown shrubbery and seriously contemplated scrambling over it to avoid any awkward questions.

"Maybe she saw the fight and went back in to find us?" I heard Shane say and a few murmurs of agreement.

Go inside, please go inside.

"Okay, we'll do a sweep of the floor again. It really isn't like her..." I heard Mia telling them as they walked away.

I gave myself a few minutes, my hands patting my hair, trusting I hadn't messed my messy bun up. My hands shakily straightened my top and smoothed my skirt. With a deep breath, I collected myself as I rolled my head on my shoulders, and then with a confidence that I wasn't feeling, I went into the party to join my friends.

FRIDAY CLASSES SUCKED BALLS. NOT ONLY HAD I NOT SLEPT A WINK because all I could feel was the frustration of an impending orgasm my fingers couldn't give me, but I didn't understand why he hated me so much.

Or did he hate me? Did you do what Jett did last night if you disliked someone? I didn't know. Nor did I know how to ask the question of Mia without telling her everything, and I didn't want to say the words. I didn't want to share the shame of my crazy one-night stand.

Plus, the whole campus was alive with the *mayhem* the Devils had caused last night. No one of course was accusing them outwardly, but it was obvious they had been up to their tricks. In the early hours of the morning, three classrooms had been completely emptied of furniture. Every car parking space had a desk and a chair in it, and when people had tried to park, the pile of furniture had begun to grow as the traffic backed up.

Most of the students lived on campus, but the admin staff, the lecturers, the maintenance men, the groundskeepers, all of them commuted to work. Morning classes had been disrupted, and chaos had overtaken Cardinal Saints College.

Not only had they done this, but a devil's trident had also been tagged onto the side of the stadium, and apparently Coach Bowers had been explosive in his rage, screaming on the walkway to get the *fucking Santo shits* to his office.

They were due to travel this afternoon to Missouri for the game tomorrow, and the only time I had been alert all day was when I heard some guy in my class tell his friend that he heard both Ash and Gray were being made to stay behind.

The rumour was a false one. I happened to be behind one of the assistant coaches in the coffee queue when some guy asked him if the full offence was travelling this afternoon, and the coach had told them it was a full complement, minus QB8 of course, who was still nursing an ankle injury.

Huh, his ankle didn't look injured, I thought to myself, but I wasn't a sports therapist.

As I sat under my tree, I watched the maintenance men and groundskeepers traipse back and forth, putting the desks and chairs back inside. All the trolleys had also been "misplaced," and the poor guys were doing it by hand.

"Hey." Mia dropped beside me as she watched the to-ing and fro-ing. "Carnage," she snorted as she took out her lunch bag. "How did they do it?" she asked me curiously.

"They're claiming it wasn't them."

"It has Devils' Mayhem all over it," Mia scoffed as she uncovered her lunch. It appeared to be lettuce, cucumber and sliced avocado.

"What are you eating?" I asked her as my nose wrinkled in distaste.

"Edamame beans." She handed me a small pack of the soybeans, and I frantically shook my head. "They're full of fibre," she advised me.

I didn't doubt it but said nothing as I sipped my caramel latte, my eyes returning to the men working.

"So." Mia popped one of the beans into her mouth. "Jett and you are…" She waited expectantly.

My head snapped to hers in question. "Nothing?"

"He spoke to you at the bar, and I heard they were at the party we were, but I didn't see him, did you?"

I swallowed. "No."

"Maybe he was here playing with tables and chairs." Mia giggled.

"It would have taken them hours," I stated as I returned to watching. "Well, I guess they would have had the moving trolleys. But wouldn't someone have seen them?"

"No idea, I do know it meant my computer science class was cancelled as the professor couldn't get into the parking lot."

"Yeah, I got off without Leitch this morning. Maybe we need to thank them?" I gave her a small smile, and Mia chuckled.

My phone rang, and I looked at the unknown number.

"Hello?"

"Ms Bryant?" The woman's voice had a crisp edge to it that made me sit straighter.

"Yes?"

"This is the dean's office on campus. Can you come to the dean's office at one thirty? He would like to speak to you."

"Um, is everything okay?" I asked as I looked up at Mia, who had stopped eating.

"Is one thirty convenient?"

"Yes, of course." It wasn't, I had a class, but the lady was satisfied and hung up.

"What is it?" Mia asked me with concern.

"The dean wants to see me at one thirty."

"Why?" Mia asked as she resumed eating. "You win something?"

"What? No." I chewed my lip as I thought about it. "Why would you think I had?"

Mia shrugged. "What else could it be? You're a model student."

"Yeah." I didn't stop fretting as I thought about it. "What if I'm in trouble?"

"You look guilty!" Mia laughed. "You don't do *anything* wrong, Ava. Some underage drinking, yes, but then the whole campus would be in the dean's office."

"Yeah." I nodded again as Mia opened her phone. Looking over campus, I saw Jett and Gray standing watching the guys working the desks and chairs. Several people were calling out to them, but they remained stoic as they watched. Ash came down the steps from the law building and slung his arms over his cousins' shoulders. I saw Jett nod, and then Ash was walking towards one of the maintenance men. I heard the guy start laughing, and then with a high five to Ash, he and another guy disappeared into the building.

A few minutes later, they came out with the trolleys, and the remedial work to the grounds and parking lot was smooth.

When I looked over at where the Devils stood, Jett was watching me, his face blank. He slipped his shades on, and then the three of them walked towards the stadium.

"Hey, look, they found the trolleys," Mia exclaimed as she looked up from her phone.

"They did." Standing, I brushed off my shorts. "I have to go, you be okay?"

"Library?" Mia guessed with a smile.

Not this time. "Yeah." I nodded, and with a small wave, I hurried back to the apartment. I needed to change and be more presentable. I had a bad feeling about this afternoon's meeting, something wasn't sitting right with me.

CHAPTER 20
Jett

My leg was bouncing as I sat on the chair outside the dean's office. The guy hated me and my family; why he took this job was beyond anyone's understanding. Why he was offered this job was also beyond my comprehension. My dad told me it was because he needed to be the better man. My uncle told me it was because my dad was an idealist and eventually reality would bitch-slap him if he didn't first.

Uncle Kage was a hard bastard. I sometimes wondered how Ash was more like my dad while I was more like my uncle. Gray was a disturbing blend of both of them.

Kage and Kerr Santo. They had been born as triplets, but the third son had died days later. Dad always said that they felt his presence, but that kind of talk freaked me out. I didn't hold much faith in the supernatural or ghosts. Ash said it wasn't the supernatural I had a problem with, more like empathy in general, and I had a tendency to agree with him, not that I would ever tell him that.

Gray and Ash had boarded the team's jet to go to Missouri about an hour ago. They would be landing soon, and here I was, sitting like a chump outside this little prick's office. I was pissed at staying behind. However, I was running out of time to prove who had done the spiking, and being hauled in front of Dean Porter was not what I needed today.

"Santo," the voice beckoned me as his secretary exited the office.

Getting to my feet, I walked into the office, my face carefully blank. "Dean Porter?"

"Shut the door and sit down."

Biting my tongue, I did as instructed. When I was facing the little fuck, I sat calmly. My dad had taught us to school our emotions and never let anger rule you. I had mastered it slightly better than Gray, who was sometimes as explosive as they come, but still we were adept at it and knew how to play the game.

The dean was small in height, slight of frame, bald, thick black glasses and a crooked nose. The result of my dad, who had broken it when he punched him in his junior year of college for scratching his car. Allegedly. Dad had definitely punched him; Dennis Porter had *allegedly* scratched his brand-new Aston Martin.

Dad liked flashy things, traits my older brother picked up, but Gray and I were more...reserved. Slightly.

"The school was vandalised last night."

"I heard." I nodded.

"You heard? You didn't see?" He leaned forward in his chair, a huge brown leather thing that swallowed him.

"What would I see?" I asked calmly.

"You didn't see them taking hours this morning and afternoon, travelling back and forth with the desks and chairs?"

"I did."

Dean Porter sighed as he leaned back in his chair. "Tell me why."

I watched him watch me. "Tell you why...?"

"Don't mess with me, I'm not your coach."

"Thank God for that," I told him. When his eyebrows rose in surprise, I rubbed my jaw. "You've missed the flight to Missouri if you were coach."

"Why aren't you on that flight?" he asked me shrewdly.

"Injury."

"There's no medical record of it."

"Should you be looking at my confidential medical records?" I asked him as my head tilted to the side.

"I am your dean."

"You are, but you're not my doctor," I countered back at him.

We sat in silence for a long, drawn-out moment as he tried to think of a reason to be looking at my medical records, and I sat smugly, knowing he'd already fucked himself and whatever bullshit reason I was here for.

"If you admit to the crime, I will not penalise you." He started to talk again, and I covered my snort with a fake cough.

"What crime are we talking about?" I asked casually as I watched him. For being a bald man, he had the bushiest eyebrows I'd ever seen. Did he know what hair trimmers were?

"Vandalising school property."

"Who did?" I asked him with wide eyes.

"Don't mess me about, son," he snapped.

"See, I'm not your son," I reminded him. "I'm Kerr Santo's son, and Kerr Santo and my uncle, Kage Santo, are actually sons of the sons of the sons." I paused and pretended to count on my fingers. "Great-great-granddad, great granddad, granddad, dad, and me, so...sons of the sons of the sons, yeah, anyway, my family built this college."

"I know who your ancestors are," Dean Porter snapped.

"Okay, I wasn't sure." I grinned.

"I also recall you and your brother adamantly swearing you were good enough to get in here on your own merit without using your family connections," he said to me with scorn.

"I have a four point oh average, and Gray has a three point nine. The school's admission policy is three point seven. Our *merit* is just fine." This was bullshit. "Why am I in here?"

"You drew graffiti on school property."

"My dad's building, you mean?" I just wanted to fuck with him now.

"I'm warning you," he said as he leaned forward angrily.

"I didn't do shit," I retorted. "Even if I did, there's fuck all you can do about it." Standing, I looked down at him. "Get proof next time before you try and pull this shit." Striding to the door, I looked over my shoulder. "Have a good afternoon, *sir*."

I closed the door more forcefully than I should have and was leaving the office when I saw her sitting there, looking small and timid. Ava wasn't small or timid. Why was she here?

"Why are you here?" I asked across the office floor.

Seeing me, her eyes widened and she shook her head. "Not sure. You?"

"Bullshit."

"Tried to blame you for the chairs or the tag?" Ava looked at me knowingly.

I huffed in derision. "Both, I think." I shrugged carelessly.

"But you were seen last night," Ava said with a sly smile. "At a bar and then a party." She nodded in admiration. "Alibi. Clever."

"Or we could just be innocent?" I said as I raised my hands in front of me.

Ava's head tilted to the side as she looked at me. "I don't think you're capable of knowing the word."

My tongue ran over my teeth as I looked away from her. I recalled the sweet taste of her pussy on my fingers, and looking back at her, I watched as her cheeks flushed. "Maybe not," I murmured. Without another word, I left her sitting there.

Outside, I texted the group chat.

Me: **Which one of you told the dean Ava's earning?**

Gray: **Anonymous tip**

Me: **From who?**

Gray: **A concerned contributor to the school scholarship program**

Ash: **Dad?**

Me: **She's in the dean's office now**

Gray: **You're stalking her?**

Ash: **Thought you had better game**

Me: **Fucker pulled me in and tried to pin last night on me**

Gray: **What'd you say?**

Me: **Reminded him he needed evidence**

Ash: **Way to smooth things over**

Me: **Remember their WR just came back from a knee injury, tell Jamie to target him. Their LBs are brick shithouses, you need to be fast off the line**

Gray: **Yes coach**

With a grin, I headed down the steps from the main admin building. Curiosity got the better of me though, and I lingered to see what Ava would be like when she came out. Would he kick her out? He might, he was a dick. I'd wanted her gone, and now that it was within reach, I wasn't sure how I felt about it.

Ten minutes later, Ava came almost running out of the building. I wasn't sure if she was running because she'd just been asked to leave or because she hadn't and was putting as much distance between herself and the dean in case he changed his mind.

She paused once to scramble in her purse, and then she was on her cell, walking swiftly again. I considered following her, but Gray was right, stalking wasn't my thing, and really if she left, she left. That had been the plan.

My own cell rang, and I grinned at the caller.

"Hey, dad," I greeted my father as I headed to my afternoon class.

"The dean called me this morning, something about my sons and nephew being stupid little pricks," he told me, his voice rich with humour.

I laughed out loud. "Did he actually say that?"

"No, the bastard wouldn't dare." My dad sounded relaxed. I wasn't concerned about this call. "Mayhem?"

"Yeah, thought it was time for a reminder."

"Sounds more like a harmless prank than mayhem," dad said to me.

"That what you told Porter?" I asked him. "A harmless prank?"

"No, I asked him what proof he had." I heard my dad sigh. "Graffiti?"

"That actually wasn't us," I told him truthfully.

"But you know who?" Dad asked me knowingly.

"Of course."

"Okay, make sure your loose ends are tied," he reminded me. "The board can't ignore hard facts."

"Got it covered, dad."

"I know, son, just making sure. So…" He hesitated. "Why aren't you in Missouri?"

"Injury."

"You're benched, you mean, why?" Kerr Santo was easier going than his brother, but he was still a hard ass.

"Long story," I answered.

"Make it a short one," he countered, and I smiled in the afternoon sun. I missed my dad sometimes.

"Not a conversation for the phone, dad," I told him.

"Excellent, your mother misses you. Get your ass home for dinner. You can tell me all about it then."

"Dad…"

"Jett?"

There was no point arguing. "I'll see you at seven."

"Make it six so we can talk while mom's in the kitchen pretending to cook."

I laughed again. My mom seriously couldn't boil water. All our meals were prepared by our cook, but mom could plate like a Michelin star chef, and she took great pride in presenting us restaurant-quality-looking plates of food, whereas our cook actually made us restaurant quality food.

"She'll have your balls if she hears you," I warned him.

"Woman's had my balls from the day I met her," dad grunted.

"Too much, dad." I grinned. "See you at six. Is Onyx home?"

"Yeah, fucking furious about…who knows what. He refuses to talk about it, another reason you can come home and calm your erratic older brother down."

"Fun times with the family," I teased before we said goodbye, and I turned direction. Instead of heading to class, I went back to the dorm house. I needed to fix some things before the three-and-a-half-hour drive home. I opened my messages to the chat just between Gray and me.

Me: **Dad's summoned me home**

Gray: **Told you he would**

Me: **100% truth or fudge?**

Gray: **Bro's home too, go for the 100, Onyx will sniff the lie out**

Me: **Fine**

Gray: **You got this**

Me: **Onyx is going to bust my balls**

Gray: **Bust his head?**

Me: **Sound advice, dickhead**

Gray sent me the one finger emoji back, and I laughed again as I put the phone away. Our older brother was intense. In a good way to us, but to everyone else, he was just fucking brutal. But Gray was right, he would smell a lie on me before I even walked into the house. I thought about it. I needed a distraction, and then I pulled the phone out of my back pocket again.

"Yeah, it's me. Dad wants a family supper, you up for a drive home?" I waited until Quinn answered. "Yeah, be outside in thirty minutes. Oh and, Quinn, Onyx is home." I heard her hesitate, and then she said she'd be ready.

When I picked her up outside her dorm, she greeted me with a warm smile as she placed her overnight bag in the back seat of the car.

"You're such a pretentious prick with this car," she said as she got into the front seat.

"It's an R8, it's cool."

"It is, you're still a prick."

I grinned at her. "You already anxious about seeing your number one fan?"

"You know he hates me because of Ash." Quinn rolled her eyes. "But I told dad you were driving me home and mentioned that your mom would want to see me, so he's coming too. At least dad will keep him on a leash."

"Nice, should be fun." I looked over at her. "You tell my mom to expect them?"

"Obviously, I told Sable." She glanced at me. "Kerr realise you should be in Missouri?" Quinn asked as she slipped her sunglasses on.

"Yeah, and Dean Prick hauled me into his office," I told her.

"For mayhem?" she asked, and I nodded. "It was hardly worth a visit to his office; it was more inconvenience than mayhem."

"That's what dad said."

"You boys losing your touch?" she teased me as I drove.

"Warm-up act, Queeny, you know better."

Her laugh was light in the car as she leaned forward to switch the music on. "I'm feeling the nineties vibe. Eddie or Kurt?"

"Hmm, both?" I suggested. "Start with Kurt."

"Come as You Are" flooded the car, and I felt myself relax as Quinn started to sing along to the lyrics.

As we drove off campus, I thought about what to say to my dad and brother about Ava. Dad would want me to forget about it and would call Coach to make the problem go away. Onyx would agree, but he would want me to make her suffer a little. I smiled to myself.

I really hoped the dean hadn't kicked her out. I wasn't finished with Ava Bryant yet.

CHAPTER 21

Jett

DINNER HAD BEEN GOOD. DAD, ONYX AND I HAD A *BOYS CATCH UP* while mom prepared the table. We had staff for that, but she liked to set the table, especially when she had guests coming.

Onyx had met my innocent stare with a knowing look when I showed up telling them I had dropped Quinn off first and the Lawrences would be over for dinner. Mom knew, but it seemed she had kept her older son in the dark. His animosity towards Quinn wasn't hidden, and he would have found a reason to bail had he been warned.

As I now sat outside Coach's office on Monday morning before practice, I thought back to the conversation with my dad and older brother.

"Why are you benched?" dad asked me as soon as the door to his study was closed.

"Failed a drug test," I told him, and when his mouth fell open in surprise, I shared a look with my older brother. "We think I drank a bottle of water with a drug called Versed in it. It's used mostly as an anaesthetic. I actually have no idea why anyone would take it recreationally."

"You think*?" Onyx asked from his chair.*

"One of the effects is memory loss. I have no recollection of the evening. I woke up the next day with no memory of the night before, of what I drank, or who gave it to me." I saw the fury on my father's face. "I didn't know I had taken it. I took some painkillers before the game that morning for what I thought was a hangover, and the water was the same one with the drug, so I failed the random drug test."

"Water? You drank spiked water*?" my dad asked me as he began to pace. "Was it opened before you drank it?"*

"I don't know."

"And Coach Bowers?"

"Doesn't believe me," I answered. "Well, he believes me kind of. I have two weeks to prove I got my drink spiked."

"If you don't remember, how are you supposed to prove this?" Dad demanded angrily.

"I assume you didn't sleep alone?" Onyx asked me with a smirk.

"You would assume right."

"The girl's connected?" my dad asked.

"Only just found out who she was. I don't remember much about her either."

"Have you asked her?" Dad looked frustrated.

"Not directly."

"Playing with your food, little brother?" Onyx took a sip of his whisky as he watched me.

"A little," I admitted.

"Women aren't playthings," dad grumbled as he sat in his chair. He missed the look between my brother and me, which begged to differ with dad's view. "I'll call Bowers. This is bullshit."

"I can handle this, dad," I told him quietly.

"You've been training to get to the draft since you were three. This isn't just an obsession, Jett, it's your passion. One that I am happy to support, and I will not allow some girl and a bottle of fucking water to jeopardise that."

"I'm not sure she's connected," I told him. What the fuck?

"I suggest you find out," Onyx said dryly. "Pussy's pussy. There's always another tight one to fill."

"Onyx," my dad protested weakly. "We raised you better than that."

Onyx winked at me as he took another drink of his whisky, and I schooled my expression so dad didn't see my answering grin.

"Jett," my dad said, giving me his full attention. "Find out who did this, do whatever you think is best to deal with it, but I will speak to Bowers and get this bullshit benching lifted. I will make sure that there is no record of this anywhere."

"Careful, dad." Onyx leaned back in his seat as he appraised our father. "Sounds like you're willing to step in and alter school records."

My dad levelled him with a hard stare. "When it is merited, I will protect my son's future," he told him angrily. "Any of my sons. Even when it isn't merited, I would do what is necessary."

Onyx dipped his head slightly in acknowledgement of his past fuck up, which dad fixed then too.

"Jett?" my dad asked me.

"Yeah, thank you, I need to play." I looked between the two of them. "It's all I want." Being this open and vulnerable wasn't something that came easily, and I saw them both acknowledge my honesty. "I will find out who did this though," I promised them, and I saw the gleam in my older brother's eyes as he saluted me with his drink.

"Santo!" Coach called, and I went into his office, closing the door behind me. "Your father called me in the middle of my Sunday barbeque."

"He wasn't happy with my benching," I told him as I sat down.

Coach Bowers considered me for a long moment. "Coaching is hard," he began, and I kept my opinion about his large salary to myself. "There are eighty-five men on my roster. Do you know the most important thing a coach can have from his team?"

"Respect."

"Exactly. *Honesty* and respect." He sat back and looked at me. "You ran to your daddy because you didn't like my coaching method?"

I smiled. "I went home to my father, who requested my presence because he didn't understand why I wasn't playing on Saturday. You see, my *daddy* has my respect too. I told him exactly what I told you. The difference is, *Coach,* he believed me."

Coach Bowers glared at me. I didn't flinch from the stare. "You're out for Saturday."

Bastard. "And the week after?"

"I told the team you were out for two weeks with an injury. After Saturday, your two weeks are up."

"Thank you, Coach." I stood at the jerk of his head in acknowledgement. I hesitated at the door. "If I deserved this, I would take it." I looked over at him. "I didn't know I had taken it."

Coach Bowers rubbed his jaw. "I believe you," he grudgingly admitted. "I didn't need the fifteen-minute reaming out of my ass on Sunday from your father."

"He can be passionate."

Coach snorted. "Will we have a problem going forward?"

"Absolutely not, Coach. You still get to give me shit, and I'll still take it." I grinned at him, and he laughed. "I *do* respect you, but when your head's up your ass, well..." I half shrugged and ducked when he threw his foam football stress ball at me.

"Out!"

Laughing, I went back to the locker room feeling a lot lighter than I had.

"Fixed?" Gray asked me as he looked up from putting his cleats on.

"Yeah, the ankle will be ready for Sunday," I told him, the hidden message clear.

I saw him frown, but as he rubbed his shoulder, he looked to the coach's door. "We did think it would be two weeks to completely heal."

"Exactly," I replied. "So, I'm going to go to class, and you can all enjoy four hours of training."

"Dick," Gray muttered as he pulled his jersey on. As I left the locker room, I wondered if my brother knew I would rather be doing the practice session than sitting in economics, learning about foreign trading patterns. Putting my shades on, I realised of course he did.

Ash had seen Ava earlier, so we knew she hadn't been told to leave; however, I wondered what she *had* been told. I was back on the active playing roster, but that didn't mean I was any closer to knowing who had deliberately tried to ruin my career.

I recalled Onyx telling me to stop playing with my food and get it done, and I wondered if it was time to break Uptight.

There was still speculation about why I'd chased her across the campus, and although I hadn't pushed it and the talk had quietened, I knew one word from me would start the rumours again. I headed to the coffee shop, and as I waited for my coffee, I had Elise beside me.

"Baby, I missed you this weekend."

I seriously doubted it. "You did? I heard Jamie filled your… night on Saturday."

Elise gave a light laugh as we exited the shop, and she hooked her arm through mine, ignoring me when I shrugged her off. "He tried, know what I mean?" Elise raised her pinkie finger and wiggled it.

I laughed despite myself. "Ouch," I said as I took a drink of the scalding black coffee. Thank fuck Ava hadn't flung this at me, I'd have been blistered.

"You fill my *night* better," she said to me with what I think she thought was a sexy smile.

I didn't comment. She was a good lay, but once was enough for me. Elise had stage five clinger syndrome, and I didn't need a clinger in my life.

"Where were you this weekend?" she asked me curiously. "With a girl?"

See, clingy. "If that girl was my mom, then yes, I was." I spotted Quinn crossing the grass and saw her hand lifting in a wave when she saw me. "And Quinn, of course."

"Of course." Elise had lost her smile when she saw Quinn approaching.

"Yeah, Quinn really helped me with that girl, you remember the one who stole from me."

Elise's eyes lit up. "Yes, I was wondering what happened there."

Quinn was now beside me, and without a word, I handed her my coffee. She took a drink gratefully. I noticed Elise's eyes widen at the sharing, but she said nothing. She had been burned before by Quinn and hadn't quite recovered.

"You know, the usual." I shrugged carelessly.

"You fucked her?" Elise said in surprise.

"Fucked her? Nah, but I didn't protest when she apologised."

Quinn snorted and handed me my coffee back.

"You accepted an apology?" Elise looked scandalised.

"She was on her knees for a while, know what I'm saying? In fact she keeps wanting to apologise to me, over and over." I smirked as Elise filled in the blanks, and as Quinn and I walked away, Quinn looked over her shoulder.

"She's already on her phone," she said with disgust.

"Excellent."

"You throwing your blonde to the wolves?" Quinn asked casually.

"Yeah, see how she fares. She doesn't like attention."

"So...you're just putting her in the spotlight."

Slinging my arm around Quinn's shoulders, I pulled her into me. "I'm a giver," I teased her.

"You're a bastard," Quinn told me playfully.

"I am." I kissed the top of her head. "It's why I'm your favourite."

"It's *why* you're my best friend, dickhead." She laughed. "I never said you were my favourite."

"Onyx was reserved on Friday," I said carefully as we walked, sharing my coffee.

"I believe I have your other brother to thank for that." Quinn looked down as she spoke.

I raised my eyebrow in surprise. Gray had said nothing to me about it. "Well, if you're gonna thank him *properly,* put a cushion down first; your knees will ache before he's done."

Quinn threw her head back as she laughed at my implication. "A blow job isn't the answer." She giggled as we walked.

"It isn't?" I asked her with a grin. "Pretty sure that's always the answer."

"Your dad's such a gentleman, he would die if he knew you were such a sleazy dick," she said good-naturedly.

He probably wouldn't. He and my uncle had been no Boy Scouts when they were younger either.

"Quinn." I hesitated. Did she need to know, I asked myself.

"You didn't let it go?" she said softly as she sobered while we walked to her first class.

"We couldn't."

She held her hand out for my coffee, and I gave it to her. "And? What did you find?" She didn't look at me, and I hated that she couldn't look me in the eye.

"We haven't gotten it all together yet," I admitted. "We found more than I think we were expecting."

"If I ask you to stop?"

"It's no longer just about you," I said as I pulled her arm to get her to stop walking. "Plus, you know he was never going to let it go."

Quinn was looking away from me, and I watched her as she struggled with her emotions. "You aren't supposed to be telling me, are you?" Her dark brown eyes shone with unshed tears when she finally looked at me.

"They don't think you need to know."

"Idiots, both of them."

"That's what I said." I gave her a small smile. "Do you need to see?"

"No." Her eyes were wide with alarm. "No," she repeated softly.

"I will nail the fucker to the wall, I promise."

Quinn nodded as she drank more of my coffee. "Don't tell them I know," she whispered to me before she headed into the sports building to go to her first class.

Finishing my coffee, I tossed the cup. I was right to tell her, she needed to know.

Checking my phone, I grinned when I saw the social chat for the sports teams. There were already about a hundred messages and comments about *my* screamer, and as I read some of them while heading into class, I chuckled at the more ludicrous ones.

Ava quite obviously hated the spotlight. She wasn't an Elise, desperate to be seen. She wasn't like Quinn, who ignored the attention she received because of her looks and who her friends were. Ava actively went out of her way to avoid notice. This was going to be hell for her, she was going to get hit on by every guy who thought she was an easy lay, and every girl would be ready to rip her to shreds for *being* an easy lay.

Whistling as I headed into my class, I knew I'd enjoy seeing her reaction to the attention she was about to receive.

It was shaping up to be a good week.

CHAPTER 22

Ava

Professor Matson was in full flight as she presented her class that afternoon. Her enthusiasm was rubbing off on me, and I had caught myself leaning forward a couple of times, engaged in her lecture about the self-destructive tendencies of Romeo. But leaning forward stuck my head out of the row I was in, and at the very end of that row, perched like an Angel of Death, sat Jett Santo.

He never looked my way. He made no effort to catch my attention, but I was acutely aware of him. There had to be about ten or eleven people between us, but it felt like I could reach out and touch him. I wasn't sure he knew I was in the same row as he was, but I no longer believed in coincidences when it came to Jett.

My week had been torturous hell. Almost every person was accusing me of either being a thief or a slut. At first, I'd been confused, and then I heard that I was apparently *begging* him to sleep with me and he kept saying no. He or his psycho family had told people I was a whore, a desperate whore, who was begging to be with him. *Bastard.*

Mia had advised we ignore it and pretend like it didn't matter, and I had, but it was hard. The beginning of the week was terrible, so bad that I ended up hiding in the library. On Tuesday, the dark-haired girl from the class Shane and I had—who I now knew was called Elise—spilled her smoothie all over me in the cafeteria, and when I had jumped to my feet amid all the laughter and insults, I'd looked up at his table to see him and his brother laughing along with everyone else. He'd had the audacity to wink at me before I turned and almost ran from the cafeteria before I either burst into tears in a temper or punched his smirking face in.

But I couldn't *do* anything because I was on probation. Dean

Porter had confronted me about my side earning with Wade's band, and after he had lectured me, he looked over all my records. He even had emails from my professors about my performances in class. Professor Windsor, or Joe as I would happily call him now, had sent a really supportive email, which seemed to have impressed the dean. However, the fact of the matter was, I'd been stupid and careless with the gift that was my scholarship. The dean had me on a six-month probation, so I couldn't afford to put a foot wrong, which is why *Elise* didn't get a smack in the mouth.

There was no escape though. Today, I'd had a few comments already flung my way this morning, asking if being chased was my turn on and how many dicks I was willing to suck at once.

It was unnerving. I was the girl who blended. One night with Jett and then a sprint across the green *away* from him, and I was suddenly desirable...and it wasn't in a complimentary way. It meant I was a cheap lay. Funny, I never heard any comments from anyone asking Jett if he was willing to chase them. Double standards. Unacceptable in this day and age. Yet, still it was present. I was a cheap whore, and he was a conquering god. Pathetic.

Ducking my head back out of his line of sight in case he looked my way, I settled back in my seat. I couldn't even accuse the fucker of spreading the rumours, as I had no proof. As always, a Devil was blameless.

"Hey, hey, you."

I froze and turned to the guy behind me. "Me?"

"Yeah, you, whatsyername?"

"Why?" I whispered suspiciously as I took in his smug grin and his friend, who was also watching me.

"Is it true what you did when you got caught?" he asked with a sly grin.

Ugh, enough with the bullshit. "No," I snapped as I turned around again.

"That's not what I heard," he continued to whisper behind me.

Inching forward in my seat, I edged away from him. "Heard you blew *the* Devils. Both of them. Like they tag teamed you."

I tried to focus once again on the professor. I had been in that building for five minutes. How the fuck would I have done both of them? Realising this wasn't the point, I furiously did my best to ignore the whispers behind me as they got more and more derogatory and preposterous.

"You been double dipped?" the guy asked a little louder, causing several answering snickers, and that was it, I'd had enough. A girl could only take so much, and I had endured a *week* of this.

"Quit it!" I was on my feet, and I was so angry I didn't care that I had once again stopped Professor Matson's class. "You repulsive dick, what gives the right to talk to me like that?" I demanded with my hands on my hips.

"Is there a problem?" Professor Matson asked curiously, and when I met her enquiring look, I realised she recognised who I was. "You...again?"

"Sorry." I turned back to the guy behind me when I heard his snigger. I didn't recognise him, but that meant nothing. "Keep your mouth shut, or I'll shove my hand so far up your ass it'll be *your* tonsils that are getting tickled. Do you feel *me*, asshole?"

The lecture room was silent for a brief moment before the class erupted into laughter. My face was red from temper, whereas his was red from embarrassment. Turning back to face forward, I gave the professor an apologetic look, who acknowledged it with a slight incline of her head. I could feel *him* staring at me, and almost like a magnetic pull, I turned my head to look.

Jett sat at the end with his left leg stretched out in front of him. His left arm was draped casually along his desk, his right arm rested loosely across his armrest. His head was turned my way, and when our eyes met, that smug smirk slowly tipped his mouth upwards. He looked...triumphant. I didn't know why that was the word that I associated with him, but it was. Suddenly, it was replaced by one of coldness as his eyes flicked over me before he faced the front of the lecture room.

"Bitch," the guy whispered behind me as the professor once again resumed her lecture after I had interrupted her.

"Shut the fuck up," I snarled back at him.

I felt the kick at the back of my chair, but with my hand clutching my pen so tightly and the other one gripping my desk, I knew better than to turn around.

"Ignore it."

Turning my head slightly, I looked at the guy beside me. "It'll be over soon." He must have known I wasn't following. "The Santos will have someone new to torture, and you'll be forgotten." His look of pity made me feel worse than anything douchebag had said behind me.

With a brief smile at him for being decent, I tried my best to focus back on the lecture. But all I could think about was the horrible rumours and assumptions that people were making about me. Realising what I had been putting off, I knew I needed to talk to Jett, and then this would be over. I was sure of it.

As the lecture came to a close, the professor asked me to stay behind. It wasn't completely unexpected. I idled at her desk while she spoke briefly to her TA, and on his way out, I once again made eye contact with Jett. His trademark smirk made me want to punch him, and I hastily looked at my feet to break eye contact.

"So, again I find myself with a disrupted class," Professor Matson said as she came over to me. "Can you tell me what happened today?"

"The guy behind me was saying...unpleasant things. I tried to ignore him, but he just wouldn't quit. I didn't mean to lose my temper." I took a breath as it rushed out. "Or cause a scene."

"Another scene," she reminded me. Her long brown hair was pulled back from her face but hung in waves down her back. Black, leopard print glasses, with a white collar showing under her emerald green sweater, she was an attractive woman. I imagined that she would probably tick the boxes of the professor pin-up fantasy.

"Yeah, um, that time it was a rat."

Her head tilted to the side as she looked at me. "What's your name?"

"Ava Bryant, ma'am."

"Ava, do you think I'm blind?" she asked me curiously as she looked me over. "Do you think I don't know who the star quarterback for the Saints is?"

"Um, I..."

"And do you think I wouldn't know who his teammates are?"

The guy wasn't Jett's teammate, but I decided now was not the time to tell her that. "Um."

"Ava, let me give you some advice. Woman to woman."

Huh?

"They are not interested. They are here for football and to perform for scouts. Academia is not their priority, I know this, and I am sure you do too. What I don't know, is it yours?"

"Yes." I nodded vigorously.

"Good, ignore the boys in the class and concentrate on your degree. Unfortunately, you will mean nothing to them. Even if you're a warm body one night, it is unlikely that you will stay that way. You need to focus on you."

Oh my God, she was parenting me? It was weirdly sweet but also truly horrifyingly awkward. "Um, yeah," I stumbled. "Um, thanks."

"Good girl. No outbursts next week, okay?" Her hand rubbed my upper arm as she smiled at me, and in a cloud of awkwardness, I departed her class.

As soon as the door closed behind me, I was fishing out my phone. I needed to tell Mia.

Me: **Prof Matson just gave me the sex talk**

Me: **Like can I hashtag awkward?**

Mia: **I'm heading into class – tell me everything but I won't be able to respond**

Mia: **and it's #awkward dork**

I laughed out loud, which turned into a squeal when hands grabbed me, and I was jerked into an empty classroom.

"What the hell?" I yelled as I was pushed forward, and catching myself from stumbling, I straightened before turning with fury to feel all my rage dissipate when I met the sky-blue eyes of a Devil. "Jett?"

"I hear you wanted to talk to me?" he asked me with an almost friendly look. I watched as his right hand reached over, lazily rubbing over the bicep on his fully tattooed left arm.

"So you thought grabbing me and throwing me into an empty classroom was the best approach?" I asked him as I shook off my shock and marched to the door. One single step and he was positioned smoothly in front of the door, blocking my exit.

"What did he say to you in class?" Jett asked as he leaned against the door casually.

"Don't you know?" I glared at him. Nerves and repressed anger were causing me to be reckless. "Isn't he yet another one of your *friends*."

"You shouldn't listen to rumours." He smirked at me. "Thought you would know that."

"Have you heard what they're saying about me?" I demanded of him as I took another step forward. "It's *horrible*."

"I don't listen to gossip." Jett sneered as he spoke to me, and somehow he made even that look sexy.

"Figures, why listen when you started the shit in the first place?" I snorted as I crossed my arms over my chest. "Why am I here?" I looked around the classroom. "And how do you always know which rooms are empty?"

Jett considered me for a moment. “You came to see me last week,” he prompted me as he waited.

So much seemed to have happened since then, but I still hadn’t *actually* spoken to him. “Yes, I um...” I twisted the handle of my book bag. “So...” I faltered. I didn’t know how to approach this, where did I even start?

“Are you ready to tell me why you did it?” Jett’s look was hooded as he looked at me, and his casual consideration of me had suddenly changed to him being completely alert, and he hadn’t even moved. The guy was…intense. There was no other word for it. He just took up all the space and all of my focus. I had absolutely no idea how I had ended up in his bed, and now I had less of an idea of how I told him this. “You tell me the truth and the rumours stop. You lie…and well, you won’t like what happens next.” He grinned and I felt a sliver of fear. “I’m waiting.”

“Yeah, aren’t we all.” Running my hands over my arms, I considered him. “You’re a dick, I just want that said before I start.”

“I haven’t got all day,” he told me coldly.

“More lives to ruin?” I muttered as I felt my shoulders slump. “Okay, here goes nothing, I don’t usually drink.”

“Of course.” I heard his snort of disbelief, and wrapping my arms around myself, I looked at the point past his shoulder.

“Just…” I rolled my head on my shoulders. “Okay, this is embarrassing enough, just let me get through this, okay?” I didn’t want him to look at me as I spoke, so I turned away from him and walked further into the class. When I heard nothing to the contrary, I wet my lips and told him what I knew. “I don’t drink because I’m a hopeless drunk, but I can drink a lot. I mean a *lot*. Like my friend says I have hollow legs. But, the drawback is, I black out.” I hesitated, and hearing nothing, I ploughed on. “That Friday, I was wasted, so wasted I have no memories of it at all.”

“What?” His voice was a ferocious whisper. “You’re telling me that *you* don’t remember anything?”

"No. It happens, it's why I don't really drink, I never remember." Staring at my feet, I fidgeted. "I know I come across as coherent and sober, but...I'm not." Taking another breath, I blurted it out. "I don't know when or how I met you that night. I remember absolutely nothing."

When the silence was uncomfortable, I turned around only to find I was alone. He was gone, and I didn't even hear him leave. Well, it was over. Now he knew, and the less said the better. Weirdly, I could still feel the noose hanging around my neck, an ominous feeling that this was far from over.

SLOWLY WALKING BACK TO THE DORM, I THOUGHT OF WHAT I'D SAID to him. Did he believe me? He didn't seem to react well, but then I wasn't one hundred percent sure how he should react. Had the roles been reversed, would I believe him? Or would I have walked away to process?

"This is a nightmare," I muttered as I climbed the stairs to the apartment. As I let myself in, I welcomed the cool air inside the living room and thought about the whole entire mess that was my life over the last week. It didn't matter what I had to do or who I had to avoid, I could handle it, but what I knew I couldn't cope with was the fact I hadn't been honest with Mia, and now I had no choice but to tell her.

My phone beeping drew my attention, and dreading Mia had already heard the news about class, I pulled it out slowly from the pocket in my book bag.

Unknown: **Get your ass to my house. NOW**

Me: **Who is this?**

Unknown: **Don't fuck with me**

Me: **Jett?**

I bit my lip. I mean, I was pretty sure it was, because who else would be texting me this kind of demand? But still...better safe than sorry. I re-read the messages and laughed at myself. Yeah, because the messages were giving the impression of "safe."

Unknown: **You want me to come get you?**

No. I definitely did not want that. Standing up from the couch, I hesitated. Should I change? Should I at least brush my hair? Should I actually go? I had no doubt that he would come to me, and who was to say he would be alone? He could bring Ash, or worse...Gray.

Mind made up, I left my apartment, leaving my bag behind me and tucking the key into my shorts as I walked with no hurry to the other side of campus. I kept to the back routes. It was still mid-afternoon, so most students were on the main campus, meaning few people were hanging about their rooms or the grounds.

When the huge mansion house came into view, my feet dragged even more. The door to the house was open, and my heart told me that this was a bad thing for me. At the entrance, I hesitated. I wasn't going to walk right in. Raising my hand, I knocked on the door.

"We don't get visitors." Jamie Woods, the defensive end for the Saints, was looking at me from a doorway. With the smells coming out of it, I would hazard a guess that it was the kitchen.

"Um, I was invited." My teeth chewed my bottom lip as I shuffled my feet.

"Ash?" Jamie looked me over with interest. "You look his type."

"Is he here?" I wasn't about to be specific about which Devil wanted to speak to me. I had heard that Gray had recently punched Jamie after training, and the students who went to watch the training sessions said that Ash tackled Jamie badly during the practice session too. I noted the fading to his skin, which showed where he had recently had a black eye and bruised cheek. Seemed like Jamie had met the wrath of the Devils and not fared well.

"They live on the top floor." His head jerked to the stairs, and he went back into the kitchen.

Again, I hesitated, but I was worried another one of the football team would come home or appear out of one of the many doors and ask me more questions. With my nerves already stretched thin, I started to climb the stairs. He was waiting on the second level, and I knew with one look that he had been listening to me downstairs.

"Remember the way?" His low drawl was enough to make the butterflies in my stomach swoop.

Sometimes silence was the answer, and I chose to say nothing as I followed him up the stairs. To be truthful, had he asked me, I really didn't know the way. I had a hazy memory of cleaning up in his room and then getting the hell out of there as quickly as my hungover body allowed me. When Jett pushed open the door to his bedroom, I followed him inside before I stopped, keeping the door close to me. Just in case.

He turned and appraised me coldly. I didn't note the decor or the furnishings. I kept my eyes on him, so when a pair of arms picked me off my feet and carried me further into the room, my scream pierced the air as the door banged firmly closed behind me.

When I was set on my feet, I whirled and looked at Gray, who took a step towards me, and I immediately stepped back. "What the fuck is wrong with you?" I asked him as my shaky voice gave away how much he unnerved me.

"Bitches that fuck my brother when he's not aware of what he's doing is what's wrong with me."

I looked between the two of them. They looked so much more like twins when they were angry. Their jaws were set the same, the scowls were similar, and the dislike shone fiercely in the same pair of eyes. "I don't understand."

"Sure you do." Gray walked past me, his shoulder bump almost knocking me off my feet.

"No, I don't." I should have taken my book bag, I could have used something to throw. As it was, all I had was my wit, my sandals and my self-defence classes. Maybe I wasn't as fresh out of luck as I first thought. I had no qualms about smacking one of these assholes if I had to, the dean would have to understand.

"You recognise the room?" Jett asked me. He hadn't moved from his spot, and his almost casual stance was making me more nervous than Gray's barely restrained anger.

"Um…" Looking around, I examined it. Did I? Were the walls lighter than I remembered? I had no idea. "Look, I told you earlier, I was drunk. I don't remember much."

"Convenient." Gray snorted as he sat down on a chair beside the door. "You got amnesia?"

"No," I snapped at him. He was quite possibly worse than Jett. "It's called a hangover. I was drunk, I was doing double shots at beer pong, and I was very, very, *very* drunk. I have no recollection of this room or anything else." This wasn't true, but I wasn't telling these pricks that I was having vivid dreams of Jett and me in compromising positions.

"Your lies stop now," Jett said to me as he walked closer to me. He was so close I had to turn my head away, or my face would be pressed into his chest. "Now, tell me why you drugged me."

My head snapped back to look up at him in bewilderment. "What?" I met his hard stare. "What the fuck are you talking about?"

CHAPTER 23

Jett

I looked down at her, and the confusion was clear in her eyes. Green eyes the colour of the grass after a hard game, I noted. She glanced over at Gray, and I saw her fear of him, and I wanted to tell her that he was the least of her problems.

My hand cupped her chin, turning her attention from Gray back to me, her eyes wide as she stared up at me. She looked like she was caught in the headlights, but I was done being fooled by this girl. "Another thing you're conveniently forgetting?"

"I don't..." She shook her head from side to side as she tried to release my grip from her chin. "I don't do drugs."

"Neither do I," I bit out as I brought my face closer to hers. "But there's fuck all I can do when some little bitch spikes my drink."

Ava's eyes widened fractionally more, and then they narrowed as her hands came up and pushed at my chest. "Get off of me. You need my permission to touch me, and your touch is not welcome."

My hand was wrapped around her throat, and I dragged her nearer, my head bent more so my lips were almost on hers. "I don't remember the night completely, not yet, but I will, and from what I *do* remember, you have absolutely no issue with me touching you. In fact, this whole house knows how much you want *more* of me touching you." I leaned forward, my lips hovering over hers. "I didn't hear you protesting when I finger fucked you last week either."

"Take your hands off me," Ava demanded. Her voice was low and wavered, but her look was steady.

Her gasp when Gray pressed up behind her, forcing her closer to me went straight to my dick, and I couldn't deny that she still affected me. Which pissed me off only more. "You don't seem to mind being touched," I said as I looked quickly at my brother behind her. He nodded once, and his arms closed around her, holding her sandwiched between us.

"Stop this." Ava's eyes were wide, and I noted the fury in her eyes.

"Stop what?" Gray asked as his lips skimmed her ear. "You don't like being here?" His nose ran up her neck, and Ava tried to move away from him, which caused her to press closer to me. Her reaction was odd; most girls would have thought they had died had they been pressed in between us.

"I don't know what kind of games you play, I'm sure they're heaps of fun with other girls." Her voice cracked, and I felt her swallow against my palm, and my mind instantly replayed her swallowing down my cum that Friday night. "But I'm not that girl. So I'm asking you both nicely, take your fucking hands off of me." Her body was rigid, her eyes alight with fury, and her hands had tightened into fists on my shirt.

"Or what?" I taunted her quietly, and I couldn't deny she was turning me on as she met my look defiantly.

"Or I will report you both for sexual harassment, and I hope you have good lawyers, *Devils*, because this shit doesn't fly *anywhere* and most definitely not in the NFL."

Gray grabbed her ponytail and yanked her head back, and I saw her wince in pain or surprise, I wasn't sure. "Sexual harassment? Is that your play? Is that why you took it?"

"Took *what*?" She glared at him, and he pressed closer to her. I saw her temper break at Gray's manhandling of her. "I really, *really* wish this was you," she said to him through gritted teeth before the little snake kneed me in the balls.

I hit the floor like a ton of bricks, and as I went down, she kicked me in the ribs. Spinning on her heel, her roundhouse kick struck Gray in the chest before she launched forward and punched him in the jaw. As quickly as she'd lashed out at us, she was running to the door. Yanking it open, she cried out in surprise when she ran straight into Ash.

Ash looked at both Gray and me struggling to our feet, and he automatically grabbed a hold of Ava. "Whoa! What the hell is going on?"

Ava looked over her shoulder at us, her eyes meeting mine, and she turned back, her fist already raised to punch Ash. He saw it and grabbed it and then very slowly stepped out of her space. "Are you okay?" he asked her with his hands raised to calm her.

I wasn't sure if it was her anger, her emotions, or her fear of being caught, but she stepped into the comfort my cousin was offering her. Ash looked at us both like we were the bastards here and gently took her hand. "Hey," Ash spoke quietly. "Hey, it's okay, come on, my room's here, take a minute before you go home, okay?"

The door closed as he led the girl who had drugged me out of the room and out of my sight.

Leaning against his bed, Gray gave me a rueful look. "So…she doesn't scare as easily as you thought she would."

As I tried to straighten, I rubbed my poor balls. "I was not expecting that reaction," I admitted with a derisive laugh. "Fuck, they're never going to drop again," I groaned as I sat on the bed.

"I thought she would think it was payday," Gray told me as he rubbed his chest. "Did you hear her? Sex offences? Really?" He gave me a disgusted look as he rubbed his chest. "I dunno if my ego can cope with reporting her for assault."

As my balls throbbed in agreement, I couldn't help but laugh at Gray's comment. "Man, you beat the shit out of Jamie, and then the next week, a girl the weight of a fucking twig decks you."

"Wasn't expecting it." Rolling his head, he looked me over. "You okay?"

"Yeah, I will be." I sighed as I looked at the bedroom wall, the shared wall between Gray's room and Ash's. "She didn't notice she wasn't in this room."

"Noticed that."

"I don't know if that makes her guilty or as clueless as me," I admitted.

"Is it really possible that she also drank the water?" Gray was looking at the floor as he thought it through. "She thinks she was drunk, but what if she doesn't remember because she *can't* remember?"

Tipping my head back, I stared at the ceiling. I'd considered that. My fury had only wanted her to tell me why she did it, tell me what she had hoped to gain. I never really considered she would be innocent.

As in *actually* innocent.

"I don't know."

"Maybe we need another tactic?" Gray asked me with a side grin as he headed for the door. "Just so you know, if she has no part to play in this, I'm not fucking saying sorry for this."

"Me neither," I promised as we left the room and walked into Ash's. He was on his chair at his desk, his bathroom door was closed, and I could hear the water running. "What the fuck did you do to her?" he demanded of us as we entered the room. "She was shaking so badly I almost offered to give her sugar!"

I felt a twinge of guilt and exchanged a look with Gray, who looked slightly guilty also. "What's she doing?"

"Washing her face," Ash said with a shrug.

"I'm going in," I told them as I headed to the door.

It pissed me off that I actually hesitated at the bathroom door, and telling myself to get a grip, I opened it. She was at the sink, her head buried in the towel in her hands. When she heard the door close, her head jerked upwards.

"Bastard."

"You just kneed my balls and then kicked me in the ribs," I

reminded her, and the vicious smirk she gave me caused me to realise she was not only fierce, but she was also *fearless.*

"You deserved it, what the hell was that?" Ava angrily folded the towel. "You sick fuck, you cannot treat people like that. I'm not a fucking toy."

"You drugged me, then fucked me, then got me suspended. I think we're even."

Ava stared at me with her mouth hanging open before she blinked. "I did...what? *No!*"

"You drugged me."

"No, I really didn't."

I ignored her. "You fucked me."

I saw her swallow, and she lost a bit of her bravado. "I did." Her tongue nervously wet her lips, and I watched with far too much interest for a guy who supposedly hated the woman in front of him.

"You stole from me."

Ava's eyes widened. "No, I didn't!"

"You took my sheet."

She licked her lips and looked away from me, her face flushed.

"Why?"

She shrugged and I was ready to press her when she looked back at me. "You started all those horrible rumours, you didn't deny it when people asked you if I sucked you off, and you laughed when your friend dropped her *freezing* smoothie all over me."

"I got suspended because of you."

Ava shook her head in denial. "How is that even my fault? What did *I* do?" she wailed in despair.

"Because I failed a drug test, a drug you gave me."

"Dude, I wouldn't know *how* to drug someone. I don't even know how I met you that night. All I remember is some very sordid sex scenes and then throwing up in your bathroom for what felt like eternity, buck ass naked while you and Ash watched me."

"Sordid sex scenes?"

"Did you hear the rest of anything I said?" Ava demanded angrily.

"Sure, it sounded like blah blah blah lie lie lie."

Ava barked out a sardonic laugh as she flung her hands in the air. "God, you're a massive dick. Congratulations, I genuinely thought when I heard shit about you, that no one, I mean *no one*, could be such a fucking asshole in real life...but here you are."

"I'd say it's been a pleasure, but I'd be lying."

Ava glared at me for a long moment. "I didn't drug you. I genuinely didn't know you were incapacitated that night."

"Incapacitated?" I laughed incredulously. "Is that what you're calling it?"

"I don't know!" Ava cried in frustration. "I don't know what I'm calling it, except a horrific, horrible nightmare of a mistake that I never want to think about ever again!"

I felt my head tilt to the side as I saw her cheeks redden. "But you are thinking about it?" I said smugly. "You remember the sex. Which is why my fingers were deep inside you the other night. You want me to fuck you, your pussy's so hungry for me, you were willing to let me fuck you against the side of that house."

Ava glanced at me before she resumed looking at the wall, the slight wag of her head belying her frustration. "You're unbelievable."

"Thanks." I grinned and I saw her bite down on her lower lip.

"I wasn't being complimentary."

"Weren't you?"

Her eyes flicked to mine before she shifted her position. "I don't know what happened the first night." She rubbed her forehead as she groaned. "I don't even really know how I ended up against the wall after the bar, you're…confusing."

She was confused? Join the club. "Tell me what you do know?" I suggested. She looked genuinely lost, and I decided that I could hear her out.

"I can't."

"Why?" My voice was hard.

"Because my insides are like freaking jelly!" Ava cried. "You both scared the shit out of me, and I don't want to help you, I want to go home, have a shower and never speak to either of you fuckers again."

"Tough." I crossed the short distance to her. "You don't leave until you tell me everything that I want to know."

"I have no problem hitting you again."

"I'm ready for you now. Consider those ones free."

Ava didn't back away from my words or my proximity, and I realised she had absolutely no issue being close to me. "You're nothing but a bully."

"No, I'm not. All I want is the truth."

As her hand ran over her face, I watched as she then wrapped her arms around herself. "I told you the truth."

For the second time that day, my head dipped and I spoke into her ear. "I don't believe you." I caught the sharp intake of breath, I noticed her body sway into mine, and I saw her skin flush. This girl was not as averse to me as she liked to pretend.

"Jett," she began, and I have no idea why I did what I did next, but I kissed her.

Ava was shocked for one second, and then she was kissing me back. Hands tangled in my hair as she pressed into my body, her tongue stroking against mine as I pulled her closer.

Like floodgates opening in my brain, memories came rushing back to me. I remembered her touch. I remembered the sweet way her body moved into mine when I fucked her. I saw flashes of her in my bed, lying underneath me, her back arching as I slammed into her. I could hear her moans, I could taste her on my tongue. I remembered how turned on she made me. I remembered the need to own her, to own every part of her body as I fucked her again and again.

With my hands cupping her ass, I lifted her, and she eagerly wrapped her legs around me as I sat her on Ash's bathroom counter. My hands were already pushing her shirt up as my teeth nipped at her neck. My dick strained against my jeans, seemingly as eager as I was to be inside her again.

"Is this *also* sexual harassment?" Gray's dry question stopped us both in our tracks.

Jerking away from her, I didn't miss the dismay and confusion on her face as Ava slid off the counter. Without a word, she pushed past Gray, and I heard Ash's query as to where she was going when the door slammed shut behind her.

When I was back in the bedroom, Ash looked at me expectantly. "Went well?"

"Shut up."

"We learned nothing," Gray told him with a tired sigh. "Except that my brother really will fuck anyone, she's got a temper, and she has a decent right hook." Gray looked over at Ash. "In terms of how either of them ended up here, we know nothing more now than we did the morning after."

"It'll be fine, she'll be back."

"Jett..." Ash looked at the door I was staring at and then me. "Trust me, that girl isn't walking back in here anytime soon."

The smile was small, but they saw it. "I remember being here, with her. Trust me, she'll be back."

"For your dick?" Gray asked sceptically.

"She'll be back because we'll give her no choice." I looked at my brother and cousin. "The plan doesn't change. Quinn learned she's on probation. I own her fucking ass, and she will do exactly what I tell her until she either tells the truth or we find the fucker who set me up."

CHAPTER 24

Ava

My recollection of the walk home was fuzzy. My hands were shaking the whole way, and twice I needed to stop myself from turning around and going back to punch Gray again and his stupid brother. I knew they were Devils, I knew it. I'd heard the stories, I'd witnessed their douchebaggery when I was in high school—but, oh my God, the nerve.

The actual goddamn nerve of them. Squeezing me in between them like that, what was their intent? Did they think I was one of their bed-hoppers that would bounce from one dick to the next as long as it was a Santo's?

And drugged him? *Drugged him*? Was he for real? By the time I was back at the apartment, angry tears had spilled, and I wasn't sure if I was furious or hyperventilating. I was so thrown by the afternoon that I completely forgot my roommate and best friend would be home, and as I burst through the door, I startled Mia so much she gave a yelp of alarm.

"Ava?" Her hazel eyes were full of concern as she took in my appearance, and then I was wrapped in the comfort of her arms. "Oh my gracious, what happened?"

The adrenaline from *them,* the confusion of kissing Jett—and liking it—the mere bizarreness of it all combined with my temper, and I burst into tears. Mia held me as I sobbed on her shoulder, and her soothing voice and serene stroking of my hair calmed me enough to know I was going to be okay.

"Shh, tell me what's happening," Mia spoke evenly as my crying eased and I started to get a hold of myself again. My sniffles subsided, and hearing that I was semi in control again, my best friend stepped back and looked at me. "Want to talk?"

The dry humour and the quirked eyebrow were enough to make me smile, and grabbing my hand, she led me to our sofa.

"I've not been completely honest with you," I started, and when she frowned, I jumped back off the sofa. "I need a drink for this."

"Water or hard stuff?" Mia asked me curiously.

"Hard, definitely hard," I grumbled as I grabbed two bottles, one of José and one of Jack, and held them up to her.

Her legs were folded underneath her, and with her daisy print skirt and soft white T-shirt, she looked as if she should be ordering tea rather than deliberating the choices of tequila or whisky. Mia pointed at the whisky, and I poured us two healthy shots with ice.

As I handed her the glass, I sat back down beside her, and we clinked our glasses. "You okay?" she asked me.

"No." Taking a sip of the liquor, I grimaced. "I think I should have put Coke in this."

"Nah, this way we'll get hairs on our chest," Mia teased.

I grinned as I settled my head on her shoulder. "I had sex with Jett Santo."

I felt her body stiffen in surprise, and I heard the faint choking and knew she was probably stopping herself from spitting out her drink. "Excuse me?"

"That Friday when I left you and walked home. I don't know how I met him or when I met him, but we hooked up and I spent the night with him."

Mia inched slowly away from me, and she turned slightly as I raised my head to meet her incredulous stare. "Ava, I...girl! You're gonna have to tell me from the beginning. Okay? I..." She took another drink before she stood and went to the kitchen, grabbing the bottle of whisky and two cans of Coke from the fridge. Topping up both glasses, she added a splash of Coke to each. "Okay, spill."

"Wade said I played beer pong, and I vaguely remembered the game once he told me. I definitely tasted the tequila the next morning," I started dryly. "I don't remember the boy you said I spoke to, I can't even picture his face. I was drunk. Like I don't even know how bad, but it was bad."

"I didn't think it was that drunk." Mia frowned as she sipped her drink. "I feel so bad that I didn't know."

"It's fine, it would have been fine. I should know better than to do shots, especially ol' José."

"Why can't you be a fall-down drunk like normal people?" Mia demanded as she swatted me with her hand.

"I want to say that my way is less embarrassing, but you know, the whole 'I slept with the devil' kinda puts a new slant on things."

"This was over a week ago," Mia scolded me. "Why are you only telling me now? Because of the horrible things guys are saying?" I knew when she realised, because her hand flew to her mouth and she stared at me in horror. "You're his thief?"

"I'm the thief."

"Ava!" Mia's look was searching. It was like she didn't know me. "I...my goodness, I just...okay, no more interruptions, tell me what you remember."

"I don't," I snorted. "That's my problem. I don't remember much of the party after agreeing to play beer pong, and I only remember that because Wade mentioned it last week, and that's when I knew I'd played. I don't remember leaving, I don't remember trying to get home or how I met Sir Fuckalot." Mia snorted at my terminology but said nothing to interrupt me. "I do remember waking up the next morning half dead, naked and hungover."

"Ava..." Her look spoke volumes, and I shook my head quickly to assure her.

"I also remember the flashbacks of me having sex with him, and I was a full participant in the act." Looking away from her, I squirmed in embarrassment. "It was definitely consensual and apparently, much to my grief, loud."

"I did hear that his bedroom activities that Friday were, shall we say, more *robust* than normal."

"Yeah, well, that's me, the screamer." I felt another tear slip over, and I wiped it away hurriedly as I took a gulp of my drink.

"Ava, you shouldn't joke like that." Mia clasped my hand as she smiled at me sadly. "Tell me more."

"I woke up on Saturday morning, and I didn't know where I was, and then I heard him in his shower, which is the first I realised that I wasn't in bed here. I was under the sheet, so when he came out, I pretended I wasn't awake. He didn't see me. Well, not my face."

"I don't understand," Mia interrupted me. "When you left, he would have seen you?"

"No, because I threw up all over his bathroom, naked, in front of him and Ash, and all they saw was my butt."

Mia's startled laugh was enough to make me grin humourlessly. "Yup, I spent a long time on his bathroom floor, throwing up with my ass in the air."

Mia's two hands were pressed to her mouth, but I saw her shoulders shaking with laughter.

"Oh, it gets better. He had to leave for the game, so while I was dying at his toilet bowl, he locked up all his valuables."

"Oh my lord, this is so bad," Mia told me as she tried to restrain her laughter. "I'm sorry that I'm laughing, I can't help it!"

I chuckled too because, even though it was horrible, it was a little bit funny. "Mia, I didn't know who he was until he told me not to use his shower and be gone by the time he got back."

Her grin faded as she narrowed her eyes at Jett's words. "What a cracking butthole."

Nodding, I reached for my glass. "He is." Pulling my hair over my shoulder, I sighed. "So, I took a shower." I grinned when she high-fived me. "And then I made my way home. Where I took another shower and basically lay down here and felt like death."

"You should have told me."

"I didn't know what to say," I confessed. *"Hey, Mia, so last night, I lost my virginity to Jett Santo, but I don't know how or why because I don't remember?"* I looked at her as I shrugged. "You would have had me at campus police in a heartbeat."

Mia chewed her fingernail as she considered my words. "I still might," she confessed.

"No. I was definitely happy to be there at the time."

"How do you know?" Mia asked me gently.

"Because since Sunday I've been having complete replays in my head of our time together." My cheeks were bright red, and I couldn't meet her eye.

"Good?" Mia asked lightly.

Nodding self-consciously as I flamed red, I was surprised when she reached out and grabbed me and pulled me into a hug. "Oh, Ava, I am glad it was, but, sweetie...it's just so...sad!"

"It is." I nestled into her side again with my head once again resting on her shoulder.

"But why are you a thief?" Mia asked in bewilderment.

I sat up and looked at her. Jesus, I had to say it out loud. "I took his bedsheet."

Mia stared blankly at me. "Huh?"

"It had…" I ran a hand over my eyes in despair. "You know."

"Oh, Ava." Mia's eyes were full of sympathy.

I tried to shrug it off. Instead, I laid my head on her shoulder again. "And the Monday after, I spoke to Ash, and he didn't recognise me, even though he's technically seen me naked. And of course, I blurt out *naked* to him!"

It eased the tension at least as Mia giggled as her hand stroked my hair.

"And then I sat on the girl giving Jett a blow job, and he talks to me, and I knew as soon as he looked at me, he had no idea who I was."

"What a jerk!" Mia tsked as she listened.

"And then he was here that same night."

Again, I was dislodged off her shoulder as she looked at me in question. "How?"

"I couldn't sleep because of...him. So I went outside, and as I was trying to cool down, he appeared like a bad fairy."

"The night the generator died?"

"Yeah." I glanced at her once and grimaced. "It was Jett who got it fixed."

Mia's eyebrows rose in surprise. "Oh," was all she said as she looked at me before taking another sip of her drink.

"I didn't want to talk about it, and I thought I may never have to," I admitted as I shifted uncomfortably on the couch.

"I understand."

"You do?" I asked hopefully.

"Not really, but I want to." Her hand made the *carry on* motion, so I did.

"Then later that day, Ben Kowoski hit me on the head with a football, and I met Jett again!" I rubbed my head where he'd hit me, and I sat straighter on the couch. "We agreed to never talk again." I frowned as I thought about it. "I think. But then I saw him at the bar, and then the party after and…" I trailed off.

"And today?"

"Well, I knew he was injured, and you and Wade seemed to think the girl who 'stole' from him was the reason, and I've been trying to work up the courage to talk to him. But I didn't hurt him, that Friday, that is."

"Friday? You hurt him another time?" Mia asked me curiously.

"I kneed him in the balls and kicked him in the ribs today."

"Ava!" Mia's hand was once more over her mouth in shock.

"I know, I'm a terrible person." As my hands rubbed the back of my neck, I hung my head before I thought about it more. "Actually, screw that, I'm not. He is."

Mia nodded, but she looked uncertain. "How does he not remember you?"

"Oh, Mia, that's the worst part."

"How?" Mia asked in surprise.

"Because someone drugged him, and he thinks it was me!"

I felt the tears well, and Mia looked at me in confusion before she was on her feet, pacing. "So, you don't remember him, he doesn't remember you, and both of you don't really remember the night?"

"I think so," I sniffled. "Well, I'm remembering some of it, the...you know."

Mia stopped her pacing as she looked at me. "Could you both have been drugged?"

"I was drunk. That's why I don't remember."

"But were you?" Mia sat back down beside me, her hands reaching out to take mine. "Sweetie, you both could be victims of a horrible, *horrible* prank."

"I don't even know how I met him." I leaned forward, my arms wrapping around myself. "If I knew where and how, I'm sure I would remember more."

"And he knows you don't know?" Mia asked me.

"Yes," I sighed. "Neither he or his douchebag brother believes me."

"Well, they wouldn't." Mia looked thoughtfully out the window. "I mean, no offence, if I didn't know you and know this is way out of your comfort zone, I wouldn't believe you either."

"Thanks."

"You understand what I mean," she replied as she resumed pacing. "What did he do to make you hit him?"

Leaning back onto the sofa, I scrunched up my nose as I considered the best way to tell her. "So, they thought to bully me. Kind of. I think. Anyway, Jett made me go to his dorm house today, and he was in my space, and then Gray was pressing into me from behind, and I asked them to move, because it was really uncomfortable and intimidating, and neither one of them did, and Gray licked my ear! So..."

"So you lashed out," Mia finished for me in resignation. "Ava, violence isn't the answer."

"They had me pressed between them like one of their whores."

"Ava!"

"Sorry." I wasn't—not really.

Mia gave a light chuckle as she looked at me. "You're so wonderfully you." After she filled our glasses again, she handed me mine. "Only you would protest being pressed between the Devils."

"They're assholes."

"I know," she said as she sipped her drink.

"I had wild sex with the devil himself. He doesn't remember. He thinks I drugged him, he doesn't believe I didn't, I kneed him in the balls, and that's not even the worst part."

Mia hesitated slightly as she put her drink down. "There's more?"

"I made out with him this afternoon in Ash's bathroom."

She was silent for a few moments before her head dropped into her hands. "Ava, I...none of this makes sense to me!" she wailed. "How? And more importantly...*why?*"

"I don't know!" I groaned as I fell to my side on the couch and buried my head under a cushion. "He's so hot! And I hate him, and he kisses like...I don't even know. And he kissed me, and I was upset, and I just...I kissed him back."

When there was silence, I peeked at her from under my cushion. She was sipping her drink and looking at me in slight amusement. Or exasperation. I wasn't sure. "Who stopped the kiss?"

"Gray."

Mia whistled as she sat back down. "Awkward."

"You have no idea."

"Girl, you are screwed."

"Yup."

"Like I don't even know how to fix this."

"Nope."

"Wanna lock ourselves in so we can't escape and get drunk?"

"Sounds like a plan." I reached for the bottle of Jack.

CHAPTER 25

Jett

Saturday morning, I was livid because it was game day and I wasn't playing. Coach had offered to let me sit on the bus and accompany my teammates. I had refrained from telling him where he could stick his offer and his bus, but I was pretty confident he wasn't a stupid man, and it didn't need to be said.

Sitting in my bedroom, I debated about finding Ava and more or less threatening her until she told me what I wanted to know. I had almost left the house twice to go hunt her down, but then I thought more about it, and I didn't trust myself to be alone with her. If you asked what I didn't trust, I wasn't sure if it was because I would strangle her or fuck her. Maybe both?

And while that made me snort out in disgust at myself, it gave me no assurance that she didn't drive me insane enough to actually do it. Either option.

Last night, I had lain awake as more and more of my memory returned. I still wasn't clear on where we had met, but the time in here, in my bed, was playing like a full-blown porno in HD. And if I were honest, I wouldn't mind a *live* replay, one where I remembered and I didn't have to wait until I was asleep to remember the feel of her riding me.

"This is fucked up," I said to the empty room as I stood. "Why would I want her again? I don't even like her."

I rubbed my crotch as I thought about her kneeing me in the balls. "She's definitely a handful," I mused as I walked aimlessly around my room. Checking the time, I noted that it was an hour before kick-off. I refused to watch. Our opponents today were okay but nothing great. As long as Ben passed to Gray or Ash, they'd hold the offence. Jamie and his defence could handle the rest.

They would be back late evening, and even though there was a party to attend, we had other business first. Ash had tracked down another one of the guys in the films we had uncovered. Even with all the shit going on with me this week, he had been busy.

My job this afternoon was to do some recon and then figure out if the dick had a safe in his house. I usually liked longer to plan, and having sight of blueprints never went amiss, but this was a curveball and one we weren't supposed to be catching. However, that film was imprinted on our brain and not in a good way like Ava was.

Growling at myself for thinking of her again, I headed to the kitchen. No game day meant I could eat more than I normally would.

I was in the middle of a huge bowl of pasta with chicken, green beans and tomatoes with Jamie's pesto sauce when I heard the door get knocked. The guys had a habit of keeping the door open, but I didn't encourage it. Four times in freshman year, I'd found some random guys sitting on our sofas, watching TV. I wasn't a fan of strangers. I wasn't a fan of anyone really.

I debated about ignoring it, and then my phone beeped.

Uptight: **I know you're in there, open the door, I need to talk to you**

Me: **Fuck off**

Uptight: **Just open the door or I'm coming in anyway**

They hadn't locked the door. I had checked it was closed, but I hadn't checked it was locked. *Fucking woman.*

As I strode to the front door, she stood there, hair in a messy ponytail, wearing denim shorts and a yellow T-shirt that read *your drama gives me trauma.*

"What do you want?"

"I was hoping we could talk? Without, you know..."

"My brother?" I suggested.

"Yeah."

"You're scared of Gray?"

"No, I just don't think he needs to be present for a private conversation." Ava rocked back on her heels, and I squinted at her in thought.

"You drunk again? This one of your 'I look sober, but I'm not' pretences?"

"It's *not* a pretence, it happens, but no, I'm sober now."

"Now?"

"Last night, when I went home, I may have had more of the bottle than I should have." She shrugged like it wasn't a big deal, and it wasn't. Not to me. "Slept longer than normal, or I'd have been here sooner."

I grunted as we stared at each other. She wasn't going to leave. Fuck it. "I'm eating lunch."

"Okay." Ava hesitated and then seemed to make the decision. She walked into the house and closed the door behind her. "Just telling you now. This isn't anything, and you touch me and I'll cut it off."

"My hand?"

"Any of it." Her look was meaningful, and I couldn't help but feel slight respect at her no-nonsense attitude.

"Yeah? Well, don't flatter yourself."

Turning on my heel, I went back to the kitchen, and as I sat at the counter, I resumed eating my food.

"Hungry?" Her dry tone and raised eyebrow at the size of my plate didn't bother me.

"It's why I'm eating."

Ava's hands went into her back pockets, and she looked away from me with her eyebrows raised. "Okaaay," she drew the word out, and I ignored her tone. "So, I spoke to my roommate about what happened the other week."

"Congratulations."

"Will you quit it? You're being a complete dick," Ava snapped at me as her temper frayed. She jumped when I tossed my fork onto the counter.

"Will I quit it?" I asked her angrily. "Do you know what day it is?"

Her cheeks reddened as she nodded and wouldn't meet my stare. "Game day."

"*Game day* and I'm here, not playing, not on the field, but here, with you, because I'm suspended." I stood up as I leaned over the counter to stare at her dead-on. "So no, *Ava*, I won't *quit* it."

"I didn't do this to you," she whispered after a moment of quiet.

"Tell me who did."

"I don't *know*." When she saw my anger mounting, she put her hands up to slow me down. "Dude, seriously, I do *not* know. But... I'm willing to tell your coach what I remember. If you think that would help you."

Why would she do that? I watched her as she looked at me. She held my stare, and when I cocked my head to the side to consider her further, she rolled her eyes. "What happened?" I asked her curiously.

"What do you mean?" Ava's face showed her confusion before she schooled her complexion back to smoothness.

"You're usually uptight and angry, now you're almost..." I considered my words. "Pleasant."

Ava snorted as she relaxed slightly. "I'm not the evil bitch you think I am," she told me as her shoulder lifted in a shrug. "My roommate is trying to convince me that whatever you got given to you, I may have had as well." Ava dipped her head to look at her feet. "I think, with my history of being so wasted as not to remember the night, she's reaching, but"—with a quick vulnerable glance up at me, she dipped her head again—"I guess I need to consider it."

"So what are you proposing? You go and speak to my coach and what? Tell him we had a night of sex that neither of us has a clear memory of how we landed in bed together, just that we did?"

Ava rubbed her nose, and I noted it was to hide her smile at my sarcasm. "I was thinking we didn't need to mention the sex bit and just that I also have no clear memory of the night."

"I already told him I woke beside a girl who I don't remember fucking."

Ava's startled gasp at my crudeness made her choke, and she coughed violently. Without thought, I was getting her a bottle of water and thumping her back, placing the water beside her as she rested her palms on the counter. I realised I was rubbing soothing circles between her shoulder blades.

Her head turned to the side as she looked at me, and I stepped back, picking up the water and handing it to her. Wordlessly she took a sip and then another. Subtly, she took a step away from me.

"You scared?" I taunted her, and I felt a grim sense of satisfaction as I saw her hand tighten on the bottle.

"Of you? No."

God, what the fuck was it with this woman? Her words were like a flag to a bull. I stepped closer to her, and I saw her eyes widen in alarm. "You sure about that?"

"You sure you want to test me? Again?" Her taunting words and reminder of her knocking me on my ass yesterday didn't have the desired effect she wanted. Instead of backing off, I had her pinned against the counter, both hands behind her back, pulling them down so her back arched and her tits pressed into my chest. When she moved to strike me with her knee, I was ready for her, and I thrust one leg between hers, pressing up. Her small gasp and the flare of heat in her eyes told me I hit the spot.

"Now what?" With slow, measured movements, I dipped my head into her neck and trailed my nose slowly up the column of her throat. "Tell me, Ava, what are you going to do?"

"This is bullshit," she told me angrily.

I felt her test my hold on her wrists, and I skimmed along her jawline. "You have a mouth on you, don't you?" I asked as my head moved and I placed my lips next to her ear. "And I remember how hot that sweet little mouth is. I remember you sucking my dick and swallowing me down that tight throat."

I could feel her heart hammering her chest, and her breathing was becoming slightly heavier. I knew how she felt. My dick was beginning to wake up, and although I didn't want her to know that I was as turned on as she was, I was also reluctant to step back.

Instead of protesting or trying to get away, she stretched as much as she could in my hold, rising up on her toes to reach my ear, and her soft breath against my skin almost caused me to make a mistake. "I thought you had no memory," Ava mocked me as she moved her head to look at me, and her green eyes met mine. "Or do *you* protest too much? Devil."

We stayed like that, neither willing to back down. Her legs were trembling from the strain she was putting on them, and slowly she lowered herself until she was steady on her feet, but her eyes still held mine in challenge. With a sharp push, I pressed into her more and was rewarded when her eyes widened in alarm. There was no denying she could feel me pressing against her. My dick was so hard it was painful.

"Be careful, Ava, you don't want to do this. You won't like the way I play." Swiftly, I stepped back, and when she stumbled, I caught her and turned her quickly, pressing her over the counter, her ass rubbing into my crotch exactly as it was supposed to. Slowly I moved until I was almost lying on top of her. "I remember this...I remember how you begged for more." My teeth nipped her earlobe, and I felt her body shiver. "Now you either want a replay no matter how much *you* protest, or you want to get the fuck out of my house. Which one?"

"I want out." Her quick breathless reply made me grin as I slowly uncoiled and rolled up and off her body.

"I think I like you better like this," I mused as my hand trailed along her spine. Letting her go, I stepped back out of reach of her punch should she attack. And I was right, her swing was as wild as the fury in her eyes.

"You speak to my coach about what happened between us and I'll ruin you, do you understand?" I asked her as I watched her shaking hands smooth back her hair as she tried desperately to compose herself.

"Fuck you." Angrily, she stormed away from me, heading for the kitchen door. "I offered to help you, but maybe I'm hungover after all."

"Seems to be a theme," I snorted. "I'll be in touch."

"Go to hell." The front door slamming shut behind her made me chuckle. I checked the time, the first quarter would be starting. I was in a better mood to watch the game now.

By the time the second half had started, I had gotten into three arguments on Twitter, two on Instagram, and had sent both Gray and Ash several angry messages about the mistakes they were making on the field. Knowing they wouldn't see the texts until after the game just pissed me off more.

As the final minutes of the last quarter played out, I was grateful that we would be taking home the win. My phone alerted me to a new message.

Replying to @DevilsASaint#8 You sound like a spoiled brat, how's the ankle or can't you remember? @UptightKickedYourAss

I stared at it, knowing exactly who the tweeter was, even though when I checked the account it was newly opened. I couldn't believe her. She had balls. I also had to be careful, because what I wanted to say to her, even I knew I couldn't put on social media.

Replying to @UptightKickedYourAss Ankle's good, thanks for being a such a "giving" fan @DevilsASaint#8

I quickly opened my texts and opened our message thread.

Me: **Don't fucking dare**

Uptight: **Or what?**

Me: **Don't**

Uptight: **I told you, you don't scare me asshole**

She also sent me the one fingered emoji.

Replying to @DevilsASaint#8 You're delusional. Alabama is gonna kick your ass...whether you play or not #DanteSpenceis#1 #GoLions #BlueandWhiteforthewin

Within seconds, my Twitter blew up. And then it was my text messages.

Gray: **Put the fucking phone down**

Ash: **Dude you're tripping, get off SM**

Gray: **So help me brother, I will kick your ass! Do not fucking reply to her**

Ash: **Is this dick on Twitter Ava?**

Me: **Yeah I think so**

Me: **You both played like shit**

Gray: **Didn't miss you on the field - dick**

Ash: **Ben throws better than you**

Me: **@Ash then why can you still not catch the fucking ball?**

Gray: **We're cutting you off SM**

My social media went dead, and I called Gray. It went to voicemail. I tried Ash. Same thing. *Fuckers*. They'd blocked me from my accounts.

Heading up to my room, I reluctantly agreed I probably did need to be cut off and should stay in the house until they came home where I could vent my frustration on my brother, my cousin, or both. Opting to ignore good sense, I headed to the shower. Tonight's plan was cancelled. I texted them both to tell them, and then I turned the phone off. Brushing my teeth, I stared at myself in the mirror, my head running through the routes and plays they should have made today. Picking out black jeans with the knees ripped out and a black V-neck T-shirt, I got ready to leave.

I was restless, and I was pissed, and only two things calmed me down. One was football, which was currently being denied to me, and the other was sex. That wasn't being denied to me, and I had a mind to get laid. Fucking someone else would get a certain blonde out of my head. I hoped.

As I headed out of the house, I made sure to leave my phone behind me. As pissed off as I was at mostly everyone, I knew better than anyone how ruthless I could be when I wanted something.

And right now? I wanted to punish Ava and remind her who the fuck she was playing against.

CHAPTER 26

Ava

THE MUSIC WAS LOUD AND THUMPING, BUT IT WAS SATURDAY, THE football team had won, and the college spirit was high. Mia had scolded me for riling up Jett on Twitter. I wasn't sure that it had been my smartest move, but he pissed me off. So, watching the game and seeing Kowoski make schoolboy errors that the Santo quarterback wouldn't, weirdly made me angry. And I didn't even root for this team. Them playing like they'd never flung the ball before was good for Alabama.

But…I knew if I was pissed at the way they were playing, Jett would be furious. He was already furious about not playing today and was a dick. A huge dick that needed to be reminded he was not God. No matter how much he loved himself.

His tweets and comments on Twitter had been downright insulting, and feeling self-righteous on behalf of strangers, who I would normally believe were also assholes, I created a fake account and got involved.

Just because I knew it would wind him up. And it did.

And I felt…triumphant.

Especially when he immediately texted me to tell me to quit it.

Big mistake. Huge. He may as well have handed me his direct Twitter access. And I called him out, and I declared my team colours.

And now in the corner of a large living room, at a college party, I may have been regretting my choices. Because the smart, funny shit stopped being funny when Twitter basically imploded on my phone, and I had ended up having to hide my phone as the hate got to be too much.

On the upside, Mia, after her lecture about my recklessness, had come bounding in my room to tell me that Alex had invited her to go to a party and that Shane had asked if I would go too. He'd texted, but I hadn't answered, as my phone was still buried and in hiding.

However, I felt like I needed to get Jett out of my mind, and before I knew it, I said yes. I was strictly alcohol-free though. That Friday and last night had been as much as I'd drunk the whole summer, never mind in a couple of weeks. I was happy with my soda in the corner, watching Mia talk to a group of people on the other side of the room as Alex watched her, completely mesmerised. Shane had gone to the bathroom, and he hadn't come back. I thought he'd ditched me....or the line was so incredibly long, he was still stuck in it.

The party was big. Students kept pouring into the house and were now spilling over to the backyard.

I wondered if Mia would mind if I bailed and went home. She was having a good time, and I watched with a smile as she laughed at something said in the group she was talking to. I edged towards the door to the hallway, leaving the sanctuary of my corner.

"Uptight kicked your ass?"

I turned to look at the tall girl who was often seen with Jett and Gray. Black hair spilled over her shoulders. Her height made her stand out, but I think even had she been four feet tall, you would notice her.

"I'm sorry?" Denial was my preferred way to do this.

A small smile crossed her lips, but it was not friendly. "You will be."

I looked her over quickly. Skinny black jeans, a black loose top with a wide neck that slipped off her shoulder. The top had a thin red glittery thread running through it, it was pretty. Wearing black heeled boots, which only gave her more height, she was stunning. Wearing hardly any makeup except for a winged eyeliner made her almond-shaped eyes pop even more, and I felt like a grub beside her. My jeans and blouse I had picked out to wear tonight, which I thought were girly and pretty, now made me feel like I was dressed like a kindergarten teacher. Whereas she was sexy and classy and I could dislike her on that alone, I decided, even though it went against my whole entire nature, but for this girl, I would make an exception.

"Did you just threaten me?"

Dark brown eyes met mine, and there was no friendliness from this girl. Not towards me. "I'd have to care to threaten you. I don't care." She raised her red Solo cup to her lips. She even made drinking from a Solo cup look sophisticated. "But I do find that intense stupidity can be quite intriguing. I mean, does the creature know they are so incredibly dense that they don't recognise the danger? Or do they simply lack the brain capacity to care?" Dark eyes met mine again, and she smirked.

"Creature?" I asked, giving her my full attention. "Dense? I don't know who the fuck you are, but you can go now."

She huffed out a laugh as she looked over the room, and then some guy walked past her, and she handed him her cup like he was a waiter. She didn't even make eye contact with him. And he took it! I wasn't sure which one I was going to smack first, her and her stupid attitude or him for being a sucker for the elitist bitch.

Looking down at me, her eyes narrowed. I hated how much taller than me she was, the heels giving her inches she didn't need. "Is it a ploy? Do you want to get his attention, or do you just want to fuck him again?"

My mouth dropped open at her callousness. I swore all the time. I was me, Ava; swearing was part of me. This girl didn't look like she should know swear words, never mind say them. "I don't want to be anywhere near him again," I spluttered. "Any of them, they're sick, twisted shits." I immediately felt guilty, as Ash had been nice to me. "Well, Ash is different."

Her peal of laughter was heard by others even with the music being so loud. Long slender fingers pushed her hair over her shoulder as she gave me a condescending smile. "I'm no longer intrigued. You're an idiot."

"You're a bitch." Her eyebrow rose in question at my statement, and I shrugged with an indifference I wasn't feeling. "What? I thought we were just saying what we thought with no holds barred," I told her.

Cold eyes held mine, and I actually felt more threatened by her than I did with either of the Santo boys, and they had trapped me in a meat sandwich for crap's sake.

"He will destroy you. He will literally ruin you for what you've done to him. He may have been lenient. I believe he may actually have been kinder, but you fucked yourself this afternoon with your desperate need to be seen by him."

"He isn't a god." I tried to keep my voice steady, but her look and her words had my insides trembling with fear. She was as psycho as the others. Was she their sister? "He can do nothing to me that he's not already done." I mean, he'd already spread the rumours I had stolen from him. His housemates knew I slept with him, and now my reputation was in ruin, and I'd been reprimanded in class because of him. What else could he do? Really? I said as much to the psycho bitch in front of me, and she smiled.

Her hand reached out, and instinctively I jerked back. Her victorious smile at my reaction made me curse inwardly at myself for reacting to her, but it didn't help my nerves when she rubbed a lock of my hair between her fingers before tucking it behind my ear. Her head lowered, and she spoke into my ear, ensuring she'd be heard over the music.

"You're a fool. Jett will eat you up and spit you out, and you won't even know he's done with you until you're back home in your two-bed apartment in Knoxville with your mama, attending community college." Stepping back, she smiled a wide bright smile. "It will be fun to watch though. Be seeing you, Ava. Be seeing you *real* soon."

She walked by me, making sure not to touch me, and with grace, she crossed the room to join a group of girls, who all welcomed her like she was the queen.

My eyes stayed glued to her for a few minutes, watching her interact. She never looked back, and it was as if I hadn't existed.

"Hey." Mia had joined me, and Alex had followed. "You were talking to Quinn Lawrence; how do you know her?" Mia was smiling and happy. It was not the time to tell Mia that I didn't know her or to reiterate what she had said to me.

"I just met her," I mumbled into my cup of soda, wishing it held something harder. "I think I need a drink." Heading to the kitchen area, I surveyed the range of alcohol. There was no way in hell I was touching the large bowl of punch, I had no idea what was in there. Opting for safety, I took a bottle of beer from one of the ice coolers.

"She's besties with your friend," Mia told me as she accepted a beer from me. Alex shook his head and held up his bottle of water.

"Designated driver," he told me.

"Cool." Twisting the cap off the bottle, I looked at Mia. "I'm aware of who she's friends with," I told Mia dryly. And if I hadn't been before, I surely was now.

"Quinn's cool," Alex said easily as he looked over in the direction of the bitch from hell. "She's in my sociology class. Smart too."

Mia gave him a sly grin as she looked at him and then over at Quinn. "Brainy and drop dead gorgeous," she said as she turned to me. "Can we hate her on principle?" she joked with a good-natured laugh.

Easy. "Consider it done." I took a large swig of beer as I listened to Mia assure Alex we weren't bitches, we were merely joking. I kept my comments to myself.

"Where's Shane?" Alex suddenly seemed to realise his bandmate was missing.

"Bathroom."

"Sounds like a plan," Alex said, putting his empty water bottle down. He tugged Mia closer to him, placing a chaste kiss on her temple. "Don't let me lose you," he murmured. Her face flushed with warmth, and I saw the shy smile she gave him as he walked away from us to find the bathrooms.

"Smitten?" I teased her. Her happiness and the fact she was having a good time soothed my own rancour at the words I had exchanged with Quinn.

Mia bit her lip as she swayed slightly to the music. "He is kinda hot. And sweet."

"Hmm." I nodded. "So...I can go?"

The dancing stopped, and Mia grabbed my arm, her eyes wide with concern. "No! Why! Are you not having fun?"

She looked so distraught that I was going to leave her I felt guilty. "I'm not feeling it, Mee," I admitted.

"Because of those tweets, isn't it?" Her hands rested on her hips. "You're not that person, Ava. You can't be a catty kitty and not feel bad. Just apologise."

I blinked in shock. "No. I have nothing to be sorry for." And if she had heard what the witch over in the corner had said to me, she wouldn't be asking me to.

"You need to fix this. He's bound to be feeling as confused as you." Her eyes were so full of sincerity that I wanted to hug her and beg her never to change. Even if she was delusional.

"I don't think he had a problem with his self-esteem, sweets." I tried for lighthearted, but it came out more maliciously than I intended.

"You know what you need?" Mia asked, reaching forward, and I was already stepping backwards. "You need to dance."

I didn't. I never needed to dance. Dancing was for people who enjoyed being sweaty and free and pressed close to strangers who had no boundaries nor the understanding of personal space.

"No," I warned her as her fingers laced through mine. Mia was slight, but my God, she had upper body strength when she wanted it. "Mia, you know I hate it." My pleading landed on deaf ears, and when my best friend took great care to ensure I was at the edge of the dancing area and no immediate person was beside me, she started to dance. So I was either the weirdo standing at the edge of the dance floor, staring at her, or she was the weirdo at the edge of the dance floor dancing by herself, which would only invite guys over to her.

Reluctantly, I moved my feet in the semblance of a shuffle. Mia rolled her eyes and grabbed my hips, encouraging me to move them in time to the music.

Leaning into me, she shouted, "Ava! Loosen up, forget about this and just relax!"

Easy for her to say, she hadn't just been told by Jett's friend that he was out to get me. With a loud groan, I decided she was right. Fuck them. He was just a guy, what could he actually do to me? At the end of the day, he was only a footballer.

We danced for four songs. I kept to my spot and actually enjoyed myself, or I enjoyed seeing Mia let loose. The girl had moves. Which I noticed Alex was very happy to watch. He had returned with Shane, and the two of them were talking between themselves and waiting patiently for us. I liked that neither of them tried to join us on the dance floor. I liked that they stayed to the edge and were happy to let us do our thing.

"Mia, I need to pee," I shouted to her just as the last song finished.

"Yeah? I need a drink!" Grabbing my hand, she pulled me through the throng back to the guys. Alex handed her a beer, cap still on, which she took happily, and I noticed her subtle check to make sure it was. Christ, how jaded were we that we trusted nothing at a college party? Was it sad or smart? Or both?

"Can I get you something, Ava?" Shane asked me as he pointed over his shoulder to the kitchen.

"I'm going to find the bathroom," I told him, and he casually took my hand.

"I can show you, I found one that you don't need to wait for an hour in." His rueful smile told me my earlier concern that he had ditched me was unfounded.

I wasn't completely sure how I felt about holding his hand, but I said nothing as I followed him to the back of the room. I passed Quinn again, who was now with another group of people, and I saw her contemptuous look at my hand in Shane's. I was prepared for her scorn and happy to ignore her.

What I wasn't prepared for was the three guys who just walked into the party and stood in the doorway. The three of them surveyed the room, effectively blocking our way out.

What I also wasn't prepared for was Jett, locking eyes on me immediately, or the sneer on his face when he, too, saw my hand in Shane's.

Shane carried on towards them, and when he said "excuse me" to get through them, he seemed genuinely confused when Gray looked him up and down before turning his head to say something to his brother, who laughed.

Ash moved aside to let us past, and even as I followed Shane numbly, I could feel eyes boring into my back. Unable to stop myself as Shane led me to the staircase, I looked over my shoulder and met Jett's flat stare. Quinn walked up behind them, and when she saw me looking back at them, I saw the small smirk, as if to say *I told you so,* before she touched Jett's shoulder and he turned, giving her his attention.

Maybe I would be lucky and the bathroom would have a window beside a drainpipe that I could shimmy down to escape. Because going down back into that room would be a mistake, and I had made enough mistakes when it came to Jett Santo.

CHAPTER 27

Ava

I was quietly confident that I shouldn't be there in the bathroom, which was actually in someone's bedroom, but as I cooled down, I did my best to calm down. His malice when he looked at me was unnerving. Gray had been cold, and Ash, although he had been as unnerving as the twins, he had at least been decent enough to move to let us past. I knew with certainty that there was no way Jett nor Gray would have moved.

The three of them were dressed similarly, but each stood out. Their family was definitely blessed in the genes department, shame they had crazy in their DNA. I wet my lips as I contemplated the window. *Dramatic much, Ava? I thought he was just a guy?* I was nodding to my inner self that he *was* just a guy when the door was knocked lightly.

"You okay?" Shane asked me with concern. "You've been in there a while."

Great, now he thought I was pooping. As I threw the door open with gusto, the poor guy stepped back in alarm.

"Sorry, I needed to cool down." I grinned and I knew it was manic, so the wary look he gave me was warranted, causing me to dial it down a bit, and I watched him visibly relax.

"That's okay." His easy smile was calming, and he glanced over his shoulder to the main bedroom door, which was half closed. "I just don't think we should be in here longer than we need," he confessed, and if possible, his contrite look made him cuter.

"Noted." I checked I'd turned the tap off in the bathroom and then headed to the door. "Let's go." When we were in the hallway, Shane tugged at my hand, pulling me to a stop. "You okay?" I asked him as he walked around me and stood in front of me.

"Yeah, there's just no rush to go back down...is there?"

Oh. I wasn't sure what to do now, did he mean one of the rooms or stay here? "You want to stay up here, in the hall?"

"Yeah." Shane looked around the empty hall. "It's quieter and cooler, and now the football team's turned up"—he rolled his eyes —"we're never going to get near the drinks again."

Go downstairs and meet the wrath of the triad with their resident bitch, or stay up here and hide with a nice safe guy, who wasn't pushing for me to go into a bedroom? Hmm, the decision was a tough one.

"I'm good to stay up here and talk," I told him as I considered the wooden floor and whether I should sit on it. "You think it's safe to sit?" I asked Shane with a smile, and as he thought about it, he bent down to look closer. Which is how I saw Jett stride up the stairs, his eyes already locked on mine, his dark look sending a shiver down my spine. If I was honest, my reaction wasn't from fear.

Shane straightened when he felt the foreboding presence behind him, and with a glance at me in confusion, he turned to see who was behind him.

"Oh hey, was I in the way?" Shane asked as he looked around the wide hallway in which Jett could easily have moved around him.

Jett's eyes flicked to mine, and then his attention was back to Shane. "Need a minute with her," he told him.

Her? Asshole.

"Oh." Shane was looking at me curiously, and I knew I was scarlet. "I didn't know you were friends."

My strangled laugh caught both their attention, and Shane took a step towards me. "You okay?" he asked me with concern.

Jett raised an eyebrow, daring me to say otherwise.

"Yeah, absolutely." I nodded, not making eye contact with either of them. One could see right through me and the other, well...I didn't want to lie to his face. "I'm really thirsty, would you mind getting me some water?"

"Of course." Shane smiled, and his hand ran down my arm in a familiar way, which caused Jett to narrow his eyes and my cheeks to burn brighter. "You sure you'll be okay?" When I nodded, he stepped back. "Meet you back downstairs?"

"Absolutely, I'll be right behind you."

Jett didn't have to speak. His face told me I may have been hasty with my assumption on the speed of this next conversation.

Shane lingered for a moment more before the Saints number eight turned his head and stared right at him. The message to move along was loud and clear. With a gulp, Shane dashed down the stairs.

"Nice," I snarked as I watched Shane's retreating back.

"How's your Twitter?"

Embarrassment flushed my face this time. "Haven't checked."

"Hiding?" The smirk was back, and he looked far too pleased with himself.

"Never." *Liar.*

"I told you not to do it," Jett said casually. Almost *too* casually, as if he thought being friendly towards me was going to ease my nerves. Well, he didn't know me that well.

"Well, thank Christ I don't have to listen to you."

The friendliness vanished as quickly as it had come. Hard blue eyes travelled over me before he made eye contact again. "Don't you?"

"No." Defiantly I met his stare, Quinn's words from earlier in my head.

"We'll see." Jett leaned into me, and I pressed myself up against the wall, my breath leaving my body in a rush in my haste to get out of his space. With that smirk in place and humour dancing in his eyes at my reaction, he pushed past me as he entered the room I had used the bathroom in.

My hand grabbing his arm surprised him, and well it should, because it shocked the hell out of me. "Wait." My voice cracked, and I couldn't take my eyes off my hand curled around his forearm. "You don't need to be a dick, you don't need to try to intimidate me or send your psycho girlfriend to give me veiled threats." With confidence I wasn't feeling, I looked up at him. "I didn't do this to you, but I told you, I'm willing to tell whoever you need about what I remember if it helps you. *I'm* willing to help you."

Jett's hand covered mine, plucking my hand off his arm and dropping it like it personally offended him. "Who were you with?"

"When?"

He looked over my shoulder, jerking his head towards the stairs. "Boyfriend?"

"Shane?" I looked towards the stairs. "No."

"Fuck buddy?"

My head snapped back at him in disbelief. "No, what is *wrong* with you?"

"Got drugged, fucked a girl, got suspended from football." Jett said it so matter-of-factly without a flinch, but *I* did at the brutality of his words. "What's wrong with *you*?"

Asshole. "Got wasted, fucked a guy, got threatened." I could play his game even if I didn't match his coldness.

Jett smirked as he leaned forward, and this time I didn't move away from him. "Who said it was a threat?" With a low chuckle as he saw my face pale, he went into the room, closing the door firmly behind him.

As I hurried down the stairs, I was not at all surprised to see Gray standing at the foot of the stairs, blocking anyone from going up. His eyes met mine, and I looked away as he stepped aside, and I rushed back to the main room.

They said there was safety in numbers? Well, I needed numbers, because I did not feel safe. Quinn had unsettled me with her little speech earlier, Gray looked menacing, and Jett...well, he confused me. Because while he completely intimidated me, he also made my pulse throb in anticipation any time I was near him. Our hook-up in his bathroom still made no sense to me. I mean, we went from freezing to hot to cold again within the space of twenty-four hours. Twenty-four hours? Twenty-four seconds felt more like it.

"Did you see who are here?" Mia asked me quietly as she handed me a beer.

"Hard to miss," I replied as I purposefully turned my back on the Devils who I could see.

"We can go, we don't need to stay," she assured me with a quick smile. I looked at Alex, who had been talking to someone else. With a fist bump to the guy, he turned back to Mia, his arm slipping around her waist. I said nothing, but I noted Mia wasn't stepping out of his touch.

"I'm not running from him."

"Who's him?" Alex had heard my comment as the music dipped into the next song. "Did you ditch Shane?" he asked me curiously as he looked around the room.

"No, I was in the bathroom, and he said he'd meet me down here." Over a week of knowing Jett Santo, and I'd become a habitual liar.

"There he is," Mia said as she pointed over to Shane, who was talking to Wade and Bea. Finally, the numbers I needed to stay away from shithead and crew.

"My girl!" Wade greeted me with a hug, which I returned before hugging Bea. "This place is packed, music's shit though. I'll be back. Why don't you all head outside, get us some air." With a kiss to Bea's cheek, he went off in search of whoever was in charge of music.

"How are you, Ava?" Bea asked me with a smile as she watched Wade make his way through the crowd before we moved our little group outside, and Wade was right; it was better, not as noisy but still crowded.

"Good thanks." Another lie. "How are you? I love your outfit." Bea had on a tight black pencil skirt, butterfly clasp elastic belt, and a red and white gingham short-sleeved top with a sweetheart neckline and tiny red heart buttons. It was perfectly retro and fit her slender figure like a glove.

"I made this top in class, and I'm telling you, Ava, I thought I'd given myself at least a half inch more room than I have. These girls are ready to greet the world if I'm not careful!"

With a glance down at the cleavage on display, I laughed. "No dancing for you," I agreed with a wink.

As Bea told me what else she had been making, I could feel him behind me. Self-consciously I looked over my shoulder quickly, and there he was. Leaning against a low wall in the yard, a bottle of beer in his hand, listening to Quinn, who was standing close to him but not touching. Were they together? Because if I'd hooked up with her boyfriend, well, I kind of understood her dislike of me.

Jett's eyes flicked my way and held. Jesus. He was intense.

"Ava!"

The loud shout in my ear made me jump. "What?" I turned back to look at Mia, who was shaking my arm.

"Ava, look!"

Turning my head in the direction of her stare, my jaw dropped open. Dante Spence had just come into the yard through a side gate.

"Oh fuck," I gasped. He looked as flawless as always with thick light blond hair that was in a low fade, square jaw, and perfect white smile. He was slightly smaller in height than Jett, his six one height nothing to complain about. His shoulders weren't as broad, and he was a slimmer frame. Jett had more bulk, which was surprising for his QB status, especially as he used his feet as much as his arm. Dante stayed within the safety of the pocket more, but as a result, he had a slightly better throwing arm.

"You need to talk to him this time," Mia urged me. "Not about football, but about girl things."

"Periods?" I blurted, and Bea burst out laughing.

"No, you lunatic," Mia scolded me. She quickly checked for Shane, who had migrated to a group where Wade had stopped to talk on his way to join us, with Alex following. "We'll distract Shane. This could be your chance, Ava," she added excitedly.

Bea glanced at Shane and then me. "You collecting a harem, Ava?" she teased.

"Yeah, that's me, the collector." I noted that Dante was with his friend, Dustin Slater, and I saw Dustin see Mia at the same time as I saw Dustin. "Eh, Mee, *you* may need the distraction," I warned her.

Dustin was the wide receiver for the Lions, and with agile footwork, he was weaving through the crowd to Mia like he ran his routes to the end zone, with speed and precision.

"Red, I was hoping to see you," he greeted, and Mia's smile could have lit the backyard. Dante was three steps behind Dustin, and I saw him recognise me at the same time as I saw the Devils move into my line of sight, and the only word to describe *them* was murderous.

"Hey," Dante said as he reached forward and gave me an awkward hug.

Dante Spence hugged me. Willingly. Without provocation. Like he wanted to. Why didn't this make me as happy as it should?

"Hi, Dante." My voice squeaked, but he didn't notice.

"Did you see the game today?" he asked me, and for the first time in his college football career, I hadn't. Because I'd been watching the Saints. Because I knew Jett would be watching, alone.

"Mm-hmm." Lie lie lie. Was I ever going to tell the truth again?

"So," Dante teased, his smile easy, "hit me with my stats."

"Yeah, Ava, tell me Dante's stats from today's game."

Whoever I pissed off, whoever I hurt, I'm sorry. This is not karma. I do not deserve this. I am a good person. Please, will you fuck off?

"Santo?" Dante lost his easy smile.

"You look surprised to see me." Jett's voice had no friendliness. "But why? I'm at a party in my college campus. Why wouldn't *I* be here?"

"You didn't play today," Dante answered as two more of his team arrived behind him. "Heard you were injured."

"Heard wrong," Jett answered tersely.

Dante and he held a long stare off, and I had absolutely no idea how I was in the middle of this.

"The party seems big enough for both of us," Dustin said with a forced casualness, and the two grunts from each quarterback could be heard over the music, which I was sure had been lowered.

"Good game you had," Ash said to Dustin, reaffirming my belief Ash was the only decent Santo there was.

"Yeah, everything was coming my way today," Dustin told him. "Saw your catch in the end zone, good footwork."

"Thanks," Ash replied, and then they were silent again.

"I bet you know all the stats today," Dustin said with a knowing smile at me. "C'mon, tell us who had the better passing rate."

"Uh," I stumbled. I had all the attention, and I never in a million years wanted it. "For your game?"

Dante frowned. "Yeah, although remember that night you told me all the stats for that weekend? That was impressive."

I could feel Jett as he moved beside me. A hand touched my lower back, and I tensed. "How do you know, Ava?" Jett asked as his hand pressed into my back, his fingers twisting into my top, and I knew it was to stop me from bolting.

"Huge Lions fan, aren't you, girl?" Dustin had no idea he was making this worse for me.

"I'm more a lover of the game itself," I croaked out.

"Lions for the win?" Gray growled.

Prick.

"Oh man," Dustin laughed. "Did you see that shit on Twitter?" He laughed loudly. "Dude, you were a genius with the trash talking," he said to Jett. "Our upcoming game's got so much hype around it. We already obliterated every other team this week in the press."

I noted that Dante didn't seem to be impressed at his wide receiver's easy friendship with the opposition, and then my panicked brain remembered that Dustin had gone to the same high school as the Santos.

"Got to play to the crowd," Ash spoke for Jett, who was still in a stare off with Dante.

Dustin looked around the party. Many were staring at the small group that I was still the centre of, but most were partying like normal people on a Saturday at a college party. "My kid sister's boyfriend is here. We agreed to detour on the way home and pick him up."

"All of you?" Gray asked as he looked over the four players.

"Well." Dante looked at me. "I came hoping to see you."

"You did?" Jett spoke before I had a chance to. I felt him turn slightly into me, and I knew my cheeks were on fire. "Why?"

"Don't." The plea was out before I could stop myself. Fingers tightened on my top, digging into my flesh.

"Don't?"

"Girl, did you switch teams on us?" Dustin asked with a wide-eyed look as he clutched his chest in mock horror. His teammates laughed, and I was grateful for the attempt at the easing of the tension. Dante didn't laugh.

"She more than switched," Gray said with a smirk as he took a swig of his beer. I felt Jett's chuckle, and I looked over at Mia, who looked as helpless as I felt as I stood there caught in between the two larger-than-life egos. "We've all *heard* how much she switched."

Bastard.

"Your stats today, I'm sure you know," I said suddenly to Dante before any other Santo could make a dig at my night with Jett. "Best player of the game, although Dustin definitely brought his A game. You'll need to be quicker though next week, Slater; the Saints linebacker Brown was on fire today." I turned my attention back to Dante. "And you? You better hope that pocket protects you. Woods is on point. He had four sacks today alone. Saints defence may just be enough to win it."

Dante gave me a good-natured smile. "That your take? Saints going to take down the Lions?"

"Defence wins championships," I answered blithely. "Offence can only take you so far." Those fingers were going to leave a bruise on my back if he dug in any tighter.

"Offence takes it to the end zone," Jett answered me before he spoke to Dustin. "Well, we shouldn't hold you up on your search for...whoever."

Dante held his stare and then turned his attention back to me. "Can we talk?"

"No."

I blinked. With a small shake of my head as if to clear the fog, I looked up at Jett. "I believe he was talking to me."

Jett glanced down at me, and I swallowed as his cold mask slipped, revealing his anger. *Jaaaysus Lord.*

"I was," Dante said. "Talking to you, that is."

"She'll talk to you if you can tell me her name." Mia stepped forward, and my jaw dropped open along with Dante's. His lack of response only frustrated her more. "Seriously, dude, how many times has it been now?"

"*Mia!*" I protested as I looked at her with a clear *what the fuck* look.

Jett was grinning like he'd already received the Heisman Trophy. "Shh now," he hushed me. "We're all waiting, Spence. Impress us."

Was my whole entire existence just for his entertainment?

Dante stood silent until it became uncomfortable for him, never mind me. He looked furious, and with a grunt, he spun on his heel and barged through the backyard to go inside, with his teammates following him.

Dustin looked at me in apology. "Sorry, Ava." He sounded sincere, and I could only jerk my head once in a nod. "Red, don't be a stranger," he said to Mia with a wink, completely ignoring the fact that Alex had glued himself to Mia's side. "See you on the field, guys."

When they were in the house, Jett's fingers loosened, and I wrenched myself free of his hold.

"So, how often do you hang out with the competition?" Jett asked me coldly.

"They're not competition to me."

"Is that right?" His tone was deceptively calm.

"That's right," I snapped back angrily.

"And that, my friends, is what we call motive." Gray snorted. "We're out." Tapping Jett on the shoulder, he turned away.

Jett stood for a moment longer. His left hand stroked his chin before his fingers ran over his lips and down his chin as he considered me thoughtfully. "Pity." He and Ash followed Gray.

"What did he mean?" Alex asked in the quiet that followed.

"It means nothing," I answered softly. Nothing good anyway.

CHAPTER 28

Ava

GETTING READY FOR BED AFTER BRUSHING MY TEETH AND GARGLING my mouthwash, I felt slightly sorry for myself on how the night had ended for me. Not long after the Devils had left us outside, I'd felt exhausted and made my way home. Mia and Bea were happy to stay, Alex was trying to convince Mia musicians were more fun than footballers, and things with Shane were slightly awkward after Jett's manhandling of me. I knew everyone was thinking of the "blonde" Jett had been looking for and the rumours circulating about me, and I knew that they were eventually going to ask if I was her.

I hadn't wanted to answer any questions in regards to the bizarre encounter with the Alabama guys, and Mia had been tight-lipped when I questioned her about her outburst towards Dante.

Overall, the night had lost the fun factor for me, and I knew the more my friends had to drink, the more questions I'd have to avoid. Home had been the more desirable option. Climbing into bed, I lay on my back, staring at the ceiling. Being an obvious glutton for punishment, I had stalked Dante's Facebook and felt happy there was no mention of awkward parties on their rival's campus.

Gray's less than subtle accusation of motive pissed me off. They still thought I had drugged Jett, and I was of a mind to no longer defend myself to the assholes. They didn't believe me. Me knowing Dante worsened my case, but did his lack of knowing *me* in some way help me? Or did it make me look even more suspect?

I could hear Quinn now, whispering into Jett's ear about me doing it for attention. In my head, I punched her.

"You can't lie here and worry about this," I told the room. "Go to sleep, it won't be as bad in the morning." Advice my mom gave me all the time. Nothing was as bad as it seemed after a good night's sleep.

Closing my eyes, I listened to my mom, eventually drifting off to sleep.

The thud of something being kicked woke me. Blearily, I lifted my head and peered into the dark.

"Mia?"

"You wish."

"Jett?" I bolted upright, sleep forgotten as I leaned over and flicked my sidelight on. There he sat at my desk, in his armour of black clothing, hair messy, and his boots on my floor. "How?" I stuttered. "Why are you here? How did you get in here?"

"Not important," he said as he studied me. "How long have you known Spence?"

"No." I was out of bed, hands on hips, ready to do battle. "Get out of my bedroom!"

Jett looked around lazily, taking in the pale walls, the three shelves of textbooks, the bed, the desk and the small closet. "No," he mocked me.

"This is insanity, this is *illegal*," I told him. "You broke into my apartment."

"Did I?" He cocked his head as he looked at me. "I say you let me in."

"I say you're full of shit."

"See how it works?" Jett's gaze travelled over me slowly, and I felt the goose bumps as he did so. "I say you drugged me."

"I say I didn't."

Jett's eyes fixated on my chest, causing my nipples to harden, and I hastily crossed my arms. His slow smile caused my tummy to somersault. "I say I may fuck you again."

My throat closed. "I say not likely."

He was on his feet and in front of me in one stride. A hand cupped my chin, tilting my head back as he stared down at me, his face clear of emotion. "I say you drop to your knees and suck my dick."

"I say you kiss my ass."

He smirked, and seeing that familiar expression almost relaxed me until I was spun and my pyjama shorts were tugged down. Fluidly, I was bent over, and my cry of alarm was swallowed by my cry of pain when the bastard bit my ass. "Ow, you fuck!"

His lips and tongue soothed the bite, causing my core to heat, before he bit the other cheek, causing me to cry out again before he soothed the bite again. His lips moved over my ass, and my head was reeling from his touch. His hand skimmed the inside of my thigh before it lightly traced over my pussy.

"So wet," he murmured as he bit my ass cheek again, and his fingers ran through my folds. "Did I do this to you that night?" he asked me as his thumb rubbed over my clit. "Did I eat this pussy until you screamed for me?"

Yes. "I..." I gasped when his tongue replaced his thumb. "Oh Jesus," I groaned as he ate me out, my legs spreading to give him room. His tongue was merciless, like him. As he licked me, his fingers stretched me open before his tongue dipped inside me. "Shit." It felt so good. My cry of protest when he stopped stroking me would have embarrassed me, but Jett flipped me around, and pushing me onto the bed into a sitting position, his hands grabbed my thighs and pulled me to the edge where he got on his knees and buried his head between my thighs. I could say nothing as my hands curled into his hair, feeling his breath against my most sensitive area before he licked and sucked me until I was begging him not to stop. Not this time, he couldn't leave me like this again.

My hand was in my mouth, trying to stop my scream as his fingers pushed inside me, and my whole body arched at the exquisite sensation.

"Your roommate isn't here," Jett told me gruffly just before he took my clit into his mouth, sucking hard as his fingers picked up speed.

My orgasm burst inside me, and my legs clasped around his head as I screamed out in ecstasy, crying his name. Gentle licks lapped over me until I got my breath back. The heels of my palms were pressed against my eyes, and I fought to get control of myself. As I struggled to recover from my orgasm, hearing the click of a belt, I removed my hands from my face. A strong hand slipped around my throat to the nape of my neck, and Jett pulled me up into a sitting position once more.

His dick pressed against my closed lips, and with no hesitation, I opened for him. He filled my mouth before he slid out, leaving just the crown of the head in my mouth, and my tongue flicked against it. I heard his low moan, and I took him in my hand and started to move him in and out of my mouth, my tongue stroking his shaft and flicking against the sensitive head.

"More," he grunted as he pushed his hips into my face. "Swallow it, I remember *this*." His voice was thick with lust, and breathing through my nose, I did, I took him deeper. Shocked that I could, I looked up at him, and his heady stare with his eyes glazed with desire made my thighs clench. I kept going, and he let me, moaning encouragement as I sucked him.

"Like that," he encouraged as he started to thrust into my mouth. "I'm going to come down your tight throat." His hips picked up speed, and I intuitively knew to stop moving and let him dictate the pace, his hand tightening in my hair. "Fuck," he mumbled as his hips stilled, and I felt him pulse in my mouth, his head thrown back as he groaned his release.

As he withdrew, he stared down at me. His thumb caressed my lips before he pushed it into my mouth, and without thought, I sucked as his look became flat once more. Jett straightened and buttoned his jeans before tightening his belt. "You better not be lying," he grunted. "Be at the stadium at eight on Monday morning."

"Why?" I asked as I pulled my sheet over the lower half of my body.

"Because I said so." He gave me an indiscernible look, and then picking up his boots, he walked out of my bedroom. The door thudded closed behind him, and I sat on my bed for a few minutes before I had the sense to go lock the door.

Climbing back into bed, I wondered how that had escalated from a break-in into a spontaneous sex session. Curling up in bed, I fought the urge to scream before I got up and went to brush my teeth again. Staring at myself in the mirror, I didn't know what the hell was happening anymore.

But with Jett, had I ever?

ON MONDAY MORNING, I STOOD OUTSIDE THE PLAYER DOORS TO THE stadium nervously. While I waited as the minute hand ticked closer and closer to eight, my tummy was ready to upend my coffee and banana I'd had for breakfast.

I still had no idea why I was here. I could only guess it was because he wanted me to tell his coach about the night he was drugged. I was so nervous I had put on skinny white jeans and a cream short-sleeved top with a floral pattern, and I'd even cleaned my Chucks.

"You look like you're going to church," Jett said to me when he pushed the door open from inside the stadium.

"Morning," I greeted him as I walked towards him. "You seem breezy." I hoped he understood sarcasm.

In practice pants and his jersey pulled up over his pads, he looked like my version of a porn star. A rather inappropriate memory of his head between my legs made me shiver, and I saw his smirk as he watched me.

"Coach is in a bitch of a mood," Jett spoke easily as he secured the door behind me. His eyes ran over me, and his tongue licked his bottom lip. "You looking all innocent may not help," he mused as he led me towards the office.

I looked around eagerly. I'd been to the stadium many times, but this was restricted access, and my football junkie self lapped up the inside tour.

"You really are a football fan?" Jett asked me as he hesitated at the door that was signposted Lockers.

"Yeah," I admitted as he waited.

"That probably shouldn't make my dick as hard as it is."

I blinked in shock, and my tummy somersaulted once more when he gave me a slow smile. Why was I reacting to him like this? The pull to step into him was strong, and I was grateful when he opened the door and led me down a corridor.

We passed the locker room, and I had no desire to peek inside since the black football pants Jett was wearing were moulded to his ass and thighs, and I was having a hard time taking my eyes off his butt.

"You done staring at my ass?" he asked me when he stopped outside another door.

"I don't think so," I admitted without thought. My eyes flew to his, and I saw his pleased look as he laughed. It softened him, and I drank in this version of Jett hungrily.

"Coach is waiting," he said, sobering as he knocked, and when the call to enter came, he gave me a questioning look.

"I'm ready," I told him.

"Let's get it over with."

We walked into an office, which I think was bigger than it appeared. It was just so cluttered I immediately felt claustrophobic. I recognised Coach Bowers, of course. I didn't recognise the woman beside him, but I did falter when I saw Ash and Gray.

"Hi," I greeted weakly.

Coach Bowers stood up and offered me his hand, and I shook it as he told me who he was.

"She's a football fan," Jett told him as he rested against a wall. It seemed to be the only spare piece of wall that wasn't covered, and I knew I should have been looking at Coach, but I was drinking in the pictures on the wall.

"Holy shit, this is Devonte Carlson," I said, whirling to look at Coach Bowers.

He looked at me in confusion before he nodded. "Yeah, good player."

"Good player? Are you joking?" I moved to the wall. "He's the GOAT! Over a thousand passing and rushing yards three seasons in a row, the guy moves like a hot knife through butter."

"As I said," Jett said dryly, "she likes football."

Aware that all eyes were on me, I flushed. "I'm sorry," I rushed out. "I'm not here to stare at your wall." My eyes darted back to it, and I felt a pair of hands on my shoulders as Jett pushed me down into a chair.

"Focus," he said quietly into my ear.

"Sorry."

Coach was looking between the two of us, his eyes curious, but his lips were pressed together tightly.

"You know why you're here?" he asked me.

"I think so," I told him.

"This is the team's doctor, Isabell Sanchez. She was the one who tested the sample from Santo that Saturday morning." Coach pointed towards Ash and Gray. "These two are here because it seems private meeting means shit to them."

Looking at the two of them, I saw Ash grin and Gray stare impassively back at me.

"My understanding is they come as a package." I opted for light and cheerful.

Coach snorted and leaned back in his seat as his hands clasped in front of him. "I've had your school records looked at."

"Why?" I asked. He now had my full attention.

"You're one of three people in this school on a full ride."

I shifted uncomfortably in my seat. "My understanding was that this school didn't discriminate against the scholarship kids." It was true. Sure, you could spot the money kids, but that was true in any walk of life. In some colleges, they gave you a card that declared to all whenever you used it what your college payment plan was. Cardinal Saints didn't. When I handed my card over to pay for books, food, hell, even a coffee, it was the same card as anyone else's.

"We don't." Coach watched me. "But I also know you got pulled into the dean's office last week for making a side profit."

I glanced at the silent observers to my right. "Yes," I answered.

"Which tells me you're either stupid to throw away a full scholarship or desperate." Coach didn't break my eye contact. "You don't strike me as stupid."

"That's what Dean Porter said," I muttered as I fidgeted in my seat. "I'll tell you what I told him, which is the truth, and trust me, if you'd received the call I got from my mom afterwards, you'd feel bad for me."

"Explain."

Looking at Jett again, I flinched at his hard stare before I turned to look at Coach and the doctor. She looked nice. "I'm a fully funded scholarship recipient," I began. "I applied here on a whim, and the school must have liked what I had to offer, because as you rightly said, I got the whole shebang." My finger rubbed over my eyebrow. "But…" I sighed as I thought of my reasoning. "I get my tuition paid, my books, my housing and my food."

"Nice," Ash murmured.

"Yeah, well, have you eaten in the cafeteria?" I asked him. When he nodded, I turned back to Coach. "It's the same food every week. For a seventy-five grand tuition cost per student, the food could be better. I got a side income so I can buy and make my own food."

I sat in the silence and waited. Dean Porter had also been silent, but the doctor lady leaned forward.

"You risked it all so you could eat in your apartment?"

I nodded. "Look, my mom sends me an allowance, and I know I sound like a whiny shit, but I wasn't asking her to break the bank so I can eat fresh pasta. My friend offered me cash if I provided a service for him, and it meant I earned fifty bucks at a time and my mom didn't have to waste any more money on me."

"You risked a full ride for fifty bucks?" Ash asked me in disbelief.

"What kind of service?" the doctor asked at the same time, and it was she who I answered as I saw she had made an entirely wrong assumption.

"I draw." I hastily pulled out my phone and opened my photo gallery. "I make posters and flyers for his band."

"Oh." She looked entirely too relieved. "You're very talented," she said as she passed me the phone back.

"So you're stupid after all," Coach Bowers commented.

I grimaced as I looked at him. "Guess so," I admitted. "My mom definitely called me that several times when she got hold of me."

"What did Dean Porter say?" Gray asked me. It was the first time he had spoken to me.

"Um, I have to stop, obviously. I'm on probation so I have to behave even when I want to smack someone," I said as I glared at him, and he actually grinned. "And he's making me spend Saturday mornings teaching art to underprivileged kids as penance." I sat on my hands to stop from fidgeting. "'Making me' sounds harsh; it's been fun so far."

"And the incident with my quarterback?" Coach asked me.

"I was really drunk," I admitted. "I don't remember meeting him, I don't remember being with him, I *do* remember the hangover."

The coach studied me, and then he stood. "We've been looking into the drug that was administered to Jett. I need to go coach my team. Doctor Sanchez wishes to talk you through everything. It's entirely possible you were also under the influence."

I opened my mouth to protest, but Jett's hard look made me stop. "Okay."

"Before I leave, I have one more question for Ms Bryant."

"Okay," I said as I swallowed.

"Should it be found that you were also drugged, will you be seeking damages against my quarterback?"

My eyes widened, and I shook my head. "No, sir."

"The team?"

"No."

"The school?"

"No."

He considered me, and I realised this is why he was so sought after as a coach. It was as if he could pull the truth from me. I saw him nod once.

"I hope you were only drunk, Ava," Coach said quietly. "Thank you for your time today."

He left without a backwards glance, and then Gray and Ash followed him. Jett hesitated, his eyes on mine.

"Santo! Move it!" Coach's voice bellowed down the hall, and Jett rolled his eyes before he left the office, closing the door behind me.

I turned back to the doctor. "He's intense."

"He's my dad."

Oh. "Um…"

She smiled at me. "Let's get this over with. Do you want someone here with you?"

"No," I answered, and then I looked at her. "Do I need someone?"

"This is unofficial," she admitted. "You're here under your own choice. You can answer or you can decline, it's entirely your call."

I rested my elbows on the desk. "I have nothing to hide," I told her honestly.

"Then let's begin."

CHAPTER 29

Jett

I WATCHED THE BALL AS IT SAILED THROUGH THE AIR, BOUNCING OFF the padding at the end of the stadium.

"Santo!"

"Jesus," I muttered as I turned to Coach. "Yeah?"

"What in hell's name was that?" he barked as he marched towards me. When he was alongside me, his finger jabbed me in the chest. "Your head is here, but your dick is in there?"

Licking my lips, I took my helmet off. "My head's in there too," I admitted as I stared down the tunnel.

"Boy, that girl is innocent. Open, honest, genuine," Coach said to me. "I hate to tell you, I think you're going to find she's fallen foul of the same as you." He rubbed his forehead. "What's worse, she's never going to know if she was."

"I know." I tapped my helmet off my thigh. "I was so sure she was in on it until…"

"You got to know her," he said gruffly. "I can see that."

I frowned as I looked back towards the tunnel until Coach reached up and knocked the back of my head. "She's there, you're here, practice. You throw another ball like that and Kowoski's back starting against Texas."

Slipping my helmet back on, I looked at him with a scowl. "No need for threats," I muttered as I picked up the next ball.

"Game head only on my field," he told me as he walked off.

I threw balls for another hour until my arm ached. Then we ran routes, passing to Gray or Ash as Jamie made it his personal mission in life to take me down on the field.

By the time practice was finished, I ached everywhere. I still had afternoon classes to go to, and as I lay on the turf after being flattened by our linebacker, I stared up at the cloudless sky.

Two shadows stood over me, and I looked up at Ash and Gray. "Still miss practice?" Gray asked as he extended his arm and helped me up to my feet.

"What the fuck's up Woods's ass?" I grumbled as we headed to the showers.

Ash grinned as he pulled his jersey off. "He didn't even touch you," he said as we stripped.

"Not for the lack of trying," I told him gruffly.

"He took Ben down six times last Thursday in practice. Seriously started to think it was personal," Ash told me.

"He wants to win the conference, we all do," Gray grumbled as he turned the shower on. "Let's hope he brings this all week and still has enough for Spence next Saturday."

I nodded as I stepped under the hot spray.

Pulling on clothes after I was washed and dried, I already felt my muscles stiffening in protest. "Fuck, is this what time off means?"

Jamie was lacing up his sneakers when he heard me. "Sore, Santo?"

"Fucking aching," I told him as I pulled my T-shirt over my head.

"You want the defence to go easy on you?" he asked as he stood, his broad frame filling the space.

"Fuck no, I want to win."

Jamie nodded in respect, and then he and his fellow henchmen, *defence*, left the locker room.

"Santo!"

All three of us turned to see Coach at the door. "Office."

"Me?" I asked him as I picked up my book bag.

"All of you."

Exchanging looks, we piled into his office. Coach was looking at the photo Ava had almost creamed over.

"She's inconclusive," Coach started with no preamble. "Izzy

doesn't know if she was an unfortunate drunk or targeted also." He sighed. "She did say she can tell you almost every statistic in the history of football though." Coach's eyes gleamed in approval. "And for that, Ms Bryant is your proven alibi."

I glanced at Gray, who was frowning. "I don't understand."

"She's a Lions fan. Blood runs blue and white, and when she's not supporting the Lions, she isn't even a Titans fan, but a Panthers one, something to do with her grandfather." Coach looked personally offended. "There is no way in hell you and this girl hooked up with her *only* drunk."

Ash snort laughed, and I saw Gray hide his smile. "Coach, are you saying she would have to be *drugged* before she slept with me?" I asked incredulously.

"Sure as shit am."

Ash let out a loud laugh, and Gray joined him. I looked at Coach, who was grinning. "Fuckers, all of you." I walked out of the office to the sound of them laughing their asses off behind me.

Heading to class, I ignored the calls from my brother and cousin to wait for them. Ava needed to be under the influence to fuck me? Is that what she told the doc? I'd see about that.

The first class of the afternoon passed quickly, and then I was in the class where I got a blow job the other week. I scanned the seats for the little turncoat, and when I spotted her blending into the wall, I stalked towards her.

As I dropped down beside her, Ava wordlessly stared at me before her eyes darted around the room. "What are you doing?"

Pointing at the large white screen in front of the room, I told her, "Learning."

"Why are you beside me?" Ava demanded quietly. Her eyes kept flicking to the door.

"Do you want me to move?"

"Yes!"

Turning, I looked at her, and she sat back, her head dropping to break the eye contact. "Excuse me?"

"This professor thinks I'm already a team bunny. You sitting beside me is only going to condemn me further."

"What the fuck is a team bunny?" I asked her in amusement.

"Jett!" Ava's eyes were wide with pleading.

"You want me to move?" I asked again, and when she nodded too enthusiastically for my liking, I stood.

Her relief was palpable, and I bent over her, my lips on her ear. "You can thank me for this later, on your knees, rabbit."

I was laughing as I made my way up the stairs to the back row. Now that I knew where she was in the class, I had no idea why I hadn't noticed her before. Her face was red from embarrassment, and when the dude who had given her grief last week started on her again, I took special note of who he was.

Five minutes into his shit and Ava was on her feet. This time, she didn't confront him but merely packed her books and climbed the stairs. I watched her silently as she took the empty seat beside me. When she eventually made eye contact, she gave a slight shrug.

"Better the devil you know," she murmured as the lights dimmed and the professor started class.

The darkness hid my smile.

The week passed quickly, and although I saw her once or twice on campus, she didn't seek me out, nor I her.

But she was all I could think about.

Ash had her in one class, and at dinner on Thursday night, he commented that their professor seemed to hold a personal vendetta against her. As he ate his chicken and spaghetti, he shook his head. "You can see he intimidates her, but every time he picks on her, she answers." He shovelled his food into his mouth. "You gotta admire her spunk."

Gray grunted but said nothing.

"What is it?" I asked him as I ate my own dinner, carefully pushing the asparagus to the side. I growled when my brother reached over and pushed it back into my food.

"Eat your greens," he told me.

"Fuck you. I hate asparagus."

"Eat it," both he and Ash told me.

"It tastes like fucking feet," I muttered, biting into the spear on my fork and forcing myself to chew and swallow.

"Why would you know what feet taste like?" Ash asked with a quick grin to Gray, who huffed out a laugh.

"You ain't been laid in over a week," Gray said slyly. "You been tamed?"

Ash snickered as he drank his water. "You caught the feelings?" he mocked me.

"You're both assholes," I said to them as I kept my eyes on my food.

"This will help," Gray said as he pushed his phone across the table at me.

I stared at it and then looked at both him and my cousin. "What the fuck is this?"

"Told you before," Gray said as he ate more of his supper. "Motive."

"It could be nothing," Ash said quietly. Gray huffed in contempt, and I studied the phone again.

"She played us?" I asked. "All of us? We already settled this."

"Wasn't Coach who questioned her," Gray said. "Izzy's soft." He looked over at Ash. "She's given him more hand jobs than he can count."

Ash swatted the back of Gray's head. "Hey, she massages the ache. It's for medicinal purposes."

Gray rolled his eyes as he finished his dinner. He took the phone off me as he stood. "Don't lose sight of the bigger picture," he reminded me as he took his plate to the sink.

I opened my own Instagram and looked at the pic and the caption. Dante Spence had posted a pic of a blonde girl, her face turned away from the camera, wearing a Lions shirt, and the caption read *objects of my desire* with the hashtag *Uptightkickedyourass*.

It was hard to tell if it was Ava, but the message was clear, Spence was making a move on her.

I remembered her red-haired friend challenging him when he said he wanted to talk to Ava. The friend knew immediately he had no intention of being there for Ava until I was in the same space as her. When she demanded he tell Ava he knew her name, his epic fail had been funny as fuck to witness, but I *had* registered the brief look of hurt on Ava's face.

It was one of the reasons I went to see her later. I had no intention of putting my lips on her body, any part of her body, nor did I expect her to wrap her perfect lips around any part of mine.

When I was in the same room with her, sometimes I forgot what my goal was, and I ended up either kissing her or playing with her sweet body.

"What you going to do?" Ash asked me quietly as he set his fork down.

I swallowed as I looked at the picture again. With a slight shake of my head, I rubbed my lips together. "Nothing," I told him as I closed it down.

"No retaliation?" Ash looked over his shoulder at Gray, who stood facing me, his hands resting on the sink behind him.

"I'm cleared, Coach believes me, and even if he didn't, it was fixed." I ate the last bite of my chicken, ignoring the remaining asparagus that lay on my plate. "As for her part, she cemented the fact to Coach I was duped."

"That's it?" Ash looked sceptical.

"Pussy is pussy," I told him as I schooled my features. "He won't beat me on the field, and this?" I tossed the phone onto the table. "This tells me he's desperate."

"Okay." Ash looked unconvinced.

Gray watched me, and with a small smirk, he turned back to the sink. The fact my little brother thought I was losing my head over a girl was sobering.

A girl who didn't even like me.

A girl *I* didn't even like.

Did I?

My foot tapped off the floor, and I watched Ash as he took our plates to Gray, who frowned at my uneaten vegetables before scraping my plate in the trash.

"You both ready for Houston?" I asked them as I stood. When they nodded, I headed to the front door. "Going to hit Quinn up," I called over my shoulder as I left.

The walk to Quinn's dorm house was quick. Her dad had scored her a single-room apartment. She shared a kitchen with three other girls, but her room, living room and bathroom were her own.

Taking the stairs two at a time, I rapped my knuckles against her doorframe, and she opened it with a smile.

"What's up?" she asked when I closed the door behind me, and she folded herself into her easy chair.

Wordlessly, I handed her the phone with the Instagram pic. Quinn sniffed in dislike, but she handed it back to me. "It isn't her."

I felt my chest ease, and I was more surprised I'd had anxiety about this. "You sure?"

"Yes," she said as she stood. "Hey, look at this." She tugged my arm, pulling me to her desk. Picking up one of her textbooks, she showed me a diagram, and I turned both my head and the book to figure out the position.

"This is porn."

Quinn gave a delighted laugh. "No, it's deep tissue massage. Be my guinea pig?"

"No." I studied the pic again. It still looked like porn. "Gross, no."

"You would do this with Ava in a heartbeat!" Quinn scolded me with a pout.

"Yeah, cause my dick would get hard and then be wet as she or anyone else would be riding it. You?" I shook my head. "That's like asking me to tongue Aunt Charlotte."

Quinn started to giggle and ended up holding her sides as she laughed. "Fuck, I think I'm going to vomit." She wiped her eyes as she straightened and fixed me with a stern glare. "It's not flattering that you're not attracted to me."

"Are you on glue?" I asked her, bewildered. "You're like my sister, for fuck's sake."

Quinn spontaneously hugged me. "And you're the best brother ever." She planted a sloppy kiss on my cheek.

"Why you being weird?" I asked as I went and sat down, turning the TV onto the sports channel.

Her smile dimmed, but she forced herself to remain upbeat. "You ready for Saturday?"

"Always."

She closed her book and stretched out in her easy chair. "You eat?"

"Gray made chicken and spaghetti."

"Nice." I watched her as she started to play with her hair. "He make you eat your veg?"

"Tried. He made asparagus."

Quinn gagged, and I laughed. "Ash eat his supper?"

"He did, mom."

"You know he fixates," she said quietly.

"We do, Gray weighed his portion first."

Quinn nodded, and we relaxed into a comfortable silence. As I listened to the sports news, she came over and settled beside me on her small couch. Her head rested on my shoulder, and I wrapped my arm around her.

"What is it?" I asked her quietly.

"It would have been his birthday soon," she told me, and I felt the tear hit my arm.

"I'm sorry, Queeny." I kissed her head. "I got you, you can cry, no one else is here."

And she did, as I watched the news and held her loosely, she cried into my shoulder. When she got up to dry her eyes and wash her face, I texted my brother.

Ten minutes later, I opened the door to him, and he pushed past me into the apartment, enfolding her into his arms, and I shut the door behind me as I left.

Feeling helpless, I headed back home. Some sorrow wasn't for me to fix, no matter how much I wanted to.

CHAPTER 30

Ava

Turning the TV off, I watched Twitter as the shit talking started about who was going to win between the Lions and the Saints next week. I had watched the Saints today and felt guilty for it, but I needed to see if he won.

If *he* won. Not they won.

Mia was shopping in Cardinal. We had a party tonight at Jett's house, and she needed new clothes. She didn't, but her mom had sent her an allowance, and Mia had already blown through half of it.

I'd been to Cardinal earlier to help with the art class, and although I'd helped, the actual art teacher blew my mind with her skill. The kids loved it though. Ranging from ages seven to eleven, they spent three hours on a Saturday morning in the community hall to give their parents time to do what they needed or to have a break from their parents.

I was home with some groceries and had made myself lunch when Mia declared she needed new clothes. There was no way in hell she was getting me away from the game, and she knew it. Having blown me a kiss, she assured me she would eat in Cardinal.

Jett had been precision perfect today. Seriously, I hadn't even seen top NFL quarterbacks play like he did today. The Lions were in for a fight next week. The hype and speculation were already rampant, and the rest of the league didn't really exist at this point. Given that they were archenemies didn't help either.

The party tonight was at the football team's house, and as I stared at my small wardrobe, I wondered if I should have gone to the store with Mia and gotten some new clothes. I thought about what Quinn wore and considered my options. With the best will in the world, I couldn't hope to achieve the same level as Quinn. She was model-like and had obviously always been that way. The ship had sailed for me to suddenly become glamourous overnight.

I pulled out a black dress. Every wardrobe should have an LBD as my mom called them. Was tonight the night to wear my little black dress? It was pretty. As plain black went. A sleeveless fit and flare dress with a square neckline, and the skirt came mid-thigh. Remembering what happened last time I wore a skirt with Jett around, I blushed.

Chewing my bottom lip, I put the dress back. I was not putting in a special effort for Jett Santo on the off chance he would want to talk to me as much as I wanted him to talk to me.

The dress came back out. I was wearing this dress for *me*, not him. He did not dictate my wardrobe.

The dress went back. I was wearing jeans, I was more comfortable in jeans. Dressy shorts? I looked at my shorts, and then I went to Mia's closet. She had a nice pair of black dress shorts with a turn up, and they were classy. I could wear dress shorts. They showed more leg, but they were *shorts*.

I took them back to my room and then spent the next hour trying to find anything to match them.

"Holy gumdrops." Mia stood in my doorway and looked at the clothes on my bed and on my floor. "I thought I was the one who went shopping," she teased.

Looking around my room, I groaned. "I have nothing to wear!"

"Are those my shorts?" Mia said as she leaned over my bed and picked up her discarded clothing. "And my top?" She looked at me with an amused glint in her eye. "Ava, are you freaking out over the football player?"

I was so close to denying it, but she was my best friend, and I couldn't lie to myself anymore. "I'm freaking out over the football player."

"The Devil or the Lion?" she asked me with a curious look.

"The Devil." I sighed long and hard. "The Lion doesn't even

know my name. And the Devil…well he knows too much." My face flushed red as I met Mia's amused look.

Mia snort laughed and then grinned at me. "My black shorts will look good with your lovely legs and…" She pulled something out of her shopping bag. "I may have bought you this to wear."

"Mia!" My eyes widened in excitement. "Ooh, it's so pretty." It was, it was a long black top, and across the front was a large heart made up of words with a silver matte splash across it, like paint. Mia held her finger up and turned the top. It was backless. The neck was three buttons and then dropped to a wide band at the bottom, but from my shoulders to my ass, my back would be bare.

"Shit," I whispered. "I can't…can I?"

"Paired with my black dressy shorts, you will be smoking hot."

"My feet?"

"Not your Chucks." Mia crossed to my closet and pulled out a pair of ankle boots. "Perfect."

"No bra?" I worried my lip, but my eyes stayed glued to the top.

"You can carry it off," Mia told me with confidence. "You like?"

Nodding, I looked at her. "I think so."

"We'll style your hair down," she said as she gave me a reassuring smile. "That way you can hide your back with your hair if you're nervous. Or your boobs," she added dryly.

"Mia!"

"What? You think I don't see them nipples pointing up and saluting him whenever he's near you?" She grinned as she pulled a slinky dark green playsuit out of the bag. "You like?"

"Whoa, that is *short*."

"See? You're not the only shorts girl tonight."

I frowned. "But my shorts will actually cover my ass."

Mia laughed as she headed to her room. "So will mine, *prude*."

Looking around the room, I stared at the chaos I created, and with a heavy sigh, I started to tidy the mess. When I was finished, I looked at the bag pushed to the back of my closet. Shutting the closet door, I decided I would worry about it later.

I showered first and let my hair half dry before I blow-dried it as Mia sang country songs in the shower.

Getting ready was always fun with Mia. I loved watching her style her hair. She had deft fingers, and I watched as she quickly parted her hair into two French braids. Her plaits pulled her hair off her face, leaving the perfectly oval face stark and bare, and she opted for only eyeliner and mascara and then a deep pink lipstick. It was so plain but so in-your-face attention-grabbing. I knew Alex would die of lust as soon as he saw her tonight.

"Same for me?" I asked as I dutifully sat in front of her.

"No, but you do get braids. Viking ones for you, I think."

I watched as she parted my hair at the side of my head and wove in two small tight braids. The loose hair at the top, she brushed back, and then with a skill I would never possess, she intertwined the braids at the back of my head so they would not only hold, but also keep the top of my hair in place.

She applied dark smoky eyeshadow, sweeping the colour across my eyelids while she hummed happily. On the instruction not to move, Mia applied my eyeliner, and then I was instructed to give each eye three coats of mascara. She cleaned off my cheeks with a tissue and then applied a tinted moisturiser over my cheeks and forehead before I got a sweep of pale bronze on my cheeks. My lips, she left nude, and when she stepped back, I looked good.

I looked better than good.

"Wow."

"You look hot," she said proudly. "If number eight doesn't die on the spot, he isn't worth your time." Holding my top up, she grinned. "And the beauty of this top?" Unbuttoning the three buttons at the neck, she let the top fall away. "You can *step* into it." Handing it to me, she pointed at my room. "Bra off, sexy panties on."

"Mia," I protested as my cheeks flamed.

"Lace ones, make him want to tear them off you."

"Mia! Will you stop?" I laughed as I headed to my room. "I'm dressing for me, no one else."

"Course you are, make sure you wear the G-string."

"I don't own a..." I stared at the lacy, flimsy thing on my bed. Holding it up, I examined it.

"You're welcome," she said to me as she stood in the doorway.

"I owe you money," I said as I glanced at the panties again.

"Presents," Mia answered. "Mom got a royalty cheque."

Mia's mom was an actress, not a very well-known one or, if we were honest, any good either. But she had a part in a bad TV show when Mia was much younger, and it had a cult following now, so her royalty cheque was regular.

"You shouldn't use your money on me."

"Shush, put them on. Get dressed. I'll meet you in the kitchen. I'm making mocktails."

"I love mocktails!" I said as I closed my door so I could get undressed. A few minutes later, staring at myself in the mirror, I turned once more as I looked at my back. There was no denying I was braless.

"Are you going to come out?"

"I have no bra on," I said instead.

The door swung open, and Mia looked jaw droppingly stunning. Her deep green playsuit set off her beautiful auburn hair, while her legs were slim and elongated in the nude high heels she wore.

"Whoa, mama." I whistled. "You look amazing."

Mia grinned as she looked me over. "Well, baby, you went and grew up on me," she said playfully as she crossed the room to stand beside me. We stood side by side, and I swallowed as I looked at us both. We looked hot.

"Your boobs look amazing."

"They're doing okay," I agreed. "I shall be standing beside the AC all night so I don't get boob sweat patches or sweat running down my back!"

"And the moment is officially ruined." Mia laughed as she nudged me with her shoulder. "I have the drinks ready."

The beauty of dress shorts? Deep pockets. Slipping my wallet into one and my phone and key in the other, I dropped my nude lip gloss into Mia's tiny purse.

"Do you think you'll be home tonight?" I asked her as we tidied up the glass pitcher and the glasses.

"If I'm lucky? No." Mia winked at me, and I laughed at her openness. "And if *you're* lucky, there are condoms in the bathroom cabinet, remember."

"I think I'll be okay," I said as I stared at my boots.

"Looking like you do tonight, you'll be more than *okay*."

We walked slowly to the house party, Mia's heels slowing us down. The sun had set, and the night air was slightly cooler. It was a beautiful night for a stroll.

When we arrived, we both got appreciative looks from the guys at the door. It wasn't usual for the house parties to have official guys standing guard, but this was the active football team's house, plus they had won today and this was a big party. All the furniture was pushed to one side of the room, leaving a large open space for the festivity.

"You definitely drinking water?" Mia asked me over the music as we headed to the kitchen.

"Absolutely." I nodded as I looked around, already conscious of my backless top.

"Don't sweat it," Mia told me with a firm look. "You look hot."

We weaved through the crowd, and I spotted Wade and Bea. They waved, and after we both received compliments about our appearances, I felt myself start to relax.

We'd been at the party for over an hour when the cheers and

hollering started, and I knew that the football players who mattered had arrived. I saw them greet a few people, and they were running up the stairs. That was odd. I turned to question it, but I was with couples.

Alex had found Mia not long after we arrived, and they were giggling together in a corner. Wade was currently wrapped around Bea, and Shane had given me a wave from the other side of the room when we came in. He stood with Sticks and a couple of girls I didn't know, and I didn't have to be a genius to know he had ventured elsewhere. I didn't have any bad feelings that he seemed to have moved on. So it wasn't really my fault my eyes turned to see them come down the stairs.

I saw Ash first as he came into the huge space. He was wearing his jersey and black jeans. The black uniform top, with only a silver stripe on the arms and the Saints logo on the chest, looked good on him. Gray was already talking to a girl, I noticed, and as I saw the other players, I felt slight disappointment that Jett wasn't there.

Until he was. He came down last. My heart plummeted when I saw a brunette waiting at the foot of the stairs, ready to latch onto him, and I saw him laugh at something someone said to him.

His hair was messy, he was wearing a sleeveless Saints practice top, and he was also in black jeans. I noted a few scrapes on his arm that was free of tattoos from the knocks he had taken in practice. The Saints logo on his jersey made me look quickly to Gray. I hadn't noticed it before, but Gray was also in a black uniform top, moulded to his body, and I searched the other players. Only five or six more were wearing their football tops.

I turned to get Mia's attention, but she was now kissing Alex, and I didn't know how to interrupt her.

"What is it?" Bea asked me curiously.

"It's mayhem."

Wade's head snapped up from his girlfriend's neck, and he took in the scene. "Shit, so it is."

Turning my attention back across the room, I realised Jett had noticed me. I saw his eyes run down me slowly before they trailed leisurely up and over my body. My whole body felt hot, and when he fixed on my chest, I really wished I had a bra on to hide the pebbling of my nipples. When he finally met my eyes again, there was a hunger in them that I couldn't look away from.

His grin was wicked when suddenly the lights went out and the music cut off.

"*Mayhem!*" It was shouted all around us, and I flinched as people either shouted in glee or screamed in fright at the sudden change to the evening.

I'd been to one party before where the Devils caused mayhem, and I'd learned from that night. They put the lights out, the music stopped, and the trick was *not* to run. If you ran, you were fair game to be chased.

I waited in the dark, bodies jostled around me, and then I heard it. A sinister whisper all around us. "*Run!*"

I wanted to screech and bolt, but I stood firm. Nervously I rubbed my hands over my shorts, and I reached out for Mia, but she was gone.

"Mee?"

She knew better than anyone not to run. She was in heels for fuck's sake. "Mia?"

I moved to where she had been and stretched my arms out, hoping to find her. Suddenly I was pulled back into a hard chest.

"You running, Uptight?"

"No." I shook my head, and I stiffened when cool hands slipped into my top from behind, gliding over my skin to my front and curving upwards, brushing under my breasts.

"I think you should run," Jett whispered in my ear.

"No," I said as someone else bumped into me, and Jett tightened his hold on me, his fingers grazing over my nipple.

"Yes." He tightened his hold on me as his fingers played with my breast. "Or the lights are going to come on, and you'll be bent over with my dick filling you for everyone to see."

It was wrong that my body clenched at the thought, but his low chuckle in my ear had my heart racing.

A hard slap to my ass caused me to jump, and panic seized my body, causing me to be reckless.

I ran.

CHAPTER 31

Ava

I MOVED BLINDLY THROUGH THE HOUSE, BUMPING INTO PEOPLE, crying out when hands grabbed at me, and when I lost my balance at the foot of the stairs, I made the decision, and then I was running up them. I knew the way after all. He wouldn't expect me to be bold, he wouldn't expect me to run *upwards*.

At the top of the stairs, I hesitated. I didn't know which room was his. Hands grabbed me, and I screamed as I was turned deftly and pressed against the wall. His lips covered mine, and tentatively I reached for him, my hands searching and *checking* it was Jett kissing me.

"It's me," he confirmed before his lips covered mine again, and this time, I parted my lips for him. Jett crouched as his hands slipped under my ass, and he lifted me, my legs wrapping around him as he carried me, his lips never leaving mine.

A door opened, and then he moved through it, closing it behind him. I heard a click, and then there were screams of surprise, laughter and outrage from downstairs as the lights were back on. It wasn't unheard of for some girls and guys to be kissing when the lights went on. The point of mayhem was to cause as much disruption as possible, and it was common to find your girlfriend or boyfriend kissing someone else. It was also common for mayhem to *cause* mayhem, and fights usually broke out.

Jett pulled back and looked down at me as his hands squeezed my ass before letting me go, and I slowly slid down his body to stand in front of him.

"Turn around."

Swallowing, I did as he asked.

"That top can never be worn again," he muttered as his hands once again slid inside, and he pulled me into him. His head dipped, and his lips were on my neck, and I moaned softly in appreciation as he started to rub his hands over my breasts.

I could feel his hard length press against my ass, but I couldn't think as his mouth moved over my neck, and his fingers plucked my hard nipples between his fingers.

"Recognise the room?"

Opening my eyes, I looked around. "Maybe?" I wasn't sure. It wasn't Ash's room, but I couldn't tell if it was the room from the other day.

"Not even the bed?" His voice was husky as his hands worked on the buttons of my top.

The bed I recognised from my dreams. "I remember the bed," I said, feeling shy.

"Good, because I'm about to fuck you in it."

His crudeness didn't upset me. As he undid the last button, my top fell away from my body, and he turned me to face him before his head lowered and his tongue and mouth were licking and sucking on my breasts.

Quick hands made short work of my shorts, and within minutes of entering his room, I was in ankle boots and a black lacy G-string. Jett ran a hand over his mouth as he took me in.

"Boots off and get on the bed."

Silently, I did as he said. Kicking my boots off, I turned and crawled onto the bed. The dark grey sheets felt crisp under my skin.

I heard his hiss of appreciation as he took in the G-string, and a calloused palm ran over the globe of my ass.

"On your knees."

Frowning, I raised myself onto my knees. With one hand, Jett pulled his top off over his head. I don't know why that made me pant with need, but it was so indescribably sexy I wanted to pounce on him. I drank in his abs and broad shoulders as he kicked his sneakers off and started to unbutton his jeans where the hard V was leading to his happy trail.

Pushing his jeans down, he stood in his boxer briefs, and my eyes were on his body. Jett kneeled on the bed and looked at me as he rubbed himself, my eyes greedy to see past the final barrier of his boxer briefs.

"Suck."

I went to move, to lie down, and his hand caught in my hair. "Stay on your knees, like you did last time."

"I don't remember," I whispered, my throat so dry my voice was raspy.

"I do." He pushed on my shoulders. "I see it every time I close my eyes. You on your knees, crouched over my dick, sucking me down that perfect throat." His hand dipped into his boxers, and he pulled himself out. "Show me."

Tentatively I leaned forward. It was awkward in this position, but my tongue came out, and I flicked it over his head. He tasted fresh, and with a moan of approval, I tasted him again. Jett was silent as I opened wider and took more of him in. I didn't remember doing this the first time, and I was so high from my own orgasm last time we were together I only had a dim recollection of what I'd done that night too.

Tonight, I was sober and eager. I was learning what he liked as I tasted him, my hand and my tongue working him in and out of my mouth to the sounds of his pleasure.

"Take it all," he told me as he pressed forward. I fought the gag reflex, and then I felt him in my throat. His hiss of pleasure made me double my efforts.

Managing to move him in and out, I caressed the underside of his dick with my tongue each time before I deepthroated him.

"Fuck, you're too good at this." Hands tightened in my hair, causing me to lose my balance a little, but Jett held me up. "Look at me."

It was slightly impossible at this difficult angle, but I tried. It was enough for Jett, who looked almost feverish with need.

"Swallow it all," he commanded as he started to fuck my throat. His hand grabbed around my throat as his hips moved faster. Had we really done this the first time? As he pushed further and further down my throat, I felt the panic. I couldn't breathe. His hand was wrapped around my throat as he literally choked me on his dick.

His guttural cry of release as he pulsed in my throat made me almost sag with relief. Backing off him, I straightened, not prepared for the look in his eye.

"What is it?" I asked self-consciously.

"Nothing." He smiled, but his eyes remained hooded. "Lie down."

Confused at his tone, I did so.

"Did I eat you out with you on your back? Or did you ride my face?"

I sat up and saw him push his boxers down, kicking them off as he got back on the bed again. "There's no way I didn't tongue fuck you," he said as he took the G-string off, tapping my thigh to let me know to raise my ass.

"I don't know," I told him as he undressed the last remaining piece of my clothing with an almost clinical detachment. "Why are you mad at me?" Sitting up, I grabbed a pillow and covered my nakedness. "You seem pissed off."

Jett pushed me back down on the bed, taking the pillow off me. His hand dipped between my legs, finding me soaked for him as his fingers slid through me slowly. "I want to do what we did the first time."

"I don't know what that was," I told him quietly. "Can't we just do what feels right *now*?"

He'd been staring at my pussy as he moved his fingers through my folds, but when I spoke, he looked up at me, and I saw his eyes soften. Moving up, he caught my lips in a soul-searching kiss. His tongue stroked mine, and his hands tangled in my hair as he moved over me, nestling in between my thighs. My legs curled up around him, and I felt him move his body over mine, his dick sliding through my wetness, and my body arched with need. The need to have him fill me was overwhelming.

"Not yet," he whispered against my mouth. "I need to taste you first."

Moving back down my body, his hands softly pushed my thighs wider apart, and then his tongue was there, lapping at the mess between my legs, licking me and sucking me as his fingers slid inside me.

"Jett," I gasped as he stroked over my clit. "That's so good," I moaned as he covered my pussy with his mouth. His tongue was running hungrily over me, and I felt him push it inside me before it flicked in and out of me, causing me to moan louder as my body tightened in response. I was going to explode, I knew it and so did Jett. He murmured his approval at my reaction, and the soft vibrations of his mouth pushed me over unexpectedly. My hands clutched his hair as my lower body raised itself to his mouth, and I rode out my orgasm on his tongue as I screamed his name.

Dimly I heard the foil wrapper, and then he was pushing into me, my body not quite willing to stretch to accommodate his size.

"You're so fucking tight," he muttered as he pushed again. "I know you're no virgin." He gave me a grin, and whatever he saw on my face caused his eyes to widen in horror as realisation dawned on him. "Ava, *no*."

Gritting my teeth, I pressed the heels of my feet into his ass, and I pushed him in. My cry of discomfort was quiet, but it felt like it echoed in the quiet of the room. Jett was frozen above me as his eyes roamed over my face.

"That's why you took the sheet?" he asked me as his hands braced on either side of me. I nodded once. "I took your virginity?" he asked me incredulously.

Did he know he needed to move? My body had stretched to fit him, and now I needed friction that only he could give me. "You have to move," I told him hoarsely. Jett hurriedly tried to pull out, and my feet stopped him once again. "No, I mean *move*." My hips bucked under him, and my pussy clenched around him. I heard his low growl.

"Ava, don't," he whispered as his head dropped to my shoulder. "You're fucking killing me."

"I'll kill you if you don't *move* your ass," I whispered furiously at him, and I heard his low chuckle before his lips were moving over my shoulder, kissing and nibbling my neck. He licked the sensitive part of my neck before he bit gently, and my hips surged upwards again, causing him to groan as he slowly, so fucking slowly, started to roll his hips.

My fingers dug into his shoulders, sculpted from years of training into the perfection that was Jett, as he slowly picked up speed. Hands hooked under my ass, lifting me up to meet his slow thrusts, my body clenching around him as he hit something deep within me that caused my eyes to flutter closed.

"Open. Keep your eyes on me," Jett whispered gruffly.

His slow thrusts morphed into deep long strokes, and my hips were eagerly meeting his, stroke for stroke. "Fucking hell, you've got me like a vise," he mumbled against my mouth. "I need to fuck you." His tongue swept into my mouth as his hips picked up speed. "I need to fuck you hard."

Sky blue eyes, clouded with lust, bore into mine as Jett moved over me, driving deep into me, and I felt my orgasm building as he moved faster. Jett growled, and suddenly I was on top of him, his hips pumping upwards in powerful thrusts as I rolled my hips over him in answer. His hands grabbed onto me as he pushed me over his body, and I could feel the tightness in my belly as he fucked me. My hands trailed down his chest as they gathered on his stomach, and I used him to raise my body over and over as I pushed down, again and again. I was losing control, and Jett was wild beneath me. I cried out his name as I reached the precipice, and I felt my pussy clench tightly around him.

Jett surged upwards one more time before he let out a loud grunt, his body stiffening as I felt him jerk inside me, following me over the edge. My body slumped, and strong hands caught me, laying me over him. His kiss was soft and sweet against my lips before my head nestled into his shoulder, and I studied the arch of his throat as his head dropped back on his pillows.

We lay in silence for a long moment, catching our breath, as I slowly became aware of the sounds of the party still happening downstairs. We'd need to separate eventually, but I selfishly wanted to relish the moment a little bit longer.

Jett must have heard my thoughts. "You need to move," he told me as his hands cupped my ass, and he lifted me off him. His hand caught the base of the condom before he was pulling it off, pinching the end.

I watched as he knotted it with a practiced move before he was on his feet and walking to the bathroom. I heard the flush and then the running water as he washed his hands.

I really wanted to put my clothes back on, but there was no way in hell my legs were going to hold me up right now.

Jett came back out of the bathroom and pulled on his boxers. "So," he said with a hard look in his eye. "Tell me how the fuck you were a virgin?"

Swallowing, I pulled his bedcover over me as I sat up slightly. "You look offended."

"You think?" he snapped as he glared at me.

"I don't know what your problem is," I said as my euphoria from the sex was being rapidly replaced with irritation over his attitude.

"My problem is that I took your virginity."

"So?" I decided I needed clothes for this conversation. "It was mine to give."

"You don't even fucking remember!" Jett roared angrily. "*I* don't fucking remember."

"Is that why you're mad?" I asked him as I threw the cover off me and stood, no longer giving a shit I was naked as the day I was born. "You wish you could remember?" I asked him scathingly.

"Yes!" Jett was on his feet. "Why aren't *you* mad?"

"Haven't we made up for it?" I asked as I pointed at the crumpled bed as I stalked over to my shorts and looked around for my panties.

"No, you stupid girl," he growled at me as he threw my panties at me. "Why the fuck would you *want* to fuck me again?" he asked in bewilderment. "I *know* I wouldn't have been careful with you."

This was horrifyingly awkward. I had just had some mind-blowing sex, which had now turned into this third-degree scorn I wasn't prepared for. Forgoing the flimsy panties, I pulled the shorts up my legs. "Well, I came back for more, you can relax." I fastened the top button as I looked for my top.

"Ava?" Jett took a step towards me. "Ava." His finger slipped under my chin, tilting my head back to look at him. "How do you know I didn't hurt you?" he asked me gently. "How do you know you *gave* me it? What if I *took* it? Fuck, Ava, what if I took it?"

I couldn't cope with his uncertainty. He was so vulnerable right now. He looked like *I* had been the one to cause *him* pain. "I know you never forced me." My hand caught his, and I placed it over my naked breast so he could feel my heart pounding. "My mind doesn't remember," I told him as I searched his eyes so that he would understand what I was telling him was the truth. My hand cupped the side of his face as I tried to give him comfort. "But my body *does*, my *body* remembers you, and that's how I know." I sighed as I stared into his eyes. "I know you would never have hurt me, not like that, or asked me to do anything I wasn't *willing* to do. You only took what I gave, Jett."

Jett's mouth crashed down on mine, his lips devouring me as his hands slid into my hair, moving my head, angling where he wanted it, allowing him to deepen the kiss. His moan was low in his throat as one of his hands slid down my side, tearing at the button on my shorts, pushing them to the ground.

I was turned and lifted, pressed against the wall, and then he was pushing inside me again.

"Condom," I gasped as I tore my mouth from him.

"You're a virgin, and I'm clean," he growled against my skin as he moved further inside me, my body still not used to his size stretching me. "Shit, I never knew it could feel this fucking good."

"I'm your first without a condom?" I asked in surprise as my back arched and he began to piston his hips into mine.

"Yeah." Jett's head was lowered as he watched himself fuck me. "Your pussy's gonna suck me dry," he moaned as his head lifted and he met my gaze. His hand on my hip dug into my skin, but his other hand caressed my face softly. "You okay?"

I nodded as I moved in rhythm with him. "I'm good," I promised.

"Yeah, you are." His lips covered mine, and there was nothing more to be said as we both took what we needed from the other, falling apart together, over and over until we finally fell asleep, exhausted.

CHAPTER 32

Jett

I WOKE UP TO AVA CURLED AROUND ME, HER HEAD ON MY CHEST, her hair splayed out over my shoulder, her leg hooked around mine. She was fast asleep, and I wasn't complaining about how right it felt to have her lying on me, sleeping beside me.

My hand trailed down her spine, relishing in the touch of her soft skin. Her slender body pressed into mine was comfortable. More than comfortable.

I took her virginity. I'd almost fucking died when she told me last night. It made sense now, the complete awkwardness of her, the hard angry stares. I took her innocence on the Friday, was a complete fucking bastard to her the morning after, and then on the Monday afternoon, she sees me with my dick in someone else's mouth.

Why the hell was she in my bed now? I'd been a complete asshole to her. Her head moved on my chest, and I felt the soft kiss press to my chest.

"Hey," I spoke to her softly. "You awake?"

"Mm-hmm." Ava stretched, which only made my body more aware of hers.

My dick woke up. I'd fucked her so much last night I was surprised it stirred. Ava moaned softly as she felt me harden.

"Does it ever stop?" she groaned as she burrowed her head into my neck.

"You make me want to fuck you," I teased her as I eased her off me. I didn't expect her flush to make me happy. "You sore?" I asked her as my hand was already smoothing over her hips, cupping her ass.

"Yes." Ava opened her eyes and laughed at me. "Have we slept at all? You went *all* night."

"*We* went all night," I corrected her as I moved my head to lap at her breast. "The time in the shower was your fault." I sucked her nipple into my mouth, my teeth grazing her slightly. Ava's back arched in pleasure, her body rising to meet me. "The last time was your fault because you wanted to be, and I quote, *adventurous*." I grinned as she hid her face as she laughed in embarrassment.

"I always wanted to know what reverse cowgirl felt like," she mumbled behind her hands.

"And now you know." I moved up her body again, noting the marks from the bites and the bruises from either my mouth or my hands gripping her to me. She was the poster girl for freshly fucked, and I knew any guy would take one look at her and think it was open season. I wasn't ready for the surge of possession I felt for her. It was so strong it shocked me slightly.

"What is it?" Ava asked me, her hand reaching out and stroking my face. "Why the frown?"

"You okay?" I asked instead, avoiding her question.

"I think I'm hungry," Ava said honestly with a small chuckle, which turned to a gasp when my fingers slid between her thighs. "Jett," she groaned, her lids already fluttering closed.

"I'm hungry," I whispered against her throat as I bit her skin softly.

"You're insatiable," she growled as her hips rolled to meet the rhythm of my fingers.

"I am," I admitted as I ran my nose along her jawline. "I'll stop if you want," I asked her as I slowed my fingers.

Ava's eyes flew open, piercing me with outrage. "You better not," she warned me.

"Thank fuck," I muttered with relief. I was hard as a rock, and my dick was eager to settle back into its new favourite place. I kissed the hollow of her throat as Ava widened her legs, and I moved in between them. "If it hurts, tell me," I told her as I guided myself inside.

Even after the many times she took me last night, her pussy still protested to let me in easily. The resistance just made me want to push into her more, and I heard Ava moan in appreciation as I worked myself in.

"You feel so good," she whispered as her fingers dug into my shoulders. She wasn't the only one who would bear the marks of our night together.

Fully seated inside her, I paused as I took her in. She was beautiful, her body was perfect, her tits the perfect size. She was soft everywhere, and again I felt the overwhelming need to claim her.

"Why are you staring at me?" Ava asked me with a gentle smile.

"You're beautiful."

It was out before I realised. I didn't spout that kind of talk, but Ava's happy blush made me smile as she saw right inside me.

"You're not too bad yourself." She grinned. "Want me to flip? Avoids awkward morning breath," she teased me with a raised eyebrow, making me laugh out loud.

I nodded as I withdrew, still marvelling at the feel of her without that rubber layer between us. When I came inside her the first time, unprotected, I panicked, and she reassured me she was on the shot. My inner cynic had warned me not to be stupid, but I'd realised very early on with Ava, she was completely genuine.

Now, all I wanted was to feel her walls clenching around me and milking my dick of every drop I had to give.

On her hands and knees, she looked over her shoulder at me in question. "Stop staring at me and do me already," she demanded playfully as she wagged her ass back and forth. "I need you." Her plea was thick with lust, and I felt immense satisfaction at her words.

How I never came there and then was probably the result of a long night of sex. With a single thrust, I pushed into her, and I heard her moan of pleasure as I started to move. Jesus fuck, she was already gripping onto me as I moved inside her. Pushing her head into my pillows, I leaned over her.

"People are still sleeping, babe, don't scream."

Babe? Who the fuck was I?

Ava's pussy clenched around me as she clutched the pillow to her mouth to stop her moans as her ass pushed back into me. I was no longer sure who was fucking who, all I knew was I needed to come, and I wasn't starting off the day without giving Ava her orgasm first.

My hips picked up speed, and I wondered at my own stamina. Thank the good Lord, Coach didn't train on Sunday. I would never last on the practice field today.

"Jett," Ava whispered at me, trying to control her moans. "Jett, harder, I'm so close." Her voice picked up in volume, and I pushed her back into the pillows.

"I know," I told her as my hands gripped her hips. "Don't fucking scream," I grated as I moved harder and deeper into her. I felt the familiar quiver at the base of my spine as my head tipped back, and I stared sightlessly at the ceiling. Her walls clamped down on me so tightly I swear I saw fucking stars before she did it again, and clenching my jaw so firmly that I may have cracked teeth to stop my own groan as my body seized up, I came hard deep inside her. I'd definitely bruised her this time, but as my dick pulsed its release, I didn't care. I was aware Ava's own body had locked up as she came, and I doubted she cared either.

I collapsed beside her. She hadn't moved, and I tiredly covered us both with my sheet.

"Need to clean," she murmured, her voice heavy with exhaustion, and I ran my hand over her ass.

"Sleep." My eyes were already closed. "Wash later."

"Mm-kay." I felt her move into me slightly. "Don't judge me for being sticky." Her whisper was soft, and I was sure she was already asleep before she finished, and I laughed softly at her ridiculousness.

Reaching out, I pulled her further into me. I didn't question my need to have her close, I just knew I needed to be touching her. I may never stop needing to touch her. The thought didn't even scare me.

WHEN WE WOKE THE SECOND TIME, I WAS CURLED INTO HER BACK, my arm around her holding her to me, and Ava's head was resting on my arm. She was tracing lazy patterns over my arm, and I felt her smile against my skin when she realised I was awake.

"Hey," she greeted softly.

"You're wearing your panties?" I questioned as my hand moved over her hip.

"Yeah, needed a barrier of protection against you," she teased as her head turned and she met my look with a grin.

"You smell like me," I said as I burrowed into her neck.

"Cleaned up." She gave a happy sigh as she wiggled back into my embrace.

"How long was I asleep?" I rolled away from her, reaching for my phone.

"Not sure, I've only been awake twenty minutes or so." Ava sat up, covering her chest as she did so.

"I'm fucking starving," I admitted as I stood. I didn't miss her hungry look down my body as I headed to the bathroom. "I'll be ten minutes, and then we can eat," I told her over my shoulder, and I heard her murmur her consent.

Once I was showered and was brushing my teeth, I took in all the nips and marks on my body. I wasn't sure which were yesterday's game and which were Ava's. Wrapping my towel around my waist, I went back into the bedroom. She was trying to pile her hair up on her head in a bun, scowling at the visible marks on her neck and shoulders. Her eyes met mine in the mirror.

"What is it?" Ava asked as she turned when she saw my frown, dropping her hair to fall loose around her shoulders.

"The top comes off."

"We *just* got showered."

I smirked at her assumption. "No, that top never gets worn again." I strode towards her, and she backed up in alarm, her eyes wide. Catching a lock of her hair in my fingers, I tugged her towards me. "Do you know how hard that top made me last night?" I whispered against her lips. "I saw you and thought you looked good, and then you turned and spoke to your friend, and I realised you were practically naked." My thumbs rubbed over her nipples as I spoke. "My dick almost punched through my jeans. I already knew you would be mine last night, but this top…fuck, Ava." My lips caressed hers, and she kissed me back, her teeth pulling my lower lip into her mouth.

"It's either this top or no top," she teased as her tongue stroked my lower lip. "And I don't have a bra."

My mouth captured hers as I pushed her back against the wall. With a sharp jerk, I pulled the buttons apart and heard the rip of fabric. Ava made a sound of protest, which was swallowed when I dipped my head and sucked her nipple into my mouth. I pushed the band of the fabric down over her slim hips, and then I straightened, looking at her in triumph.

"No top?" Ava looked scandalised. "*Naked?*"

Grinning, I walked to the closet and tossed a practice jersey at her. "Not naked."

Ava looked at the Saints top with a frown before she looked up at me in uncertainty. "You want me to wear your shirt?"

Shit, did I? Yes. I did. I wanted her to wear it and never take it off.

"I can give you a T-shirt if you prefer?"

Ava clutched the shirt closer to her chest as she bit her lip. "No, I want to wear this."

"You sure?" I flinched at the vulnerability in my voice. This pussy wasn't me. "It's just a shirt."

"Is it?" Ava saw through my bullshit, and I smiled ruefully as I looked away from her, my hand running through my hair.

"No." I wanted to cross the room to her, but I stayed where I was. "You okay with it?"

"It?" Ava looked down at the top again and then back up at me. "Or this?"

"Both?" Our eyes locked and held. I was nervous. What the fuck was I nervous for? It was *just* a jersey. It was *so* much more than a jersey.

She lifted the top up and went to put it on. I held my breath, and as she pulled it over her head, I crossed the room. Ava froze, her hands stilled, her head was clear of the neckline, but her breasts were still bare.

"Before you put it on, I need to tell you something," I blurted.

"Okay." Ava looked down at her top. "Will it take long?"

I huffed out a laugh as my hands rested on her bare shoulders. "It was us who told the dean you were earning."

Ava rolled her eyes, and stepping back, she pulled the jersey down her body. "Yeah, I guessed."

"You guessed?" I hadn't been expecting that. "Why aren't you screaming at me?"

Ava shrugged as she pulled her hair out from under the jersey. "Who else would it be? No one else cares enough about me making fifty dollars here and there when I shouldn't." Ava looked down at the length of the jersey. With a frown, she started to tuck it into her shorts. "I was pissed, I was, but then you tell me it's 'cause I drugged you? Well…" She glanced up at me. "It's a severe reaction, but I understood why."

"You could have gotten kicked out of school," I said to her, not understanding her calmness. "I would have done that to you, made you lose your scholarship."

Ava ran her hands through her hair, fluffing it up around her shoulders. "Who actually told?"

"Why?"

"Because I know it wasn't you." Ava stood back and looked in the mirror. The jersey was too big, but she'd tucked the front in her shorts, the rest covering her ass. "I may be pissed at Gray, but you..." Her head dipped as she looked at her feet. "I was certain it wasn't you."

"I let the girls spread the rumours about you being a thief and a slut."

Her breath caught, and she didn't look my way. "I know, that was hard, but I assume that stops...now? After..."

"Yes. Yes!" I repeated when I saw her doubtful look. "I'm sorry."

Ava's eyes searched mine as she looked for any duplicity. "Okay."

Pulling her into me, I tipped her head to look up at me. "You sure?"

"Yeah." Her smile was slow, and I saw the mischievous glint in her eye. "I'm not apologising for punching you or for the tweets."

My laughter rumbled out of me as I buried my head in her neck. "My balls have been sucked dry by your pussy and treated well, they're fine. Apology to *them* is accepted."

"Jett!" Ava whispered in mortification.

I straightened once more and looked her over. "And you're wearing *my* jersey, I think we both know who *Uptight's* been really rooting for."

With a laugh, she pushed me away from her. "Egotistical dick!" She held her hand out to me as she headed to the door. "Come, you promised me food."

We headed downstairs together, and I felt slightly cavemanish for how much satisfaction I was getting from her wearing my number.

The kitchen was fuller than I was expecting, and I felt her hesitate before she dropped my hand. Ash and Gray were sitting at the breakfast bar, both of them looking far too amused at what Ava was wearing. Jamie was making pancakes and bacon, and he stopped when he took her in before he resumed what he was doing. Two other guys on the defence shared a grin but resumed eating their cereal.

Derrick moved from the counter where he'd been resting his elbows.

"Ava?" He looked her over in concern, and then his face hardened when he noted my jersey.

"Hi, Derrick." I saw her smile at him as she smoothed her hands over her shorts. "Um, hey, team." Her face was on fire, but she stood firm.

I felt her relax slightly as my arm wound itself around her waist, and she leaned into me. "You want some pancakes?" I asked her softly.

"Is that okay?" Ava asked, looking at Jamie. "If I have some?"

"Aren't you a Lions fan?" Jamie asked her with a scowl as he flipped his pancakes.

"I've been persuaded to consider my options," Ava said to him with an easy smile and a twinkle in her eye and the guys laughed. It was as if all the tension in the room dissipated as Ava visibly relaxed.

Jamie smiled widely and poured more batter into the pan. "How many you want?"

"You okay there?" I asked Derrick, who was still watching Ava.

"Yeah, I wasn't expecting…never mind."

Ava caught his tone and playfully punched his shoulder. "Why so glum? I haven't seen you since the party at Oakwood a few weeks ago."

"I think you're mistaken."

Why was he acting like a dick? My eyes flicked to my brother, who was already giving our corner his full attention.

"No, I'm not," Ava said as she accepted some bacon from Jamie. "Remember, you'd lost your keys." I saw her frown as if she was remembering something. "No, not keys," she murmured to herself.

"You're mistaken," he snapped at her.

Ava shook her head, and I watched it happen. "You were going to walk me home," she whispered, the bacon falling from her fingers. "You gave me a bottle of…" Her eyes flew to mine, and my eyes snapped to Derrick's.

"Water," I growled as I surged forward, my fist scrunching his shirt as I hauled him towards me.

"It was you."

CHAPTER 33

Jett

"Easy, brother," Gray said calmly behind me.

"You fucking piece of shit," I grated out through my teeth. "You drugged me?"

Derrick's eyes glanced to Ava, and I banged his head off the wall. "Her? It was for Ava?" My fist connected with his jaw, but I kept him standing, and I punched him again and again and again.

"Jett!" Ash's hand was on my arm, and I shook him off. "Your hand," he warned me quietly as he made me take a step back.

"Talk." Shoving him into the wall, I stepped back and watched as he wiped the blood from his nose.

"Why are we listening to the little slut?" He tried to laugh it off. I leaped forward again, but Gray was there, his arm across Derrick's throat, pinning him to the wall.

"I suggest you speak fast," he said, his voice low and steady.

"Who was the water for?" I asked Derrick. I needed him to say it, and I felt Ash clasp firmly onto my shoulder, holding me back.

He licked his lips, and I was sure he was going to say nothing, and then Ava moved in front of me, her eyes wide with unshed tears as she looked at him.

"Why?" she whispered. "I'm nobody, I've spoken to you maybe three, four times?" Shaky hands pushed her hair back, and if my cousin wasn't holding me back, I would have gone to her.

"You're not nobody," Derrick said. The change in his demeanour was quietly terrifying. "You're beautiful. You're kind. But you have shit choices in friends." Scorn curled his lip upwards, and he looked at me. "And guys. I could have shown you."

It was his look that was the trigger for my memory, and I remembered. He'd been in my ear for too long at the party, and the guy I was looking for wasn't there. I said as much to Derrick, and he told me the person he was looking for wasn't there either. His tone had caused me to look at him, and I remembered asking who he was looking for. He had laughed it off and said he'd see me later.

He had gone to the kitchen and studied the bottles of water so long I asked him if he was okay. He'd jumped like he'd been caught doing something, and then he asked if I was going back to the house. I said yes, and he had handed me a bottle of water for the walk home. He'd told me he'd be back soon—he needed to find his keys—and then picked two bottles of water up and hurried out the door.

The whole situation was weird, and sensing something was off, I followed him. He didn't head back to the dorm house, and curious, I stayed back and then felt like a paranoid dick when I heard the music coming from Oakwood. He was going to another party, no big deal. It was probably to get his keys that he'd mentioned. I opened the water and drank as I turned to head back to the house.

I saw her at the same time he did. Blonde, pretty, wearing simple jeans and a T-shirt, and at first, I thought she was hammered. Her feet tripped over themselves, and Derrick launched forward and caught her.

Her voice and hand movements were completely contradictory to a drunk person, and I realised she was maybe just clumsy. She sounded clear, but the more I watched her, her body started to tell a different story. Moving closer, I saw him cop a feel of her ass as she spoke to him animatedly, she didn't seem to notice he'd just felt her ass. It didn't sit right with me, his hands on her body, and I moved into the light so he knew I was there.

"Ava recognised me," I told him. "She gave me some shit about fluffing up three of my passes against Kentucky." I looked at her, and she wiped her eyes hurriedly. "I remember now, I couldn't figure out if you were drunk, high or just annoying." I scoffed a laugh. "You spoke so clearly."

"I told you that," Ava whispered with a sad smile.

"You couldn't keep your hands off her." My attention went back to Derrick. "I didn't like it, it wasn't right."

He said nothing as he stared at me, only wiping his nose every now and then when the blood from his busted nose trickled into his mouth.

"You offered us *both* a bottle of water," Ava said to him sadly. "For the heat."

"You were dehydrated," he grumbled.

"I was about to be more than fucking *thirsty* though, if you got your way," she yelled, suddenly stepping forward in her anger. "You piece of shit, you were going to what? Wait until I passed out?"

Derrick's eyes snapped in anger. He must have forgotten Gray was at his throat. "Slut!" he screamed at her. "The whole fucking house *heard* you screaming like a whore. Don't stand there and act like you're innocent. You make me sick, you're just another whore."

Ava lunged for him and thank fuck Gray remembered her speed and saw it coming as he stepped back before she elbowed Derrick in the face and then brought her knee to his balls, dropping him to the floor.

"I'm not a whore, I was a *virgin,* you sick fuck." Her foot slammed into his ribs. "You fucking bastard." She shook her head in disgust. "You have no fucking right to judge me."

My arms circled her as I pulled her back. "It's okay. I'm here." Turning her in my arms, I wrapped my arms around her when I saw the tears spill over, and I looked to my brother and Ash. "Call Coach."

"I already did," Jamie said as he stepped forward, and I turned to him cautiously. Ava must have felt me tense, as she stopped crying.

"Who for?" I asked Jamie, and I felt Ash and Gray move behind me.

"For him." He spat on Derrick's prone form. "I suggest you clean your hands; he'll go fucking nuts when he sees them."

I looked at the rest of the team in the kitchen as they stood stoically. "You're not going to say anything?"

"Didn't see anything," the safety said. "You see anything?" he asked his friend, and he shook his head.

"And me?" Ava said quietly.

"I saw self-defence," Jamie answered her gently. Ava nodded once and leaned back into my chest. "I reckon you have ten minutes," Jamie said. "Clean up and be ready."

"Got it."

Gray and Ash stayed behind to watch Derrick, and I pulled Ava into my bathroom. Silently, I washed my hands, and when I winced at the cuts on them, she took over drying them and asked me where the alcohol wipes were.

Pointing to the cabinet under the sink, I sat on the counter as she cleaned my scrapes. "I offered to walk you home," I said quietly. "I didn't like the way he was looking at you." Ava said nothing as she cleaned my hands. "You saw Wade, you didn't want him to see you with me." I huffed out a disgruntled laugh. "You ducked out of sight, and I had no idea what to say to him, so I said I lost my keys." I pushed her away from me as I remembered. "All I wanted was him gone." I watched her as she shuffled on her feet. "I walked you home, you drank all your water and were still thirsty. I shared mine with you." Shaking my head, I remembered her standing outside her dorm, her boldness and no shits attitude had intrigued me. "You gave me *so* much shit about my game, you weren't like any other girl who was interested in my football career. *You* actually cared about the game, it was a nice change." Her eyes flicked to mine before she gave a half-hearted shrug. "I wanted to fuck you."

Ava inhaled sharply at my words but she didn't flinch. "I wanted it too," she admitted. "I wanted to know what it felt like to be kissed by Jett Santo."

"You told me you lived with a roommate, I suggested we go to my place. And then, well, we have our hazy memories." I couldn't hide my disgust at myself.

Finally, skittish green eyes lifted to meet mine. "I'm sorry."

I blinked. "Why are *you* sorry?"

"I really was the reason you got suspended," she whispered as a tear slipped over.

Was she kidding me? "Ava? You were…assaulted." I couldn't look at her, I felt like scum.

Cool hands clasped my cheeks. "No," she whispered as she rose onto her tiptoes and brushed her lips over mine. "I told you, it wasn't like that. My body *knew* you, I wanted you. I want you."

"And how do you know?" I asked as I pushed her away. "How do you know if I hadn't come along, you wouldn't have *wanted* Derrick?"

Ava bit her lip as she shook her head. "I don't know—"

I snorted in disgust before she stepped back into my space.

"I don't know how to make you believe me," she continued. "I need you to *trust* me, I would know the difference. I know how you touched me, I know you didn't force me, I know you took your time with me, I know what you made me feel." Her hands reached for me. "Jett, please listen to me."

My head dropped into my hands as I ran them through my hair in frustration. "You can't know." I sighed. "You'll probably never know."

"So that's it?" Ava asked me tiredly. "You'll always think this?"

I met her look, and I shrugged. "What else can I think? I'm no better than him."

I heard the knock on the door as Ash told me Coach was here. With a sad smile, I left her in my bathroom. I didn't know how I could ever look at her again, as the guilt was already weighing me down.

Derrick was taken by Coach and campus police to the real police. I had no idea how the school's PR team would handle this, but my dad phoned and insisted all three of us come home, which meant the board already knew.

The drive home was silent, and I had to fight the urge to turn around and see if Ava was okay. I shouldn't have left her, but I didn't want to be there when she realised that I was no better than Derrick. Coach told me that the school would reach out to her and see what she needed but he agreed that I needed to give her space.

Space I could give her.

In the kitchen at home, my parents and my aunt and uncle demanded all the details. I hadn't really wanted to talk about it, so Gray and Ash filled them in as I sat and stared at the wall. Every touch with her, every smile, every captured gasp replayed in my head as I analysed every moment with her.

Now that Derrick had been revealed as the missing piece, I remembered mostly everything and I was sure that Ava would too.

"Jett," my mom spoke softly to me. "Jett, honey, can we talk?"

I looked around the kitchen. Everyone was gone except mom. "Where are they?"

She sighed as she reached out to stroke my arm. "I think Gray is punching the shit out of something in the gym, and your dad is waiting to pick him up, and then I guess the two of them will run on the treadmill until they collapse." She tried to smile. "You know, Santo men shit."

I snorted out a laugh. "And Ash?"

"Kage will be punching the shit out of something, and Ash will be waiting to pick him up, then they'll swim laps until Aunt Charlotte needs to rescue them," mom said dryly. "Same Santo, same man shit." She lost her smile as she looked back at me. "I hate that this happened to you."

"Ava, it happened to *Ava*, mom."

"I know, I know that, sweetie…but it happened to you too."

"I still don't remember it like I should, I didn't think I drank that much of the second bottle," I told her quietly.

"But you must have." She answered me gently. "You don't remember the night at all?" she asked me curiously.

"Now I do." I stood from the table. "Now I have it in full Imax surround sound in my head."

"And what does it tell you?" she asked me as she gave me her full attention.

"That she was as willing as I was."

Mom nodded and plucked at her sleeve. "So, what we need to know is if you both would have been that way if you weren't drugged."

I shrugged. I didn't know.

"And your brother and cousin tell me that you and Ava are a very *hands-on* couple."

Couple?

"They do?" I asked cautiously.

"Yes, Gray says you're drawn to her like a moth to the flame, and Ash says he's never seen you happier than you were this morning with her." Her smile was full of love. "Drugged water or not, Jett, you and Ava would have ended up together."

"She's an Alabama Lions fan," I blurted out.

My mom laughed. "And now we know how you were attracted to each other: she poked your QB ego."

I grinned despite myself. She probably did. Ava was definitely ballsy enough to spike my interest.

"She sounds nice," mom said.

"She is," I agreed.

"We could send you both to couples therapy?"

"I think that's too soon, mom," I replied as I rolled my eyes.

"Quinn is extending the invitation to Ava," mom said as she stood.

"What invitation?" I asked in alarm. "Quinn is not exactly *friendly* towards her."

"She needs to talk to someone about this, a professional. We're sending you to one too." Mom poured me a glass of water from the fridge. "Don't bullshit me, you need to talk about this. Either together or separately, I don't mind, but it is happening."

"I'm not going," I told her adamantly. "But I think it's good if Ava does, thank you."

"Your father can speak to you about it."

I wisely said nothing. My mom was sweet and kind but stubborn as an ox when she wanted something. I already knew dad would agree with me, and then I would have an appointment anyway. Sable Santo was very protective of her children. Whether I went or not was a battle for another day.

"Should we check on them?" I said instead.

"No, your hand's already a mess, you don't need to hit anything else," mom scolded. "You will eat."

"I'm not hungry."

Dark blue eyes met mine. "You'll eat the sandwich I made for you, and then you will complain to me that you shouldn't have had so many carbs the week of the Alabama game." She tossed her black hair over her shoulder. "You will then proceed to tease me that I didn't make the sandwich and that cook did, and you will then heckle me until I confess."

I felt myself smile despite the horrible day. "Is that right?" I asked her.

"Yes, that, my dear boy, is right." Her eyes twinkled as she took a plate out of the fridge, placing it down beside me and then putting a small dish of pasta salad beside it. I saw her bite her cheek thoughtfully as my fork dug into the pasta. "I *did* make that."

My fork froze.

Mom looked at me and then the dish. "Yeah, don't eat it. It's horrible." She patted my shoulder as she took it off me. "Eat your sandwich."

Later, when Gray and my dad both looked like they'd gone ten rounds in the boxing ring, I had the same conversation with dad about a therapist.

I was happy to let him fight that battle for me with my mom. Not tonight though, we really weren't masochists.

My phone was beside me, a heavy presence in the room, and giving up the pretence of ignoring it, I switched it on. I had several messages from Quinn, and I felt guilty all over again. I had two from Jamie, which surprised me, but he came through for me today. I had some other bullshit but nothing from Ava.

Had such a short time away from me already made her hate me?

Me: **Are you okay?**

I waited. No reply.

Gray came into the room, his eyes dark with concern.

"You okay?" he asked as he lay down beside me.

"Yeah." I hesitated. "No? I don't know."

"Shit sucks," he said as we both stared at the ceiling.

"Yes, it does."

"She'll come around." He sounded confident. "Or you will. You'll realise you're being a dick."

Turning my head, I looked at my brother. "Wow."

"You know what I mean, you're spiting your nose for your face." He frowned. "Or whatever they say."

"Cutting off my nose to spite my face," I told him dryly.

"That's it."

"You're very supportive," I mocked him.

"You like her, she likes you, a *lot*. This will pass, and it'll work out." He sat up and swung his legs off the bed. "What *won't* pass is we need to win against Alabama, and we need to keep going on the *other* thing."

"I won't drop the ball on either," I assured him quietly to his back.

He looked over his shoulder at me and frowned. "She needs this to happen."

"She does, or you do?" I asked him softly. I already knew the answer.

"Both." He got off my bed and walked out of my room. I didn't go after him. My brother didn't need me chasing him as he chased his own demons.

My phone lit up.

Ava: **I am. Are we?**

Well, that was the million-dollar question.

CHAPTER 34

Ava

The week had been surreal. People who had never spoken to me before were nice to me, but I soon realised it wasn't because of the whole drugged water thing, it was because Quinn Lawrence had come to my apartment on Sunday with a bizarre offer about a therapist, and then on Monday morning, she met me at the coffee shop and proceeded to have coffee with me as she walked me to class. She then sat with Mia and me at lunch, and I hadn't known how to tell her to go away.

When someone asked her how we were suddenly friends, her smile could have blinded the sun, and I spat out my soda when she told them I was Jett's girlfriend.

When I asked her what the fuck was wrong with her, she'd grinned in delight and told me the best way to deal with a Santo was ignore him until he listened.

Quinn Lawrence was mentally unhinged. I was sure of it.

Ash sat beside me in Leitch's class and when Leitch had been about to rail my ass because I hadn't done the reading over the weekend, Ash had reamed *him* out. Leitch had been speechless, I'd been struck dumb. Ash was back to my favourite Santo. Kind of.

In Professor Matson's class, Jett had sat in the seat beside the guy who usually gave me shit, and the guy had been so nervous he had left the classroom. Jett hadn't spoken to me or looked at me, but when he left the class, his hand had trailed over the back of my neck once.

Mia was watching my week unfold like she was binge-watching her favourite TV show. I swore, at one point, she was going to ask me if she could get popcorn.

Of Derrick, there was no mention. It was my first time ever witnessing money at work. I knew there was an investigation, because I heard the hint of a rumour about spiked water, but from what I could discern, it was an opposing college's trick to mess with the team. I was in the cafeteria, using my card like I promised the dean and my mom before I sat down to eat my lunch. Quinn was sitting beside me, separating her Skittles into colours and counting them out. When I couldn't take it anymore, I felt the need to ask her.

"What if there were other girls he tried this with? How will anyone ever know?"

She paused in her counting. I noted all odd numbers were in a pile themselves.

"Trust me, they've put out feelers," she told me without looking up. "It's not being forgotten."

"It feels like it," I muttered.

Quinn raised her head to fix me with that dark stare of hers. "You think the board advocates women being abused?"

"No." I shook my head as she raised a perfect eyebrow. "No," I stressed again. "I just thought…I don't know."

"You're right, you don't know, but that doesn't mean nothing is happening." Quinn bowed her head again as she resumed splitting her Skittles up.

"Have you got OCD?" I asked her curiously.

"No. I just like even numbers."

I was pretty sure that was some kind of OCD, but Quinn kind of scared me, so I said nothing until my mouth worked before my brain. "But you're friends with the Devils."

I saw her grin as she pushed a lonely green Skittle to the pile. "Your point?"

"There's three of them."

"And I make four."

Right.

A large hand reached over her shoulder, and Gray scooped all her odd Skittles into his hand. "You done?" She nodded once, and he tossed the handful into his mouth. "Glad to be of service," he teased as he walked away. She didn't lift her head, she didn't watch him walk away, but I did see her small smile.

I didn't understand their relationship. "What if the odd pile was now an even number?" I asked her curiously.

Quinn blinked at me once. "But the colours didn't match."

She was definitely insane. "Of course." I nodded as my head screamed *what the fuck kind of logic was that?*

Quinn started to eat her Skittles. Two at a time. The colours didn't mix. It was like watching a lab rat perform tricks; she was weirdly fascinating.

"So," she spoke as she watched me shrewdly, "are you done thinking he's going to come around on his own?"

This time I blinked. "What?"

She popped two orange Skittles in her mouth and shrugged. "Jett, he's a tricky one."

"Have you slept with him?"

She stared and my face burned. Slowly she swallowed her Skittles before she reached for another two. Purple this time.

"Jett is like a brother to me," she answered carefully.

"Is Gray?" My brain and I needed to have a conversation.

Two green Skittles were selected, and then she skipped them for yellow. "Why is this a question?"

"You're right, it's not my business." I looked around the cafeteria. I needed Mia.

"It's not." Quinn stood fluidly. Eight green Skittles sat on her tray. "I don't like green."

She walked away, and I sat there looking after her as I deliberately ate the remaining Skittles, one by one.

After lunch, I walked leisurely to class. The school was a beehive of activity for the Saints home game against the Lions. School spirit was high, and there wasn't a person in the campus not rooting for the Cardinal Saints.

Even me.

Yup, I was full on black and silver. I had no idea how I would break it to my mom.

I heard the chanting and turned as I saw Jett, Ash, Jamie and some others walking across campus. They all had their football jerseys on, but my eyes were glued to number eight. He looked incredible as he crossed the green. He was smiling at something Ash said, and I saw him shake his head at his cousin as Jamie laughed.

They were headed to the stadium. They had practice, and classes for them were off. We needed the win against Alabama to make it to the conference championships. Resting against a wall, I watched them. I saw him turn his head as his brother joined them. From here, they looked more like twins.

Jett dipped his head to hear his brother, and then he was looking across the campus to look at me. Well, I wasn't sure if it was me, but it felt like it. He held my stare for a moment, and then he was turning away.

I let out the sigh I was holding as sadness washed over me, and when my phone vibrated in my pocket, I pulled it out, disheartened.

Jett: **You look good today**

Looking at my jean skirt and T-shirt, I doubted it. My T-shirt was plain blue, and it wasn't until I went to class that I realised it was the same colour of his eyes.

I woke that night to him in my bedroom. He was on the chair at my desk, the bedsheet that I had taken from his bed in his hands. I'd kept it, in a bag at the back of my closet. I had no idea why. Panic? I had just known on that Saturday morning, he couldn't come home to a bloodstained sheet. He'd have been looking for me. He thinks he wouldn't, but he would have.

"I should have thrown it away," I spoke quietly.

Jett said nothing as he stared at me, and then he stood fluidly, his face void of emotion. "Burn it," he said before he went to the door. "I'm sorry."

"For what?" I asked as I raised myself onto my elbows to look at him. "For having sex with me? Then or later? Or both?"

"For being a bastard."

He left me without another word, and I stared at the ceiling, wondering when in the hell did I fall for the Devil, and how was I going to make him understand he cared for me as much as I did him?

"IF YOU DON'T WEAR IT, I WILL NEVER TALK TO YOU AGAIN."

Looking at my best friend, I fought the eye roll. "Mia, no."

"But I got it made!" she wailed. "You need this, *he* needs this."

I looked at the T-shirt. It was black with the Saints mascot—an actual saint—on the front holding a red devil's trident. On the back was a large silver number eight, and although I loved the T-shirt, she knew as well as I did that I couldn't wear it.

"I cannot claim to be *his*," I hissed at her. "What if he hooks up with someone and I'm wearing this like a loser?"

"He isn't going to *hook up* with anyone!" Mia wagged her head back and forth as she threw her hands in the air. "You owe me a top."

That was kind of mean. I couldn't believe she went there; it wasn't my fault that Jett had ripped the top she bought me last week. As I stared at her and she rolled her eyes back at me, I knew she would get her way, so I held my hand out in resignation. "Give it to me."

Mia crowed in triumph, and I shrugged out of my tank top and pulled the T-shirt on. "Sizes are small," I told her.

"No, you need to let him remember you have curves *and* remind him how much he loves your curves."

"Mia!"

"Hush, I think high ponytail for effect." Her hands were already in my hair, and I decided to give in and let her do what she wanted. My nerves were already shot for today, so worrying about Jett not liking my T-shirt was not a big deal. Jett getting injured or, worse, hooking up with someone else...that made me feel sick.

Eventually when she was finished putting makeup on me for a football game, she let me leave the apartment.

Like all the other thousands of supporters, we walked to the stadium, black and silver mixing with blue and white. Balloons and decorations dominated the campus, and it was so hard to not get caught up in the buzz.

At the stadium, Quinn was at the entrance, and she rolled her eyes as she saw us. "Finally, I almost sent someone to get you!" she snapped as she fastened two wrist bands around our arms. Her hair was also in a ponytail. Black jeans and a Saints jersey completed her outfit. I noted that there was no number on her back. She turned me swiftly to admire my T-shirt. "Nice."

"Mia made it," I told her.

"Sure." Quinn pulled me forward.

I looked back at Mia, who looked sheepish. "It was her idea."

They ganged up on me? When did this happen?

"Where are we going?" I asked as I was hauled through a crowd.

"To the seats. If I miss them warming up, I will *not* be happy."

She was happy *now*? I trailed after her, reaching behind me to grab Mia, who was grinning in excitement.

We were in the family seats, and I felt anxious again as I looked around nervously. "Quinn?"

"Our parents are in the box, but I like to be down here for warm-up," she told me as she watched the tunnel. "They need to know they have support all *through* the game, including warm-ups."

I nodded. Whatever reservations I had about Quinn, it was clear she was fiercely loyal to her friends.

The crowd that was already in the stadium cheered when the Saints came running out to practice. Quinn definitely sounded like the loudest. I saw their heads turn, and I saw number eight stumble. I wanted to run. This was a bad idea.

"Best he sees you now and gets over it," Quinn said to me with a satisfied smirk.

Coach Bowers was already yelling at them, and I watched the team go through their paces. Jett threw the ball repeatedly down field as Ash and Gray did quick sprints to limber up. I knew the rest of the team was doing things, but all I could watch was the Saints QB.

His jersey was tucked up over his pads, and his black undershirt was already sticking to his body. Black pants sculpted his thighs and ass, and I knew I was completely objectifying him.

"Your tongue's out," Mia whispered to me as she giggled.

"He's just so goddamn sexy. I want to lick him all over," I told her loudly over the noise.

"Hello, we're the twins' parents."

My eyes closed, and I felt Quinn laugh beside me. Turning, I plastered a smile on my face.

"Hi."

"Ava?" Jett's mom looked exactly like Jett, only softer.

"Yeah, um, hi." I jerked my thumb over my shoulder. "Sorry."

"It's fine," she assured me as she hugged me.

"Oh, right." I hesitantly returned the hug.

"Your shirt's amazing. Quinn, you've been *decorating* again?" Jett's mom quickly hugged the dark-haired girl.

"It's not like it's graffiti." Quinn shrugged.

"You're the tagger?" I said as my mouth dropped open.

"Shh," Quinn shushed me. "You want to get me in trouble?"

I never in a million years imagined it would be Quinn. Would anyone?

"I hear you like football, Ava," Jett's dad said to me.

"Yes, very much, sir."

"Kerr is fine," he corrected. "Who's your money on today?"

I licked my lips. I hesitated. Kerr Santo nodded thoughtfully as he watched his family on the field. "I agree." He turned to me. "Follow me."

I had no reasonable objection, and as Quinn stood there introducing Jett's mom to Mia, I followed his dad off the bleachers and down into the stadium and into a small office.

"You have five minutes, Ava, use it wisely."

As he shut me in, I looked around the room in confusion before the door opened again and Jett was there. His hair was already messy from warm-up, and his cheeks were flushed. Two black grease marks ran across his cheeks, and I watched him as he slowly closed the door.

"Ava," he growled as he crossed the room, and then his hands were in my hair, his lips were devouring me, and my hands were clutching him to me. "I don't have much time," he whispered against my lips.

"What do you need to win?" I asked without hesitation.

"You. On my tongue."

Honestly, I'd been thinking pep talk or something, and my jaw slackened.

Jett grinned, and then I was laughing along with him. He wrapped his arms around me. "I think I've been a dick." He pulled me tight into him.

"You need to think of the game," I told him seriously. "You can do this today. Seriously, the defence is so good Spence won't know what hit him."

Jett stood back and looked down at me. "You're putting the win today in the hands of Woods?" he asked me.

"Jamie's been really bringing his A game," I said to him with a completely straight face.

Jett stared at me for a long moment before he fisted my T-shirt and dragged me up to meet his lips. "You'll pay for that," he promised as he kissed me.

"Bring it," I teased him as I kissed him back. "*After* you beat the Lions today."

"I missed you," he whispered as his arms wrapped around me again. "I missed this." I smiled at his words before he slapped my ass hard. "Defence will win it, like fuck they will," Jett scoffed with a grin as he headed to the door. He looked back at me, sobering. "You're okay?"

"I am now," I told him with a happy smile.

He smiled back but his eyes still showed his doubt. "You sure you're okay?"

"I'm perfect." I nodded, his concern for me was touching.

"You are." He hesitated one more time. "We're going to be okay." His smile was so confident, I melted as I realised that he wanted *us* as much as I did.

"We're going to be more than okay," I promised him. "I switched football teams for you, don't make me regret it."

He was back in front of me, and his lips covered mine. "Because you're mine," he growled. "I need to go." He kissed me quickly once more. "Your ass is mine after this," he called over his shoulder as he flashed me a grin before he left me there to go win the game.

And they did.

EPILOGUE

Quinn

I WATCHED HER COME BACK FROM THE OFFICE, HER LIPS BRUISED from kisses, her cheeks flushed from happiness, and when she smiled at me, I returned it. I had gotten so good at plastering a smile on my face, no one cared anymore if it was real. Only one person saw through my fakeness, and he was on the field, catching balls.

"He treat you right?" I asked her, making my tone light.

"I think he will." She beamed at me. I felt a small sliver of happiness for them. Jett needed someone wholesome like Ava. Someone who was fierce in her own right but needed protecting.

They told me she had put Derrick on the ground. She looked so slight, but she had fight, and that's why my best friend was falling in love with her. He hadn't admitted it yet, but he was. She was already head over heels for him. She wore her heart on her sleeve, and I wondered at her bravery to show her emotions so openly.

The Santos huddled together for the first play of the game. Ash stood slightly taller than his cousins, but he was by no means the tallest on the field.

"Ash has really slimmed down and toned up," I heard Kerr compliment Kage, and I forced my face to remain blank.

"Yeah, he says Gray's been really careful with what they're eating," Kage answered. I felt him nudge me. "They keep this up, they may not need you," he teased.

Never. They would always need me.

"Who do you think is telling my son what to cook," Sable said with a laugh. Her arm circled my shoulders. "They'll always need you," she said as she kissed my head. I smiled up at her.

I was a Santo in everything but name. We'd had a rough two years since I broke up with Ash—well, he broke up with me, but we were disastrous from the start. Ash had refused to be in the same room as me, and Onyx, the twins' older, *wilder* brother, had taken Ash's side because Onyx was a fucking sociopath. Gray had kept silent, which Ash had taken as solidarity, and Jett had been neutral. Jett would never turn his back on me; I was his best friend, and although he would never understand why I did what I did, he would always be there for me.

"I thought you did sports therapy?" Ava asked me as her eyes stayed trained on number eight.

"Nutrition too," I answered.

"That's awesome." She was nodding, but she may as well have been on the field. Jett had passed the ball, and Ash was already breaking away to race down the field.

A tackle took him out, and the pass was ruled incomplete. The stadium mumbled as he bounced back to his feet and gave the player who tackled him a friendly pat on the shoulder as he ran back to the line of scrimmage.

"He's fit," I heard the red-haired one murmur to Ava.

Leaning over, I smiled at her. "He's a manwhore."

"Okaaay."

I didn't miss the wide-eyed *what the fuck* look she sent to Ava. I also didn't care.

Straightening, I watched as Jett shouted out the play, and then the ball was in his hands. Running back a few steps, he faked the throw, and I saw the handoff to Gray. The running back took off down the field. His speed always surprised people, and I watched him eat up the yards. Urging him on, I heard the stadium yell for him to make it. At the twenty-five, he swerved the oncoming safeties, and then Ash was beside him, blocking any of the defence that rushed them as they both raced down the field.

They were at the twenty.

The fifteen.

Holy shit, he was at the ten.

Five-yard line.

And then he was in the end zone.

The stadium went wild. I saw him bounce off Ash's chest as Jett ran down to meet him in the end zone. Jett's hands clutched Gray's face guard as their helmets clashed and he congratulated his brother, Ash bouncing beside them with excitement.

The big screen showed the replay, and when the grin spread across Gray's face as he reached the end zone, my heart stuttered.

He was so gorgeous. He didn't have Jett's hard lines and planes. His face was softer, but his eyes were hard. Always stern, always unyielding, always careful.

Only when he played football did his mask slip.

Or the night he told me he loved me, and I walked away from him and broke his heart.

Since then, football was Gray's only desire, and the urge for revenge on what was done to me. His revenge would never replace what I'd lost.

I smiled along with the others as they cheered and clapped for the touchdown. Gray allowed his mask to slip when he played. I couldn't afford that same luxury. My mask stayed in place even though it no longer had anything to hide. I'd been empty inside for so long the mask protected nothing but a shell.

Only one man could fill that void, and he turned his back on me the same way as I once turned my back on him. All I had left was my fake smile and a desire in my heart for him to see me once again.

The way he used to, before I lost it all.

Playlist

'Unsteady' - *X Ambassadors*
'Fire' - *Barns Courtney*
'Rebel Yell' - *Billy Idol*
'We Don't Have To Dance' - *Andy Black*
'Demons' - *Imagine Dragons*
'Ten Million Voices' - *Shamen's Harvest*
'Way Down We Go' - *Kaleo*
'Counting Stars' - *OneRepublic*
'Come As You Are' - *Nirvana*
'Castle of Glass' - *Linkin Park*
'Hellfire' - *Barns Courtney*
'A Girl Like You' - *Edwyn Collins*
'Life to Fix' - *The Record Company*
'Falling Like The Stars' - *James Arthur*
'Legendary' - *Welshly Arms*

From the Author

Hello! Thank you so much for reading this book and my word, what a story it was for me to write!

The Santo boys have been in my head for a long time, playing it cool and biding their time. However, just before Christmas 2020, they started causing *Mayhem* in their allotted spot in my brain. They wanted their story told, each story completely unique but irrevocably interwoven with each others, which is *why* these books are not simply standalone books with a common theme. They will, and do need to be read as a series. While I was writing this book, I was also listening to what was happening in books 2 and 3, and it may be that alcohol may be needed going forward.

Ava and Jett's story is a classic enemies-to-lovers story, and I did think I was going to write a bully romance. But, I have never been able to tell my characters what to do, they listen to the thought process, they nod at the outline and then as soon as I type *Chapter 1,* they run and scatter off in different directions and then it's like herding cats to get them back on the page. By the time they settled down, I was halfway into the book with new grey hairs and no sleep.

So, it's not a bully romance but I think I love it even more because of that. They told their story how it was for them and that's all I can ask of them.

Although Jett has his asshole moments, for those of you who were looking for a shade darker and more of a complete asshole, I think Gray may fill that role and his book's next in the series.

Also I would like to state here, Versed is a drug and it is used for 'twilight sedation' - the only thing I have used artistic licence on, is the amount of time lapsed before memory returns and of course, the *animated state* of the recipients, for want of a better term. Wink wink, nudge nudge.

I really hope you love all of my characters as much as I do, if you feel inclined to do so, a review on your favourite retailers site would be awesome sauce.

Eve x

Acknowledgements

I would like to thank everyone who supported me in getting this book out, but first I want to clarify two things. One, it is absolutely possible to get very drunk, and have no recollection of the night before and wake up the next morning with no hangover. I know this firsthand, it's how I sailed through my late teenage years, twenties and early thirties with never experiencing a hangover. My late thirties…not so much. Also, eating Skittles in colour order and in twos is not insanity, no matter what Ava thinks…and I have no judgement of Quinn in leaving the green ones behind.

Glad we cleared that up! :)

As always, it may be only me that writes the story (with the aid of the maniacs in my head), but it takes so much more than me to present and publish a book.

Firstly, Jay, another fantastic cover, you keep bringing it every time. Thank you so much for seeing my vision and then giving me what I *actually* want. We make a great team.

To the ladies at the Next Step PR, thanks for all your promotion work and spreading the word about this book. You are incredibly supportive and enthusiastic and I absolutely love that about you all.

To Brenna, for once again listening to my insanity and then sharing your medical knowledge with me. I may have used artistic license but the foundation of the knowledge is all Brenna. You rock Glitter Girl.

To Helayna, thank you for your editing skills. One day I promise I'll learn about dangling modifiers...maybe. Until then, I know I can count on you. I know I drive you insane, but you know you love me.

To my beta readers, Amber, Julie, Katy & Renee - still rocking it girls, thank you. You read this whole book in one weekend, even though you have families and other commitments and the fact you willing lose sleep just to read my words, it's the biggest compliment I can receive. I love you all. Thank you so much for being my girls.

To the bloggers, reviewers, and bookstagrammers out there who have supported this launch, thank you so much. I appreciate each and every one of you.

To my readers, thank you always for your support. It means so much to me, and I will never be able to thank you enough.

And finally, Mr M, thank you for the coffee and the snacks and the hours of leaving me alone so I could write this book, but mainly, for just looking after me. For keeping me sane, reminding me how to breathe when I panic the books aren't good enough, and for being an endless supplier of hugs. I love you.

Eve x

About the Author

Eve L. Mitchell is a USA Today Bestselling author who writes contemporary romance and urban fantasy.

Being an avid reader from a young age, Eve still considers herself to be a reader first. She believes there is nothing better than getting that new book either on your e-reader or in your hands, and the fact she may bring that excitement to a fellow reader, fills her with wonder. She writes under a pen name because otherwise her Secret Agent status will be revoked.

Eve lives in the North East of Scotland, with her three coffee machines and her significant other, Mr. M. She enjoys NFL Football, music and having long conversations with the voices in her head, which sometimes turn into the stories she writes.

If you want to keep up to date with all things Eve, to be the first to hear about updates from Eve sign up for her newsletter.

All the books; both fantasy and contemporary:
https://bit.ly/Evesnewsletter
Just contemporary romance book news:
https://bit.ly/Evesromancenewsletter
Just Fantasy books news:
https://bit.ly/Evesfantasynewsletter

Connect with all things Eve: linktr.ee/EveLMitchell

THE BOULDER SERIES

FROM BOOK 1: You'd think the universe would toss me a break after the year I'd had.

I made a plan, one that would give me a fresh start in a new town where no one knew me.
It should have been simple, but nothing is ever as easy as it should be when starting over.
New town, new school, and a new life. It sounded easy enough, or I'd thought it had.

It wasn't.

THE DENVER SERIES

FROM BOOK 1: *Be careful what you wish for.* Isn't that what they say? In my defence, what woman *wouldn't* wish for a handsome, intense, and successful man? Aiden is all of these things and more.

He is also a jerk of epic proportions.

He is blunt, closed-off, and secretive. I know there's more to him than just his good looks, but he refuses to open up. So why do I keep going back for more?

GET THE SERIES
WWW.EVELMITCHELL.COM

THE RUTHLESS DEVILS SERIES

FROM BOOK 1: She is his enemy. He is her nightmare.

They say there's a thin line between love and hate, and neither is prepared for the consequences when they cross that line.

Three guys, three girls, one game. Are you ready to meet the Devils?

GET THE SERIES

WWW.EVELMITCHELL.COM

THE AKRHYN SERIES

Creatures of evil roam the shadows - the Drakhyn. They may look like humans, but their taloned hands and razor-sharp teeth serve one purpose only; killing.

A Sentinel's purpose is to patrol and protect. They are highly trained soldiers with superior skills and abilities. Whether they be Vampyres, Lycan, Castors or gifted Akrhyn, their purpose is the same; hunt the Drakhyn and rid the world of their evil presence.

THE WATCHER SERIES

FROM BOOK 1:

One psychic. Six demons. And a whole lot of trouble.

I am a typical, though admittedly anti-social, woman who lives alone in the rural Highlands of Scotland. I also happen to be a clairvoyant who can summon the dead. It's a pity the souls I see didn't give me a heads-up, nor did I glimpse my own future on the night six demons came hunting for me.

GET THE SERIES

WWW.EVELMITCHELL.COM

Printed in Great Britain
by Amazon

83884474R00202